
★

Something was missing…

He went over the words again in his head: *It's your fault Jill and…died the way she did…all the others. Now it's your turn. Chief Inspector.*

Jill *and* what? Why couldn't he remember what came after *and?* And why was someone blaming him for her death?

It didn't make any sense at all, he thought as he drifted off to sleep.

He was awakened by the ringing of the phone. He switched on the light, squinting at the time. Twenty past twelve! Who on earth was calling him at this time of night? Still half-asleep, he answered, "Paget."

Silence. He struggled upright in the bed. "Paget," he said again. "Who is this?"

"You think it's over, don't you, Chief Inspector?" a voice said harshly. *"But it's not, you know. You still have to pay for what you did, so think about it as you try to sleep tonight."*

★

ACTS OF VENGEANCE

FRANK SMITH

TORONTO • NEW YORK • LONDON
AMSTERDAM • PARIS • SYDNEY • HAMBURG
STOCKHOLM • ATHENS • TOKYO • MILAN
MADRID • WARSAW • BUDAPEST • AUCKLAND

ACTS OF VENGEANCE

A Worldwide Mystery/July 2004

First published by St. Martin's Press, LLC.

ISBN 0-373-26499-2

Printed in U.S.A.

ACTS OF VENGEANCE

ONE

DETECTIVE CHIEF INSPECTOR Neil Paget stuffed another folder into an already bulging briefcase, and snapped it shut. Eight o'clock, and still at least two hours' work ahead of him when he got home. He paused, listening to the rain slashing at the windows, and wondered if it was ever going to stop. Fourteen days into November, and already they'd had three more inches of rain than had fallen in the entire month a year ago. He looked down at his shoes and grimaced. Fine state they'd be in by the time he reached his car. The antiquated sewer line into the building was being replaced at long last, and what used to be the car park was awash with mud.

Paget hoisted the briefcase off the desk, plucked his furled umbrella from the hat stand, and turned out the light. His footsteps echoed hollowly on the worn linoleum as he made his way past cluttered desks and silent phones to the head of the stairs and descended to the ground floor. He nodded his good-night to Broughton, the duty sergeant at the desk.

"Bit of flooding out your way, sir," Broughton called after him. "Nothing serious yet, but best be warned." Paget raised a weary arm in response and moved on down the corridor to the double doors of the main entrance. On nights like this he wished he lived in town, but the thought, as always, would vanish with the dawn.

A woman wearing a blue plastic mac stood at the door, face pressed against the glass as she peered into the night. So intent was she on whatever it was she was looking for that she jumped when he said, "I thought you'd left some time ago, Constable,'' then took a step backward as she gasped and whirled to face him. "Sorry," he said. "I didn't mean to startle you, Regan. Are you waiting for someone to pick you up?"

Kate Regan put a hand to her chest, took in a deep breath and shook her head. "No. That is, no, sir. I was just looking out to see if it was still raining."

It was an odd answer, considering the rain was bouncing six inches off the concrete steps outside, something he could see even from where he stood. "I think you'll find it is," he said drily as he opened the door.

"Is your car around the back, sir?"

"That's right. Yours?"

She nodded. "Mind if I walk round with you?"

"Not at all, but... Is there something wrong, Constable?"

"Oh, no, sir." Kate shook her head vigorously, then laughed self-consciously. "It's just that these shoes are not exactly the best for walking through mud, and I could use a steadying hand over some of the puddles out there. That is if you don't mind, sir?" she added quickly, as if fearing she might have overstepped the bounds.

"Not at all, Constable."

They paused on the top step beneath the canopy above the door while Paget opened his umbrella. Kate Regan pulled the hood of her mac over her head, tugging the drawstrings tight beneath her chin, creating a frame for her face. With her pale skin, luminous eyes, and a sprinkling of freckles across her nose, he thought she looked more like a little girl than a twenty-nine-year-old seasoned constable.

PC Kathleen Regan had come to them from Tenborough, where she was being considered for promotion. After she had passed her sergeant's exams, it had been decided to send her to CID for further training while she waited for an opening. At least, that was the official version. In fact, the Broadminster CID was short by at least four people, so under the guise of training, Chief Superintendent Brock had arranged to have

PC Regan transferred on temporary duty to help make up the numbers, and—he hoped—stop Superintendent Alcott from whingeing on and on about lack of staff.

"Take my arm," Paget told her as they descended the steps together. Kate glanced around as if afraid someone might see her and think she was cosying up to the chief inspector, then grasped his arm. They picked their way along the side of the building, half jumping runnels of muddy water flowing from the shoulder-high embankment of sodden earth. Tarpaulins had been draped over the mound in an effort to prevent the earth from washing away, but they merely served to slow the process rather than stop it. What had once been a parking area for some thirty cars was now reduced to a narrow lane barely wide enough to allow the passage of a single car.

"Thank goodness!" Kate breathed as they reached the end of the building and turned the corner. "At least there's no mud back here." She stopped abruptly. "It's so dark. What happened to the lights?"

The area behind the building was poorly lit by two old-fashioned lamps at the best of times, but now both lights were out. If it hadn't been for the feebly blinking red-and-amber lamps marking the edge of the earthworks beside the trench, there would have been no light at all.

"Probably shorted out by the rain," Paget observed. He took out his car keys, attached to which was a tiny torch. The bulb was no more than a few millimetres in diameter, but it threw a surprising amount of light. They came abreast of a silver Escort, and Paget held the torch while Kate fished inside her handbag for her car keys. She opened the door, and the interior light came on. She looked down at her shoes and shook her head. "Ruined," she observed sadly.

"Should have brought your wellies," Paget told her, wishing he'd done the same.

"I did," Kate told him ruefully. "They're in the boot." She slid into the seat. "Good night, sir. And thanks."

"Good night, Constable." Paget stepped back as Kate

closed the door and started the engine, then moved on to where his own car was parked at the far corner of the building. Behind him, he heard the nervous grate of gears as Kate Regan backed the car out, spinning her wheels on the wet surface as she set off. She braked at the corner and then was gone.

Something was bothering that woman, he thought as he continued on. She'd denied that there was anything wrong, but she'd been on edge. He'd felt the tremor in her hand as she clutched his arm. He hoped it was nothing serious. Whatever it was, it hadn't shown up in her work, but he made a mental note to keep a close eye on her during the next few days.

He had almost reached his car when he was blinded by a blaze of light. The umbrella was torn from his grasp, and his head exploded. Steel fingers grasped his hair, forcing his head back as he stumbled to his knees. Rain pounded in his face as he stared blindly into the light, arms flailing uselessly at his sides.

He sensed rather than saw movement behind the light. He tried to pull away, but his head was in a vice. A gloved hand appeared from behind the light. He tried to get his feet under him, tried to push himself away, but there was no feeling in his legs. He saw the flash of steel; felt the rush of blood; felt it run down his throat. The blade flashed again....

Someone shouted as if from far away. So very far away. A figure, shiny, ghostly, seemed to float in front of him, then disappear. He fell face down, tasted blood. He must try to... The thought eluded him. Like a thousand tiny icicles, rain slashed against his face. He felt the water seeping through his clothes. His suit... So cold, so dark, such a lonely place to die.

AUDREY TREGALLES draped a sheet over the ironing board and tested the iron. She enjoyed ironing sheets. Not many people ironed their sheets nowadays, but her mother had always done it, and Audrey had simply carried on. She liked the warm smell of the material, and the way the wrinkles disappeared. The pure whiteness reminded her of snow…and Christmas.

"Less than six weeks till Christmas," she observed. "It will be nice to see Philip and Lilian again, won't it, love? Pity they can't stay longer."

Hidden behind the newspaper he was reading, Detective Sergeant John Tregalles's normally pleasant if somewhat rumpled features became set. Black hair and a dark complexion bespoke his Cornish ancestry, as well as Cornish stubbornness at times, despite the fact that he'd been born and raised in London.

"Umm," he grunted neutrally.

"I shall have to make the cake this week," Audrey continued. "I meant to do it last week, but…" She sighed and shook her head. "I really don't know where the time goes; do you, love? I mean we've only just had bonfire night, and now it's nearly Christmas." She frowned as another thought occurred. "Best get that order in for Lilian's wine as well."

Tregalles sighed. "There's lots of time," he said.

"Not if they have to special-order it, there isn't. You know what happened last time when you left it till the last minute. Not that Lilian ever said, but you could see she didn't like that Bulgarian stuff you brought home."

Tregalles snorted. "Didn't stop her from tossing it back, though, did it?"

"Now, you know that's not fair, love. She has a heart condition, so she has to drink wine with her meals. The doctor told her it was good for her."

"It should be, at that price," Tregalles muttered. The truth was, Lilian was an alcoholic, but you couldn't tell Audrey that.

"Don't be like that, love. They don't come that often, and it will be nice to see them again. You shouldn't begrudge Lilian a little wine. She's such a sweet little thing, and it is only for a few days each year."

And thank God for that! Ever since last Christmas, Tregalles had been dreading the thought of another encounter with Audrey's brother and his wife, or more specifically, with Lilian. Philip was the only one of Audrey's four brothers who had gone to university, and now he worked for—sorry, Tregalles corrected himself silently, *held a position with*—the BBC, which, he seemed to think, gave him the right to talk down to everyone. Tregalles didn't like Philip, but he was prepared to put up with him for a few days for Audrey's sake. But Lilian was something else again. Even now, just thinking about last Christmas was enough to bring out a prickle of sweat across his brow. Lilian, a neatly packaged, slightly buxom blonde with the face of an angel and a strong sense of the dramatic, tended to become amorous when she'd had too much to drink, and last Christmas she'd taken a fancy to him. Philip hadn't seemed to notice—or hadn't cared—and Audrey had scoffed at the idea when he'd tried to tell her he was literally being stalked by her sister-in-law.

"So you think she's after your body?" she said, chuckling, as they got ready for bed on Christmas Eve. "More like a bit of wishful thinking, I'd say," she added slyly. "Lilian's just a big tease, messing with your hair and patting your cheek and such. She's an actress. They do that sort of thing. They don't mean anything by it. It's just their way. And you *were* under the mistletoe when she kissed you. I don't know why you made such a fuss over a friendly little kiss, gasping and making such noises. It's all in good fun. It's Christmas."

But the mistletoe wasn't the half of it, he thought as he slid down in bed beside his wife. It hadn't been the kiss that brought tears to his eyes and made him gasp; it was when he'd tried to pull away, and she'd slid her hand between his legs and squeezed. He'd mumbled some excuse about her catching him by surprise, and Lilian had smiled wickedly and said perhaps they should try again when he was more prepared.

"I'll order the wine on Saturday," he said, and sighed.

There was nothing to be gained by starting an argument he was bound to lose.

The telephone rang. "I'll get it," he said, tossing the paper aside and scrambling to his feet. Audrey followed him with her eyes. She wished John and Philip had more in common, but there it was. It was hardly Philip's fault that he'd had more education than John, but John always seemed subdued when Philip was in the house. It was almost as if he were ashamed of his job compared to Philip's, and he shouldn't be. John's job was every bit as important as Philip's, and she would remind him of that before they came.

Tregalles appeared in the doorway. His face was pale. He seemed to have aged ten years since leaving the room. "I've got to go," he said, his voice little more than a whisper. "That was Alcott on the phone. It's Paget. He was attacked in the car park. Some bastard cut his throat!"

WHEN TREGALLES ARRIVED at the hospital, he found Detective Superintendent Thomas Alcott in one of the lounges, where he'd been firmly directed by a staff nurse when she discovered him smoking in the corridor. Called from a retirement dinner for one of the town's councillors, he'd come straight to the hospital, where he now awaited word on Paget's condition. The superintendent's normally sallow features looked positively grey beneath the harsh fluorescent lights, and his eyes were bleak. His dinner jacket hung open, his tie was askew, and flecks of fallen ash dotted the otherwise pristine whiteness of his pleated shirt as he paced nervously back and forth.

"They're still working on him," Alcott greeted Tregalles as he ground out his cigarette. He fired the words like bullets. "He's lost a hell of a lot of blood; in fact it's a wonder he's alive at all, from what they tell me. Hit on the head and slashed across the throat. Cut an artery. He'd have been dead if it hadn't been for some quick thinking by one of the new lads Uniforms took on last month. Chap by the name of Redfern. Seems he kept his head and put pressure on the artery while his mate called for an ambulance. Stayed with Paget all the way into Casualty. He was still here when I arrived, soaked to the skin and blood all over his clothes, so I sent him home to change. Told him to get back to the station as soon as he could and bring all his clothing in a bin bag for Forensic and wait for me there." Alcott fumbled for another cigarette, lit it, and sat down. He leaned his head against the wall and blew a stream of smoke into the air.

Tregalles sat down facing the superintendent. "Look, sir, all I know about this is what you told me on the phone. What did happen, exactly?"

Alcott shook his head. "All I know at the moment is what Redfern told me. He says they were bringing in a drunk and disorderly who'd passed out in the back of the car, but there was no room to park near the front door, so they drove around the back, where they saw two men struggling beside a car. Redfern said they both had their backs to him, but it looked to him as if the man closest to him had the other man on his knees and was pulling him backward by the hair.

"Redfern jumped out of the car and yelled at the man to stop where he was, but of course he didn't. He took off into the trees next to the playing fields. Redfern said he was about to go after him when he saw the man on the ground was bleeding badly, and he could see his throat was cut. He told his mate to call an ambulance, then did what he said he'd been taught to do in first aid class, and put pressure on the artery. It was only then he recognized the man as Paget. Fortunately, the ambulance arrived promptly, and then it was only a matter of minutes to the hospital. Redfern stayed with Paget and kept the pressure on all the way up to the operating room, where the surgeon took over."

Alcott sucked deeply on his cigarette. "The people in Casualty said if he hadn't done what he did, Paget would have been dead long before they got there."

"Thank God he did," Tregalles breathed. "Any sort of description of the man who got away?"

"No. All Redfern could tell me was that he was fairly tall and was wearing a dark mac. Black plastic, he thinks."

"There was only the one man?"

"He didn't see anyone else."

"What about the weapon? Any sign of that?"

Alcott cocked a quizzical brow at the sergeant through a haze of smoke, and Tregalles suddenly became conscious of his position. He had been virtually interrogating his own superintendent. "Sorry, sir," he said. "I didn't mean to… It's just that, well, being DCI Paget…" He stumbled to a halt, not quite knowing what to say.

But Alcott nodded understandingly. "It's all right, Tregalles," he said quietly. "We all want the answer to those questions." He fell silent for a moment, and when he spoke again it was in a thoughtful tone. "I asked Redfern the same question, but what he told me doesn't seem right. He said he was quite sure the man had something like a bar in his hand when he first saw him. He only saw it for a split second, but it was his impression that the man was holding a short metal bar, or possibly a length of pipe, but not a knife."

"But Paget's throat was cut."

Alcott shrugged. "I know. Doesn't make sense, does it? Paget still had his wallet on him when Casualty took charge of his possessions, and Redfern says Paget's briefcase and umbrella were lying beside the car."

"He could have been interrupted before he had a chance to take anything," Tregalles observed. But he was puzzled. Why would anyone be waiting behind the building? No mugger in his right mind would hang about out there, even if it wasn't pouring with rain. There was nothing there, unless of course the man had been after Paget's car. It could be that Paget had caught someone trying to break into his car, and tackled him. But if the man was after the car or even the contents, there were better pickings elsewhere. "It sounds to me as if this bloke was lying in wait for Paget," he said.

"Which is why I wanted you down here." Alcott drew heavily on his cigarette. "You're probably as close to the man as anyone. Was he worried about anything? Have there been any threats? Anything arising from recent cases?"

Tregalles shook his head. "Not that I know of," he said. "Mind you, I'm not sure he would have let on if there had been. He's not exactly a talker, is he? At least, not when it comes to himself."

"What about his personal life?"

Tregalles grimaced. "To be honest, sir, I don't think he has one. He's always at work. He's mentioned the garden the odd time, and he has a daily housekeeper, but I've never heard him mention anything or anyone else. His mother and father are both dead, and the only woman I've ever seen him out with is one of the doctors here. Dr. McMillan. Audrey and I saw him having dinner with her one night a month or so back, and they seemed pretty chummy. I thought at one time that he might have something going with Grace Lovett, you know, from SOCO, but nothing seems to have come of that."

Alcott nodded glumly. Paget had always been reticent about his private life. "I've been on to Len Ormside," he told Tregalles. "Told him to get down to Charter Lane immediately and set up an incident room. SOCO's been alerted, but I'll be surprised if they find anything out there in all this rain."

"Superintendent Alcott?" A tall young man in blue surgical garb stood in the open doorway. His face was pale, his eyes dark, and he looked desperately tired. The superintendent rose to his feet. "I'm Alcott," he said quietly, "and this is Sergeant Tregalles."

"My name is Livingstone. Mr. Livingstone," the surgeon emphasized, establishing his credentials, "and the best thing I can say at the moment is that your man is still alive, which is something of a miracle in itself, considering the enormous amount of blood that was lost. The damage to the neck and throat has been repaired, and he has been given a transfusion, but it will be some time before we know how well he will respond. Unfortunately, the head injury complicates matters. Intracranial haemorrhaging is putting pressure on the brain, but the full extent of that damage cannot be determined until our neurologist has had a chance to examine him. And, if he recommends it, we may have to wait for the results of a CT scan.''

The surgeon paused. "In short, gentlemen, the patient is in very serious condition. Because of the damage to his throat and internal bruising, we had to perform a tracheotomy, which simply means that he is breathing through a tube inserted in his throat. He is, of course, unconscious, and no doubt will remain so for some time to come.''

"This head injury," Tregalles ventured, "will it mean an operation?''

Livingstone shook his head. "I don't know," he said. "There are a number of less invasive techniques for reducing the pressure, but it's too early to say exactly how we will proceed. The only thing I can tell you at the moment is that the patient is stable, but it could still go either way, and I think it would be advisable to notify his next of kin.''

"There are no close relatives as far as we know," Alcott told him.

"Mrs. Wentworth, his housekeeper, should be told," Tregalles put in. "I've never met her, but I gather she is a long-time friend as well as his housekeeper.''

Alcott glanced at his watch. "It's late," he said. "Let the woman have a good night's sleep. It's not as if she can do anything. We'll send Molly Forsythe out there first thing tomorrow morning.''

"There is Dr. McMillan," Tregalles offered.

Livingstone frowned. "What about Dr. McMillan?" he asked. "She isn't involved in this case.''

"It's just that I thought she might like to know, since she

and the chief inspector... Well, I don't know how close they are, but I believe they are on friendly terms."

"Really?" Livingstone seemed mildly surprised. "In that case, I'll have someone ring her."

"I'll be posting an officer outside Paget's door," Alcott told Livingstone. "I trust you'll have no objection to that?"

Livingstone eyed the superintendent suspiciously. "It depends," he said. "I realize that you must be anxious to talk to Mr. Paget, but I cannot allow his recovery to be put at risk. His life literally hangs in the balance."

But Alcott was shaking his head. "As you say, the sooner we can talk to Paget, the better, but that's not why I want someone here. We don't know why Paget was attacked, but the way in which it was carried out suggests to me that it was deliberate and, I suspect, premeditated, so I'll feel a lot better if someone is stationed outside his door. As well, I'd appreciate it if you would let the officer know of any change in Paget's condition so he can keep me informed."

"I'm sure that can be arranged," said Livingstone, his mind already on other things as he glanced at the time. "I must go. It's been a very busy night, and it shows no signs of letting up." He turned to leave, then paused. "I don't know if this will be of any help to you, but in my opinion the wound to the throat was caused by something much thinner than a knife. Possibly a razor—or a scalpel."

"Bloody hell," Tregalles breathed softly as Livingstone left the room and they followed him out. Knife wounds were common enough in Broadminster, as everywhere, but razors? No. Even the gangs who invaded Broadminster from time to time used knives or more sophisticated weapons. As for scalpels, Tregalles wasn't quite sure whether the surgeon was being facetious or not, but Livingstone didn't strike him as someone who would make frivolous remarks.

"As you so succinctly put it," said Alcott grimly, "we have to find this man, and we have to find him fast. Obviously, Paget isn't going to be able to help us, so we'll be working blind as far as motive is concerned. I'll have someone go through our office records, and you can do the same on Paget's case notes. If he did receive a threat of any kind, he may have logged it. Meanwhile, you and I will begin questioning anyone who saw or spoke to Paget just before he left the building. And when Forsythe goes out there to see Mrs. Wentworth first thing tomorrow, I want her to find out everything she can about Paget's private life. There has to be a strong motive for such a vicious attack. I want to know if Paget was worried about anything—money troubles, women, anything at all.'' Alcott flapped his hands helplessly. "To tell you the truth, Tregalles, it wasn't until tonight that I realized how little we know about the man once he leaves the office.''

"Who will I be reporting to?" Tregalles asked as they left the hospital, suddenly conscious of the fact that he would no longer be working for Paget. *And might never work for him again!* came the insidious thought.

It was still raining. Alcott paused at the top of the steps to take one last drag at the cigarette he'd been cupping in his hands as they walked along the corridors, before flicking it into the night. "You'll be reporting directly to me," he said. "We have two DIs off sick, one on course, and we're stretched to the limit, so I'm counting on you, Tregalles. You probably know more about Paget than anyone else here, including me, so in effect, this is your case. I'll see you back in the office in ten minutes. There'll be no sleep for any of us tonight.''

TWO

"I WANT YOU TO run through it one more time for Sergeant Tregalles's benefit," Alcott said. "Beginning with you, Davis."

The two uniformed constables, Les Davis and Barry Redfern, sat facing Alcott and Tregalles across the table in interview room number 1. Davis, the driver of the patrol car, was the older of the two: dark-haired, heavyset, a Welshman from Llanelli.

"From the time we entered the yard, like, sir?"

Alcott nodded.

"Right, sir. Well, like I said, we were bringing in this drunk and disorderly, but what with the barricades around the trench, and the space being so narrow at the front, I didn't want to try to park the car there, so I went round the back."

"After almost getting hit by that Escort as we came in," Redfern muttered, then shrugged apologetically. "Sorry, didn't mean to interrupt, sir."

"No, no, that's all right," Alcott told him. "This Escort, where was it coming from?"

"From round the back. It came down the side of the building and cut out into the road as we were coming in. I don't think she even saw us until it was almost too late."

"She? Did you recognize the driver?"

Davis shot a glance at his partner, and Redfern shifted uncomfortably in his seat. "It wasn't *that* close," Davis said, distancing himself from Redfern's statement. "It's just that I wasn't expecting anyone coming down there that time of night. I mean, there was no danger.''

Alcott brushed that aside. "So who was it?" he demanded.

"It was that WPC from Tenborough. Constable Regan."

"You're quite sure?"

"It's hard to miss that red hair, sir."

"And she came out as you drove in?"

"That's right, sir. In a bit of a hurry, too."

"Go on."

"Well, like I said, we drove round the back, and as we turned the corner we could see there was some sort of donnybrook going on, so I flicked my high beams on to get a better look, and as soon as I did, young Barry here jumped out of the car and started running toward the two men."

"Two men?" Tregalles repeated. "You mean Mr. Paget and his assailant? Or do you mean two men in addition to Mr. Paget?"

"Just the one man attacking the other," said Davis firmly. "I didn't know it was Mr. Paget at the time. How about you, Barry?"

"I only saw one man, sir, apart from Mr. Paget, that is," Redfern said. "Mr. Paget was on his knees, and the man attacking him was holding him by his hair."

Alcott leaned forward. "Using one hand or two?" he asked sharply.

Redfern squinted into the middle distance as he tried to recall the scene. "One hand," he said decisively. "His left hand. He had some sort of weapon in his right hand—a metal bar, I think—so I shouted at him to drop it."

"A metal bar? Not a razor?"

"A razor?" Redfern looked startled by the question. "No, sir, definitely not a razor. Is that what he used? Jesus! No wonder there was so much blood!"

With some prompting, Redfern described again what he'd done while waiting for the ambulance. For his part, Davis had called for an ambulance from the car before running into the station to get help and pick up a blanket to keep Paget warm until the ambulance arrived.

"Anything else?"

Davis frowned in thought. "I picked up Mr. Paget's brief-case and umbrella and tossed them into the car."

"Where are they now?"

"Turned them over to the duty sergeant, sir. I believe he bagged them in case there were prints on them."

Alcott grunted his approval as Tregalles directed a question to Redfern. "You say the man ran off into the trees? Was he carrying anything?"

"Like what, sir?"

"Like the metal bar, for example."

"Not that I could see, but then it's only a few yards to the trees, and when I saw how badly injured the man on the ground was, I stopped to attend to him instead of giving chase."

Tregalles looked puzzled. "So, we have an attacker holding Paget by his hair with one hand while holding an iron bar in the other. Where was the razor? And how did he manage to cut Paget's throat? Are you quite sure there wasn't someone else out there?"

Redfern shook his head. "If there was, I didn't see him," he said firmly.

"Me neither," his partner said. "There was just the one."

Alcott broke in to question them further, insisting on more detail, but the answers remained the same. He knew there was something wrong, but he was convinced the two men were telling the truth—at least as they saw it. "Very well," he said at last. "Make sure you put everything in your report."

The superintendent rose to his feet as the men stood up to leave. "How long have you been here, Redfern?" he asked.

"Four weeks, sir," the man said warily.

"Four weeks," Alcott repeated. "Well, I'll tell you, lad, you've made a damned good start. Your quick thinking and subsequent action may well have saved a man's life tonight, and it will be noted on your record.''

Redfern looked embarrassed as the superintendent shook his hand. "Just doing what they taught me, sir," he mumbled. "Is Mr. Paget going to be all right?"

Alcott drew in his breath and shook his head. "I'm afraid that remains to be seen," he said, "but you'll be told as soon as we know anything for sure." He turned to Davis. "You're to be congratulated, too," he said as Redfern moved away, "and it will be noted. Looks like you've got a good lad, there."

"I have, sir," Davis agreed. "And thank you."

As the two men left the room, Alcott sank back into his chair and rubbed his face with both hands. "Not a good start, Tregalles," he said bleakly, "so let's hope to God that SOCO finds something more to go on than we have at present, because as of now, we have nothing!"

ALL THOSE ON the afternoon shift had been asked to stay behind, and now it was the duty officer, Sergeant Sam Broughton, who sat opposite the superintendent and Tregalles. A heavyset grey-haired man, he sat stiffly in his chair, one leg outstretched to relieve the throbbing in an arthritic knee.

Alcott lit a cigarette. Broughton's eyes flicked to the No Smoking sign on the wall, but he said nothing. "You can smoke if you wish, Sam," Alcott told him. The two men had known each other a long time. Broughton thought about it, then shook his head.

"So you saw Paget leave," the superintendent said. "What time was that?"

"Six minutes past eight by my clock," said Broughton promptly. "I'd just finished clocking in a domestic. The time's on the sheet."

"He was alone?"

Broughton nodded. "That is, he was when he passed the desk, but he stopped to chat with Regan at the door."

"What was she doing there?"

"Don't know, really. She came down about ten minutes before Mr. Paget did, and stopped to have a word with Linda Bryce. I thought she'd left the building, but next thing I see is her talking to Mr. Paget at the door. They left together."

"Bryce? I don't think I know her, do I?" said Alcott.

"She's one of our clerks. Civilian. Works afternoon shifts mostly. I understand that DC Regan is staying with Bryce while she's here in Broadminster."

"But Regan lives in Broadminster," Tregalles objected. "She's married and lives right here in town with her husband. She told me when she first came."

Broughton shrugged. "Don't know about that," he said. "As far as I know, she's been staying with Linda Bryce for some time now."

"Is Bryce still here?"

"That she is, sir," said Broughton with a smile, "and a right fuss she made when I told her she had to stay. Big date, apparently. Wanted to know if she'd be paid overtime."

Alcott snorted. "Davis told us that Regan was in a hurry when she left the car park," he said, "and it was only a matter of seconds later that he and Redfern saw Paget being attacked." He glanced in Tregalles's direction. "Sounds to me as if she might have seen that something was going on, and ran away rather than tried to help."

But Tregalles shook his head. "I've been working closely with Kate Regan for the past month," he said, "and I don't believe that. She's not afraid to wade right in if necessary. If she'd seen Paget being attacked, I'm sure that she would have either gone to help him herself, or at least come in here to get help. She wouldn't just drive away."

Alcott grunted non-committally. "That's the last you saw of either Regan or Paget?" he asked Broughton, and when the sergeant nodded, he said, "Right, then. Let's have this woman, Bryce, in, and see if she knows why Regan left in such a hurry."

WHILE THEY WERE waiting for Linda Bryce to be brought in, Charlie Dobbs, the man in charge of SOCO, knocked and entered the room. He was a tall, lean, cadaverous-looking man with a droll sense of humour—some would even say macabre. His rank was that of inspector, but for as long as anyone could remember, no one, from the highest to the lowest, had ever used his title. He was known and referred to by one and all as Charlie.

Charlie's upper half was protected by a yellow cape, but the legs of his trousers were soaked through, and he was in his stocking feet.

"Left my wellies at the front door," he explained. "It's still pissing down out there, and Broughton doesn't like mud all over his floor." He stood there, just inside the door, dripping water. "We've cordoned the entire area off, but it's useless even trying to search the ground until daylight. Even then, between the rain, the ambulance men, and the uniforms tramping around out there, I doubt if we'll find very much."

"What about the trees?" Alcott asked. "Redfern said the man took off toward the playing fields through the trees."

"We've cordoned them off," Charlie assured him. "Anything in particular we're looking for?"

"The weapon," said Alcott. "Or weapons. And anything that suggests that more than one man was involved in the attack. It seems we have either a man with three arms, or someone else was there. Anyway, see what you can find."

Charlie was halfway out the door when Alcott called out after him: "And don't forget the ditch. If the weapon's there, I want it found."

Charlie nodded dolefully. "Bloody thing's full of water," he said. "We'll have to pump. Could take a while."

"Then pump!" Alcott told him. "And let's make sure the contractor understands that no one goes near the site until we give the OK."

As Charlie left the room, Linda Bryce entered hesitantly. "Sergeant Broughton said you wanted to see me, sir?"

Alcott remembered the woman now; he just hadn't known her name. She was tall and slender and extremely well endowed. She wore tight skirts, ending several inches above the knees, and if ever there was a gathering of men around a desk in the front office, you could be fairly certain it would be hers.

"Sit down, Miss Bryce," Alcott told her. "We'll try not to hold you up for long, and we do appreciate your volunteering to stay behind to help us."

A smile tugged at the corner of Linda Bryce's lips as she sat down opposite the two men. She sat up very straight on the wooden chair, knees pressed together, smoothing nonexistent wrinkles from her skirt with long, caressing strokes of her slender fingers. Alcott eyed her for a long moment through a plume of smoke, then sat back in his chair and nodded to Tregalles.

The sergeant, who appreciated beauty in all its forms, shifted his gaze and found the woman's soft grey eyes upon him. She wasn't what he would call beautiful, but she certainly was attractive, and those legs... He looked down at his notes to break the spell.

"Sergeant Broughton tells us that Constable Regan stopped to have a word with you before she left," he said. "Do you mind telling us what that was about, Miss Bryce?"

Linda hesitated, looked down at her hands folded in her lap. "I was just telling her that I might be home late after work and not to wait up for me, that's all," she said.

"I was under the impression that Kate Regan lived with her husband here in Broadminster, but now I'm told that she's living with you. Is that correct?"

"That's right, sir."

"And why is that?"

Again, Linda hesitated. "It's just that... Well, you know how it is, sir. Things weren't going all that well at home, so I suggested she come and stay with me for a while until things could be sorted out."

"Things? Such as…?"

"With respect, sir, I think that's something you should be asking her."

"But you do know why?"

"Well, yes. At least…" Linda Bryce pursed her lips as if trying to decide how much to say; her eyes remained steady on the sergeant's face for a long moment. "At least," she continued slowly, "I know what Kate *says* is wrong."

Tregalles raised a quizzical eyebrow.

Linda moved uncomfortably beneath his gaze. "It's just that… Well, to be honest, I think she's overreacting. I mean, yeah, Paul's upset, but you can hardly blame him, what with the way he lost his job and all. But she claims he flies into uncontrollable rages, swearing and ranting on about her and her job, and she's afraid of what he might do."

"But you don't believe her?"

"It's not that I don't believe her," the woman said carefully, "it's just that I think she's got it wrong. Paul is such a sweet man. I can't believe he would ever harm Kate."

"You know him, then?"

"Yes. Well, I haven't actually seen Paul these past few months, but I've spoken to him on the phone. He just wants Kate to come back to him, that's all. He says he can't understand why she left him."

"And what does Kate say?"

"She says that he's gone strange since he lost his job; she says he drinks a lot, yet I've never seen him drunk, and she says he's accused her of having an affair with someone at work. She says he wants her to pack her job in and stay home with him. Which, if that's true, is pretty ridiculous, isn't it? I mean, what would they live on if she did that?"

"An affair? Do you have a name?"

"No. Kate never said."

Alcott leaned forward and butted his cigarette in a makeshift ashtray. "What else did you and Regan talk about before she left this evening?" he asked.

Linda shrugged. "Just a bit of idle chat, that's all, sir," she said.

"About what, Miss Bryce? Why was she waiting at the door? Was she waiting for Paget?"

Linda frowned, seemingly perplexed by the question, but then began to nod. "I don't know about Mr. Paget, but she may have been waiting for someone to come along. Someone who would walk with her to her car."

"Because?"

Linda Bryce took in a deep breath slowly, then let it out again. "Because she thought Paul was out there. She told me that she thought she'd seen him from the upstairs window just before she was ready to leave. That's why she was waiting inside the door, I expect. Trying to see if he was still there before going out."

"I see. Then Paget came along and the two of them went out together."

"I don't know, sir. I didn't see that. My desk is over in the corner by the window."

Superintendent Alcott leaned back in his chair and lit another cigarette. "I think it's time we had a chat with Constable Regan," he said quietly. "You haven't phoned her about what happened, have you, Miss Bryce?" The woman shook her head. "Good. Then let's get her down here now," he told Tregalles. "No doubt Miss Bryce will give you the number."

THREE

KATE GLANCED AT the time as she turned into Charter Lane. Twenty-eight minutes past midnight. Sergeant Tregalles hadn't said why he wanted her to come in. Just that he needed her down there immediately. Said he'd explain when she got there, but it must be something big to be called back in at this hour.

There were lights ahead. Dozens of them. A uniformed constable waving a torch stepped out into the road. "You can't stop here, miss," he told her. "Please drive on."

Kate flashed her card. "I'm wanted inside," she told him. "What's going on? Why is all this blocked off?"

"If you'll follow me, I'll show you where you can leave the car," the man told her, and moved off without answering the question.

Kate parked the car and picked her way between lines of yellow tape and entered the building. She was surprised to see Sergeant Broughton still there, and even more surprised to see some of the afternoon staff huddled around their desks. "What is it?" she asked the sergeant. "What's happened?"

"No doubt the superintendent will tell you what it's all about," he said. "He and Sergeant Tregalles are waiting for you in there." He pointed to the door of interview room number 1. Behind Broughton, she saw Linda standing beside her desk; she tried to catch her eye, but Linda turned away. Puzzled, Kate walked toward the interview room, and was suddenly afraid.

KATE STARED AT Alcott in disbelief. "Mr. Paget, sir? Attacked? In the car park? But he was just going to his car when I left. Is he... Is he all right? Was he hurt?"

"He's on the critical list in hospital," Alcott said tersely. "Now, I'm told that you and DCI Paget left the building together. Did you see anyone else out there? Anyone at all?" Kate hesitated for only a fraction of a second before shaking her head, but it didn't go unnoticed by the superintendent. "Tell me," he said sharply, "how did you and Paget happen to leave together? Broughton tells me that you came downstairs several minutes before Paget. Why did you wait for him at the door?"

"I wasn't waiting for him, sir. I wasn't waiting for anyone. I was simply standing there looking out, hoping the rain would ease up a bit before going round the back to get my car. I'd just decided there was no point in waiting any longer when the chief inspector came along, and since his car was also round the back, we left together. We reached my car first, and Mr. Paget went on to his. That's the last I saw of him."

"Where was he exactly when you last saw him?"

"As I said, walking to his car."

"Was he close to it?"

"He must have been. I lost sight of him as soon as I got in my car, but he didn't have far to go. From then on, I was concentrating on getting the car around the corner without running over one of those silly little lights they have out there beside the trench."

"You didn't see anything in the rearview mirror?"

Kate was irritated by the question. "As I said, sir, it was as black as pitch out there. There was nothing to see."

"That lane beside the building is narrow," Alcott observed, "yet I understand you were travelling so fast when you came out of there that you almost hit a patrol car. Why were you in such a hurry, Constable?"

A slow flush crept into Kate's face. She remembered now. Remembered trying to peer into the shadows as she drove past the heavy machinery where she'd seen movement earlier. Trying to see if Paul was there. "I may have been going a *bit* fast," she admitted grudgingly, "but I don't think there was any danger of a collision, sir. If there was, I apologize. I can only say that I was tired and wet, and I just wanted to get home and soak in a hot tub."

"Who else was in the car park besides you and Paget?"

"No one, sir." She thought of Paul, and mentally crossed her fingers. "At least not as far as I know," she amended.

"Not your husband, then?"

Linda! Damn her anyway! Why could she never keep her mouth shut? The colour deepened in Kate's face. "I don't understand, sir," she said weakly.

"Don't you?" Alcott blew smoke into the air above her head. "I think you do," he said harshly. He sat back in his chair and nodded for Tregalles to continue.

The sergeant leaned forward, elbows resting on the table, hands clasped in front of him. "What happened out there, Kate?" he asked quietly. "Why were you going so fast? What were you afraid of?"

Kate chewed on her lower lip. This was all going wrong. She'd tried so hard to keep her personal problems away from work. It was no one else's business. Here she was, a police-woman, damned good at her job and on the way to becoming a sergeant, yet it would look as if she couldn't even handle her own husband. How was that going to look on her record?

She met the sergeant's gaze with troubled eyes, but before she had a chance to speak, Tregalles spoke again. "This is no time for holding back," he told her. "Mr. Paget's life is hanging by a thread tonight. But for the grace of God and a constable with his wits about him, he would have died out there. Now, did you see someone out there? And if so, was it your husband?"

Kate Regan closed her eyes. Not Paul. It couldn't be. Surely to God he wouldn't be so stupid! And yet... "Answer the question, Constable!"

Kate's eyes flew open. "I—I honestly don't know. I saw a shadow...."

"Has your husband done this before? Waited outside for you to come out?"

"Yes."

"Did you see any sign of him when you walked with Mr. Paget round the back?"

"No."

"Has he ever threatened you? Threatened to harm you physically?"

"Yes, but he wouldn't... He's not himself. You don't understand!"

Alcott leaned forward, his sharp eyes fixed intently on her face. "Then make us understand, Constable," he said softly, "because you are not leaving this room until we do!"

IN THE INCIDENT ROOM across the hall, Sergeant Ormside sat at his desk. All the lights were on, but he was alone, there to begin the process of setting a major investigation in motion. A lean, sharp-featured man with a ruddy complexion, Len Ormside had spent more than thirty years in the service. He knew virtually everyone from the chief constable down, and no one could touch him for his intimate knowledge of the area. While the ultimate responsibility lay with Superintendent Alcott, it was Ormside who would direct the day-to-day operations and keep things moving. In the past, Alcott had left the supervision of the incident room to Paget, but now it was Paget who was the victim, and it seemed strange to Ormside to be working without the DCI's direction. It wasn't that Ormside didn't know what to do, or even needed direction—he'd been doing the job long before Paget came—but it just didn't *feel* right somehow.

The sergeant sighed heavily and roused himself. There was a lot to be done, preparatory work for the most part, because there was little anyone could do until daylight. Charlie Dobbs seemed to think it would be a waste of time going over the ground at the rear of the building, but then, Charlie always looked on the black side. Ormside hoped he was wrong, because without more to go on than they had at the moment, it was going to be a hard slog.

But first things first. The sergeant turned to the computer beside his desk and clicked on "Media." A menu appeared, and he clicked on "Appeals, Public," then selected one of the standard formats. He filled in the blanks—times, date, location, etc.—then switched to the fax programme. The appeal for public assistance would go out immediately. It was too late for the morning papers, but the radio and TV stations would have it on the early news. There would be the usual rash of calls, of course, most of which would take up time and lead absolutely nowhere, but even if it produced one small gem, it would be well worth the trouble.

Ormside brought up the duty roster on the screen and began checking off names and setting assignments. He'd work till three, he decided, then put his head down on the cot in the first aid room for two or three hours' sleep before starting to call in extra staff. They'd be needed for the wide-area search across the playing fields, and for knocking on every door in the immediate vicinity of Charter Lane.

THE TOWN HALL CLOCK was striking two as Alcott and Tregalles left Charter Lane in the sergeant's car. Regan had been reluctant to talk to them about what she considered to be her private life, but Alcott had soon set her straight on that score, and once she started talking, it was as if she wanted to clear the air completely, and held back nothing.

She told them that she and Paul Marshall had been married for four years. Like many couples, they both worked; she travelled back and forth each day to her job in Tenborough, while he worked for Scofield Box and Paper, an aggressive local firm with customers throughout western England and much of Wales. Then, six months ago, Paul was made redundant.

"It came as a terrible shock to both of us," Kate said. "There was no warning. Nothing. Paul had worked for Scofield's for almost twenty years, and suddenly he was out. What made it even worse was that he'd just been promoted to sales manager for the South-West Region, after years on the road as a sales rep."

Apparently, unknown to almost everyone who worked there, the firm had overextended itself and gone deeply into debt. A corporation by the name of Trimble-Dexter had taken over their debt and scooped them up. There was a wholesale change in management, and Paul was out.

"He simply couldn't believe that the company he'd served so faithfully for all that time would toss him aside like that," said Kate. "He couldn't get it through his head that, apart from the name, Scofield's no longer existed, and the decision to let him go had been made in some corporate boardroom in Wolverhampton. He kept saying they'd made a mistake, and they would call him back, but of course that didn't happen, and he was forced to face the fact that he would have to look for another job."

The trouble was, Kate explained, his age was against him. Paul was forty-one years old, twelve years older than Kate, and no one was prepared to take him on. He'd tried everything, even taking computer courses at the college to try to make himself more marketable, but nothing had worked. Résumés he sent out went unanswered, and he'd become more and more despondent. Always a quiet man, he withdrew even further into himself, and flared up when Kate tried to talk to him. "He resented the fact that I was going off to work each day, while he was stuck at home," she explained.

Within months, their relationship had deteriorated to the point where they were barely civil to each other. But Kate said she became really worried when Paul began to disappear for days at a time. When he did come home, she could see that he'd been drinking, but when she tried to talk to him about it, he turned on her and said it was all her fault for not supporting him, and blamed her for being away all day. He said that if she loved him, she should quit her job and stay with him.

"There was no reasoning with him," said Kate, her eyes moist as she looked at the two men. "I finally had to admit that things were out of control. I couldn't handle him; he needed professional help, but he refused to see a doctor. I tried to get someone out to see him, but you know what that's like these days, so things just went from bad to worse."

From that time on, Kate said, all Paul would talk about was her leaving her job. She had a duty to stay home with him, he insisted. When she refused and tried to reason with him, he said she must have another reason for not wanting to stay at home with him, and accused her of using her job as a blind for carrying on an affair. The more she denied it, the more he screamed at her, and said if he ever caught her with another man, he'd kill him.

Kate fell silent. Her eyes met those of the superintendent. "There was no one else," she told him. "There never has been, but Paul wouldn't believe that. I couldn't stand it anymore, so I left him and went to stay with Linda until I could try to sort things out. But he's still stalking me. Sometimes he's there outside the house at night when I get home, just standing there across the street." Kate shivered. "He never speaks, just watches. He phones Linda and pleads with her to persuade me to go back to him. She thinks he's harmless, and I know she doesn't believe me when I tell her what Paul is *really* like."

Kate Regan stopped speaking and sat back in her chair. She closed her eyes. Her face was paper-white. She looked exhausted.

But Alcott wasn't prepared to let her rest, at least not yet. "And you believed he was out there tonight?" he said.

Kate opened her eyes. "I *thought* I saw someone out there, sir," she said carefully. "I couldn't see properly because of the poor light and the rain, but it looked as if someone was standing in the shadow of that big Cat they have beside the trench. I assumed it was Paul. I couldn't think why someone else would be standing out there in the rain like that.''

"So you waited by the door until Paget came along because you were afraid to leave the building alone."

"I didn't know it would be Mr. Paget," said Kate wretchedly. "I just hoped someone would come along so that I didn't have to walk to my car alone."

"You didn't know it would be Paget," Alcott repeated softly. "Are you quite sure about that, Constable?"

"I—I don't understand, sir."

"Then let me make it absolutely clear. Who else's car was parked behind the building, apart from your own?"

"Just Mr. Paget's."

"Exactly! And isn't that why you waited at the door? Because you knew that Paget would be along in a few minutes?" Alcott leaned across the table. "Is it not true that you had arranged to wait for him there? That perhaps your husband had good reason to believe you were having an affair?"

"No!" Kate Regan's hands slammed the table so hard that Alcott recoiled. Her eyes blazed, and bright red spots appeared in the middle of her cheeks. "That is not true," she shouted at him. "I told you I waited there in the hope that someone would come along, but, if necessary, I was prepared to wait until I was sure that Paul had left. Then Mr. Paget came along. I didn't know he was coming. It was simply a coincidence, and I looked upon it as a godsend, and took advantage of it."

Alcott's voice was pitched dangerously low when he spoke again. "So what you are telling us is that you walked out there with Paget, knowing your husband might be out there, knowing he had threatened to kill the lover you say doesn't exist, and you didn't tell him? You didn't warn him?"

Kate shook her head.

"For God's sake, why not?" Alcott exploded.

"Because I didn't think it was anyone else's business,"

Kate flared. "Besides, it never occurred to me that Paul might think that Mr. Paget... I didn't think..." Kate stopped and shook her head despairingly.

"Precisely!" snapped Alcott. "Paget was damned near killed tonight because you didn't bloody well think!" His eyes never left the face of the hapless woman as he stood up. "Where's your husband now?" he demanded.

Kate shrugged helplessly. "I don't know. At home, I suppose." She, too, rose to her feet. "I know it sounds bad, sir, and I know Paul made those threats, but I don't believe he could have attacked Mr. Paget, not like that; not so savagely. Paul's not like that. He—"

But Alcott cut her off. "Frankly, Constable, I'm not interested in what you believe or don't believe. As far as I'm concerned, your husband is the prime suspect in this case, and the sooner we have a talk with him the better. Meanwhile, you will remain here under supervision, and write out everything you've told us. And there will be no phone calls to your husband, or anyone else for that matter. Understood?"

Kate felt the colour rising in her face. The hostility emanating from Superintendent Alcott was palpable, and she knew, at least as far as he was concerned, her career could well be over.

She sucked in her breath and nodded grimly. "Understood, sir," she said through gritted teeth.

ANDREA MCMILLAN STOOD beside the bed, listening to the dry, rasping sound of air flowing through the tube in Paget's throat. The young constable had exerted so much pressure on the artery to stop the flow of blood that he'd bruised the throat, which had almost swollen shut by the time they reached the hospital, hence the tube.

"To be honest, Andrea, I thought we'd lost him a couple of times on the operating table," Geoff Livingstone had confided, "but he came back. Says a lot for the man's stamina. Close friend of yours, is he?"

"A *good* friend, yes," said Andrea, barely conscious that she'd corrected him. It was as if she had to make that distinction clear, not only to Livingstone, but to herself. Neil Paget *was* a good friend, steady, understanding, patient, reliable—all the attributes she would look for in a husband, and in a father for Sarah. She enjoyed his company, and she was fond of him, but even now, seeing him lying there, fighting for his very life, she could not bring herself to say she *loved* him. She wished she could, for she felt sure that Neil was in love with her. He'd never actually told her so, but she had seen it in his eyes, felt it in his touch, and it wasn't as if she hadn't wanted him. There'd been times when she had ached to let him take her in his arms, to hold her, but something had always held her back.

She sighed. Was she being unreasonable? she asked herself. Was it simply a case of being afraid of making another mistake as she had with Sarah's father?

Livingstone had reached out and touched her arm. "There's nothing you can do by staying here," he told her. "Whatever happens now is very much up to him. Why don't you go home and get some rest?" He glanced at his watch. "What time are you on this morning?"

Andrea cleared her throat. "Not till nine," she said huskily.

"There's still time to get three or four hours' sleep if you go now," he urged. "Mr. Stone is not going to take kindly to a registrar who falls asleep during rounds, no matter what the reason, so go home now, Andrea. Please."

"I will," she'd assured him, "in a few minutes."

That had been an hour ago, and still she stayed, unable to leave the man who, in every way but one, was closest to her heart.

FOUR

THE SIGN SAID Bridgewater Road. "This is it," said Alcott unnecessarily as Tregalles turned the corner. "And I think that's number twenty-eight," he added a few moments later. "The one with the light in the window."

"Odd," Tregalles observed as he pulled in and stopped the car. It was the only lighted window in the street. "I wonder if someone warned him we were coming?"

"They hadn't better," Alcott muttered as he got out of the car. He pulled up his collar against the rain and led the way up the short path to the door. The front-room curtains were partly drawn, and they could hear the muffled sound of TV voices as they stood in the shelter of the tiny porch and rang the bell. No answer. Alcott stuck his finger on the bell and kept it there.

The TV went off, a light came on in the hall, and a shadow appeared behind the frosted glass in the door.

"Who is it?" a voice called from behind the door. "What do you want?"

Alcott bent down and pushed the letterbox open. "Police," he shouted. "We need to talk to you, Mr. Marshall."

"Police? Can't it wait till morning? I'm on my way to bed."

"Sorry, sir, but no, it can't wait till morning. We need to talk to you now. It's important."

There was an audible sigh of resignation from the other side of the door. A chain rattled, and the door opened a few inches. Alcott held up his warrant card. "My name is Alcott,

Superintendent Alcott, CID," he said, "and this is Sergeant Tregalles. Please open the door."

The chain remained in place. "If it's next door complaining about the TV being too loud, I turned it down an hour ago, so you can bugger off. I'm going to bed!" The door began to close, but Alcott put his shoulder to it and wedged his foot between the door and the jamb.

"This has nothing to do with the TV," he snapped. "This is a serious matter involving your wife. Now, please open the door."

"Kate? What's happened?" The voice rose. "Is she all right?" The door closed as the chain was slipped off, then opened wider to reveal a man of indeterminate age silhouetted against the light.

"Mr. Marshall? Mr. Paul Marshall?" Alcott stepped over the sill, forcing the man to step back as Tregalles followed and closed the door.

"That's right. Now, what's this about Kate? Where is she? What's happened?" Narrowed eyes searched their faces for answers.

"All in good time, sir. Shall we go inside?" Alcott began to advance down the narrow hall, all but pushing the man toward an open door.

"Do I have a choice?" Marshall asked resentfully as he turned and led the way into the sitting room.

It was a barren, airless room that smelt of… what? The stale, acidic odour reminded Alcott of the cells after weekend revellers had been cleared out on a Monday morning. Apart from a single armchair, a dining table with two matching straight-backed chairs, and a television set, the room appeared to have been stripped of everything movable. A single bar of the electric fire glowed bright orange, and a pair of shoes with socks draped over them stood on the hearth, presumably placed there to dry.

Marshall crossed the room to stand in front of the armchair as if afraid the superintendent might want to claim it for himself. "All right, so you're in," he said truculently as he sat down. "Now, what's happened to Kate?"

Alcott remained silent, taking his time to unbutton his coat. His nose wrinkled in distaste as his eyes swept the room and settled on the man facing him.

When Alcott first set eyes on Paul Marshall, he thought there must be some mistake. It was only on closer inspection that he realized this was the same man whose picture Kate Regan had shown them, a photograph taken at the time of their wedding. "He was different, then," Kate had said wistfully, "but he's changed; he's not the same man I married."

In the photograph, Paul Marshall looked very smart in his double-breasted suit, hair short and neatly styled. He had a pleasant, friendly face and an engaging smile. Alcott could understand why Kate had been attracted to him, and why Marshall had been successful as a salesman. What had puzzled him was why Marshall had found it so hard to find another job. But seeing the man now, he was beginning to understand some of the things Kate had told them. This thin, stooped man, with unkempt hair and sallow skin, bore little resemblance to the photograph taken four years ago. His face was gaunt, his eyes like chips of coal, deep-set and watchful, and he hadn't shaved for days. He wore a shapeless cardigan over a stained shirt, both far too big for him, and his trousers were so badly creased and rumpled that Alcott wondered if the man had slept in them.

"I think you know very well why we're here, Mr. Marshall," he said quietly. "Tell me, where were you earlier this evening around eight o'clock?"

"I'm not answering anything until you tell me what's happened to Kate," the man said belligerently. "Is she hurt? You said it was serious."

"I said it was a serious matter involving your wife," Alcott corrected. "Now, sir, please answer the question. Where were you earlier this evening?"

"I was here. Where else would I be on a night like this?"

Alcott moved to the hearth and bent to look closely at the shoes. "Hardly the way to treat good brogues," he observed mildly. "Too much heat cracks the leather." He picked them up and turned them over. "Mud," he said. "Looks to me like the clay down at Charter Lane. We'll take them with us when we leave, Sergeant. And the socks. I'm sure Mr. Marshall has others he can wear." He set them down again and stood facing Marshall. "Now then, sir, shall we begin again? What were you doing in Charter Lane earlier this evening?"

Tregalles took out his notebook, brushed crumbs from the seat of one of the chairs, and sat down at the table.

"That *is* where the mud came from, is it not?" Alcott prompted.

Marshall's brows drew together in a frown. "Charter Lane? I'm afraid I don't know what you're talking about." He spoke carefully, like a man who knows he has had too much to drink and is trying to hide it. "The only time I was out was when I went down to the corner shop for something for my tea."

"What time was that?"

"Six, seven o'clock. Something like that. I don't know exactly." His lip curled. "I didn't know then that I'd have to account for my time."

"A bit late to be going for something for your tea, wasn't it?"

"So I fell asleep. Is that a crime now?"

"Is that the corner shop at the bottom of the road?" Tregalles asked.

"That's right."

"So you won't mind if we ask them if they remember what time it was you came in?"

Marshall shrugged. "Do what you like," he said. "I'm sure you will anyway."

Alcott pulled out the remaining chair and sat down in front of Marshall. "Save your lies for your solicitor, Marshall," he said curtly. "You were seen in Charter Lane."

"I don't see how. I wasn't there. Who says I was?"

"Your wife."

"Kate?" Marshall groaned and shook his head as if in weary disbelief. "So that's what this is all about. All right, what's she been saying about me? What is it I'm supposed to have done now?"

"Why don't you tell me?"

Marshall raised his head. "That's just it. I haven't done anything, but Kate keeps making up these stories...." He broke off and looked hard at Alcott. "You've come to warn me off, haven't you?" he accused. "She tells you some cock-and-bull story about my being in the yard at Charter Lane, and you come out here in the middle of the night to try to put the fear of God into me. Isn't that how it works? What do you plan to do? Arrest me?"

In the yard! Tregalles wrote in his book, and underlined it.

"Do you deny that you have been stalking your wife ever since she left you?"

Marshall snorted. "Stalking? Is that what she calls it? If you mean have I tried to *talk* to my wife on a number of occasions, yes, I have, but she just turns her back and walks away." He sat forward in his chair. "Look, Superintendent, all I want is my wife back here with me where she belongs, but you've put so much pressure on her, demanded so much of her time, and made her feel so guilty about leaving the job, that she's confused. You've got her thinking that you can't do without her down there, when I'm the one who can't do without her. I'm her husband, for God's sake! She should be here to look after me as she promised."

Tregalles raised his head, pen poised above his notes. "Promised, sir?" he echoed.

"That's right, promised before God when we were married. In sickness and in health. That's a sacred promise, and it's her duty to come home to look after me."

"You've been ill, then, have you, sir?"

"Sick, more like. Sick to death of being out of a job. Sick of being told I'm too old. Sick of having to look after myself when my wife should be here to look after me, except she thinks more of her job than she does of me, thanks to being brainwashed into thinking she is actually useful down there. And as for her being made a sergeant, well…'' He dismissed that idea with a shrug. ''It's a numbers game with you lot, isn't it? Got to have so many women, so many blacks, and so on. Right?''

His voice changed to one of earnest pleading. ''Just for once, couldn't you look at it from my point of view? See, I didn't mind Kate going off to Tenborough every day when we were first married. I was on the road most of the week, and we had our weekends together, so it wasn't a problem then. But it was different when I became a manager. I expected her to stay home, to be there when I got home each night, but by then she'd become so wrapped up in the job that she didn't want to leave. I didn't like it, but I put up with it because I thought sooner or later she'd realize it was her duty to give up her job and stay home. I mean, that's her place, isn't it? Here with me. Then, when I was made redundant, I thought that would settle it. There'd be no question; she'd see that she had to stay home. But she didn't.''

Marshall's eyes were moist. ''I pleaded with her, but she wouldn't listen. She said there was no need to leave, because she was being moved back here to Broadminster for special training, and everything would be all right. She'd be close to home. But it wasn't all right. She was still away when I needed her, gone all hours of the day and night. I pleaded with her, but this time she had another excuse. She said they were going to make her a sergeant if she stayed on, and she'd be making more money, so I wouldn't have to worry about not having a job.''

His voice rose to an angry pitch, his words beginning to slur. ''How do you think that made me feel, eh? Sitting here without a job? It isn't *fair,* her having a job while I'm stuck here, day in, day out. *I'm* the one who should be making the money. It's *my* job to look after *her*. I'm the one who should have a job, not Kate!''

Marshall's expression hardened. His voice dropped to little more than a whisper, and his eyes became slits. ''But then, I didn't know the half of it, did I? Didn't realize what had been going on behind my back. I still thought it was all about the job, about her wanting a career. I trusted her, but I should have known by the way she kept going on about him.''

''Him?'' said Alcott sharply. ''Who are you talking about?''

''As if you didn't know,'' Marshall sneered. ''You know damned well who I mean. The one she was always talking about before she left. Day after day, he was all she ever talked about after she was transferred to Broadminster. It was DCI Paget this and DCI Paget that—I'm surprised you need anybody else down there from the way she used to go on about him, he's so bloody marvellous.'' Marshall sighed heavily and rubbed his face with his hands. ''I'll admit I lost my temper,'' he continued. ''I told her if that was the way it was, if she thought more of the job and this bloke Paget than she did of me and her duty to me, then she might as well stop there with him instead of coming home.'' His eyes glistened as he looked at Alcott. ''So she did,'' he ended.

Alcott shot a questioning glance at Tregalles: did he know anything about this? it said. The sergeant shrugged and shook his head, but the question hung in the air between them. Kate Regan was an attractive woman, and she had been working closely with Paget. In fact, now that Tregalles came to think of it, she had often volunteered to stay behind when she could have gone home. As for Paget, he always stayed late, had done so as long as Tregalles could remember. He'd thought little of it at the time, but now…

''Are you suggesting that your wife is having an affair with Paget?'' Alcott's voice was dangerously low.

Marshall met the superintendent's stare head-on. ''What do you think?'' he said defiantly. He looked down at his hands.

"It's not Kate's fault. She's such a trusting soul. It's his fault. He's got her mesmerized."

"So you decided to do something about it," Alcott prompted. "Which is why you were waiting outside the building earlier tonight, waiting for your wife to come out, hoping to catch her with Paget. And when you saw the two of them together, you followed them round the back, waited for your wife to—"

"I didn't—" Marshall interrupted, but Alcott cut him off.

"Waited for your wife to leave," he continued as if Marshall hadn't spoken, "then followed Paget to his car, where you attacked him and tried to kill him. Isn't that right, sir?"

Paul Marshall looked stunned. He sat very still. "Tried to *kill* him?" he breathed. "I don't even *know* the man; I wouldn't know him if I saw him. How could I...?"

"Don't know the man?" Alcott shouted. "You sit there and tell me your wife is having an affair with one of my men, then expect me to believe you don't know him after following your wife about for weeks?" He rose to his feet and crossed the floor to stand in front of Marshall. The superintendent was not a big man, but he seemed to tower over the cringing Marshall. "Do you know what I think?" he said. "I think you went down to Charter Lane to spy on your wife, and when you saw her leave the building with Chief Inspector Paget, you waited until she'd gone, then tried to smash his head in and cut his throat. If a police car hadn't arrived on the scene just then, he would have died. In fact, that is still a very real possibility, and if that happens, you'll be looking at a charge of murder."

Marshall refused to look up. "I told you I wasn't there," he whispered hoarsely. "I've never even met this man Paget. I don't know what you're talking about."

Alcott turned to Tregalles. "Mr. Marshall will be accompanying us to the station," he said. "See if you can find him some other shoes and socks." He took out his cigarettes, lit one, and inhaled deeply. "Oh, yes," he added as Tregalles was about to leave the room, "and while you're at it, Sergeant, you might take a look at Mr. Marshall's shaving gear."

"YOU WERE RIGHT to have me examine him," the doctor told Alcott, "but he isn't ill—at least, not in the conventional sense of the word. He is undernourished and he seems confused, but that may be due to the drink. I've never seen anything like it; the reading is off the scale. By rights, the man should be unconscious, yet he walks and talks as if he's had nothing more than a couple of pints. Do you know what he's been drinking?"

"Vodka," Alcott told him. "He had a bottle down beside his chair. It was almost empty, and there were others in the house."

The doctor nodded. "I hope you weren't planning on questioning him tonight, because I've given him something to help him sleep. He'll be out for some six or seven hours, and when he does wake up, he's going to feel like hell. Try to get some liquids down him. Food if possible, but I doubt if he'll want that, so concentrate on the liquids." He picked up his bag. "Meanwhile, I suggest you get some sleep yourself."

"We will," Alcott assured him, and turned to Tregalles. "I want you back here by seven-thirty," he told him, "but first, I want you to write up your notes while they're fresh in your mind. Give Ormside a chance to look them over before the briefing in the morning."

Tregalles glanced at the time as Alcott strode off down the hall. So much for sleep, he thought as he took out his notebook.

ALTHOUGH SHE HAD hardly slept at all, Kate Regan was one of the first to arrive in the office that morning. She was desperately tired, but she was determined to do everything she could to regain the confidence and the trust of her superiors, if it wasn't already too late. The thought that she might have been responsible for the attack on Paget, no matter how innocently, continued to haunt her. A part of her clung desperately to the belief that Paul could not have done such a terrible thing, that someone else had been lurking out there, waiting for Paget. All she had seen was movement—it could have been anyone—but then she had to ask herself: how likely would it be for someone other than Paul to be standing out there in the rain?

A cold chill touched Kate's spine as she thought of their brief encounter in the hall as she was leaving. She had come face-to-face with Paul as they were bringing him in for questioning, and she'd been shocked by his appearance. It was the first time she had been that close to him since leaving the house, and she could hardly believe it was the same man. He was gaunt and hollow-eyed, and he seemed smaller than she remembered.

He'd stopped in front of her, forcing Alcott and Tregalles to stop as well. "Kate," he said sorrowfully. "Why are you doing this to me? Please wait. Please come back home."

She remembered standing there, unable to speak, unable to move. He looked so slight and helpless between the two detectives, his eyes fixed on her face, soft yet earnest in their pleading. For a fleeting moment she glimpsed the man she'd married, and felt a tug at her heart. She wanted to reach out…

But Alcott had glared at her as if he thought it her fault for being there. "Move on," he said roughly, nudging Paul sharply in the back. "We haven't got all night."

They'd moved on. Kate followed them with her eyes. Paul turned to look back. It was only a glance, but she would never forget the look on his face. Gone was the gentle, pleading look; instead, his eyes were full of hatred as they bored into her own.

Kate didn't remember going to her car, but she did remember sitting there with the doors locked, listening to the drumming of the rain and trying to stop her hands from shaking.

It was while she was on her way back to Linda's place that the idea came to her. She could use Paul's absence to return to the house for the things she'd left behind in her haste to get away. Things such as clothing, personal belongings, shoes—especially shoes. She still had a key.

The first thing that hit her when she opened the door was the smell. No matter how many hours she'd worked in the past, and no matter how demanding the job, Kate had always prided herself on keeping the house neat and clean and fresh, even if it meant working late into the night, and it had never smelt like this. The door to the living room was ajar. She went in, turned on the light, and stopped dead in her tracks.

What had once been a comfortable if somewhat cluttered room had now been stripped almost bare. There were no pictures on the walls; the big mirror over the fireplace was gone; the sofa and an armchair had disappeared, lamps, and... "Oh my God! The Welsh dresser!" she cried aloud. She had given pride of place to the wedding gift from her mother.

Kate felt a rising sense of panic as she made her way through the rest of the house. It was the same in every room. The bed and chest of drawers from the second bedroom were gone. The room itself sounded hollow, and Kate realized that she was walking on bare boards. The carpets! Those lovely carpets—all gone. In fact, anything that wasn't needed had disappeared; even the cooker, along with various pots and pans, had been removed from the kitchen; only the microwave and fridge remained. Discarded TV-dinner trays and pizza boxes were stacked high in one corner of the kitchen, and the whole house smelt of stale food and unwashed clothes.

And there were empty vodka bottles everywhere.

Some of her own clothes were still there, but she couldn't bring herself to touch them, let alone take them with her. She forced herself to take several pairs of shoes, but once she had them she couldn't get out of the house fast enough.

Now, as she sat at her desk, afraid to look her colleagues in the eye as they drifted in to work, she wondered how she could possibly get through the day.

IT FELT MORE LIKE the end of the day than the beginning, Tregalles thought as he prepared for the morning briefing. After less than two hours of sleep, he'd returned to work at seven o'clock to work with Ormside on the assignments for the day. The sergeant, as always, had matters well in hand, but even so Tregalles felt the need to check everything himself, because this time things were different. There would be no buffer in the form of DCI Paget between Alcott and himself, and he was very much aware that Alcott would be watching him closely every step of the way. But, as he'd told Audrey over a hurried breakfast, "The trouble is, we have no clues. A suspect, yes, but no real evidence."

"I don't see why you should worry, love," said Audrey soothingly. "I mean, you've got the bloke in custody already, so…"

But Tregalles was shaking his head. "I don't know that we have. We only have the word of his wife that he was there outside the station, and even she is by no means certain. He denies it, and there's no tangible evidence to link him to the crime. Mind you," he continued, more in hopes of convincing himself than his wife, "I suppose Charlie's people could come up with something this morning—not that there's much chance of that with all this rain."

"You're a good detective," Audrey told him firmly. "Mr. Paget told you that himself, so just buck up and tackle it the same way you've always done with him. Mr. Alcott wouldn't have given you the job if he thought you weren't up to it, now would he?"

Which was all very well, thought Tregalles nervously as he stood by the door and watched a subdued group of detectives filing into the room, but he wasn't looking forward to what he had to do today.

Kate was the last to arrive, having deliberately remained at her desk until everyone had gone before following them downstairs. She'd kept her head down, pretending to be absorbed in reading, but she was sure they were talking about her, perhaps even blaming her for what had happened to Paget.

She was about to follow the others inside when Tregalles put out his hand and stopped her. "A word, Kate," he said quietly. "Come with me." He led the way across the corridor to one of the interview rooms.

"Close the door and have a seat," he told her as he moved round behind the table in order to face her. He remained silent for a long moment, thinking about what he had to say. Kate, for her part, sat with hands folded in her lap, trying to mask her apprehension.

Tregalles eyed her across the desk, then blew out his cheeks and took the plunge. "The long and the short of it, Kate, is that, for obvious reasons, you cannot be allowed to have anything to do with this case. Your husband is a suspect—the only suspect at the moment—and as long as that is true, I'm afraid you will have to be sidelined."

Kate flinched when she heard the words. The thought had crossed her mind, but she had thrust it away, hoping against hope they would realize that she had distanced herself from Paul. But, apparently, that wasn't enough. Whether Paul was guilty or not, everyone believed he was, and, even though she no longer lived with him, in their eyes she was still his wife, and therefore not to be trusted. Her first black mark, she thought bitterly, and it wasn't her fault. But whether it was or not, they wanted to be rid of her, so the sooner she collected her things and reported back to Tenborough, the better.

"I understand," she said stiffly as she rose to leave. Her eyes met those of Tregalles. "I know it's not nearly enough to say I'm sorry for what happened, but I am sorry, and I blame myself for not telling Mr. Paget that Paul might be out there. I wish…" Kate felt the sting of tears behind her eyes, and bit her lip. "Does Tenborough know I'm coming back?" she asked.

But Tregalles was shaking his head. "When I said sidelined, Kate, I didn't mean that you were going back to Tenborough. I'm sorry if I didn't make myself clear, but as of this moment, you are on indefinite paid leave."

Colour flared in Kate Regan's face. "I know no one will want me around here anymore," she burst out more forcefully than she'd intended, "but on leave, when I could at least be back there doing my old job? Or don't they want me in Tenborough either? Is that it?"

"No, that is not it, Constable," Tregalles said sharply. "Believe me, if there was any way we could keep you on, we would, but this is a small region, and even in Tenborough you would have access to information regarding the investigation into your husband's activities. You know that as well as I do. I discussed this with Superintendent Alcott earlier this morning, and he agreed there is no alternative."

Tregalles stood up. He liked Kate, and he hated having to do this to her. She had more than pulled her weight in the short time she'd been there, but he had no choice. "Look, Kate," he said, "if it's any consolation, you have done well here. I know that Mr. Paget was pleased with your work, but with your husband as prime suspect…" He shrugged and left the rest unsaid. "Is there anything you need from your locker?" Kate shook her head. "In that case, if you will give me your warrant card, I'll go with you to your car. Sorry it has to be this way, but I have to see you off the premises myself."

FIVE

"WHOEVER COULD THAT BE?" Mrs. Wentworth muttered to herself as she made her way to the door. Too early for the post, and it wasn't Friday, so it couldn't be the eggs. She wiped her hands on her apron and opened the door.

"Mrs. Wentworth?"

A young woman stood there. Slim, short dark hair, nicely dressed. Nothing in her hands, no case on the step, although she did have quite a large bag slung over her shoulder. She didn't *look* the sort to be selling something, but one could never be sure these days.

Mrs. Wentworth nodded cautiously. "That's right."

"My name is Forsythe. Detective Constable Molly Forsythe," the woman said, holding up her warrant card.

Mrs. Wentworth reached into the pocket of her apron, took out her reading glasses, and put them on. "Let me see," she said as she bent to take a closer look. "Ah, yes. Something to do with Mr. Paget, is it? I did wonder, since his bed's not been slept in. Called away, was he? Must have been very sudden, or he would have let me know. He's always been very good that way."

"May I come in?"

"Yes, of course, my dear. Would you like a cup of tea? I'll put the kettle on. It will only take a tick, and I could do with a cup myself." Mrs. Wentworth held the door wide and ushered Molly in, then led the way into the kitchen. "You just sit there while I put the kettle on," she directed as she busied herself filling it with water, setting out cups and saucers, and warming the teapot. "There," she said, surveying the table with a critical eye. "That's done. Now then, Miss...? I'm sorry, my dear, I should have said 'Detective,' shouldn't I? Forsythe, did you say?"

"Please, just call me Molly, Mrs. Wentworth. I prefer that."

The housekeeper smiled benignly. "Right you are then, Molly," she said. "Now then, what's this about Mr. Paget? Will he be gone long?"

There was no easy way to break the news. "I'm afraid he may be gone for some time," said Molly. "I'm sorry to have to tell you this, but he was badly injured last night, and he's in hospital."

Mrs. Wentworth became still. "Badly injured?" she repeated softly. "How bad, Molly? In the car, was it?"

"Pretty bad, I'm afraid," the young woman told her, and went on to explain what had happened.

Mrs. Wentworth's hand fluttered to her ample bosom. "Oh, my goodness! Oh, my!" she said breathlessly. "Right outside the police station, you say? Really, I don't know what this world is coming to, I really don't." She glanced around the kitchen uncertainly, as if trying to decide what to do next. "I must go and see him. He'll need his shaver and clean pyjamas, and his toothbrush, and—"

"I'm afraid no one is allowed to see him at the moment," Molly broke in gently. "He's still unconscious, and the doctors say it may be some time before he's able to have visitors. In the meantime, I'm afraid I have to ask you a few questions. Please sit down. And don't worry about the kettle," she went on, seeing the housekeeper's worried glance. "I'll get the tea when it boils."

Mrs. Wentworth sank into a chair and faced Molly across the kitchen table. "I don't see how I can help you," she said in a dazed fashion. "Are you sure he's going to be all right? I mean, you are telling me the truth. He's not...?"

Molly reached out across the table and took the woman's

hand. "No, he is not dead," she assured her, "but I'd be lying if I told you his condition wasn't serious—very serious indeed. Which is why I need to know if Mr. Paget has any relatives who should be notified. Even distant ones. We don't show any on our files."

Mrs. Wentworth shook her head. Her eyes were moist as she looked at Molly. "There's no one, not since his father died a few years back. His wife was killed in an explosion in London, and they didn't have any children. His mother died when he was just a lad, and he doesn't have any brothers or sisters, so he's all alone in the world."

"No uncles, aunts, cousins?"

"None I've ever heard him speak of."

The kettle began to boil. Molly started to get up to see to it, but Mrs. Wentworth was on her feet immediately. "You sit still, my girl," she told Molly firmly. "I know where everything is, and I shall feel better if I'm doing something. Poor Mr. Paget. I feel so…" Words failed her as she wiped tears from her eyes.

Molly waited until the tea had been poured and Mrs. Wentworth was sitting down again before asking the next question. "Do you know if Mr. Paget had any enemies? Anyone who might have threatened him in some way, perhaps here at the house, by letter or over the phone?"

"Enemies? Mr. Paget?" Mrs. Wentworth shook her head emphatically. "He's not the sort, is he?" she said. "I mean, in all the time he's been here, I've never known him to have anybody in. Keeps very much to himself, he does. Except for the odd walk into the village, and perhaps a quiet drink in the White Hart, he hardly ever leaves the place except to go to work. I doubt if he knows more than half a dozen people in the whole village."

"Still, his job is putting away criminals," Molly reminded the housekeeper. "Has anyone whose voice you don't know been asking for him over the phone recently?"

"No, not that I can think of. Of course, I'm only here

during the day, Monday to Friday, but the phone hardly ever rings while I'm here, and when it does it's usually Mr. Paget letting me know he'll be late or that he's had his dinner out.''

''And no one's been to the door? No strangers? No one asking questions?''

Mrs. Wentworth eyed Molly shrewdly. ''When you first told me what happened, I thought you meant that Mr. Paget just happened to be the unlucky one, like somebody was trying to rob him,'' she said. ''But that's not what you think at all, is it? You think somebody was after him, that it was deliberate. That's why you're asking all these questions, isn't it?''

''We don't know, Mrs. Wentworth,'' Molly told her. ''We really don't. So we have to examine every possibility. It's just that the attack was so vicious, and the fact that it did take place right outside the police station lends weight to the theory that someone who had a grudge against him was lying in wait out there.''

Mrs. Wentworth dabbed at her eyes with a tiny handkerchief. ''I still can't believe it,'' she said. ''Not Mr. Paget. He's always been such a gentleman. He is going to be all right, isn't he?''

''The doctors are optimistic,'' said Molly, mentally crossing her fingers and hoping that by now they were. ''You were going to tell me…''

''He'll need his pyjamas.'' Mrs. Wentworth pushed her chair back and stood up. ''And his electric shaver, and… Oh, dear, now let me think. Would you mind, Molly? Dropping them off at the hospital on your way back? He's going to need his things.''

''I don't mind at all, Mrs. Wentworth,'' Molly told her, ''but perhaps you can get them when I leave. You were going to tell me if there had been anyone at the door recently,'' she prompted. ''Any strangers.''

The housekeeper sat down again. ''No, nobody like that, except…'' She paused, then dismissed the thought with a wave of the hand. "No, she wouldn't be the sort of person you mean."

"Tell me anyway," said Molly.

"It's nothing, really. It's just that I remembered this woman who came round a couple of weeks ago, that's all."

"She came to the door?"

"That's right. Doing some sort of survey for..." Mrs. Wentworth frowned and clucked her tongue. "I'm afraid I don't remember now, but she wanted to know all the usual things, like the number of people living in the house; married or single; number of children; where I did my shopping, and did I buy this or that brand of soap powder—you know the sort of things they ask. As a matter of fact, I gave her a cup of tea, poor thing. She was sat right where you are now. Looked proper worn out, she did."

And no doubt the woman had learned far more than she would ever need to know, thought Molly, not unkindly. "Young woman, was she?" she asked.

"No. More like middle-aged. Her hair was turning grey. Nice woman. Bit down on her luck, I'd say, and she had a terrible cold. She did say she hadn't done this sort of thing before, but she'd taken it on to earn a bit of extra money."

"Did she tell you anything else?"

Mrs. Wentworth thought. "Not that I remember. We had a nice long chat, though."

"Local, was she?"

"No. At least, I don't think so. She sounded like she might be from London or somewhere like that. Nicely spoken, and she had nice clothes, but they'd seen better days."

"Did she leave a card or anything like that?"

"No. She had this clipboard and a bunch of forms she filled in while we talked, but she didn't leave anything behind."

"You said she came round a couple of weeks ago. Do you remember what day it was?"

Mrs. Wentworth thought, then got up and went to a calendar on the wall. "I remember the boy with the eggs coming later the same day, so it would be a Friday. Yes, that's right. Friday the third.''

"Did she say who she was working for?''

Mrs. Wentworth sat down again. "I'm sorry, my dear, but if she said, I'm afraid I've forgotten. But surely you don't think that someone like that could have anything to do with what happened to Mr. Paget last night?''

"It doesn't seem likely, does it?'' said Molly. "But as I said, we have to check every possibility, no matter how far-fetched it may seem. Which brings me to another question: what about women friends? Do you know if Mr. Paget is in any sort of relationship with a particular woman?''

Molly half expected Mrs. Wentworth to object to such a question about her employer, but the housekeeper surprised her. "I wish I could say yes to that,'' she said, somewhat wistfully, "but I can't. It's a shame, because he needs someone to look after him. Oh, I look after him as far as the house goes, but I don't mean that. He's still a young man—well, youngish—and he shouldn't be here all on his own. If he goes on like this much longer, it will be too late. The trouble is, he's never really got over losing his wife, which is only natural, I suppose—I know I still miss my Bert, and he's been gone a good while now—but it's not the same for a man like Mr. Paget. He needs someone.''

"But there is no one, as far as you know?''

A memory stirred in Mrs. Wentworth's mind. The memory of a torn pair of tights she'd found in the bin when she'd come to empty it a couple of months ago. The sort of tights worn by a young woman, and one with long legs at that, and she remembered exactly when it was; it was the Monday after the big storm that had taken trees down and flooded parts of Ashton Prior. Mr. Paget had never mentioned it, and it wasn't her place to ask, but she was sure that someone had slept in the spare bedroom that weekend. And the fact that he'd never mentioned anyone staying over made it all the more mysterious.

Mrs. Wentworth shook her head. "No," she said firmly as she rose to her feet. "Can I get you another cup of tea, my dear?"

GRACE LOVETT couldn't take her eyes away from the dark stain on the concrete beside the marked-off area where Paget's car had stood. She kept coming back to it, hardly able to believe how much blood he'd lost, considering that the rain must have washed most of it away. More than anything, she wanted to see him, to be there beside his bed even if he didn't know that she was there.

But she knew she wouldn't be allowed in; that had been made clear to everyone, and there was nothing she could do about that. But there was something she could do about finding the person who had attacked him, because that was her job, and she was good at what she did.

The trouble was, the rain had continued well into the early morning, and if there had been any evidence of what had taken place, it had been washed away by now. The car had been examined before it was taken away, but there was nothing to indicate it had been tampered with. It would be examined more closely by Forensic once it was in their shop, but Grace didn't hold out much hope of their finding anything that would help in the investigation. Meanwhile, all that was left to work on was an empty car park, and the probable path of flight taken by the assailant—or assailants.

Grace and the others on the team had listened closely to the taped interview in which Davis and Redfern had described the scene, and both of them had insisted they had seen only one person. But, as Alcott had been quick to point out, that didn't make sense.

"You say the man was holding Paget by the hair with his left hand, and he had something that looked like a metal bar in his right hand. Is that correct?"

"Yes, sir."

"Then what?"

"He seemed to freeze when the headlights hit him. Then, when I jumped out of the car and shouted at him, he let go of Mr. Paget and started running toward the trees."

"What happened to the bar?"

"Don't know, sir. I assume he took it with him."

"You didn't see him strike Paget?"

"No, sir."

"If that's the case, then Paget must have been struck on the head and had his throat cut *before* you arrived on the scene. Did he appear to be struggling?"

"His legs were sort of thrashing around as if he was trying to get his feet under him."

"All right, so let's take what we know and reconstruct the scene. We know that Paget was hit on the head with some sort of heavy object. You say it didn't happen while you were closing in on the man, so it must have happened before. Let's assume, then, that the assailant came up behind Paget in the dark and hit him over the head with a metal bar. Now, he could have finished him off by hitting him again, but no, he doesn't do that. He sticks the bar in his pocket, takes out a razor, opens it, and cuts Paget's throat. He then folds the razor and puts it away, takes out the bar again, and tries to haul Paget to his feet while preparing to strike again. Except he didn't get the chance because you and Davis turned up, and he had to make a run for it. Sound reasonable, Constable?"

Grace could imagine the young constable's discomfiture, but he'd held his ground. "No, sir," he said quietly, "it doesn't sound reasonable, but that doesn't alter the fact that I only saw one person. If there was another person involved, they managed to stay hidden from me."

"You saw or heard no one else running away?"

"No, sir."

"The person you did see—how tall was he?"

"It was hard to tell. As I said earlier, he was wearing a black plastic mac with a hood, but I'd say he was a bit shorter than me."

"You keep saying 'he.' What makes you so sure it was a man?"

"The way he ran, sir. He was really legging it, and apart from sprinters, I've never seen a woman run like that." There was a pause before Redfern spoke again. "But there is one thing I don't understand," he said hesitantly.

"Yes?"

"Well, sir, I don't understand how he was able to see DCI Paget well enough to hit him over the head in the first place. It's like a black hole back there, except for those safety lights along the trench, and Mr. Paget's car was well away from those."

"Good point," Alcott agreed. "So what's the answer?"

"Even though I didn't see anyone else, there had to have been a second person there. It's the only explanation that makes sense to me, sir. Someone with a torch or a light of some kind. If they were lying in wait for him back there, they would have come prepared. Which would also explain the two different weapons. The man I saw had the metal bar; the other one must have had the razor."

The rain had stopped, and the monotonous sound of the pump draining the trench echoed off the building like a heartbeat as Grace walked back to the markers indicating where Redfern had jumped out of the car. She paused there, then walked farther back, to the corner of the building where the two policemen would have had their first glimpse of the attack. She stood there for a moment, visualizing the scene, then walked slowly toward the place where Paget's car had stood. Yes, she decided, it was possible. There *could* have been a second person there. He would have been hidden by Paget and his assailant, both of whom had their backs to the police car. In order to use the razor, the second person would have to be facing Paget, so he would have seen the approaching lights *before* the car rounded the corner, and before the man with the bar became aware of them. In which case, he had ample time to duck behind Paget's car before the lights swept round to illuminate the scene completely.

But, assuming that was so, where had the second person gone? If he had made for the trees, Redfern would have seen him. But the young constable had been adamant: he had seen only one man.

Grace stood where she thought a second person would have been in order to use the razor. The thought of it slicing at Neil's throat... She closed her eyes and breathed deeply, forcing herself to stay focused on the job at hand.

If the second man had ducked out of sight behind the car, and *hadn't* made a dash for the trees, then the only place he could have gone was along the far side of the building. It wouldn't have been easy. A chain-link fence no more than five feet from the building ran the full length of the property, and the space between it and the building had become a convenient place to dump rubbish among the matted weeds. Anyone making his way through there would find it hazardous enough in daylight, let alone when it was pitch-black and raining, but it was better than being caught.

On the other hand, with the constables preoccupied with Paget, if that second person had kept his nerve, he could have picked his way slowly and carefully down the length of the building, then walked calmly out into Charter Lane. If that was what had happened, it was possible he had left some evidence of his passage.

It would be painstaking work, and it would take time, but Grace felt it would be worth it. Now all she had to do was convince Charlie.

"I'LL SAY ONE THING for him," said Charlie Dobbs as he perched on the corner of Ormside's desk. "The bastard had it all worked out so he'd stay warm and dry while he waited for Paget. He broke into the portable office used by the workers installing the new sewer line. The padlock is intact, but the hasp has been snapped off at the base. According to the foreman, nothing appears to have been taken, but there was fresh mud on the floor, and a chair has been moved to a position just inside the door. Someone sitting there with the door partly open would be able to see or hear anyone approaching Paget's car.''

"Just one chair?" asked Tregalles.

Charlie nodded. "Mind you, that's all there's room for between the wall and the desk, but there is another chair behind the desk, and we found a small amount of fresh mud there. It doesn't *prove* there were two people, but it does suggest that there were.''

"Any cigarette butts? Toffee wrappers? Anything like that? He or they had to be doing something while they waited.''

"Nothing out of place, according to the foreman, but he said he'll let me know if he finds anything as the day goes on. Oh, yes, and the two lights on the building were broken deliberately. We found the glass on the ground." Charlie paused while he rummaged around inside a plastic bin bag he'd been holding. "I saved the best till last," he said smugly. "We think this is the weapon Redfern saw." He displayed a piece of one-inch gas pipe, about eighteen inches long, sealed neatly in a clear plastic bag. "It was some distance from where we think the man entered the trees, but he could have tossed it as he ran.''

Alcott eyed the gas pipe dubiously. "Any sign of blood or hair?''

"I can't see any. Still, if there is anything there, Forensic will find it. Any luck with the house-to-house?''

"Not a damned thing, so far. Ormside has the whole area covered, but it was such a miserable night that almost no one was about. What we need is a witness who saw Marshall out there last night, because, apart from Regan's statement, which isn't worth much, considering her emotional involvement, we have nothing that ties her husband to the attack.''

"But he has to be involved," said Charlie. "I mean, assuming Regan's right, and she did see him there, Marshall would believe his suspicions were confirmed when he saw the two of them come out together. He could have followed them round the back, then gone after Paget as soon as his wife drove off.''

Alcott butted a cigarette and lit another. ''So who was sitting in the portable office watching the car?'' he asked. ''A friend of Marshall's? He'd have to be a bloody good friend to join Marshall in the murder of a copper. Not only that, but it was as black as Toby's arse out there, so how did they coordinate the attack? There's something wrong with this whole set-up, and we need to do a lot more digging.''

Charlie nodded slowly in his ponderous way. ''Speaking of this second man,'' he said, ''Lovett has a theory about how someone might have escaped detection. I'm not sure it's worth the effort, but since we have so little else to go on, I told her to go ahead and check it out.''

''Mr. Talbot? Mr. Frank Talbot?'' asked Tregalles.

''That's right,'' the man said cautiously. He was a big man, barrel-chested, iron grey hair combed straight back.

Tregalles introduced himself. ''I'd like to talk to you about a man who used to work for you. May I come in?''

Talbot hesitated. ''I suppose you know I've been retired for almost a year? Which employee are we talking about?''

''Paul Marshall.''

''Ah! In trouble, is he?''

''Why do you say that?''

''Because you wouldn't be here otherwise. Better come inside.'' Talbot led the way into a small kitchen, very neat, very tidy. ''Coffee?'' he offered. ''Just brewed it a few minutes ago. Take a pew.''

''Sounds good to me,'' Tregalles said gratefully as he sat down at the kitchen table.

''So what's this about Paul?'' Talbot set a mug of coffee in front of Tregalles, then sat down to face the sergeant.

''It's a routine matter,'' Tregalles said, ''but what I'd really

like to know is why Paul Marshall lost his job if he was one
of Scofield's top salesmen for years, and then a sales manager.''

"I see. Well, Paul did work for me for about seven years,
and you're right, he was the best salesman I ever had. I just
wish to God I'd let well enough alone and kept him on the
road. I should never have brought him inside.''

"To become a manager?''

Talbot nodded. ''Worst thing I could have done for him as
it turned out, although I suppose it would have all come to a
head sooner or later.''

"Could you explain that for me, sir?''

"Paul Marshall was a born salesman,'' Talbot explained.
"Pleasant, likeable, never pushy. He built a relationship with
his customers, and he was innovative, always suggesting ways
by which they might increase their sales, and that, of course,
allowed him to sell them more of our products.''

Talbot paused, fiddled with his coffee mug, then looked at
Tregalles. "I'd always known that Paul liked a drink,'' he
continued, "but I thought nothing of it. It's part of the job
when you're in sales: a drink in the bar with a customer, a
pint with lunch, a little wine with dinner; it's expected when
you're on the road. And yet I can't say I ever saw him drunk.
But then, I only saw him on Mondays and Fridays, and only
briefly then. He was always the first one out and the last one
back, a sales manager's dream, which was why I recommended him for the regional manager's job when it became
vacant.''

Talbot paused. "More coffee?'' he offered, but Tregalles
shook his head. "This one's fine,'' he said. The brew was
strong enough to be used as oven cleaner, but obviously Talbot liked it that way, because he filled his mug again.

"I should have spotted it earlier, but I didn't. It's a major
change, coming in off the road, and I simply thought that Paul
was taking a bit longer than usual to adjust. But it gradually
dawned on me that something was seriously wrong. He'd dis-

appear for hours at a time, make excuses for missing sales and strategy meetings, and his work was falling behind, and it was only then I realized that Paul had a serious drinking problem.''

Talbot spread his broad hands. ''Like most alcoholics—because that's what he was—he denied he had a problem. I told him the firm would pay for a course of treatment, and after several sessions with him, I thought I'd finally talked him into taking the programme. But less than two weeks into it, he stopped going; said he didn't need it. He said he could do it on his own. Trouble was, he *couldn't* do it on his own, but he refused to admit it.''

Talbot sat back in his chair and shook his head. ''Unfortunately, that's when Trimble-Dexter came along. Came out of the blue. Took everyone by surprise. There hadn't been so much as a whisper, but suddenly they were there, along with their new management. My new boss was a woman by the name of Craddock, Jane Craddock, and one of the first things she did was have me go through the personnel files with her. When she saw my recommendation for a course of treatment for Paul, there wasn't the slightest hesitation—Paul was out. I pointed out that he had served us well for almost twenty years, but that didn't make a scrap of difference to her. When I continued to try to change her mind about Paul, she said she understood perfectly how difficult it might be for me to adjust to what she called 'the reality of the business world' in the new organization, and that I might prefer early retirement.''

Talbot drew in his breath and let it out again. ''So I took the hint,'' he concluded, ''and I'm glad I'm out of it. As for Paul, I heard that he'd been round a number of local firms looking for a job—in fact, one or two phoned me to ask what I thought of the man. I tried to give them as fair an assessment as I could, but I've known these people for years, done business with them, so I felt obliged to give them the full picture. Of course, as soon as I mentioned drink, that finished it, and

Paul didn't stand a chance. I hated to do it—I mean, he was a good man once—but he is his own worst enemy, and until he straightens out, there's not much anyone can do. Even so, I was appalled by the way he looked the last time he came round.''

"He came round here?''

"That's right. He came one afternoon, pissed to the gills. Damned near knocked the door down, shouting and screaming. Kept saying that it was all my fault, and if it hadn't been for me he'd still have a job. I got him inside and managed to calm him down. He sat there where you're sitting now. Ended up crying like a baby. I called a taxi and had him taken home.''

"Did you report this to anyone?''

"No, of course not. It was the drink talking, not Paul.''

"When was this?''

"About a month ago. Apparently what triggered him was the fact that his wife had left him.''

SIX

THE TABLETS the doctor had given him had helped—but not nearly enough. Paul Marshall's head throbbed with pain, but he was determined not to show it. His mouth was dry, and his tongue felt like a wad of cotton wool. They'd offered him food, coffee, tea, water, anything he wanted, but he'd refused because he knew from bitter experience that he would only spew his guts out, and he wasn't having that. Not in front of them. Bastards! They were probably still over at the pub having lunch, just killing time while he sat in here on a hard wooden chair bolted to the floor, his only company a uniformed copper who stood by the door, pretending to be deaf and dumb.

He looked at the clock on the wall. Twenty past two. He should just walk out, he told himself. They hadn't charged him with anything—at least he didn't think they had. He tried hard to remember what had happened after the doctor had examined him, but it was all a bit vague now. Marshall closed his eyes, trying to remember, trying to think. He wished he'd paid more attention to some of the things Kate had always been on about at mealtimes—such as what his rights were.

He *should* get up and leave. Tell the copper on the door that he'd had enough. If anyone wanted to talk to him, they could come to the house, and *he* would decide whether he wanted to talk to them or not. The trouble was, he wasn't sure if he had the right to leave. That was the sort of thing a solicitor would know, but he didn't want to ask for one, because that would make them think he had something to hide.

Besides, he wasn't sure how much they knew—really knew—and how much was bullshit. He was worried about the shoes. Could they *really* tell where the mud came from? he wondered. After all, mud was mud, wasn't it?

But what worried him most of all were the blank spots, the bits he couldn't remember.

THE INTERVIEW had begun at 14:33, according to the information entered on the tape, and ended at 16:08. They'd hammered at the man for more than an hour and a half, yet Alcott and Tregalles were no further ahead. Marshall, it seemed, had found his second wind. No, he had not been stalking his wife, although he admitted once again to trying to talk to her on several occasions, but he insisted he had never approached her at work. As for her claim that she had seen him watching the office window last night, he said he'd been thinking about that and suggested that Kate might have made the story up to explain why she and Paget had left the building together.

"She does that, you know," he said. "Makes up lies like the ones she tells about me stalking her."

Alcott had challenged him on that. "How did you know they left together, unless you were there, watching the door?"

Marshall smiled. "You told me they did last night, or at least early this morning. You accused me of waiting for Kate to appear, and when she came out with Paget I'm supposed to have followed them or some such thing. I forget the rest, but no doubt the sergeant will have it in his notes. Besides, as I told you, I wouldn't know Paget if I fell over him."

Before Alcott could respond, Tregalles broke in hastily. "When you were told that you had been seen outside Charter Lane last night, you replied, and I quote: 'She'—meaning your wife—'tells you some cock-and-bull story about my being *in the yard at Charter Lane.*' Yet nothing had been said about your being in the yard up to that point. How do you explain that?"

Marshall shrugged. "Stands to reason, doesn't it? If I'd

been out in the street, no one could have seen me because of the machinery and the trees out front, so I'd have to be in the yard."

The mud on the shoes? He'd explained that, he said. He must have picked it up when he went to the corner shop. But Alcott wasn't buying that explanation. "The shopkeeper doesn't remember you coming in last night," he told Marshall. "You said you bought something for your tea. What was it?"

Marshall frowned. "Frozen potpie," he said. "At least I think it was. Could have been chicken, I don't remember. Those things all taste the same anyway. I don't pay much attention any more so long as they can be done in the microwave."

"You have the bill?"

"Oh, for Christ's sake! I don't know. It's one of those little slips off the till. They don't give it to you half the time."

And so it had gone. In fact, Marshall seemed to gain more confidence the longer the interview went on.

SUPERINTENDENT ALCOTT drummed nicotine-stained fingers on his desk, a sign of growing frustration, as he listened to the dry, pedantic tones of Allan Hobbs from the Crown Prosecution Service. Hobbs was a short, chunky man in his early forties. His face was round and pink, his mouth cherubic, and he wore gold-rimmed glasses that looked as if they had come from another age.

"I'm afraid you're going to have to let him go, Tom," Hobbs concluded. "I know how badly you want to nail the person responsible for the attack on Paget—we all want that— but there simply isn't enough evidence to proceed with charges at this stage. You have a witness who can't swear it was her husband she *thought* she saw out there last night; the only mackintosh you could find in Marshall's house doesn't. match the description given by Redfern—he described a black plastic mac; and even if Forensic identifies the mud on Marshall's shoes as coming from here, we have no idea *when* it was acquired. You found nothing incriminating in the house; you don't have a weapon, and even his wife says she has never seen him use anything but an electric razor. In short," he concluded as he rose to leave, "you have no case."

As Hobbs left the office, Tregalles, who had remained silent throughout, felt a sense of relief. He had tried to warn Alcott that they were skating on thin ice, but once the superintendent had the bit between his teeth, it was hard to rein him in—especially if you were only a sergeant. Tregalles was as anxious as anyone to see Paget's attacker put away, and Marshall was the prime suspect, but there were troubling aspects about the case, not the least of which was: who was the second person, and why would he join Marshall in such a risky enterprise?

Tregalles had asked Kate about that, but she'd had no answer. "Paul has no friends," she told him. "A couple of people he used to work with came round when he first lost his job, but he drove them away with his constant moaning. Come to think of it, I don't think Paul ever had any close friends. We used to meet other couples now and again, all in some way connected with his work, and they were friendly enough, but with both of us working, we never seemed to have time to make real friends."

"What about school friends? People he grew up with? Relatives?"

"He's an only child, and as I explained when I showed you the wedding photographs, his parents died when he was quite young, and he was brought up in a foster home, and not a very pleasant one. He left when he was sixteen."

Tregalles stood up. "I'm afraid Mr. Hobbs is right, sir," he said quietly. "Marshall may well be our man, but we have nothing that ties him to the attack on Paget. Although he denies it, I believe Regan is telling the truth when she says he threatened her. Talbot told me this morning that Marshall was in a terrible rage when he arrived at Talbot's door, banging on it and screaming abuse. Fortunately, Talbot is a big man, and he was able to calm Marshall down, but I'm not sure Kate could handle him if he came after her.''

Alcott butted a cigarette and swung his chair round to face the window overlooking the playing fields below. It was almost dark, but about a dozen children were still out there kicking a ball about, boys and girls, the girls equally ferocious in their tackling.

''Funny how things change,'' he observed. ''When I was a lad, we wouldn't be caught dead playing soccer with girls. We'd have never lived it down. Now look at 'em.''

Behind him, Tregalles coughed discreetly, but he knew Alcott would not turn round until he was ready. It was the superintendent's way of delaying a decision, especially one he didn't want to make.

''Those kids are going to be sopping wet and mud from head to foot by the time they're finished,'' Alcott continued. ''Then they'll tell their parents someone pushed them down. Your kids ever do that, Tregalles?''

''Don't all kids?'' Tregalles countered.

Alcott swung back to face him. ''I suppose there's nothing for it but to let the bastard go,'' he muttered. ''The trouble is, we don't have the manpower for round-the-clock surveillance, so we'll have to settle for having the patrol cars swing by the house as often as they can. If they see *anything* suspicious, I want to know about it.''

''Right, sir.''

Tregalles turned to leave, but Alcott stopped him. ''And make sure Marshall understands that if he goes anywhere near Regan, we'll have him back in custody so fast his head will spin.''

Tregalles hesitated. ''She is his wife,'' he said, ''and, strictly speaking, we don't have a reason to interfere.''

''She may be his wife,'' Alcott growled, ''but first and foremost she's one of ours, and we can't afford to lose good people. Make sure she's informed of his release, and tell her she's to let us know immediately if he comes near her.''

Now that *was* a surprise, thought Tregalles as he left the office. After the way Alcott had torn into Kate in the early hours of the morning, compassion was the last thing he'd expected from the superintendent. Perhaps there was hope for Regan yet. The sergeant crossed his fingers and wished her luck as he made his way down the stairs.

GRACE LOVETT PARTED the tangle of weeds and moved a piece of rotting wood carefully to one side. It had taken her all afternoon to work her way down the side of the building, picking her way through half-buried planks, broken bricks, reinforcing rods, and lumps of concrete left over from some building job of long ago. She was soaked through, and her hands, covered only by thin latex gloves, were frozen. Five more minutes, she had promised herself fifteen minutes ago, and still she searched.

The light was almost gone when she caught a glimpse of an object that didn't look as if it belonged there. It lay close to the wall, and would no doubt have lain there undiscovered for years if Grace had not persuaded Charlie that this line of escape was worth pursuing.

She took a roll of yellow plastic tape from her pocket and tore a short piece off, tying it to the chain-link fence to mark the spot. Then, taking a small camera from one of the many pockets in her boiler suit, she took a series of photographs before gently lifting the torch from its resting place.

That it had been dropped there recently there could be little doubt—dropped by someone in his haste to get away. And, unlike the length of gas pipe, it might be traceable.

SERGEANT LEN ORMSIDE tilted his chair back at a dangerous angle and put his hands behind his head. ''So,'' he said, ''what do you want us to do about Marshall now we've had to let him go?''

Tregalles shrugged. "Nothing we can do," he sighed. "CPS is right. There's not enough evidence to charge him; we can't justify the cost of surveillance, so all we can do is keep on looking and hope for a break."

"And Regan has been told to let us know if he bothers her again?"

"She's been told," Tregalles confirmed, "but whether she will or not is open to question. She didn't say anything before because she didn't want us to get the idea that she's incapable of handling her own problems."

"Right, then." Ormside glanced up at the DC who had been hovering near the desk for the past couple of minutes. 'What is it, Proudfoot?" he demanded testily.

"Today's reports from Westcombe Road, Birch Lane, and the houses round the playing fields, Sarge."

"Anything worthwhile?"

"Not as far as I can see, but you might want to look through them yourself."

"Leave 'em on the desk," Ormside told him. "I'll look at them later."

Detective Constable Rick Proudfoot set the folder on the corner of the desk and returned to his own place on the far side of the room. He sat down and thought about what he'd just heard. No surveillance on Marshall? Bloody ridiculous! Chances were he wouldn't try anything in broad daylight, but there was nothing stopping him from going after Kate at night.

Upstairs, in their regular office, Rick's desk faced that of Kate Regan, and they'd worked together a number of times. He liked Kate; she was easy to work with, pleasant, helpful, and good at her job, and the thought of her being stalked by a vindictive husband stirred his blood.

By nature, he was somewhat shy. He was broad-shouldered and stockily built, but his fair complexion and naturally curly hair made him look younger than his twenty-six years, and some of his older colleagues tended to treat him as the baby of the squad. But not Kate; she'd accepted him for himself, even drawn on his experience and local knowledge, which, perhaps, explained why he felt about her the way he did.

Sitting directly across from her, as he did, he had sensed there was something wrong, that she was unhappy about something. He had tried, in a roundabout way, to find out what it was, but she had brushed aside his concern, saying she was simply tired. He'd known there was more to it than that, but there was nothing he could do if she refused to confide in him.

And now she'd been suspended, while Marshall was free to go wherever he pleased, which meant that she could be at risk. Look at what had happened to Paget.

Sitting there at his desk, face flushed with anger, Rick Proudfoot decided that Kate Regan would not go unprotected; not if he had anything to do with it.

ANDREA MCMILLAN bent over the still figure in the bed. "I see, according to his chart, he hasn't regained consciousness," she said, "but has there been any movement at all?" The ICU nurse shook her head. She was a big girl, fresh-faced and buxom, who looked as if she might be more at home on a farm than in an intensive care unit. "But Mr. Livingstone wants him kept under sedation for at least the next forty-eight hours because of the intracranial pressure. The scan showed extensive haemorrhaging, so he doesn't want the patient to move until the pressure is lowered. Still, at least the skull wasn't fractured," she concluded cheerfully.

Impulsively, the girl reached out and touched Andrea's arm. "Don't worry, Doctor," she said, "we'll take good care of him. We've had worse cases than this to deal with, and they survived." Comforting words—until the girl spoiled the moment by adding, "Well, most of them did."

As Andrea left the ICU, she found the constable, who sat outside the door, talking to a young woman. She was tall, blonde, and strikingly beautiful, but there was tension in her face as she turned to Andrea. "Are you Neil Paget's doctor?"

she asked anxiously. "How is he? Is he going to be all right? Is there any chance that I may see him?"

"Are you a relative?" Andrea countered, noting that the woman had called Paget by his first name.

The woman shook her head. "A colleague," she said, "But I—"

"Miss Lovett is a Scene of Crimes officer," the constable broke in as if anxious to establish her credentials. "She's involved with the investigation."

The woman thrust out her hand. "Grace Lovett," she said, and Andrea found herself responding to a firm handshake.

"Dr. McMillan," she replied, "and since you're involved in the investigation, you must be aware that Mr. Paget's condition is critical, and only close relatives are permitted to see him."

"I understand that, Doctor. And it's because I know he has no close relatives that I thought I might act as...well, a sort of substitute, and perhaps be allowed to see him, if only for a moment." There was a catch in her voice, but her deep blue eyes remained steady on Andrea's face as she waited for a response.

"I'm sorry, but I can't do that," Andrea said gently. "I'm not Mr. Paget's doctor, but as it happens, I have just seen Mr. Paget, and I can tell you that he is stable; he's in very good hands, and everything possible is being done to ensure his recovery." She took Grace Lovett by the arm and began to walk with her down the corridor.

She was intrigued by this colleague of Neil's. Grace Lovett's concern for him seemed rather more than one might expect from someone who simply worked with him. "Have you known Mr. Paget long?" she asked.

Grace glanced at Andrea. "About a year," she said. "Why do you ask?"

Andrea shrugged. "It just struck me that, judging by your concern for him, you might be more than colleagues. I'm sorry, I didn't mean to pry." *Liar!* said a tiny voice.

Grace looked away. "Perhaps friends would be a better word," she said. "It's just that I hate to think of Neil lying there with no one to visit him, no one to…" She fell silent, unable to trust her voice.

"Care?" supplied Andrea. Grace nodded. Her eyes were moist.

And you care very much, thought Andrea, and felt a twinge of jealousy.

She wondered why she had never heard of Grace Lovett before. Neil had never spoken of her. Could it be that there was more to this quiet man than she had imagined? Or was he unaware that this woman, this colleague, cared so much for him?

DC PROUDFOOT UPENDED the flask and shook it. Empty. Still, perhaps it was for the best. Between the coffee and the cold, it would be a wonder if his bladder didn't burst before he got home. He looked at the time. Twenty to twelve; the light in the living room had gone out, and the bedroom light was on. He put the top back on the flask and lit a cigarette.

He'd give it half an hour more, just in case the man was being cagey, but it didn't look as if Marshall would be going walkabout tonight.

SEVEN

BY MIDAFTERNOON the following day, as Tregalles scanned the information boards, he had the uneasy feeling that things were not going well. True, they were only partway through the second day of the investigation, but he sensed a loss of momentum, and it worried him. Nothing new was coming in. Apart from a handful of callbacks, every door in the immediate area had been knocked on and the people questioned, but it seemed that no one had seen or heard anything that might prove to be of value, and the same applied to calls in response to the broader appeal to the public through the media.

The route taken by the assailant through the trees and beyond had been searched without result. Last night, uniformed police had manned roadblocks in the streets around Charter Lane, stopping anyone walking or driving through the area to ask if he or she had been there the night before. If the answer was yes, the police questioned the person further regarding anything he or she might have seen around the time of the attack on Paget, but so far they had drawn a blank. The same thing would be done again tonight and for several nights if necessary, but the sergeant wasn't optimistic about the result.

Forensic could find nothing to link the short length of gas pipe to the attack on Paget, and it remained to be seen if they could do any better with the torch. It was a cheap, long-barrelled job, mass-produced in China, and while a few had been sold through local outlets in the past few months, no records of the sales had been kept. And, working on the assumption that the weapon used was a straight razor, local shopkeepers, barbers, and antique dealers were contacted and asked about recent sales or even thefts—without result.

"Nothing new on Paget's condition, I suppose?" he asked Ormside hopefully.

The sergeant shook his head. "I spoke to the laddie on duty at the hospital no more than an hour ago, and he said there had been no change."

"If only he could *talk* to us," Tregalles burst out. "He might know who attacked him, or at the very least, give us a clue where to start looking."

"It was pretty dark out there," Ormside cautioned. "I doubt if he could see much, especially if that torch was shining in his face. But at least finding that bolsters the argument that there was another person besides Marshall involved in the attack."

"I don't think he was."

"Marshall? You don't think he was involved? He had motive and opportunity. Kate saw him out there."

"*Thought* she saw him out there," Tregalles corrected. "She could have been mistaken. He's got her so wound up she's jumping at shadows, and as for opportunity, tell me this: if Marshall was standing in the shadow of the excavator opposite the front door and saw Kate come out with Paget, how did he get round the back without being seen by either of them, and join up with a mate who just happened to be there with a torch and a razor? It doesn't make sense."

"He could have gone round the back before they came out. There was mud on his shoes, and there was fresh mud inside the shed where someone was keeping an eye on Paget's car."

Tregalles grunted non-committally as he continued to scan the boards. "What's this thing Fletcher's on?"

"He's trying to trace the woman Paget's housekeeper told Molly about. The one who said she was doing some sort of survey. She probably doesn't have anything to do with all this, but we won't know that for certain until we find her.

Anyway," he continued, "if Marshall didn't do it, who did? And what was the motive?"

"Damned if I know, Len," Tregalles confessed, "but we can't afford to overlook other possibilities. Maybe Paget has some deep, dark secret we know nothing about. I mean, what *do* we know about his private life? I've worked with the man for close to four years, and I still don't know anything about him. So I'm going to spend the rest of the day going through the case files to see if there have been any threats made against him, perhaps by someone he put away." He paused as another possibility struck him. "Unless, of course, it's someone he put away while he was in the Met. Someone who's been released recently."

"I'll get on to his old divisional HQ," said Ormside. "They should be able to dig out that information for us. Brompton, wasn't it?"

"That's right. See if you can find someone there who remembers Paget. Tell them how serious his condition is; it might just get them moving a bit faster."

"OH, NOT AGAIN!" sighed Audrey as she dropped her knitting in her lap. "It's no use brooding, love. I mean, you said yourself you're doing everything you can, so stop worrying about it. Besides, I've made three mistakes watching you go round and round this room, and I'll never get this pullover done in time for Christmas."

"But that's just it, *am* I doing everything I can?" Tregalles flopped into a fireside chair. "I can't help feeling that I'm letting Paget down. He's lying there, unconscious, and yet it's as if he's with me all the time, looking over my shoulder, depending on me to find whoever did this to him. But it's not only that; I feel I'm letting Alcott down as well."

"Now, you *are* being silly," Audrey told him. "You said yourself it's only been two days, and even Mr. Alcott can't expect miracles."

"Feels more like two weeks," Tregalles muttered as he sat

staring at the floor. He was dreading the morning briefing, with everyone looking at him, waiting for his direction and wondering if he was up to it. At least Ormside would be there, and thank God for that. But even Ormside couldn't produce evidence that wasn't there. There had to be *something* they'd overlooked.

He stood up and stretched, then moved toward the door. "Think I'll just pop back to the office for a bit," he said. "You won't mind, will you, love?"

"You didn't get in till seven as it is, so..." Audrey broke off and shook her head. "Might as well talk to myself," she said as Tregalles disappeared into the hall.

"Won't be long, love, I promise," he called. "But don't wait up."

Audrey heard the front door close. She sighed as she began to unravel the last three rows, and wondered, not for the first time, which her husband would choose if it ever came down to his family or his job.

HIS THROAT WAS DRY, burning. He could smell the smoke, smell the sickly odour of burnt flesh, and he knew that if he opened his eyes he would see the blackened figure that was once his wife. A voice inside his head was screaming NO! and yet he couldn't blot out the words. "...happened yesterday. No one knew who she was until this morning...."

He was choking...the smell... Oh, God, please let it be a dream....

THE NIGHT NURSE coming on duty picked up the chart. "You've taped his arm to the rail?" she observed. "Has there been a problem?"

The nurse she was relieving shook her head. "Not really, but he kept trying to raise his hand as if trying to push something away. I was afraid he might pull the IV out."

"He hasn't regained consciousness, then?"

"No."

"No other movement?"

"No, but he's tense, and as you can see by the chart, his temperature is up slightly. It may mean nothing, but I'd keep a sharp eye on him tonight if I were you." The evening nurse stood looking down at the unconscious man. "Looks a bit different to when I used to see him striding down the corridor on four," she said. "To tell you the truth, I used to envy McMillan."

"Dr. McMillan? Why?"

"Didn't you know? The two of them...you know."

"*Our* Dr. McMillan?" Eyebrows shot up. "Get away! You're making this up—aren't you?"

"I'm not. She's been in to see him twice. She was in last night and again tonight. She checks his chart, asks if there's been any change, then sits by the bed for a while before going on her way."

The night nurse eyed Paget critically. "Give him a shave and get him on his feet again, he'd probably not be all that bad looking," she conceded.

"He is quite good-looking, actually."

"What's he like, then?"

"A bit like McMillan, I suppose. Sort of—what's the word? Aloof? You know, all business. Very formal, very polite. A bit old-fashioned, if you know what I mean, but he has a nice smile."

"Hmm. Sounds like you've taken a bit of a fancy to him yourself."

"No, but I like him. He's nice, but you can see he only has eyes for McMillan."

"Can't think why," the night nurse said, shaking her head in disbelief. "Are you sure he's not her brother or something?"

EIGHT

SEARCHING THROUGH the case files had turned up nothing. Tregalles had gone through his own notes, and after some hesitation, he'd taken the key from its hiding place and opened the bottom drawer of Paget's desk to gain access to the DCI's personal case notes.

"It was a total waste of time," he'd confided wearily to Audrey, who had, as always, disregarded his instructions not to wait up for him. "I can't recall ever being stuck so early in a case." There was a note of desperation in his voice. "Honestly, love, I don't know what to do next. We have no leads. Nothing!"

"Well, sitting down here stewing about isn't going to do anyone any good, is it?" Audrey had told him. "Least of all you. So come to bed. Things will look better in the morning."

But now it was morning, and as he stood beside Ormside, studying the boards, things didn't look any better. The information posted there remained unchanged despite intensive enquiries throughout the area. The police had been out in force again last night, questioning drivers and pedestrians abroad in the streets around Charter Lane, but once again they'd drawn a blank.

"What about Brompton?" he asked sharply. "Anything back from them this morning?"

"Give 'em a chance," said Ormside reasonably. "We only asked them yesterday afternoon. They said they were sorry to hear about Paget, and they'd put someone on it, but it could take a while. Besides—" Whatever he was about to say was cut off by the ringing of his phone. He answered it, then handed it to Tregalles. "Alcott," he mouthed.

"Yes, sir." Tregalles reached across the sergeant's desk for a pad of paper, and began scribbling notes.

"Forensic's been on to Alcott," he told Ormside as he hung up. "The torch was clean, inside and out. Even the batteries had been wiped clean. No serial numbers or other identifying marks. However, on the brighter side, the mud on Marshall's shoes is identical to the samples taken from the area around the trench outside. It's what they call a substrata layer of clay found roughly four feet down, quite different from that found on the surface. In other words, Marshall was lying when he said he wasn't here, so Alcott wants him brought in for further questioning."

TREGALLES FLOPPED INTO a chair beside Ormside's desk and rubbed his face with both hands. "You heard?" he said. It wasn't really a question; everyone had heard.

"I heard it's best to stay out of Alcott's way," Ormside growled. "What happened?"

Tregalles grimaced. "He was ready for us. Didn't say a word until I turned the tape recorder on, then said he wanted to make a statement to set the record straight.

"It took us both by surprise. I thought I'd been wrong about Marshall, and he was about to make a confession, but that wasn't what he had in mind at all. He said he was scared when we came knocking on his door in the middle of the night, and he'd been afraid to admit to anything, so he'd lied about being anywhere near Charter Lane. Now he says he *was* down here that day, but not when Paget was attacked. According to him, he arrived about five in the afternoon, intending to catch his wife as she came off work. He said he just wanted to talk to her, to try again to persuade her to go back home with him; but after hanging around outside for over an hour, he decided she must have left before he got there, so he packed it in and went home."

"Bollocks!" Ormside snorted. "Someone would have seen him. We've questioned everyone who was working that afternoon and evening, and no one's mentioned seeing him out there."

"Which was exactly what I said, but he had an answer for that as well. He said it was raining, and he was afraid of being seen in case someone warned Kate that he was there, so he tucked himself in under the tarpaulin covering that JCB digger out there, and…"

"And it was dark and you can't prove he's lying," Ormside finished for him.

"Believe me, Len, we tried everything to catch him out, but he stuck to his story like glue, and I'm beginning to think we've underestimated Paul Marshall. I think he's cleverer than we thought, but there's something weird about him. I can't quite put my finger on it, but I think Kate has good reason to be wary of him.

"The trouble is, even if he is lying, I still have trouble seeing Marshall as the one who attacked Paget, for all the reasons I mentioned earlier, and we can't ignore the possibility that he is telling the truth. But that is not a popular idea with Alcott right now. He's got Marshall in his sights, and he wants him taken down."

Ormside sat back and locked his fingers behind his head. "Are you suggesting that Regan's lying about seeing him out there later that night?"

"No, but I am saying she could have been mistaken. I checked the view from the office window late last night, and I had someone stand beside the machine—not under the tarp, but beside it—and I couldn't even see him, let alone tell who he was. So if Kate did see something moving, it may have been nothing more than the tarp flapping in the wind, and her imagination did the rest."

Tregalles hunched forward in his seat. "Look, Len, the way I see it is this: if Marshall wanted to go after Paget because he thought he was having an affair with his wife, he could have done it on his own. Come up behind him in the dark and belted him with the pipe. This business of a second man with a torch and razor doesn't make any sense at all. And yet we know there was a second man.''

He slumped back in his chair. ''I just hope Paget wakes up soon and can tell us what happened, because I don't think we're going to get anywhere until he does.''

THE ACRID, *cloying smell of smoke! It was in his nose, his mouth, his lungs. Not just smoke, but the sweet, sickly smell of decaying flesh. Images flashed upon his inner eye. He tried to brush them away but his arms refused to move.*

Voices. A woman's voice. He couldn't make out what she was saying. Jill? No. It couldn't be. Jill was dead. The smell grew stronger; his stomach heaved. Don't look! Don't open your eyes!

His eyes were tightly shut, but that did not blot out the image. Her hair! Her lovely hair was gone. Instead, a skull, the skin strangely pale above the blackened face. Her eyes were closed beneath charred lids, and yet—how could it be?—he could see her eyes, enormous, staring blankly into his own. His stomach heaved again; he tasted bile.

A man's voice this time, distant but quite clear. ''Gently with him, Nurse. We don't want him to choke. Careful with his head.''

He felt himself slipping away. The voices faded....

WHEN GRACE LOVETT left work at five o'clock, she drove directly to the hospital. She was well aware that they wouldn't let her see Neil, but she needed to talk to someone who could tell her how he was. Perhaps that Dr. McMillan would be there. Although she'd said she wasn't Neil's doctor, she seemed to be familiar with his condition.

A policewoman lounged in the chair beside the door leading to the ICU. She had her nose buried in a magazine, but looked up as Grace approached, and scrambled to her feet.

"Miss Lovett?" she said as if surprised. "That was quick, but I'm afraid you can't go in."

"Constable"—Grace searched her memory for the girl's name—"Kendrick, isn't it?"

"That's right, miss."

"What did you mean by 'that was quick'?"

Kendrick looked at her watch. "It can't be more than ten minutes since I rang Sergeant Ormside to tell him what the doctor said about Mr. Paget."

Grace caught her breath. She felt her heart thump against her ribs. "What about Mr. Paget?" she demanded harshly. "What's happened?"

Kendrick stepped back a pace. "I—I'm sorry, but I thought you knew. He said that Mr. Paget regained consciousness for a few minutes this afternoon, and said I could pass that on, but I was to make it clear that no one would be allowed in to see him yet."

Thank God! For one brief moment, Grace felt an enormous sense of relief; then fear returned. "But he is going to be all right, isn't he? What else did the doctor say?"

Kendrick shrugged apologetically. "I did ask, but that's all he would say. So I asked one of the nurses as well, but she just said that Mr. Paget was doing as well as could be expected."

Such an idiotic phrase, thought Grace angrily. It told you nothing.

"I don't know if it means anything," Kendrick ventured hesitantly, "but Dr. McMillan was in just a few minutes ago, and I heard her say something about Mr. Paget to one of the nurses. I didn't hear what she said, exactly, but she seemed quite pleased when she came out."

"But she's not his doctor, is she?"

"I believe she's a registrar in orthopaedics. She's been in a time or two before when I've been on duty."

"To see Mr. Paget?"

"I don't know if it's to see Mr. Paget specifically; she may be seeing others in there as well, but I have heard her mention his name.''

''You say she was in a few minutes ago; do you know if she's still about?''

''Not on this floor. She went down in the lift.''

Grace thanked the girl, then went down in the lift herself. She stopped on the fourth floor to ask if Dr. McMillan was there, but was told that she had left for the day.

ANDREA MCMILLAN SETTLED herself in a comfortable chair facing Tregalles and folded her hands in her lap. ''As I told you on the telephone,'' she said, ''I am not Mr. Paget's doctor, so I'm not sure how I can help you.''

Searching desperately for another lead in an investigation that was going nowhere, Tregalles had telephoned the doctor more or less on impulse. He'd been deliberately vague about why he wished to talk to her, saying only that it concerned the chief inspector, and he thought that she might be able to help with their enquiries. Anxious to help in any way she could, Andrea had told him she was just about to leave the hospital for the day, but said if he cared to come round to her flat about eight that evening, she would be free then.

Now, facing her across a low table, he couldn't help thinking how different she appeared in these surroundings. This woman was a far cry from the Dr. McMillan he had encountered in the hospital.

The first time Tregalles had come in contact with the doctor was during an investigation into the death of a stable hand, who turned out to be her ex-husband. He hadn't interviewed her himself—Paget had done that—but he had spent some time gathering information on her, and he'd seen her around the hospital from time to time since then. But it had come as a complete surprise when he and Audrey had encountered Paget and the doctor enjoying what appeared to be an intimate dinner in one of Broadminster's finer dining rooms a couple of months ago.

If he'd thought about it at all when he'd seen her in the hospital corridors, he'd considered Andrea McMillan somewhat plain; hair pulled back, glasses stuck in her hair, hands usually thrust into the pockets of her white coat, she looked every inch the clinical professional. But seeing her with Paget, and now, seated in the comfort of this pleasant room, hair loose about her shoulders, glasses gone, and without the white coat that had masked an excellent figure, Tregalles was rapidly revising his opinion.

But now that he was here, he wasn't quite sure how to begin. Was the doctor merely a good friend, or did she mean something more to Paget? Friend or lover?

"The thing is," he began cautiously, "I came here tonight to ask for your help. I'll be honest with you, Doctor, we are not making as much progress as we would like in our investigation into the attack on Mr. Paget, and we're talking to anyone who might be able to give us a lead."

He paused, searching for the right words. "Mr. Paget has never been one to talk much about himself, so, apart from what goes on at work, we know very little about him. Mrs. Wentworth, his daily housekeeper, has been unable to help us; he has no relatives, and if he has close friends, we don't know who they are—that is, apart from you."

Andrea frowned. "I'm afraid I'm still not clear as to how I can help," she said.

"What we're looking for, Doctor, is a motive, a reason for this vicious attack." Tregalles hesitated again, then decided he had nothing to lose by taking her into his confidence. "We know that he was attacked by two people; one attacked him from behind while the other came at him from the front. One used a metal pipe, the other used a razor. Now, if the objective was simply to maim or kill him, one or the other of the weapons would have served, but the fact that there were two people, using two very different weapons, suggests something quite different. They not only wanted to kill him; they wanted to send a message."

Andrea sat forward, elbows on her knees, hands clasped, her dark eyes fixed upon his own. "I don't understand," she said. "What do you mean by a 'message'?"

Tregalles shrugged. "I was hoping that you might be able to tell me," he said. "Can you think of any reason, any reason at all, why someone would come after him in that way? Has he ever spoken to you about any enemies? Threats to his life? Anything like that?"

Andrea shook her head. "Never," she said emphatically. "But surely he would have said something to you or his superiors if he had been threatened."

Tregalles shifted uncomfortably in his seat. "Not necessarily," he said. "Especially if it had something to do with his personal life."

"His *personal* life, Sergeant? I'm not sure I follow you."

"He might have kept it to himself, for example, if it came from someone who was, let's say jealous of his—aahh—association with you."

"Jealous? Of his association with *me?*" Andrea McMillan appeared to be genuinely taken aback by the suggestion. "Wherever did you get that idea, Sergeant?"

"As I said, Doctor, we have to explore every possibility. I don't know exactly what the relationship is between you and Mr. Paget, and I'm not trying to pry into your private life, but having seen the two of you having dinner together that night the wife and I were celebrating our anniversary at the Tudor, I was hoping you might help me."

"Believe me, Sergeant, I would help you if I could, but I'm afraid I can't. I'm as concerned about him as you are, but I probably know less about him than you do. We've had dinner together a few times, but there is no 'relationship,' as you put it. Mr. Paget and I are friends, nothing more." Even as she said the words, she wondered once again if she truly believed what she was saying. But now was hardly the time for soul-searching. "Sorry I can't be of more help."

Tregalles rose to his feet. "So am I, Doctor," he said quietly, "because if we don't find these people, and find them soon, they may try again."

THE CHURCH CLOCK in Tyndall Street was striking the half-hour as Paul Marshall slipped out of the house. Eleven-thirty. The church was over a mile away, but the sound came crisp and clear on the cold night air. Inside the car, Rick Proudfoot butted his cigarette. At last! Marshall was on the move, and it wasn't likely that he would be up to any good at this hour of the night.

He got out of the car. Frost was already forming on the roof, and he was glad he'd brought his heavy jacket. He put it on, locked the car, and set out after Marshall. The man was moving quickly, and Proudfoot had to hurry to keep him in sight. Marshall was wearing trainers and dark clothing, and Proudfoot was forced to close the gap between them to avoid losing him altogether.

They reached the end of the street, and Marshall turned unhesitatingly toward the town centre. He walked with a sense of purpose, shoulders hunched forward, never once looking back as he made his way down the hill and into what was known as the Old Town.

Streetlights were few and far between, and those that did exist were old and more decorative than useful. Proudfoot shortened the distance between himself and Marshall. The man crossed the road, turned left at the next corner, and Proudfoot followed him down Westcombe Road and into Charter Lane.

A police car came out of the car park, and Marshall drew back into the shadows, waiting for it to turn the corner before slipping inside the yard to where pipes lay stacked beside a mound of earth. Proudfoot crept closer. Marshall was simply standing there in the shadow of the now silent JCB machine, hands thrust deep inside his pockets, staring at the police station.

Proudfoot drew back and waited. He was cold, but Marshall

seemed unaffected by the falling temperature. He remained there, motionless, blending into the deep shadows.

Proudfoot didn't see him go. One minute the man was there; the next minute he was gone. The constable ran across the road just in time to see a figure pass beneath a light at the far end of Charter Lane. Cursing himself for allowing Marshall to slip away, he began to run. But the road was slick where the big machines and trucks had left a film of mud, and suddenly he went down and landed hard. It happened so fast that he lay there for several seconds with the breath knocked out of him before scrambling to his feet. The front of his jacket was covered in mud; one hand was, bleeding, and one knee was painful when he tried to walk. He examined it in the light of the flickering warning lamps; the knee was grazed and bleeding, but skin would grow. What was far more serious was the six-inch gash in his designer jeans.

Proudfoot tugged a phone from his inside pocket and began to dial.

KATE REGAN WAS sound asleep when the phone rang. There was an extension in Linda's bedroom, but none in hers. She snuggled down and waited for Linda to answer, but on and on it went, more insistent with every ring.

Kate squinted at the clock. Gone midnight. Linda must still be out. Still the phone continued to ring. Muttering beneath her breath, she flung back the covers, ran into the next room, picked up the phone, and shouted, "What? If you're looking for Linda—"

"Kate! Wait, listen! It's Rick. Rick Proudfoot. I've been tracking your husband, and I've lost him. I'm afraid he might be heading your way, so lock your doors and don't let anybody in until I get there."

"Rick?" Still half asleep. "I don't understand…."

"Just do it, Kate. I'm on my way." The phone went dead.

NINE

WHEN TREGALLES HAD spoken to Paget's doctor late Friday afternoon, the man had been cautiously optimistic. "Assuming Mr. Paget continues to improve over the weekend, you should be able to talk to him on Monday or possibly Tuesday," he'd said. The news had buoyed the sergeant's spirits, and he'd looked forward eagerly to Monday morning.

But Superintendent Alcott had rung Tregalles at home on Sunday evening. "Just had a call from the hospital," he said tersely. "I'm afraid Paget's had a relapse, and his doctor is very concerned about him. Seems he started thrashing about in bed and tore out the breathing tube before anyone could stop him. They have him calmed down now, but the doctor says there is no way he can allow us to talk to him for several days."

So now they were marking time again, Tregalles thought gloomily as he and Ormside scanned the boards on Monday morning. Waiting for a break, something—anything that would give some impetus to a dying investigation. The police had been out in full force over the weekend, scouring the streets for information, but neither threats nor the promise of reward had brought so much as a whisper from the snouts, and the callbacks in the area around Charter Lane had produced nothing new.

"I suppose there's nothing back from Brompton, either?" he said glumly.

Ormside shook his head. "I checked again first thing this

morning, but the fellow I spoke to as good as told me it was not exactly high on their list of priorities.''

"Well, it bloody well ought to be," said Tregalles truculently. "I'll have a word with the super. See if he can't put a rocket up someone's arse in London."

But Alcott had problems of his own, and showed little interest in what was happening—or not happening—in Brompton when Tregalles approached him. "I haven't got time for that now," he said irritably. "The Case Review Board sits in exactly thirty minutes, and it's just my luck that it's being chaired by Chief Superintendent Brock instead of the ACC this month."

Alcott ground out a cigarette, stuffed several folders into his briefcase, and snapped it shut. "And one of the first things he's going to ask for is my progress report on this case, so I hope to God you haven't come in here empty-handed, Sergeant."

Tregalles sucked in a deep breath and blew out his cheeks. "Believe me, sir, I wish I did have something for you, but the truth is, I don't. And until we can talk to Mr. Paget, we…"

"And if he dies, Sergeant?" Alcott demanded brutally. "What then? Do we just drop the bloody case and forget it? Is that what I'm supposed to tell the board?"

"No, sir, of course not, but…"

"I don't need buts, Sergeant. I need facts! I need leads. I need evidence that will give me the people who attacked my DCI. And I need it now! It's your case, Tregalles. So what do you have for me? What do I tell the board?" He paused to light a cigarette, but his narrowed, birdlike eyes remained on the sergeant's face.

Tregalles shifted uncomfortably beneath the superintendent's steady gaze, but bad as the situation was, he felt that Alcott was being unfair, and he didn't like the implication that it was all his fault. "You tell them the truth, sir," he said baldly. "And the truth is, we have no leads, and it isn't from the lack of trying. God knows we all want to solve this case; everyone has been working flat out, and will continue to do so, but no one, not you nor Chief Superintendent Brock, can expect us to find something that isn't there. So, unless we get lucky, I think our only real hope lies with Mr. Paget himself. I'm sorry, sir, but that's the way I see it. And if that's not good enough and you want me off the case…?'' Tregalles shrugged and threw up his hands.

Alcott's eyes were like stones by the time the sergeant had finished, and Tregalles braced himself for what must surely come. What he'd said was the truth, but it most certainly was not what Alcott wanted to hear—especially from a mere sergeant.

Alcott continued to stare at Tregalles for a long moment, then shook his head resignedly as he picked up his briefcase and moved toward the door. ''What you're telling me, Sergeant,'' he said softly, ''is that I'm going to have to bullshit my way through the meeting, and pray to God that Mr. Brock doesn't have my balls.'' His voice rose sharply. ''Which,'' he continued ominously, ''is what will happen to you, Tregalles, if you ever use that tone with me again. Do I make myself clear?''

Tregalles swallowed hard. His throat was dry. ''Yes, sir,'' he said hoarsely. ''Very clear indeed.''

TREGALLES COULDN'T remember a time when he'd felt so frustrated and so powerless. ''We're just marking time,'' he told Audrey for perhaps the tenth time in the past week. ''Paget is improving, but his doctor won't let us near him for at least a few more days.''

''Well then, there's no use fretting about it, is there, love?'' said Audrey. ''You just have to be patient, that's all.''

''Try telling that to Alcott,'' Tregalles muttered darkly. ''I can feel his eyes boring into me even when he isn't there. He wants answers, and I don't have any. I went out to talk to Paget's housekeeper this afternoon to see if Molly had missed anything, but she couldn't help me. She said that since Paget's wife died, he doesn't seem to have an interest in anything but work, but we knew that already. No particular friends, no social life; the man might as well be a monk.''

''There was that woman doctor, the one we saw him with at the Tudor that night.''

Tregalles shook his head. ''I went to see her the other day, but I think they're two of a kind. They've been out together a few times, but my impression is that she doesn't know any more about him than we do. But the one thing I'm *really* afraid of is that when we do get to talk to Paget, he won't know any more than we do.''

''Well, I'm sure you've done your best, love,'' Audrey told him soothingly as they made their way to bed. ''You'll just have to be patient and wait like you've done before.''

''Wait?'' Tregalles scoffed. ''Wait for what?''

''For something to turn up. It nearly always does, doesn't it? Like you've told me time and time again, these people never know when to leave well enough alone. You'll see. Sooner or later they'll do something daft and hang themselves. I just hope they don't have another go at Mr. Paget, that's all.''

POTTER'S END, HERTFORDSHIRE

GERALD WHITE ENJOYED walking, especially on a night such as this. The sky was clear beneath a canopy of stars, and the pale light of a rising moon traced lacelike patterns across the winding country lane. The day had been unusually warm for November, but now frost was forming on the grass, glistening in the moonlight, and there was a decided nip in the air.

Friday night, and the weekend ahead of him before returning to Cambridge on Monday.

He was within a couple hundred yards of home when he heard the car approaching from behind. He moved from the centre of the road to the side; it was only prudent to give the driver plenty of room, especially if it happened to be one of the locals on his way home after a night at the pub.

His shadow leapt ahead of him as the car rounded the corner. He pressed closer to the high grass bank, shading his eyes as he glanced back to make sure the driver had seen him and was staying well over on his side of the road. The car slowed as it came alongside, and he half expected the driver to stop and offer him a lift. In fact he had begun to move closer, preparing to explain that he lived just around the corner, when the car pulled ahead and stopped.

The lights went out, and Gerald was forced to stop while he waited for his eyes to adjust to the abrupt change. Silly thing to do in a narrow lane, he thought; not that there was ever much traffic at this time of night, but it could still be dangerous.

He heard a door open, heard the driver get out. Part of his brain registered the fact that the interior light hadn't gone on when the door opened, but he sensed no danger.

"Can I help you?" he enquired tentatively. A powerful beam of light hit him square in the face, and he flung up an arm to protect his eyes.

"Gerald White?"

He didn't recognize the voice; harsh, unpleasant to the ear. "Yes, but I don't... Will you please turn off the light?"

"Just wanted to be absolutely sure."

He heard a sound behind him, began to turn, but a blow to the side of the head drove him to his knees. He tried to shout, but a gloved hand clamped itself across his mouth, choking off the sound. The light in his eyes wavered and he saw the glint of steel. Oh, God. No! They were going to cut him! It was a mistake. He struggled against the hands that held him. You've got the wrong man! he screamed inside his head.

"Get him up and hold him still!" the driver hissed, moving in closer. "Get your arm out of the way."

Strong fingers grabbed him by the hair, pulling his head back so hard he feared his neck would snap. His arms flailed wildly; his hand hit something hard—the torch—knocking it away. The light dipped, and he caught a glimpse of a figure draped in a full-length plastic mac. The light swung back. He flung up a hand as the razor slashed at his throat; felt the spreading warmth as blood ran down his arm.

"Hold him still for Christ's sake! Can't you do anything right?"

He tried once more to scream as he was lifted by his hair, but no sound came. The blade flashed again. He hardly felt its edge as it sliced across his throat, but suddenly there was no air. He saw a vivid splash of blood against the plastic mac, and then another. Someone was making the most horrible choking sounds, and he realized, as if in a dream, the sounds were coming from him.

THE COTTAGE SAT close to the road behind a bramble hedge. Made of local stone, it was a barn conversion, with double glazing, pantile roof, wooden shutters, and a two-car garage discreetly hidden around the back. Hidden because Theresa White had been forced to settle for a prefab package instead of the attached garage of matching stone she'd envisioned when she'd first sketched out the plans. It wasn't that she *couldn't* afford to have the garage built of stone, but there was Gerald's future to think of, and nothing must interfere with that. Still, the fact that she'd felt the need to compromise at all still niggled from time to time.

But now, standing in front of her bedroom window, her short, thickset body clad only in a negligé, arms raised in a symbolic gesture to greet the dawn, that was the furthest thing from her mind. Bare feet firmly planted, toes digging into the deep-piled carpet, she hugged herself, warmed by the pleasant thought that this was Saturday, and she didn't have to make the tedious journey into town today. She could do as she pleased, and she would start by having breakfast with Gerald.

Unless he'd stayed the night with Elsie. Unconsciously, the corners of her mouth turned down. Not that Elsie wasn't a pleasant enough girl in a milkmaidish sort of way, but she was local, the daughter of the man who had built the garage, and you could tell the minute she opened her mouth. Not at all suitable for Gerald—and she would insist on calling him *Ger*—rhyming with *chair,* of all things! On the other hand, Gerald was nineteen, and as long as Elsie realized that any long-term relationship was out of the question, there was no reason why he shouldn't sleep with the girl now and again. After all, she was physically attractive, and seemed clean enough in her habits, so why not? As long as he took precautions. God knows she'd warned him often enough about that, and Gerald was a sensible boy.

But no, she remembered now. Gerald had come home last night. Theresa recalled hearing the click of the metal gate as she was drifting off to sleep. She glanced at the time. Ten minutes to eight. He was usually stirring by now, but it would do him good to have a lie-in for a change. It was nice having him home for the weekend—Cambridge was only forty minutes away on the M11—and she looked forward to having him home for several weeks at Christmas.

She frowned. She hoped he hadn't been serious when he'd mentioned, almost offhandedly, that he might go skiing with some of his Cambridge friends. She didn't like that idea at all. After all, it was Christmas. He should be here at home with her. She would have to sound him out about that, but she would have to be careful. Gerald couldn't be pushed into doing anything he didn't want to do. On the other hand, he did love his mother and wouldn't want to do anything to disappoint her.

Especially as she was paying for his tuition.

Theresa sighed. His first year at Cambridge! She was so proud of him, she would have hugged him if he'd been there. And he would have said, ''Oh, *Mother!*'' and pushed her away, pretending to be embarrassed.

She watched as the sky began to lighten. It was going to

be another lovely day despite the blanket of frost that lay across the fields. Theresa frowned. Or was that snow? Surely not.

She stood on tiptoe, hands on the sill, elbows locked as she leaned into the embrasure and pressed her face against the glass. She looked down at the path below. Her heart stopped. She couldn't breathe. She stared in stricken disbelief, not *daring* to accept what her eyes were telling her. Every nerve end turned to ice. Her legs began to tremble. "Oh, God, no!" she whispered hoarsely. "Please, please, *please* God, no!" She covered her face with her hands. She was still in bed, still asleep, she told herself. It *had* to be a nightmare!

She forced herself to look again.

Spreadeagled on the flagstone path, dark and still as if laid out for sacrifice, Gerald White lay on his back, eyes closed and sunken in a waxen face. A pool of what could only be blood stained the stones around his head, its source a gaping wound beneath his chin. His skin was white, and his hair, his lovely long fair hair, was plastered to his head like some incongruous wig.

Theresa sank slowly to her knees. A keening wail rose in her throat, exploding in a searing shriek of agony.

"KILLED SOMEWHERE down the road, then half carried, half dragged inside," said the doctor. "That's my read of it, anyway. You can see where he was lifted, then set down. A lot of blood where they stopped to open the gate. Take two of 'em at least."

Detective Inspector Albert Simmonds shifted a clear mint from one side of his mouth to the other and wished he had a cigarette instead. "Thinking of taking on my job, then, are you, Phil?" he asked dourly.

The doctor snorted softly. "You don't have to be much of a detective to follow a trail of blood like that," he declared. "Vicious attack. Two cuts, both deep, but not before he put up a fight. Cuts on his hands and arms, bruises on his arms and face where someone held him, and at least one blow to the head. Not enough to kill him. Stunned him more likely. That's probably when his throat was cut. Poor bugger never stood a chance.''

"Any suggestions as to what kind of knife it was?"

"I'm not sure it was a knife. If it was, it was damnably sharp. It could have been a razor.''

Simmonds raised an eyebrow. Razors made him think of gangs. "How about time of death?"

"Rough estimate, nine to twelve hours ago. We had quite a drop in temperature last night, but they might be able to narrow that down when they do the PM.''

Simmonds looked at his watch. That would make it somewhere between nine and midnight, which tied in with what the mother had told the first men on the scene, once they'd managed to calm her down. Her son had been down to the village, she said, and she was sure she'd heard the sound of the gate closing around eleven. She went on to say that she thought she'd heard a car start up just after that, but she couldn't be sure. He'd have to talk to her later when she'd had a chance to settle down. They were lucky to have got that much out of her. Must be a hell of a jolt to look out of your bedroom window and see your son lying on the flagstones with his throat cut. It was on days like this he was glad he had no children of his own.

He moved into the road. Narrow with high hedges on both sides. Not many places to park a car. He followed the tapes around the bend. There were markers down where dark patches stained the ground. One of the Scene of Crimes officers was down on his hands and knees examining the ground. "Car stopped here, sir," he observed. "Blood all over the road. And someone's been sick. Don't think there's much doubt that this is where he was killed.''

Butchered, more like, thought Simmonds. But why? There was nothing missing. Gerald White's wallet was still in his back pocket. Fourteen pounds in it, and small change in another pocket, so robbery wasn't the motive.

Which left someone with a grudge. Jealousy? Check on his love life. Was he into drugs? Down from Cambridge for the weekend, his mother had said. Could well be drugs. This didn't look like a spur-of-the-moment thing. Whoever had killed him had meant business.

But why go to the trouble of dragging him inside the gate? There was a ditch just a few yards down the road. If they simply wanted to get the body off the road in order to delay discovery, all they had to do was roll it in there. Odd, that. It was as if it had been placed there deliberately so his mother would see it when she looked out of the window. But how would they know she would do that? He'd looked out of the window himself, and he hadn't been able to see the body until his head was almost touching the glass.

But the body was on the path where it would be seen as soon as anyone opened the front door, so perhaps that was it. Only time would tell. Too much speculation and not enough information, he decided. But he didn't like the smell of it. He didn't like the smell of it at all.

Simmonds began to shift the mint again, then spat it out in disgust. It wasn't helping one damned bit. The Scene of Crimes officer looked up at him, but said nothing as he picked up the half-sucked mint and chucked it over the hedge.

THE POLICE HAD GONE. Theresa White sat huddled in a deep armchair before the open fire, staring with unseeing eyes into the dying embers. The room was warm but Theresa was cold, bitterly cold. Her training told her she was in shock, yet she'd denied it vehemently when they'd offered to take her to the local hospital, for that would have meant leaving the house—and Gerald.

But Gerald was gone. They'd taken him away. Theresa bit hard on her lower lip to prevent herself from crying out. She'd always abhorred open displays of emotion in others, but now she found herself wanting to scream, to rail against the gods or fate or whatever malevolent force it was that ran this stinking universe. Why Gerald? Why, when he had all his life ahead of him? Why *her* son? Why not…?

The sound of the telephone cut across her thoughts, loud, insistent, urgent. Theresa huddled in her chair. She didn't want to hear it, didn't want anything to intrude upon her grief.

The phone rang ten times, then stopped, and Theresa breathed a silent sigh of relief. Her head throbbed dully. She closed her eyes. She just wanted to go to sleep, to forget, perhaps never to wake again.

She jumped as the shrill sound of the phone shattered the silence of the room again. Once more she waited for it to stop. But it didn't. Twelve…thirteen…fourteen, she counted, and when it got to twenty she could stand it no longer. Perhaps it was the police, she thought belatedly. She padded across the room, pausing for a moment to take several deep breaths before picking up the phone.

"Dr. White," she said.

"Lost your son, have you?" a voice said mockingly. "Pity. Nice-looking lad. So young, too. It's a bit different when it's one of your own, isn't it, Doctor?"

"What…? Who is this? What do you want?" Theresa White gripped the phone with shaking hands. "Who are you?" she demanded. "Why are you doing this?"

But there was no one there.

TEN

THE LINGERING SMELL of food permeated the lift and the corridors as he was being taken down to the fourth floor, though what they would be cooking at ten past nine in the morning, Paget had no idea. His stomach rumbled in response, but the last thing he wanted was solid food—not while his throat felt as it did.

They'd removed the breathing tube the day before. His throat felt raw, and swallowing took an act of faith, but apart from that, and a dull throbbing in his head, there was little pain. His neck was bandaged, there was a dressing on his head, and he had to be careful when he moved, but he considered himself lucky to be alive.

The neurologist had arrived shortly after that. He was a short, thickset man by the name of DeWitt who hummed softly to himself as he checked Paget's vision and reflexes.

"You're very fortunate that the blow to the head didn't do more damage to your skull," he told Paget. "But you will have to be extremely careful. That lump you can feel on the back of your head will go down fairly quickly, and the wound will heal, but it may take some time for the effects of the intracranial haematomas—broken blood vessels putting pressure on the brain—to subside. We could relieve some of the pressure surgically, but I prefer the less invasive techniques, which appear to be working in your case."

"Meaning what, exactly?"

DeWitt hesitated. "According to the scan, the damage isn't all that extensive, nor would I call it serious, but it is in a sensitive area, so I think the less probing we do the better. Drugs have proved to be effective in cases such as yours, and as I said, they appear to be doing their job. It may take a little longer, but provided you are careful and don't do anything foolish, I think it is the preferred course of action. However, I should warn you that you could experience a variety of sensations during the healing process, and we will be monitoring you very carefully. In addition, I want you to keep this pad beside your bed and jot down anything unusual: sharp pain, blurred vision, hallucinations, odd sounds, smells, abrupt changes in temperature—in fact, anything out of the ordinary. And don't be afraid to push your panic button and let the nurse know if you start to feel faint or experience sharp pain. That's why they're here. Perhaps you have experienced some of these sensations already?''

Smells. Hallucinations. The smell of burning flesh, and Jill's charred body. Paget almost nodded, but checked himself. Those selfsame images had haunted him following Jill's death, and he had wound up in a psychiatric ward on that occasion.

''Just the odd dream,'' he said, dismissing it as of little consequence, ''but there is a blank spot in my memory. I've been trying to remember what happened, and I can't. Is that completely lost to me, or will it come back in time? The other thing is, I can't seem to stay awake for long.''

''You're bound to feel weak, and you will sleep a lot for the next while,'' DeWitt told him. ''As for your memory, it will improve, but it's impossible to say how much you will remember. You have to give it time. Good God, man, what do you expect after surviving an attack like that? You lost an enormous amount of blood, and even though you've had a transfusion, it will take time to get your blood levels back up to where they should be. You can't force these things, so be patient.''

''Which leads me to my next question: when can I expect to get out of here?''

"You're to be moved to the fourth floor later this morning," DeWitt told him, "and you'll probably be there for five or six days at least. But when you do go home, you must continue to rest."

Paget grimaced at the thought. "How long before I can return to work?"

"Impossible to say at this stage, but I think you will have to let me be the judge of that. After you do leave hospital, I want to see you once a week until I'm satisfied that there are no residual effects. We can talk about returning to work then." DeWitt stopped Paget with an impatient gesture as he saw the protest forming on his lips. "It would be very foolish to return to work too soon," he warned sternly. "But, speaking of your work, Superintendent Alcott has been champing at the bit to talk to you, so I've told him he can come in this afternoon, but I've warned him not to stay too long."

Once Paget was transferred to his new bed, Andrea, in her capacity as registrar, visited him briefly, then turned him over to the house officer, a doctor by the name of Winfield. There was a flurry of activity and questions for about half an hour; then suddenly all was quiet and he was left alone. Whether by design or sheer good luck, he had a private room—with a uniformed PC stationed outside his door.

He lay back against his pillows, eyes closed, exhausted— annoyed with himself for feeling so weak. He'd felt quite good before the move from the ICU, but suddenly it was as if someone had pulled the plug and drained his energy away. He opened his eyes and looked at his watch, squinting. The face was blurred. The top of his head felt numb, and he could hear strange noises in his ears. He squinted harder and the watch split into two, now blurred even more. Paget felt a prickle of sweat across his brow. He closed his eyes tightly, then opened them again.

Nine fifty-three. There it was, as plain as day.

The numbness passed; the noises faded. He felt very tired, but was almost afraid to close his eyes again.

He thought of Andrea. She'd told him that he'd first re-gained consciousness more than a week ago, but he'd lost all sense of time. He did remember waking to find her sitting beside his bed, but he had no idea when that was. "Welcome back," she'd said quietly. "You had us worried for a while, Neil. How do you feel?"

"Better for seeing you," he remembered saying, before drifting off to sleep again. Later, possibly days later, they'd talked, but he couldn't remember what was said. But he did recall the feeling. It was as if there had been a wall of glass between them, and he remembered trying hard to find a way around it, but he couldn't stay awake. And when he did open his eyes again, Andrea had gone.

"I CAN'T SAY I'm looking forward to visiting Paget tomor-row," Tregalles told Audrey on Sunday night as they were getting ready for bed. "Well, what I mean is, I'm glad he's on the mend, but it's going to be hard to face him with the case being at a standstill."

Audrey pulled the duvet up under her chin. "And you think he'll blame you?" she said.

"He probably won't *say* that," Tregalles said as he slid down beside her, "but he'll be thinking it. I mean, I would if I was in his place. I'd be lying there expecting to hear that whoever had attacked me was behind bars by now, but all we can tell him is that, apart from Marshall, we haven't got a clue."

"But isn't that why you want to talk to him? I mean, he might be able to tell you exactly what happened—even tell you who did it—so why are you so worried?"

Tregalles sighed. "It's just that I feel I've let him down."

Audrey propped herself up on one elbow and looked down at her husband. "What else could you have done, then?" she demanded.

"That's just it. I don't know. Len and I have been over it time and time again, but there are no leads, nothing, except for Marshall, and the more I think about that, the less I'm inclined to believe he had anything to do with it. We certainly have no proof.''

''Well, it's no good lying there stewing about it, is it?'' she said in her practical way. ''What you need is something to take your mind off it.'' She leaned down and kissed him. It was meant to be a peck, but her husband curled an arm around her and drew her to him. ''Like what?'' he asked softly, nuzzling her neck. He pressed closer, but Audrey gasped and pulled away.

''Your hands are ice cold,'' she accused.

''Cold hands, warm heart,'' he chuckled, and reached for her again. ''Why don't you warm them up for me?''

IT WAS CLEAR BY the look on their faces that both Alcott and Tregalles were disappointed, as was Paget, that there had been so little in the way of progress in finding his attacker. ''I'm sorry,'' he said, ''but the last thing I remember is Regan backing her car out and disappearing round the corner. After that, nothing.''

''You've no idea who might have done this to you?'' said Alcott.

''Absolutely none, and believe me, I've done nothing else but think about it this last couple of days.''

''You've received no threats?''

''No.''

''Money troubles? Anything like that?''

''No.''

Tregalles spoke up. ''We've been on to your old division in the Met to ask if anyone you put away when you were there has been released recently. Someone who threatened you when they were sent down, perhaps? Any ideas, sir?''

''None that I ever took seriously. Threats like that are usually made in the heat of the moment; they're rarely followed up.''

Tregalles said, ''No doubt they're busy, but we've had nothing back from Brompton as of noon today. I was wondering if you could give us the name of someone who might stir them up a bit."

Paget closed his eyes and leaned back against the pillows. "I suppose you could contact my old boss, Superintendent Bob McKenzie," he said. "But from what you tell me, this chap Marshall seems to be the more likely suspect."

"I'm not so sure about that, sir," Tregalles began, but a glance from Alcott silenced him.

"That's a point on which we disagree," said Alcott bluntly, "but it does lead me to another question. I'm sorry I have to ask this, especially when you're in this condition, but it has to be dealt with. Are you and Regan having an affair?"

"An affair?" Paget's eyes flew open. "Whatever gave you that idea?"

"Her husband seems to think you are," Alcott countered, "and from what we've been told, she was waiting for someone by the door that night. Then you came along and the two of you left together. Had you arranged to meet her there?"

"Of course not. As a matter of fact, I thought she'd gone home. I was surprised to see she hadn't left."

Alcott eyed Paget for a long moment. "So," he said softly, "if there is nothing going on between the two of you, how do you explain the fact that Regan has been up here every day, asking about you?"

Tregalles glanced at his superior. This was the first he'd heard about it—if it was true. And then the penny dropped. Of course! Alcott must have checked the log the PCs kept of everyone who had asked to see the DCI—something he should have done himself. He groaned inwardly, and hoped that Alcott wouldn't realize that he hadn't done the same.

Paget's eyes were steady on Alcott's face as he replied. "I suggest you ask Regan," he said. "I wasn't aware that she had been asking about me, but you might tell her I appreciate the thought."

Alcott grunted. "You say that Regan was waiting at the

door when you came downstairs. Did she offer any explanation?''

Paget thought about that. "Not that I remember."

"She didn't say anything about her husband hanging about outside?"

"No."

"Well, he was. He was outside, watching for her to come out. He's been stalking her ever since she left him a month or so ago."

"We can't be sure of that, sir," Tregalles put in quietly. "Even Regan admitted she can't be sure that he was there, and we still have the problem of the second person."

"Second person?" Paget looked from one to the other for an explanation.

"We believe you were attacked by two people," Tregalles explained, and went on to tell Paget about the broken hasp on the shed, and the theory that at least one man had been waiting there for Paget to appear. "We think one of them hit you from behind, and it was the other one who..." He stopped, not wanting to come right out and say, "cut your throat." "Are you sure you don't remember any of that, sir?"

Paget shook his head. "Sorry, Tregalles, but it's a complete blank. But if Regan's husband was stalking her as she claims, it would explain why she was so nervous when we left the building. I could feel her trembling as she hung on to my arm."

Alcott's eyebrows shot up. "She was holding your arm?"

"It was dark, and it was treacherous underfoot," said Paget, visibly annoyed by Alcott's question. "There was mud all over the place, and she was wearing high-heeled shoes." He closed his eyes again. "You can check with her if you like, and—"

"Sorry, gentlemen, but Mr. Paget must have his rest." No one had noticed the nurse approach until she was standing there at the foot of the bed.

"But we've only been here—"

"Quite long enough," the nurse said firmly. "Mr. Paget only came down from ICU this morning. Perhaps tomorrow?"

"Perhaps," Alcott said ungraciously as he moved away.

Tregalles touched Paget's arm. "Glad to see you on the mend, sir, and Audrey said to wish you the best."

Paget reached out and gripped his sergeant's hand. "Thank her for me," he said. He lowered his voice. "And don't let Alcott bully you into his way of thinking. If you think you have a better idea, follow it through. He gets a bit carried away at times, and he needs someone to hold him back."

He saw the steely look in the nurse's eye, and raised his hands in mock surrender. "He's going," he assured her, and settled back on his pillows. He wanted to think about everything he'd heard today, and try once more to remember what had happened out there behind the station.

He closed his eyes—and promptly fell asleep.

"DROP ME OFF at New Street," Alcott told Tregalles as they left the hospital. "I have a meeting with Chief Superintendent Brock. He wants to hear what Paget had to say." He stuck a cigarette in his mouth, lit it, and sucked the smoke deep into his lungs. "And he is not going to be pleased when I tell him Paget claims to remember nothing of the attack," he said softly, and blew a cloud of smoke into the air.

"*Claims* to remember nothing?" Tregalles echoed, batting smoke away with his open hand.

Alcott shrugged. "We have to consider the possibility that Paget knows his attacker, but doesn't want to say who it was. Or," he continued as Tregalles started to object, "he really doesn't remember, but might in time. The trouble is, we can't afford to wait for that to happen—if it ever does."

"But if he does know who attacked him, why wouldn't he tell us?"

Alcott shook his head impatiently. "For any number of reasons," he said testily. "Face it, Tregalles. Sergeant Regan is a very attractive woman, and Paget's wife has been dead now for what—four years or more? And if it was Marshall who went after him, Paget's not likely to admit that to us, is he? Having an affair with one of his staff? Attacked by a jealous husband? Not something he'd want everyone to know, is it?''

Tregalles drew in his breath. ''I think I would know if something like that was going on,'' he said stiffly. ''And I can assure you that I don't—sir.''

Alcott shook his head again. ''I'm simply pointing out that you should not allow yourself to be blinded by some sort of personal loyalty to the man,'' he said wearily. ''Granted, DCI Paget has a fine record, but he's not a bloody automaton, even if he acts like one most of the time. He's flesh and blood. Regan is quite open about her admiration for him, and I suspect that Paget is a very lonely man. It can happen, so don't dismiss it out of hand. Whoever attacked Paget that night meant to kill him. It was no chance encounter, believe me. They knew him, knew who they were waiting for, and I believe that Paget may know who they are. Whether or not this loss of memory is genuine, I don't know, but mark my words, Tregalles, there is a link. So put someone on it. Find out if the two of them have been seen together outside office hours. If it turns out there is nothing to it, fine, no harm's been done. In other words, Sergeant, I want to be damned sure we've covered every possibility. Have you ever been to his house?''

''No, sir, I can't say I have, but—''

''Neither have I,'' Alcott cut in, ''and neither has anyone else as far as I know. So, what does he do in his spare time? Put some pressure on Regan. Put pressure on the housekeeper. If anything has been going on, chances are she would know about it, but she may be keeping quiet out of loyalty to Paget. I want answers, Tregalles, so get cracking.'' Alcott slipped off his seat belt as the car drew in to the kerb.

''No need to wait,'' he said as he got out. ''I'll walk back.'' Alcott paused only long enough to grind his cigarette beneath his heel before entering the building. Morgan Brock did not allow smoking in Head Office.

But instead of returning to Charter Lane, Tregalles drove back to the hospital, where he returned to the fourth floor and examined the PC's log. Alcott was right, Regan had been there every day, enquiring about Paget's condition. But then again, so had Grace Lovett.

ELEVEN

APART FROM THE short time they'd had him on his feet and walking a few steps, Paget slept through much of Tuesday morning. He was still on liquids, and the smell of food stirred juices in his stomach—he'd have given anything for a solid meal. Not that he would have been able to swallow it, but the thought still tantalized as mealtimes came and went.

Two o'clock, and the clatter of lunch trays and the trundle of trolleys had only just subsided when Tregalles stuck his head around the door. "Mind if I come in, boss?" he asked. "I looked in earlier, but you were asleep. How do you feel now?"

"Better," Paget told him. "Is Mr. Alcott with you?"

Tregalles swung a chair closer to the bed and sat down. "He doesn't know I'm here," he said. "Besides, I wanted to talk to you alone."

"More questions?"

Tregalles shrugged apologetically. "Can't help it, I'm afraid. I hate to say it, but we're not getting anywhere. The trouble is, the super's got it into his head that you might know who did this to you. He seems to think you *do* remember, but don't want to say."

"Why on earth…?" Paget began, then nodded slowly. "I see," he said. "He believes I lied when I said there is nothing going on between Regan and me."

Tregalles shrugged. "That's about it," he admitted. "I tried to tell him he was wrong, but he insists that I pursue that line of questioning, because he's convinced that it was Marshall who attacked you. The trouble with that is Marshall is a loner. I haven't found anyone who admits to being a friend of his, or who knows anyone who is. And yet all the evidence shows that there had to be two people involved in the attack. One behind you, and one in front, and when Grace Lovett found the torch down the side of the building—"

Paget stopped him. "What was that about Grace?" he asked. "You didn't say anything about that earlier on."

"Didn't have time before that nurse came in," Tregalles said, and went on to explain how Grace had worked out how a second person could have escaped unseen, and had found the torch among the debris beside the building. "We believe that someone came up behind you and hit you over the head," he concluded, "but there was someone else there, someone in front of you, and it was the one in front who…" He made a gesture with his hand across the throat.

A tantalizing wisp of memory stirred, a blinding light, a voice—and the smell of burnt flesh! Jill's blackened face… He thrust out his hands, palms outward, and turned his head away. The image faded, but the smell still lingered in his nostrils.

"Sir? Are you all right?" Tregalles half rose from his seat, but Paget waved him away. "It's all right," he said. "For a moment there, I thought I remembered something, but it's gone."

"About the attack? Something I said?"

How could he explain what was going on inside his head when he didn't know himself? "It was nothing," he said. "Sorry if I startled you, Tregalles, but I'm told I'll experience a number of strange sensations until the pressure on the brain subsides." He switched to another subject before the sergeant could ask more questions.

"You say it was Grace who found the torch?"

"That's right. She's good. We should get her on our team."

Paget smiled. "You'd like that, wouldn't you, Tregalles?"

Tregalles grinned. "Did you know that she came to the ICU every day while you were up there?"

"Grace did? Why?"

"I reckon that bang on the head did more damage than you think," Tregalles chuckled. "I hear she was pretty concerned about you. Pestered the uniforms outside the door, even tried to get information out of that Dr. McMillan."

"Really? That was kind of her," said Paget neutrally. "Perhaps you would thank her for me when you see her. However, I'm sure you didn't come back to tell me that, did you?"

"No, sir, but I do have more questions, if you feel up to answering them."

Paget settled himself more comfortably against the pillows and waited.

Tregalles took a deep breath and said, "I'm afraid I have to ask you again, sir, about your relationship with Regan. As I said, she has been here every day as well, asking after you. In fact, if I may say so, sir, she seems to be taking an extraordinary interest in your welfare."

Paget's eyes narrowed. "Meaning?" he said softly.

Tregalles wasn't enjoying this at all, but it had to be done. "Meaning that we are trying to put it into context," he said. "It was her husband, Paul Marshall, who first implied that you and she were having an affair. He said that she never stopped talking about you, and it was because of you that she refused to leave the service. He said he finally lost his temper and told her that if she thought so much of the job and you, she might as well stay there with you. So she did. I don't mean that literally," he amended hastily, "but she did leave him at that point, and went to stay with a friend, Linda Bryce. She works in the office."

Committed now, the sergeant pushed on. "You see, sir, it is a matter of record that Regan did stay behind to work with you on many occasions when it could be argued there was no need, if you see what I mean?"

Paget closed his eyes. He saw what Tregalles meant all right. He liked Regan, but the woman was an overachiever. She was good at her job, and she was ambitious, but she pushed too hard. He could understand her wanting to make a good impression, but there had been times when he'd wished she would go home. He often worked late, but it was because he had nothing waiting for him at home. Since Jill had gone and he'd made the transfer to Broadminster, his job was his life.

Perhaps that was the way it was for Regan. Her job was *her* life, and she was looking for an escape from a situation at home that had become unbearable.

He opened his eyes. "If there was an attraction," he told Tregalles, "I can assure you it was entirely one-sided. Kate wants to become a sergeant, and I suspect that she doesn't intend to stop there. She was always looking for more work; she wanted to impress me and everyone she worked with, but that's it! In short, Tregalles, there never was any affair or anything remotely resembling an affair. Have you talked to her about it?"

Tregalles nodded. "Yes, and Molly had a talk with her as well."

"And what was Regan's reaction?"

"She denied that anything was going on—but then, she would, wouldn't she? I mean, if there was really nothing to it, she would deny it, and if there was, she'd still deny it."

Paget smiled. "We'll make a detective out of you yet," he said, "but I think you may have missed the point. It doesn't matter whether we were having an affair or not. If, as you say, Marshall believed we were, and if he saw us leave the building together, his suspicions would be confirmed, which gives him both motive and opportunity."

"But what about the second person?"

"Just because you haven't found anyone who fits the bill doesn't mean they don't exist."

Tregalles groaned. "You're as bad as Alcott," he complained.

"Do you have any other suspects?"

The sergeant hesitated. "I know this is a bit delicate, sir, but you know how it is—I have to ask. Is there any chance that someone is jealous of your relationship with Dr. McMillan?"

Paget's face was expressionless. "Not that I'm aware of," he said. "As you know, her ex-husband is dead, and, as for a 'relationship,' as you call it, we are simply friends, that's all. I hope you haven't spoken to Dr. McMillan about this."

Tregalles shrugged uncomfortably. "We do have to look at every possibility, sir. I mean, that's what you would say, given the circumstances. Right, sir?"

Paget nodded slowly. He was a private person by nature, but now it seemed that every aspect of his life would come under close scrutiny, and he didn't like the feel of it.

Tregalles said, "If it means anything, sir, the doctor said almost exactly the same thing—about the relationship, I mean."

A tight smile tugged at the corners of Paget's mouth. "Did she, now?" he said softly. "Anything else?"

"No," Tregalles sighed, "and that's the trouble. I've been through every major case you've handled since you came here, and I can't find anything that suggests this kind of revenge. The super reckons it had to be someone who really hated you, which is why he is so sure it's Marshall. Have you thought of anyone at all who might want to see you dead?"

Put that way, it was a chilling thought, and a sobering one. Until that moment, Paget had not thought of the attack in such personal terms. It was almost as if it had happened to someone else. But now he had to face the fact that someone had waited for him out there that night with one idea in mind: to kill him in the most brutal and savage way.

"There may be any number of people who don't *like* me," he said, "but I can't think of anyone who hates me enough to try to kill me. Is that why there's a uniform outside my door? Do you think there will be an attempt to finish the job?"

"It's just a precaution, sir."

"I see." Paget put his hands to his face and rubbed his eyes. In fact, he *didn't* see. His vision had become blurred, and his head throbbed painfully. Tregalles had all but disappeared. It was as if a film had been drawn across his eyes; there was a rushing sound in his ears, and his hands were shaking. He heard the sergeant's voice as if coming from a great distance. "Sir…? Are you all right? I'm ringing for the nurse."

"No!" Paget reached out and caught the sergeant's arm as he stood up and reached for the bell. "No," he said again. "It's all right. It's nothing. The doctor told me I shouldn't overdo things, and he was right. I'm sorry, Tregalles, but I think I've had enough of this for one day."

"It's my fault for keeping you talking like this," Tregalles said. "Sorry, sir. I'll be going now. Is there anything you need?"

Paget began to shake his head, then paused. "Yes, there is something. Would you let Mrs. Wentworth know that I'm out of the ICU? She's a good soul, and she worries about me. Tell her that I'll probably be home by the weekend if all goes well, but by next Monday at the latest."

"That's a bit optimistic, isn't it, sir? I mean, is that what the doctor said?"

"They need the bed," Paget told him, avoiding a direct answer.

"I'll let her know," Tregalles promised. "Anything else?"

"I'd appreciate it if you would pop in from time to time and let me know how things are going."

"I'll do that, sir. Take care."

Paget lay back on his pillows, and brushed weakly at the band of sweat across his brow. He felt light-headed, disoriented. He reached blindly for a handful of tissues on the bedside stand, and rammed them against his nose. But no amount of tissues could rid him of the acrid smell, nor could he shut out the sight of blackened human flesh.

HE WAS DOZING when he heard a rustling sound. He opened his eyes, expecting to see one of the nurses, but it was Grace standing in the doorway. She was wearing a three-quarter-length dark blue anorak with the hood thrown back. Raindrops glistened like diamonds in her hair, and her face was flushed with colour.

"Oh, dear. Sorry if I woke you, Neil. Perhaps I should come back another time."

"No, no!" Paget brushed the sleep from his eyes and struggled to sit up. "Please come in."

Grace grimaced apologetically. "I'm afraid I'm dripping wet," she said. "It's a nasty night out there, and the temperature's dropping. We could have snow by morning." She stopped halfway into the room and eyed him critically. "Are you quite sure you feel up to a visit?"

"You're like a breath of fresh air in here," he told her, "no pun intended." Just the sight of her had raised his spirits, but then, Grace had that effect on those around her.

"Tregalles tells me that you were here before, but I'm afraid I wasn't aware of it. Thanks anyway. I appreciate the thought."

Grace tugged a package from one of the pockets of her anorak and handed it to him. "I remembered your telling me that you had never read Rutherfurd's *Sarum,* so I brought you a copy. I hope I'm not too late, and you've read it since then."

"Never seemed to have the time," he confessed, "but it looks as if I will have now. Thank you very much. It's a thick one, isn't it? I'll let you have it back as soon as I've read it."

Grace shook her head. "It's yours," she told him. "It's the sort of book you may find you want to go back to every now and again."

"In that case, thanks again."

The silence between them lengthened, then, "You are tired," she said as she began to do up her coat; "I think I'd better go and let you get your rest."

"No!" The word came out almost as a croak. His throat was dry. He coughed cautiously to clear it. He didn't want her to leave. "Please stay, that is if you have the time."

"Well, if you're quite sure?"

"I am. In fact, I could use your help. I'm supposed to walk a bit each day, but I've been lazy. I hate to bother the nurses when they're so short-staffed, but I do need someone to lean on. Would you mind?"

"Of course not." Grace slipped off her coat as Paget swung his legs over the side of the bed. "If you'll just hand me that dressing gown at the foot of the bed," he said.

Grace helped him on with it, then took his arm as he slipped his feet into hospital slippers. "Are you sure you've done this before?" she asked. "You look a bit wobbly to me."

"You should have seen me a couple of days ago," he said as they made their way out the door. Then, "Don't worry, Constable, we'll stay in sight," he told the man seated outside the door. "Miss Lovett's looking after me. Alcott's idea," he confided to Grace as they moved out of earshot. "He thinks I need some sort of guard."

Behind him, the constable smothered a yawn. "Lucky sod," he muttered as he stared after them. "She could look after me anytime."

A nurse came down the hall toward them. "Don't overdo it, Mr. Paget," she warned. "I know you can't wait to get out of here, but you've been out here twice already today, and I think that's enough for now, don't you?"

Grace looked at him. "You're a fake," she accused. "And that's the most colour I've seen in your face since I came in."

"I lied," he admitted sheepishly, "but to tell you the truth, it's so dull in here, and the only other visitors I have keep asking questions. Do you mind very much?"

Grace smiled. "Of course not. After all, what are friends for if not to lean on?"

GRACE HAD BEEN GONE about an hour when he heard what sounded like an altercation taking place outside his door. He'd been half asleep when it started, but now the voices were raised, and he felt sure one of them belonged to Kate Regan.

"What is it, Constable?" he called, then remembered they were both constables, and added, "Hadley?"

The voices stopped, and the man stepped inside the room. "It's WPC Regan, sir," he said. "She is asking to see you, but I was told she's been suspended, so…"

It had been a long and tiring day; and all he wanted to do was sleep. He was about to tell Hadley he was too tired to see anyone when Regan appeared in the doorway. "Sorry to disturb you, sir," she said breathlessly, "but when I heard you'd been moved out of the ICU, I *had* to come to tell you how sorry I am about what happened. I feel it's all my fault."

"It's all right, Hadley," Paget said wearily as he eased himself up in bed. "Let her come in now she's here."

"Well…" Hadley didn't like to give way. "I shall have to put it in the log."

"Quite right, Hadley, and I'll initial it if you wish."

"Well, I suppose in that case, sir…" The constable gave ground grudgingly.

Paget waited until Hadley had gone before motioning Kate to a chair, but she chose instead to come and stand at the foot of the bed.

"No need to apologize," he told her. "From what I've been told, I doubt if it would have made a scrap of difference, because it appears two people were involved, and they were waiting for me back there."

"So it wasn't Paul?"

"I didn't say that at all. He is still the only suspect they have, and you did say you saw him out there that night."

Kate made a helpless gesture. "I felt so sure that he was out there at the time," she said, "but the more I think about it, the less sure I am. I realize now that all I really saw was a movement, and I assumed it was Paul because he's done that before.''

''You were sure enough that you were afraid to leave the building alone,'' he reminded her. Kate winced, and Paget took pity on her. ''But I don't blame you for what happened, Kate, so there's nothing to be gained by blaming yourself.''

''You *are* going to be all right, aren't you, sir?''

''They tell me I have a very hard head,'' he said, and smiled. ''It may take some time, but, yes, I'm going to be all right.''

''Thank God for that, at least.'' Kate looked at her watch. ''Sorry to burst in on you like that, sir. I know it's late, but I had to come. I hope you understand?''

Paget nodded carefully. ''But before you go, tell me, how did you get past the desk at this hour? Didn't anyone challenge you?''

She smiled guiltily. ''I was rather hoping no one would ask that question, sir. I used this.'' She took a slim plastic envelope from her purse and flipped it open. ''It's my bank book,'' she told him. ''I just flashed it at the desk and said I had to talk to Hadley. They just waved me on.''

So much for security, he thought as he settled down for the night.

TWELVE

FOR THE SECOND TIME in two days Alcott climbed the stairs to the office of Chief Superintendent Morgan Brock. Brock had not been there the previous afternoon when Alcott had gone to report the results of his talk with Paget. "He's still getting over the flu, so he went home early," his secretary told Alcott, "but he said I was to tell you he'll be in tomorrow, and he wants to see you first thing."

Alcott had looked upon it as a reprieve, since his talk with Paget had yielded nothing new. Perhaps they would know more by morning. It had been a faint hope at best, and one that had failed to materialize.

"It's been two weeks, Superintendent," was Brock's opening statement as Alcott came through the door, "and as far as I can see, you are no further ahead than you were last week. Have you made any progress at all?"

The chief superintendent rocked gently back and forth in his swivel chair, his accusing eyes fixed on Alcott's own. Cod's eyes, Alcott called them. Pale and slightly bulbous, they matched the man. In fact everything about Brock was pale: his hair, cut short and parted in the middle, his pasty face, and eyebrows so fair that it was hard to tell they were there at all. "Well?" he prompted as Alcott sat down. "What have you got to say for yourself? Good God, man, if we can't even find someone who damned nearly killed one of our own people in our own backyard, what does that say about us, eh? Have you seen the papers? The chief constable is not pleased,

I can tell you. Not pleased at all. He wants action. He wants this matter closed.''

"We have only one suspect—" Alcott began, only to be cut off by Brock.

"And you've let him go, not once, but twice," he snapped.

"Because the evidence against him isn't strong enough to hold up in court," Alcott explained patiently, "and until it is, CPS won't touch it."

"So what are you doing about it?"

"We know there were two people involved, so we're trying to find a link to the second man. Unfortunately…''

"Unfortunately, that isn't good enough," snapped Brock. He clasped pudgy hands across his belly as he tilted back in his chair. "What does Paget have to say for himself? Is he having an affair with that Regan woman?''

"He denies it emphatically. So does Constable Regan, and I'm inclined to believe them. But whether they are or not doesn't matter if her husband believes they are. As I was about to say earlier, we know two people were involved, but we can find no evidence to suggest that Marshall knows anyone he could trust to join him in such a vicious attack. In fact, we can find no evidence that Marshall has any friends at all. The only way we might find a connection is if we put him under twenty-four-hour surveillance. If I had the resources…''

Brock ignored the probe. "And if he doesn't lead you to an accomplice? What then?"

"We have to look at other options."

"What other options? And why aren't you looking at them now?"

"We are. Someone from Paget's past, perhaps. Enemies he may have made along the way. Someone with a long-standing grudge against him. Tregalles has been digging into old cases, Paget's background, his personal life. We've even considered the possibility that it was a case of mistaken identity, that Paget was mistaken for someone else, although, to be honest,

I don't think that was the case. There is every indication that it was planned."

Brock remained silent for a long moment, fingers drumming on the desk. "What about the woman? Constable Regan. Could she have been part of this? Is it possible that she and her husband planned this between them, and this whole business of him stalking her is false? We only have her word for that, and as I understand it, she was waiting for Paget at the door, and it was she who suggested walking round the back together. Could it have been some sort of set-up between her and her husband to get Paget? Is she your second attacker?"

Brock was clutching at straws. "For what reason?" said Alcott. "And why would she implicate her husband if they were in it together? Besides, she was seen leaving in her car prior to the attack, so there is no way she could have been around the back as well."

"So what am I supposed to tell the chief constable?" Brock demanded. "Did you see yesterday's editorial in the Star? Questioning our competence, our ability to give adequate protection, suggesting that we are seriously understaffed, to—"

"Which we are," Alcott stated flatly.

"To the point where we are reduced to putting a sergeant in charge of this case, rather than an inspector," Brock continued as if Alcott hadn't spoken. "I warned you, Superintendent, that putting a sergeant in charge would set a dangerous precedent."

Alcott bristled. "With respect, sir, you know as well as I do that Tregalles is only nominally in charge of this case. I am, and I take full responsibility."

"A fact that fails to give me comfort, Superintendent," Brock shot back.

Alcott rose to his feet, jaw set, eyes narrowed as he leaned forward and placed both hands on the chief superintendent's desk. "Meaning exactly what?" he demanded in a low voice. "If you're not satisfied with my…"

Brock waved a dismissive hand. "Oh, for God's sake, sit

down,'' he said harshly. "This isn't getting us anywhere. But I need *something* to take to the chief constable. He's releasing a statement to the media this afternoon, and he's looking to me to provide it, so I am looking to you for answers.''

Alcott subsided into his chair. "Why not tell him the truth?'' he said, taking a leaf from Tregalles's book, then held up his hand as Brock's almost non-existent eyebrows shot up. "I mean it,'' he went on. "There were no witnesses to this crime. We can find no motive, and any evidence that might have been left at the scene was washed away by the rain. We are doing our best, but let's be frank and admit we have a problem, and we need the help of the public in a case such as this.''

Brock grimaced and stared into space for a long moment, glowering as he considered the kind of reception he would get if he put the case as baldly as that to the chief constable.

Alcott stirred. "If there is nothing else, sir...?'' he said, preparing to rise.

Brock's eyes changed focus, eyes narrowed. He seemed surprised to find Alcott still there. "Yes, now that you mention it, there is one more thing,'' he said brusquely. "I want to see next month's overtime cut in half.''

Alcott stared at him. "And how do you suggest I do that, sir? I'm short at least four people, so overtime is the only alternative I have.''

"That, I'm afraid, is your problem, Superintendent, but it has to be done, so you can forget about round-the-clock surveillance on Marshall for a start. You'll have to find some other way.''

Alcott rose to his feet. "Anything else, sir?'' he asked grimly.

Brock reached across the desk and pulled a file toward him. "Yes,'' he said. "Close the door on your way out. I can feel a draft.''

"I DIDN'T KNOW WHEN you would be coming out, so I've brought you some more pyjamas, and some clothes for when you do," said Mrs. Wentworth as she set a suitcase on the chair beside the bed. "Now, where can I hang them up so they won't crease? I don't expect they give you a hanger, so I brought a couple with me." She looked around and spotted hooks in a tiny alcove. "Ah, that should do nicely," she said as she began lifting each item out of the suitcase and shaking it out.

"It's very kind of you to come," Paget told her, "and I'm delighted to see you, but you shouldn't have bothered with all that, especially if you came on the bus. I was going to have someone come out and pick up some clothes once I knew when I was to be released."

"It was no trouble," Mrs. Wentworth assured him. "The bus stops right outside the hospital gates, so I didn't have to carry it far." She took out a small clothes brush and flicked it across the shoulders of his sports jacket before hanging it carefully on the hanger. "Besides, I wanted to see for myself how you were getting on. They don't tell you anything when you ring up." She eyed him critically. "Are you sure you should be out of bed? You're pale, and you've lost weight— I can see it in your face."

"I feel fine," he assured her, "in fact I feel well enough to come home, but I'm having trouble convincing the doctors of that. Hospital fare isn't bad, but it's not a patch on your cooking, Mrs. Wentworth."

"Ah." She avoided his eyes as she turned back to the suitcase. Suddenly, she seemed ill at ease, and spoke rapidly. "I've brought you some buttered scones made fresh this morning, and a pot of raspberry jam and a knife and spoon to spread it with. Oh, yes, and some sweet biscuits to nibble on when you're a bit peckish, so don't go giving them all away to the nurses, now." She set two boxes and a pot of jam on the bedside table.

Paget smiled and shook his head as he placed his hands upon her shoulders. "You shouldn't have gone to all that trouble," he told her, "but it's good to see you again, and I'm glad you came."

"I'm just happy that you're still here so I *can* do it," she said fervently. "When I heard what had happened"—tears glistened in the woman's eyes—"it was just like the day they told me about my Bert all over again. Oh my, but you did give us all a scare."

"Believe me, it wasn't by choice," Paget told her. "But that's all behind us now."

"But is it? I mean, do they know who did it? Do they know why? I rang that young Molly Forsythe to try to find out if they had caught whoever did it, but she went all round the mulberry bush without saying anything. And why is that constable sitting outside your door and asking all sorts of questions before he lets anybody in?"

"It takes time," said Paget soothingly, "and that constable is there primarily to keep me from being bothered by members of the media. It's a normal precaution, that's all."

Mrs. Wentworth eyed him suspiciously. "You're as bad as young Molly," she told him, "but I don't suppose there's any point in trying to get the truth out of you, is there?" She looked around the room. "Now then, what happened to the clothes you were wearing when they brought you in? I can put them in the case and take them back with me."

"They were taken away for forensic examination," he told her. "Besides, they were ruined anyway, so I shan't be wanting them back. Now, why don't you sit down and tell me what's been happening in the village while I've been in here."

Mrs. Wentworth sat, but she didn't look comfortable, and he could tell by her face that something was wrong. "What is it?" he asked as he sat down on the edge of the bed. "Bad news? Something wrong at home?"

"Oh, no, there's nothing wrong at home, Mr. Paget," she assured him, "but it is bad news in a way. You see, it's my sister in Bristol, my older sister. You may remember I told you about her having a leaky valve in her heart and having to wait for a year before she could have it done? Well, her doctor telephoned me last night to tell me that she collapsed yesterday and was rushed into hospital, and they had to operate right away or she would have died. She's come through, but the thing is, she's going to need someone to look after her when she comes out, and she hasn't got anyone else, not since Robert—that's her husband as was—died ten years ago, so it's up to me. She'll be eighty next year, and she's got the beginning of Parkinson's as well, so I don't have much choice but to go down there to look after her, at least until she gets over the operation. I'm ever so sorry, Mr. Paget, what with you coming home soon and me not being there to look after you, so to speak, but like I said, she is my sister and I don't have much choice.''

"For heaven's sake, Mrs. Wentworth, there's no need to apologize," Paget told her. "Of course you must go. You can see for yourself that I'm on my feet, and well on the way to full recovery, so you don't have to worry about me. Besides, it won't be that long before I'm back at work."

"Oh, but you mustn't go back too soon," Mrs. Wentworth protested. "You need time to build yourself up again."

"You worry too much," he told her. "Besides, I'll need something to do while I'm at home, and I can brush up on my cooking."

"And end up eating out of tins, most likely. I just wish it hadn't come at such a bad time. But Mrs. Baker says she's willing to come in a couple of times a week to do the washing and ironing and hoovering and such, the same as she did when I went on holidays two years ago—that is, if you want her to. She's very reliable, but she can't do more than the two days a week. Trouble is, she's not that much of a cook; she fries everything, and that's not good for you, 'specially now."

"I'm sure we shall manage," he said, "so don't you worry. Is someone keeping an eye on your place while you're away?"

"All taken care of," she assured him. "Next door will be

popping in each day to make sure everything is all right, and to see to Ginger." Ginger was a huge tomcat of indeterminate age who, having arrived on Mrs. Wentworth's doorstep several years ago, decided he was onto a good thing, and stayed. And next door, he knew, referred to Mrs. Wentworth's friend and neighbour, Mrs. Lovejoy.

Mrs. Wentworth stayed for another twenty minutes, then said she would have to leave if she was to catch the three o'clock bus. "I don't like these short days," she confided. "I like to get home before dark. Now, is there anything I can do before I leave for Bristol?"

"Not a thing," he assured her. He walked with her to the lift to demonstrate that he was indeed capable of operating under his own steam, and to assure her once again that she shouldn't feel guilty about leaving him. Even so, she let the lift go by twice while she reeled off a list of things she'd done to help him when he got home.

"I've left my sister's telephone number on the fridge," she called as the doors were closing. "Now do take…" The doors closed and she was gone.

Paget returned to his room and lay down on the bed. His head ached, and a shiver ran through him as what was now becoming a familiar feeling gripped him. Familiar yet indescribable—a sort of ethereal fog that descended on the mind, where images of the past thrust their way into the present; horrible images—accompanied always by the acrid smell of burning flesh. His eyes were closed, but suddenly a blinding light, intense and painful, flared behind closed lids. He cried out and flung his arms across his face, but the light remained, burning its way into the very core of his brain.

"It's your fault Jill and…died the way she did. Yours and all the others. Now it's your turn, Chief Inspector." He had no memory of anyone speaking the words; there was no association of time or place; they were just there, harsh metallic words, toneless, sexless, expressionless, echoing repeatedly inside his head—a pronouncement without emotion, a judgement preceding execution.

THIRTEEN

ANDREA CAME to see him Friday afternoon. Paget had seen little of her in the past few days, but he put it down to the fact that everyone on the floor was rushed off their feet. Icy streets and steps were responsible for a number of accidents resulting in a variety of fractures, breaks, and sprains, particularly among the elderly, and eight people had been brought in two nights ago as a result of a pile-up due to fog on the A49. They were short-staffed and short of beds, which was all the more reason why he felt he should get out of there and let someone else have his bed.

"You said yourself that the throat is healing well," he told her, "and the headaches have almost gone. You need the bed, so why are you keeping me here?"

Andrea remained silent for a long moment, regarding him with steady eyes as she stood there beside the bed, hands thrust into the pockets of her white coat. "To tell you the truth, I'm not quite sure," she said at last. "You have us puzzled. Mr. DeWitt and I have discussed your case at some length, and to be honest, Neil, the only explanation we can come up with is that there is something you're not telling us."

"Such as?" he asked warily.

"That's just it, we don't know. You've reported nothing out of the ordinary on the pad DeWitt left with you, and yet your temperature has been going up and down like a yo-yo, and the nurses report that you are perspiring at times even when lying still. What is going on, Neil?"

"So that's why young Rachel has been popping in to take

my temperature every couple of hours," he said lightly. "And I thought it was because she liked me."

But Andrea was not to be put off. "This could be serious, Neil," she warned. "We know it has nothing to do with infection, but it could have something to do with your head injury. What about these headaches? I know they are not uncommon in such cases, but what other symptoms do you have?"

He shrugged. "The odd bad dream when I drift off to sleep, and I often wake up sweating after something like that," he said, "but apart from that, I feel fine." He felt guilty about lying to Andrea, but what was going on inside his head was no one's business but his own. Perhaps the blow on the head was responsible for these visions, but it seemed to him that they were trying to tell him something—something about Jill and the way she died. And perhaps—just perhaps—they had something to do with why he was attacked.

Which was why he needed to get out of there and start searching for the answers.

"What kind of bad dreams?"

He shrugged again. "That's the trouble with dreams," he said. "They fade so fast when you wake up. Sometimes it has to do with trying to get away from something unseen; sometimes it's as if I'm falling—you know the sort of thing. I think everybody has dreams like that at one time or another."

"But their temperature doesn't keep jumping a couple of degrees when they do," Andrea observed drily. "However, apart from that, there is no good reason for keeping you here when we are so short of beds, so you can go home tomorrow. Can I help arrange for someone to take you? I'd offer to take you myself, but I'm afraid I'm working."

"No problem," he assured her. "Sergeant Tregalles told me to give him a call when I was ready to come out."

"You still need to take things easy," Andrea warned. "Your red-cell count is still low, and it will take time for your body to recover, so please get lots of rest. Exercise is good in moderation, but you should stop at the first sign of fatigue. Drink water, six or eight glasses a day, and you'll need to keep on with the iron supplement, and vitamin B12 as well, but someone will be in to talk to you about that before you go. Since I know you like your steak, you'll be pleased to hear that an increase in red meat in your diet will help, but don't neglect the vegetables and fruit. At least you have a housekeeper who can look after you during the day. Perhaps I should have a word with her about your food.''

"No need," he said hastily. "I'll take care of it, and I will be careful."

Andrea nodded. "Do," she said, "and I'll make sure you have your appointment times to see Mr. DeWitt before you leave tomorrow." She glanced at her watch and began moving toward the door. "Sorry I don't have more time, Neil, but I really must be off. I don't want to be late leaving, because tonight they're sorting out parts in the Christmas pageant at Sarah's school, and I promised her I'd be there."

"I understand. And thanks, Andrea, for everything."

"No trouble, Neil. Take care."

Paget put his arms behind his head as he lay back against the pillows—and winced. The back of his head was still tender, although it was much better than it had been. He wondered again whether he was being foolish in not telling Andrea or DeWitt about what was going on inside his head. But when it came right down to it, what was there to tell? Words inside his head that might or might not have meaning? Words that might have been generated by his own subconscious for all he knew.

Better to say nothing. The last thing he needed now was to be branded a nutcase.

"Are you awake?"

The voice, pitched low, was barely more than a whisper, but he recognized it immediately. "Grace," he said, opening his eyes. "Come in, come in and hear the good news."

"You're getting out," she guessed, and when he nodded, she said, "I'm so pleased for you. When?"

"Tomorrow morning."

"Great! How are you going to get home?"

"I was planning on ringing Tregalles when he gets home tonight. He'll take me."

"I'm not doing anything special tomorrow," Grace told him. "Why don't I take you? Your housekeeper doesn't come in on weekends as I recall, so I can help get you settled in, see if you need anything in the way of food, fresh milk, or whatever. I know Tregalles has been working late most nights, so if he does have time off this weekend, he would probably prefer to spend it with his family. But if you've promised to call him, I understand."

"Well, no, I haven't *promised* I'd call him," Paget admitted. "Do you know if they are getting anywhere with the case? My case, I mean?"

"They're not saying much, but going by what I hear from Charlie, I think the investigation has bogged down. Sorry, because I know how important this is to you, but I'm afraid that's the way it looks."

"I thought as much," he said. "I'm sure Tregalles would have been in to see me if they had anything new. Perhaps I should let him make the most of his weekend, so if you're sure you don't mind…?"

Grace smiled. "Not at all," she told him. "Just tell me when and I'll be here."

"PLEASE CALL ME if you need anything," Grace said as Paget escorted her to the door.

"You've done more than enough already," Paget told her. "The ride home from the hospital, and being out in the fresh air was a tonic in itself, and that was certainly the best lunch I've had in a long time. Now it seems all I want to do is sleep, though God knows why. You've done almost everything for me so far today, but I feel as if I've done a full day's work."

Grace turned to face him. "You *will* feel that way," she told him earnestly. "I saw that nice Dr. McMillan when I came in to pick you up this morning, and she said I should make sure that you have plenty of rest." Colour rose in her face as she realized what she'd said. "Well, she didn't mean *me* specifically," she amended hastily. "She meant that *someone* should keep an eye on you to make sure you followed instructions. I think she looks on you as a bit of a rebel when it comes to obeying doctors' orders."

"I can't imagine why she should think that." He smiled. "I can't do much else but rest, and what with your help today, and Mrs. Wentworth's friend coming in twice a week to do the heavy work, it will be like being on holiday."

"Good. But just to make sure, I'll be checking on you from time to time," Grace warned. She opened the front door, then turned and put her hand on his arm. "Seriously, though, Neil, do take care of yourself. You've been through a lot, so give yourself time to heal properly. And keep your doors and windows locked. Superintendent Alcott didn't have that constable sitting outside your door for nothing, so do be careful. You're a long way from help out here all by yourself."

"I doubt if I'm in any real danger of being attacked a second time," he told her. "In fact, I suspect whoever did attack me is well away from here by now."

"But you will be careful?"

"Of course I will," he said, touched by her concern. "Now, you had better get on back to town while it is still light. Some of our local drivers tend to drive with their lights on high beam in these narrow lanes after dark, and they can blind you. And thanks again for everything, Grace."

"You're quite sure you won't need me tomorrow?"

"Quite sure," Paget assured her. "Besides, Tregalles is coming out here tomorrow, so I can let him know if I need anything."

"Is this some sort of progress report, do you think?"

"I sincerely hope so, although he may be looking for more

information from me. I'm not sure that Alcott is entirely satisfied that I haven't been carrying on with Kate Regan.''

''But that's ridiculous!''

''Is it?'' Paget seemed amused by Grace's swift response.
''She is a very attractive woman, and her husband seems to
think there's truth to it.''

''Well, yes, but…''

''Anyway, that's enough of that,'' he said briskly. ''I
mustn't hold you up any longer. And thanks again for everything you've done.''

Grace went down the steps to her car. Paget watched from
the door as she backed into the road, and responded to her
wave as she set off down the hill. He closed the door and
made his way into the living room and flopped down in his
favourite chair. It was odd, he thought as looked around the
room. Since coming here from London several years ago, he'd
been quite content to be on his own, yet now that Grace had
gone, the house felt strangely empty.

But then, he was tired. Andrea had warned him that he
would be, but he hadn't expected to feel quite as drained as
this. Strange her talking to Grace like that—as if she'd assumed that Grace would be there to keep an eye on him. He
hoped Andrea hadn't got the wrong idea.

GRACE WISHED she could have stayed. Neil had looked so
pale. But she could hardly insist on staying. It was all very
well for him to say he wasn't worried, but she didn't like the
thought of him being out here with no one else in the house
or even close by. What if the damage to his head was more
serious than they thought? What if he collapsed and couldn't
reach the phone?

A car was parked on the side of the road. The bonnet was up
and a man was leaning in doing something to the engine. Grace
glanced in the rearview mirror to make sure there was nothing
behind her before she stopped and rolled the window down.

"Can I help you?" she called. "Do you need a lift into the village?"

The man lifted a hand in acknowledgement, but kept his head down. He seemed to be trying to reach something with his other arm. "No thanks," he called. "I think I've got it now."

"I have a phone in the car," Grace offered.

"Thanks all the same, but it will be fine now. It does this now and again."

"Well, all right, then if you're sure." The man waved a hand again as she pulled away. She watched in the mirror, and saw him straighten up and put the bonnet down. Good, she thought as the road curved to the left and she lost sight of him. At least she'd offered help; she could do no more. Besides, although she hadn't seen much of him, her impression was that of a young man, and it wasn't far if he did have to walk to the village.

Behind her, the man waited until she was out of sight, then slipped the car into gear and followed. No need to get too close until they got back to town.

FOURTEEN

"I DON'T KNOW HOW long I'll be," Tregalles told his wife as he dropped her and the children off at church, "but Jim next door said you could go back with them. All right?"

"I suppose," said Audrey, "but I don't see why you can't go out to see Mr. Paget this afternoon. It wouldn't hurt for you to come to church now and again." She lowered her voice as Olivia and Brian scrambled out. "I mean, what sort of example is it for the kids, John? Just this morning Brian said he'd be glad when he was old enough to be a detective so he wouldn't have to go to church either. Well, don't think you're going to get away with it at Christmas; I don't care what case you're on, you are coming to church Christmas morning with the rest of us."

Audrey got out of the car and was about to close the door when he stopped her. "What is it now?" she demanded irritably. "You'll make us late and we'll have to sit down the front."

"Have a nice pray," he said, and winked.

TREGALLES HAD NEVER been inside Paget's house, although he had made a point of driving by it one day last summer when he and Audrey had been on their way to Worcester. The house was situated close to the top of a hill, with a grand view of the valley and part of the village of Ashton Prior. "Very nice," Audrey had said, "but it seems awfully big for one man. I wonder why he keeps it?"

"It belonged to his father," Tregalles told her, "and before that it belonged to the Wentworths, but when the husband died, Mrs. Wentworth had to sell. Paget's father asked her to stay on as his housekeeper, and I think Paget sort of inherited her.''

"But she doesn't live there, does she?"

"No. She lives in the village and comes in daily. Except weekends. He said once that they rarely see one another. He's gone by the time she gets there in the morning, and she's gone by the time he gets home. And she doesn't come in on weekends. They leave notes for each other on the fridge.''

Now, as Paget ushered him inside, he took a good look round. "Very nice," he observed. "Very nice indeed." And yet, he thought as Paget took him through to the kitchen, it was a bit Spartan. The furniture, what there was of it, was good, but there were none of those little touches that made the house into what you might call a real home. Audrey would say it lacked a woman's touch, and she'd probably be right. It was a bachelor's house.

As for Paget himself, he looked thinner than he had in hospital. His eyes were bleak, and his face looked drawn and grey, the muscles set. The sergeant was reminded of a friend of his, a man plagued by migraine headaches.

"Still feeling a bit rough, are you, sir?" he asked.

"As obvious as that, is it?" said Paget, then changed the subject. "Come on through. I've just made coffee, and Mrs. Wentworth made a huge batch of shortbread before she left for Bristol. In fact, you can take some home with you if you like. I'll never eat it all.''

"So you're on your own, then?" The sergeant's active mind began to put two and two together. Paget had telephoned on Friday night to say that Grace Lovett had offered to drive him home from the hospital on Saturday, and he'd wondered whose idea that had been. He glanced around the room, half expecting to see some signs of Grace's presence there, then remembered he hadn't seen her car outside.

"For a while, at least," said Paget as he poured coffee. He

nudged the open tin of shortbread in Tregalles's direction, and went on to explain why Mrs. Wentworth had had to leave. "But you didn't come out here to talk about that," he concluded. "Are we any further ahead?"

Tregalles shook his head. "To be honest, we're going backward," he said glumly. "As of yesterday, we lost our prime suspect."

"Marshall? What do you mean, you *lost* him? You mean he's disappeared?"

"Lost him as a suspect," Tregalles explained. "He has an alibi. A neighbour says he saw Marshall in the street outside his house just after eight o'clock the night you were attacked."

"Why didn't he mention this before?"

"Because he's been away. His name is Finch, Larry Finch, and he lives two doors up from Marshall. He's been away all week in Europe at a software trade show, and didn't get back till Friday night, so yesterday was the first chance we had to talk to him."

Tregalles plucked a shortbread from the tin and began to munch.

"On the night you were attacked, he'd been working late at the office, preparing to go to Brussels the following morning, and he came home by taxi. It was raining hard, as you know, and the cab was crawling along, looking for Finch's house, when they came up behind a man walking on the pavement. Finch said the man turned to look at the taxi, lost his balance, slipped off the kerb, and fell across the bonnet. Scared the hell out of the driver, who rolled his window down and started swearing at the man. The man came to the window and started screaming at the driver, and that's when Finch saw that it was Marshall. He said things were getting a bit ugly, so he got out, paid the driver off and gave him a big tip for his trouble. He said he steered Marshall up the path to his house, then went off home himself. Early the following morning, he was off to Brussels, and that was that. I checked with the cab driver myself. He remembered the incident well enough, and when I showed him Marshall's picture, he was sure it was the same man.''

"No doubt about the time?"

"None. The company still had the record of the fare."

"Was Marshall drunk?"

"Both Finch and the driver are convinced he was."

"So where had Marshall been?"

Tregalles wiped crumbs from his fingers. "He now admits he lied; he says he didn't go to the corner shop as he told us in the first place, but went to pick up more booze. When I asked why he hadn't told us this before, he said he didn't want us to get the impression that he was a drinker."

Paget's eyebrows rose at that. "Yeah," Tregalles said. "Believe it or not, he is still clinging to the idea that no one knows he's an alcoholic."

"So we're back to square one."

"Afraid so. The only good thing to come out of it is that Kate Regan will be reinstated tomorrow. Have you thought of anything? Remembered anything?"

"Believe me, Tregalles, I've tried, but no. What about London? Anything back from them?"

"We had a fax from your Chief Superintendent McKenzie, saying that they had checked back six months on anyone who you had helped put away, but no one has been released during that time."

"*Chief* superintendent? I didn't know he'd been promoted," Paget said. "But if that's the case, the only thing left is for me to check my own diaries from my time in the Met, and I intend to start going through them this afternoon. Not that I hold out much hope that they will help, but at least it will give me something to do."

The sergeant sipped his coffee, then slowly shook his head. "If they don't, I'm damned if I know where else to look," he said. He fell silent, and when at last he did speak, he avoided looking directly at Paget. "But what I do know is this: the attack on you was no spur-of-the-moment thing. It was planned. It was a miserable night, pouring rain, yet two people waited in that shed for you to go to your car. And because you were late leaving, they probably waited a long time, but the point is, they did wait. They were both armed, one with a length of gas pipe, the other with a razor, and they meant business.'' Tregalles raised his eyes to meet those of his boss. ''Somebody went to a lot of trouble to try to kill you,'' he concluded. ''Are you *quite* certain you don't know who it is?''

Paget's eyes narrowed. ''You think I'm holding something back?''

Tregalles held his ground. ''I don't know, sir. Are you?''

''No!'' Annoyance at the sergeant's question had made his voice rise. ''And I'd like to know why you asked that question.''

Tregalles shrugged. ''It's just that if someone hated me enough to want to kill me, I think I'd have some idea who it was and why they wanted me dead.''

''Well, I don't!'' Paget snapped. ''And—'' He stopped abruptly and ran his fingers through his hair. ''Believe me, Tregalles,'' he said in a calmer voice, ''it's that very question that's been plaguing me ever since I regained consciousness. Who does want me dead? What is it I am supposed to have done? I want answers to those questions every bit as much as you do.''

Later, as Tregalles was leaving, he paused at the door. ''I was wondering if you've remembered anything else about the attack itself. When we spoke in hospital, you said you remembered nothing after seeing Regan off in her car. Has anything come back to you since then? Any small detail, perhaps?''

Paget shook his head.

''In that case, sir, do you mind if I make a suggestion?''

''Not at all.''

''I was wondering if we re-created the situation as we believe it happened, and took you through it step by step, it just might trigger memories of the actual event. It's up to you, of course, and I wouldn't expect you to do it until you're feeling up to it, but with Marshall out of the picture, we've got bugger all else to go on. If you agree, I could have someone pick you up and bring you home again.''

Paget hesitated. Perhaps it would help to jog his memory, but did he really *want* to remember? DeWitt had said it wasn't uncommon for the mind to block out painful memories; given time, they might come back to him, *might* being the operative word. ''Don't try to force it,'' he'd said.

But could he afford to wait when there was someone out there who wanted to see him dead? As Tregalles had pointed out, they had nothing else to go on.

''Arrange it,'' he told Tregalles. ''And the sooner the better as far as I'm concerned. Tomorrow if you like.''

Tregalles nodded soberly. ''Appreciate that, sir,'' he said, ''but I'd like to make sure the conditions are the same as they were that night, so I'll ring you when things look right. They're forecasting more rain this week, so we should be able to set it up soon. Which reminds me, we still have your car. Can we keep it until after we've done this?''

''Of course. I shan't be needing it for a while.''

''Good.''

When Tregalles had gone, Paget returned to the kitchen and poured himself another cup of coffee. His hand began to shake as he raised it to his lips, and he swore beneath his breath as hot liquid slopped over the edge and spilled down his shirt. The cup slipped from his hand, fell, shattered on the floor, but he was barely conscious of it as he snatched the wet shirt away from his skin. His knees began to buckle and he eased himself into a chair. His head throbbed and his vision blurred as he sat there looking at his shaking hands.

He wasn't sure how long he'd slept, head on his arms at the kitchen table, but it was getting on for three when he awoke. He rubbed the back of his neck, stretched, and saw the broken cup. Remembered. Looked at his hands. Rock steady, and his vision was absolutely clear.

PAGET SPENT the last part of the afternoon searching through boxes that had remained unopened since he'd moved into the house. They were stored in the small third bedroom, or box-room, as Mrs. Wentworth insisted on calling it. He was look-ing for his old notebooks, personal diaries containing jottings and thoughts regarding cases he'd worked on during his time with the Met. It was a slow process because he kept coming across items he'd almost forgotten, reminders of the life he'd shared with Jill.

As he carted an armful of books downstairs and made his way to the living room, his elbow caught the phone in the hall, knocking the receiver off its rest. He dumped the books beside his chair, returned to replace the phone, and remem-bered that he'd been about to phone Andrea when Tregalles arrived.

He dialled her number.

Andrea answered on the second ring. "Oh, it's you, Neil," she said. "I thought it might be Sten ringing to let me know how things were going."

"Sten…?"

Andrea made a clucking noise. "Of course, you don't know what I'm talking about, do you?" she said. "It was absolutely amazing. It's hard to believe, but when I took Sarah to the rehearsal on Friday, she introduced me to her new friend at school. She'd talked a lot about this girl, Heather, but she never mentioned her last name, so I was taken completely by surprise when it turned out she is the daughter of Sten Wallen, a boy I grew up with. In fact, we were at university together for a year before he had to leave when his father became ill and died. And he was there with Heather at the rehearsal. Talk about a small world!"

"He's only been here in Broadminster a few weeks," An-drea went on breathlessly. "In fact he's only just now getting settled into a permanent place, so I offered to have Heather for the day while he gets things sorted out. I told him he was welcome to come over here for dinner, and he said he'd ring as soon as he knew how things were going. His flat isn't five minutes from here. You'd like him, Neil. It's such a shame things didn't turn out well for him, but as he says, he has a new lease on life now. He has a good job—he's an optometrist—and he has Heather." Andrea's voice dropped, and by the tone she must have cupped her hand around the transmitter. "His ex-wife never wanted the child, so it's just as well that she's gone off and married someone else. Unfortunately, it's been very hard on Sten.

"But imagine!" she went on. "Out of all the children at the school, Sarah and Heather taking to each other like that, and Heather's father being an old friend. Talk about a coincidence. It really is amazing. But I really must get off the line in case Sten is trying to get through. What was it you wanted, Neil?"

"I think you've already answered that," he chuckled. "I called to find out how things went at the rehearsal last night."

"Oh, very well, really. A bit muddled, of course, but then that's why they have rehearsals. And Sarah is going to be a red elf, which is what she wanted. Perhaps you'll be able to make it on the night of the pageant, and you can see her for yourself."

"I'd like that," he told her.

"Good. You'll be able to meet Sten as well. Thanks for phoning, Neil. Sorry, but I must hang up now. Sten may be trying to get through. Bye."

There had been more animation in Andrea's voice than he had heard in along time, he thought as he put the phone down. Still, it must be nice for her to have met someone from her past, someone who did not bring back unpleasant memories. She'd had quite enough of those.

It wasn't until later that it occurred to him that Andrea hadn't asked how he was now that he was home. Understandable in her excitement over the discovery of an old friend, he rationalized, but on the other hand, it wasn't like Andrea to forget something like that. Not like her at all.

BOURNEMOUTH, DORSET

HE COULD HEAR them talking. It was as if they were a great distance away, and yet the words were clear: his two daughters, Harriet and Claire, speaking in hushed tones as if they were in church.

"...what it costs just to park the car, nowadays. It's a wonder they don't take your blood as well!" Harriet's voice. "You'd think they'd give you a pass or something when you're visiting every day. To say nothing of the petrol. Not that I'm complaining, mind, but it's been three months now, and it all adds up."

Three months! Was that how long he'd been lying here? Wherever here was. He felt a bit of a fraud, lying there listening with his eyes shut. It was like eavesdropping. But it would spoil everything if he opened his eyes, because it would mean rejoining them in their world, and he didn't want to do that. He tried to think why, but he felt as if he were drifting, and the reason escaped him.

"Doesn't it, just! Still, it'll be my turn to pick you up next week." That was Claire. "And speaking of picking up reminds me: I must stop at the corner shop and get some milk on the way home. Everything else will be closed by then, so do remind me or Geoff will be ever so cross if there's none for his tea in the morning. We had rice pudding tonight, and I thought I had enough, but..."

He could imagine the shrug that went with the words. Claire was always running out of something, and Harriet was always not complaining. His mind drifted. He could still hear them, but something was eluding him; he could sense its presence, but it was just beyond the fringes of his mind: something...

It hit him like a thunderbolt! He felt the jolt, felt his heart bang hard against his ribs as if trying desperately to escape. He tried to force his mind to think of something else, *anything* that would block the terror that came flooding in.

But there was no escape, and the voice he heard did not come from those around him. It came from the telephone. *"Grandpa? Please... Please help me...."* He could barely make out the words through Penny's tears. Fear gripped him as he heard his own voice ask, *"Where are you, Penny? What's wrong?"*

"At home... There's a..." She gasped as if from a stab of pain. *"Please come,"* she whimpered. *"Grandpa...?"* Her voice gathered strength, and her next words came out with a rush. *"Help! Call the—"*

Click! She was gone.

"Penny! Penny!" He screamed the words inside his head as he had screamed them into the phone. He thrashed from side to side, but only in his mind. His two daughters, still deep in conversation, saw no movement from the figure in the bed.

He remembered driving like a madman toward the seafront and Penny's flat. He was sure she'd been trying to tell him to call the police, but there was no time. He had to get to her, had to help her. For the first time in his life he wished he had a phone in the car, something he'd always dismissed in the past as an expensive toy.

Thoughts streamed through his head in disjointed order. It was he who had encouraged her to strike out on her own when she'd asked what she should do. Harriet had thought she was too young to be leaving home, but Penny was nineteen; she had a good job and a good head on her shoulders. "If that's what you want, do it!" he'd told her. "I'll help you find a flat."

More than that. He'd helped her with the rent as well. And why not? After all, he had more money than he would ever need, and she was his only grandchild.

He remembered racing up the stairs, pausing on the landing to catch his breath, gasping, cursing his infirmities. One more flight to go. He staggered to the top and flung himself at the door. "Penny!" he shouted as he grasped the handle. It turned beneath his hand.

He stood there in the doorway of the tiny flat, hand pressed to his side, his vision blurred as he took in the scene. The bed, the cooker in the corner, the small window where they had both stood admiring the view of the sea. And in the middle of the room, seated on a chair turned to face the door, was Penny.

In the confines of his mind, James J. Harmer screamed her name again and again, but the *thing* that once was Penny remained mute and lifeless. Her head had fallen forward, and her long dark hair all but covered the gaping wound beneath her chin. But there was no hiding the blood that soaked her clothes, the chair, the floor—still moist and gleaming in the evening sunlight slanting through the open window.

He lurched forward, staggered, almost fell, then knelt beside the chair. He touched her arm. Still warm. He must get help....

The sound of the telephone shattered the silence. Yes, that was it! He scrambled to his feet and snatched it up, but before he had a chance to speak, someone spoke to him. He remembered the words; he remembered the voice.

"How does it feel when it's one of your own, Grandpa? Now you will have to live with the pain!"

He remembered....

"Harriet!" It was Claire's voice. "Look at Dad. He's crying. Look, there's tears! He must be... Quick, get the nurse. He's coming round after all this time."

But before the elder sister had time to leave the room, a long, quavering sigh escaped the lips of the old man in the bed, and they didn't need a doctor or a nurse to tell them that their father had departed from this life. Silently, they held each other.

Harriet Crofton, dry-eyed, stared at her father's body. First, her daughter Penny, and now her father. The two of them had always been close—closer, perhaps, than she had been to either of them. Now both were gone, and she would never know why her daughter had been killed in such a horrible manner. It was strange, but she couldn't cry. All she could think of now was that there would be another funeral to arrange, and it was no good asking Claire to help. She was hopeless at arranging things.

FIFTEEN

As HE POTTERED about the kitchen the following morning, preparing a breakfast he didn't really want, Paget wondered if he would ever again feel truly rested. After falling asleep several times last evening while going through his notes, he'd finally given in and gone to bed early. Once there, however, he'd tossed and turned for what seemed like half the night. When at last he did fall asleep, a kaleidoscope of images tumbled through his head, and so powerful was the smell of burning in his nostrils that he'd awakened to find himself halfway out of bed, quite sure that smoke was in the house.

He propped the morning paper up in front of him as he ate, but there was little there to cheer him. A renewed threat of flooding along the Severn, with Shrewsbury, Bridgnorth, and Bewdley particularly vulnerable with the forecast of more rain. Fortunately, the main town of Broadminster sat high above the river Strathe, although people living in the area known locally as the Flats had been warned to be prepared to leave their homes if the river continued to rise.

Paget flipped the pages, only to be confronted with pictures of the aftermath of a suicide bombing in the Middle East, a train wreck in southern India, and an oil spill off the coast of Ireland. There was yet another wrangle in the House over the future of the Euro, and things were heating up again between India and Pakistan. When the weather forecast for the coming week proved to be just as gloomy—rain, heavy at times, and snow at higher elevations—he gave up and tossed the paper to the other side of the table.

He spent much of the rest of the day working his way through his notebooks, pausing at times to recall the circumstances of a particular case, but he found nothing to suggest that he might be the target of some vengeful villain. Tregalles telephoned just after two o'clock to say that heavy rain was expected that evening, and it would be as good a time as any to re-create the attack in the car park. "If you agree, sir, I can have the others here, and someone will be out to pick you up about seven o'clock."

Paget hesitated. It had seemed a good idea when Tregalles had suggested it, but now, faced with the prospect of actually going through with it, he felt uneasy. It wasn't so much the physical re-enactment of the attack that disturbed him, but rather what might surface in his mind. Why he should feel that way, he didn't know and couldn't explain. But there was something....

"Sir? Sir, are you still there?"

Paget took a deep breath. "Still here, Sergeant," he said. "What time was that again? Seven?"

"That's right, sir."

"Right. I'll be ready."

"Good. Oh, by the way, sir, wear old clothes. They could get muddy."

THEY WERE ALL assembled when he arrived. Alcott; Tregalles; the duty sergeant, Broughton; and somewhat to his surprise, Kate Regan. He hadn't expected her to be there, but as Tregalles explained, they wanted everything to be the same as it was the night Paget was attacked, and she had been reinstated now that Marshall had been cleared.

They stood around, chatting in desultory fashion, a bit self-conscious and preoccupied with thoughts of what might come of the re-enactment, marking time until eight o'clock.

At ten minutes to eight, Tregalles, who had taken upon himself the role of stage manager, asked Kate and Paget to accompany him upstairs to the office. Once there, he instructed Kate to leave as she had that night, and asked Paget to wait a few minutes before going downstairs himself.

"Broughton will be on the desk, and Regan will be at the front door," he explained to Paget. "Once you get there, stop and have a few words with Regan as you did that night, then take it from there. Any questions?"

"Just get on with it," Paget said irritably. "I may have had a knock on the head, but I think I can still remember basic instructions."

"Right, sir." Tregalles looked at his watch. "Give me a minute or two to get downstairs, then come on down when you're ready."

Paget sat on the corner of his desk, fingers drumming nervously while he waited for Tregalles to get clear. He was seeing the sergeant in a new light, a more assertive, more confident man who had taken charge. Alcott might be leading the investigation, and no doubt Tregalles would be drawing on the superintendent's experience, but it was Tregalles who had taken the initiative and was doing all the legwork. Was that why he had flared up at the sergeant? Was it because their positions had become reversed?

Or was it simply the fact that he was afraid of what was about to happen?

Eight o'clock. Paget picked up the briefcase and umbrella he'd brought with him, and walked down the corridor. He descended the stairs, then moved on past the desk to the front door. Kate was there, standing with her back to him, peering through the glass into the night.

"Kate. I thought you'd gone home," he said, and the conversation flowed from there. They moved outside, paused on the top step while Kate adjusted her hood and Paget opened the umbrella, then stepped out into the rain. Kate tucked her hand beneath Paget's arm as they moved around the side of the building, but try as they might, neither of them could think of a thing to say. When they reached the corner, the lights were out as they had been that night, and Paget flicked on his key-ring torch while Kate stood by her car and searched her handbag for the keys.

"I hope this works," she said as she opened the door. "Good luck, sir."

As he had done that night, Paget watched as Kate backed out, then disappeared from sight around the corner. It was raining hard, and he had to concentrate on avoiding puddles as he continued on toward his car.

A blaze of light flared in his face. He threw up an arm as someone grabbed him from behind and held him firmly. He saw the glint of steel....

It's your fault Jill and...died the way she did...yours and all the others. Now it's your turn, Chief Inspector. Lights appeared behind him, and whoever had been holding him eased him to the ground, then ran toward the trees. The lights grew stronger; he heard a car door slam; someone shouted, then came the sound of someone running....

"Are you all right, sir?" It was Redfern bending over him. He didn't answer. He could feel himself slipping away.

"Oh, Christ!" Redfern muttered, then raised his voice. "Someone help me," he called. "I think he's fainted."

THEY SAT IN Alcott's office, Alcott, Paget, and Tregalles. The others had gone home. Tregalles had wanted to ring for an ambulance, or at least take him to hospital, but Paget had vetoed both ideas. "I was only out for a few seconds," he insisted. "Believe me, I'm fine now."

Alcott leaned back in his chair and eyed him critically. "Has this happened before?" he asked.

Paget didn't answer the question directly. "They told me this sort of thing *might* happen," he said. "There's nothing they can do about it. It just takes time. This thing tonight..." He shrugged. "I probably overdid it."

Alcott looked unconvinced, but let it go. "The question is," he said, "did it stir up any memories?"

Paget remained silent for a long moment. Despite the fact

that he'd known what was to come, the re-enactment had shaken him more than he cared to admit, and when he did speak it was to ask a question of his own. "Who was behind the light?"

"I was," Tregalles told him. "I wanted to test out Grace Lovett's theory, so as soon as I saw the lights of the police car coming round the corner, I killed the torch and ducked down behind your car, then cut down the far side of the building. I asked Redfern if he saw me, and he said no."

"Did you say anything?"

"When?"

"When you were waving that razor about."

Tregalles smiled. "Actually, sir, it was a metal ruler. I didn't want to put the wind up you by having an actual razor in my hand."

"But did you *say* anything?"

"No, sir. Not a word. Why? Did you think I did?"

A frown creased Paget's brow as he stared into the middle distance. "Someone did," he said.

Alcott leaned forward. "Well?" he demanded impatiently. "What did they say? You *do* remember, don't you?"

Oh, yes, he remembered all too well. Even now the words were running through his head. But, perversely, he was reluctant to repeat them—especially the part about Jill. That was personal, very personal, and no one else's business.

"Someone said, 'It's your fault. Yours and all the others. Now it's your turn, Chief Inspector," he paraphrased. "Those same words have been running through my head for days, but until tonight I couldn't be sure that they were spoken at the time of the attack."

"Your fault. Yours and all the others," Alcott repeated. "Who are these 'others,' Paget? What does it mean?"

"Certainly sounds like someone out for revenge," Tregalles said. "Any ideas, sir?"

"Obviously the person who attacked me blames me for

something, but I don't know what it is, nor do I understand the reference to 'all the others.'"

"What about the voice?" Alcott demanded. "Male? Female? Local? Educated? What?"

Paget shook his head. "All I can tell you is that it was a hoarse voice, rasping, very harsh."

Alcott sank back in his chair, took out a cigarette, then put it back again. Paget looked exhausted. He seemed vague, even disoriented, and the superintendent wondered, not for the first time, whether the DCI would ever make a complete recovery. Certainly the man was nowhere near the top of his form, and the possibility had to be faced that perhaps he never would be.

TREGALLES DROVE Paget home, while a constable followed in Paget's car. The sergeant had tried once again to persuade Paget to go to the hospital to be checked out, but he'd refused. "It's not like you to faint, sir," Tregalles had persisted. "Might be a good idea for them to take a look at you."

But Paget wanted no part of the hospital. They'd probably want to keep him in, and that was the last thing he needed now. "No," he'd said again, "I'll be fine once I'm home. A good night's rest will see me right."

There was nothing to be gained by arguing with him. Paget was not a man who could be pushed, but Tregalles was still worried about him. The chief inspector looked like death; his skin was the colour of chalk, and he seemed to be having trouble staying awake.

"Here we are, sir," he said as he pulled up in front of the house. "I'll see you inside while Woods puts your car away. If I could just have the keys to your garage…?"

"I wish you'd stop treating my like a bloody invalid," Paget grumbled as he got out of the car. "Not that I don't appreciate your concern, but I'm all right. The doctors told me that I'd be a bit weak for a while, but all I need is a good night's sleep. I'm only sorry that I couldn't be of more help, but at least it made me remember something of what happened that night.''

Tregalles grimaced. ''Trouble is, sir, if the motive does lie in the past, it's *your* past, and you know more about that than we do, so unless you can come up with some sort of lead, it seems to me we're running blind.''

Later, as Paget prepared for bed, his thoughts returned to what he had told Alcott and Tregalles. He'd told them the truth—just left out the bit about Jill, that was all. But it seemed as if something was missing. He went over the words again in his head: *It's your fault Jill and...died the way she did...all the others. Now it's your turn. Chief Inspector.*

Jill and what? Why couldn't he remember what came after *and?* And why was someone blaming him for her death? God knows he'd felt guilty at the time for not being in London the day Jill died, but he knew he was being irrational. There was nothing he could have done to change events.

It didn't make any sense at all, he thought as he drifted off to sleep.

He was awakened by the ringing of the phone. He switched on the light, squinting at the time. Twenty past twelve! Who on earth was calling him at this time of night? Still half asleep, he answered, ''Paget.''

Silence. He struggled upright in the bed. ''Paget,'' he said again. ''Who is this?''

''You think it's over, don't you, Chief Inspector?'' a voice said harshly. *''But it's not, you know. You still have to pay for what you did, so think about it as you try to sleep tonight.''*

SIXTEEN

TREGALLES WASN'T THERE when Paget rang first thing the following morning, but Sergeant Ormside was. Tired as he was, Paget had spent a restless night thinking about the phone call, trying to remember every nuance, every inflection as he sought an explanation. He'd written the message down, studied the words, thought about the voice.

"The voice is being disguised in some way," he told Ormside, "so I still can't be sure if it was a man or woman. But it's the same voice that's been running through my head since the re-enactment last night, so I have to assume I first heard those words when I was attacked. The only thing I *can* tell you is that he or she wasn't local. My guess is a Londoner, or very close to it. Sorry, Len, I know it's not much, but it's the best I can do. However, if they should call again, I'll make sure I have a recorder on. Let Alcott know, and if he wants to monitor my line, tell him I have no objection."

"Right, sir. But don't you think it might be better if you were to come into town for a while? At least until we can find out who's behind this."

"Thanks for the thought, Len, but no one is going to drive me out of this house. Don't worry, I'll be keeping a sharp eye out."

"Still, you might give it some thought, sir."

"I'll do that," Paget promised, "but I don't think I'll be changing my mind."

PAGET HAD INTENDED to continue going through his old notebooks that day, but he found it hard to concentrate. Finally, he set them aside in favour of a copy of the coroner's report on Jill's death. He'd had it ever since the inquest, but could never bring himself to read it until now. He went through it carefully, searching for anything that might suggest a connection between what had happened then and what was happening now, but if there was a connection, he couldn't see it.

He found nothing. In fact, he was struck by the banality of the court procedure. He had attended many inquests, and yet it was only now, reading the words on the page, that he realized how impersonal the process was. They might have been discussing the price of fish rather than the untimely and horrific death of the woman who had been his wife.

Paget left the report on the table and went to the window. The wind was gusting heavily from the north-west, and every now and then there was a spattering of rain. No matter. He had to get out of the house. He'd been cooped up too long, and he needed to clear his head, to think about what he knew and what he had believed these past few years. He checked the sky again, then put on his warmest anorak, laced up the hiking boots he hadn't worn in years, and left the house.

The wind was cold, but he didn't mind; it helped to clear his head. But he should have brought gloves. He thrust his hands deep inside his pockets and set out on the road leading away from the village.

The blustery wind tugged at the hood of his anorak as he climbed over a stile and set off up the path that would take him past Longhill farm, where Mrs. Wentworth bought their eggs. From there he could go two ways: he could continue along the ridge to the hamlet of Upton Clees, and back home again by road, or drop down into the next valley and take the long way home.

The sky was broken to the north. It was probably foolish to go so far on his first day out, but the air was so fresh and clean…

He should have listened to his inner voice. It *had* been

foolish to take the long way home. He was soaked to the skin by the time he reached the house. The rain hadn't been heavy, but it had taken him much longer than he'd anticipated to work his way out of the valley and back to the road. He'd had to follow a stream for half a mile, slogging through knee-high grass and swampy ground before coming to a ford that allowed him to cross and reach the road once more. He was cold and exhausted, and yet he also felt exhilarated. It had been years since he'd tramped the countryside like that, and he'd forgotten how good it was for the soul.

He peeled off his wet clothes, remembering to cover the dressing on his throat with cling film before getting into the shower, then just stood there, letting the water pour over him, luxuriating in its warmth. He was feeling good as he got out and wrapped himself in a towel—and then his legs began to shake. He staggered to the bedroom and fell across the bed, every muscle twitching uncontrollably. He'd pushed himself too hard, and now his body was telling him what an idiot he'd been.

The shivering subsided, but it was as if every bit of energy had been drained from him. He closed his eyes. His body felt as if it were floating, and he wondered if this was what it felt like to be an astronaut in space.

HE WAS STILL pondering the question—or thought he was—when the ringing of the phone dragged him from the depths of sleep. It was dark, and for a moment he didn't know where he was. He reached out blindly, touched the bedside lamp and switched it on. The phone kept ringing. He groped for it and lifted the receiver. "Paget," he said groggily, half expecting to hear Alcott's voice on the other end.

"Neil?" He recognized Grace Lovett's voice. "Are you all right?"

"Grace… Yes, I'm fine," he told her. "I was out for a walk in the hills behind here today, and I must have fallen asleep. What time is it?'' He peered at his watch, but his eyes wouldn't seem to focus properly.

"It's just turned six. Are you quite sure you're all right?''

"Yes, yes, of course. Just not used to all that fresh air.'' He stifled a yawn. "Makes you hungry, too.''

"You haven't eaten?''

"No, but I will soon, believe me.''

"Look.'' said Grace, "tell you what. Put the kettle on in about fifteen minutes, and I'll bring something out. You don't sound as if you'd be safe around a cooker. See you in half an hour.''

"There's no need for that...'' he began, but Grace had gone.

Half an hour later, almost to the minute, he heard her car in the driveway. He opened the door as she came up the steps carrying what appeared to be a bundle of blankets. "I've brought my bed,'' she said, and laughed. "No, don't worry. Buried in here somewhere are the fish and chips. I hope they're still warm. If not, we can heat them up in the oven.''

He could smell them, and suddenly he was ravenous.

"I NEEDED THAT,'' he said contentedly as he raised his glass. As well as the fish and chips, Grace had produced a bottle of wine. "You must let me pay you for all this.''

"Not a hope,'' she told him flatly. "My idea, my treat. Nothing like it after hiking in the hills, especially on such a blustery day as this. You were ready for it.'' She fell silent for a moment. "But why, Neil?'' she asked worriedly. "Whatever possessed you to go out hiking in this weather when you've only just come out of hospital? Your body's not ready for that kind of strenuous exercise.''

He shook his head and grimaced in self-recrimination. "I didn't set out to go that far,'' he said, "but I needed to think things through, and it felt so good to be out in the open air that I just kept going. It was only after I returned home and had a shower that I felt weak and had to lie down.''

"It's a wonder you aren't lying in some field at the bottom of the valley," Grace told him. "I know I tried to encourage you to start hiking again, but I hardly expected you to try it so soon after coming home."

Paget picked up his glass and raised it in silent salute. "Sorry, Mum," he said gravely, "it won't happen again. I promise."

"Perhaps when you're stronger," Grace compromised, "you can come on one of our easier cross-country walks. But not yet." She eyed him speculatively for a long moment. Even now, relaxed as he appeared to be, there was tension behind those steady eyes. "Is it the case?" she asked. "The lack of progress? Is there any way I can help?"

He remained silent for so long that Grace didn't think he was going to answer, and wondered if she had overstepped the mark. "If you'd rather not talk about it…" she began, but he waved her words aside.

"Perhaps it is time to talk to someone else about it," he said. "I can't seem to make sense of it myself."

Grace waited.

"I have these"—he hesitated, balking at the word "hallucinations"—"I have these visions. I keep seeing my wife, Jill—seeing her as she was after the explosion, horribly burnt and barely recognizable—and I keep hearing words inside my head. But it wasn't until we did the re-enactment of the attack in the car park last night that it became clear to me they weren't figments of my own imagination, but actual words spoken by the person who was trying to kill me. Whoever is behind this seems to believe that I was responsible for Jill's death."

Paget sighed heavily. "The trouble is, Grace, I've always had this nagging feeling that Jill might not have died if I had been there in the city that day, and yet everything I know about her death, and my own common sense, tell me that it wouldn't have made a scrap of difference where I was. So why was I attacked? And who is behind it?"

"Did your wife have any relatives or friends who blamed you for what had happened at the time?"

"No. And I read the coroner's report just this morning, and there is nothing there to show that the accident could have been avoided. Jill simply happened to be in the wrong place at the wrong time when the boy came running out...." He stopped. "But then, you don't know what happened, do you?"

Grace shook her head. She'd heard stories about how his wife had died, but she had never asked. If Neil wanted to tell her, he would do it in his own good time.

"Jill was a detective sergeant in another division," he explained, "but she wasn't even on duty when it happened. She'd been out shopping and was on her way home, when, according to witnesses, a young boy came running out of a small shop, yelling something like, 'The gas is broken, and my mum's upstairs.' They said Jill never so much as hesitated. She dashed inside and was halfway up the stairs to the living quarters above the shop when the place exploded. She didn't stand a chance. There was a fire. She died without regaining consciousness. And the irony of it was the boy's mother wasn't upstairs at all; she was in the yard at the back stacking empty boxes, and came away unscathed.

"As for me, I happened to be in Cambridge that day on a liaison job. I came home late that night, saw Jill wasn't there, and assumed that she was working. Just about every division was short-staffed, so it wasn't at all unusual for either one of us to be working all sorts of ungodly hours.

"Next morning, I was a bit puzzled that Jill hadn't phoned, but I went in to work as usual, expecting to hear from her at work. Instead, my boss called me into the office and told me there had been an explosion and a fire the day before. A body had been recovered; they thought it might be Jill."

Paget drew a deep breath. "And ever since I received that crack on the head a couple of weeks ago, I keep seeing her as she was then, burnt and blackened, and…'' His voice broke as he looked away.

Grace reached out and touched his hand. His fingers curled around her own and held them tightly. ''It scared me, Grace,'' he said softly. ''You see, I collapsed after identifying Jill's body, and when I woke up many days later, I was in hospital—in the psychiatric wing. I was afraid that if I told anyone I was seeing things and hearing voices, I would end up there again.''

He released her hand. ''I'm sorry,'' he said in a firmer voice. ''I didn't mean to burden you with my problems, but after thinking things through on that walk today, I realized that every scrap of information I have about Jill's death came to me second-hand. I wasn't there for the investigation; I wasn't even present at the inquest or the funeral. Everything I know about my wife's death comes from such things as the coroner's report or what people told me at the time. When I was released from hospital, all I wanted to do was get away from London and everything that reminded me of how Jill died, which is why I came down here to Ashton Prior. I didn't want to talk to anyone; I didn't want to see anyone—in fact, if it hadn't been for Mrs. Wentworth, I'm sure I would have left the Service.

''But that's another story,'' he concluded briskly. ''Tomorrow morning I'm going up to London to talk to the people who were there at the time, and try to find the link between the way Jill died and what's happening now.''

THE PHONE RANG. Eleven-thirty. It would be Linda telling her she wouldn't be home again tonight, Kate thought as she picked up the phone. There had to be something seriously wrong with that girl and her seemingly never-ending round of parties and one-night stands.

''Two, three, double two,'' she said.

''Kate! Please, don't hang up. Listen to me. We have to talk.''

Paul! Kate suddenly went cold. She had almost made herself believe that Paul was no longer a threat, since he was no longer a suspect in the attack on Paget. She hadn't seen him since, and hoped that he'd finally accepted the fact that she had no intention of going back to him. Now, hearing his voice again, all the old fears came rushing back, and her first impulse was to slam the phone down. But she stayed her hand. What was there to be afraid of? Why should she allow him to intimidate her?

"Go ahead and talk," she said, mildly surprised at how steady her voice sounded.

"No. Not here on the phone like this. I mean sit down face-to-face and really talk things through. Come back, Kate. Just to talk. That's all. If you still feel the same afterward, we'll work something out. Honestly, I mean it."

He sounded sincere, but Kate suddenly pictured him standing—or sitting on the floor—beside the phone, furniture gone, carpets gone, and a shiver ran down her spine. Her voice hardened. "Do you really think I'd come back to that house now that you've stripped it bare?" she demanded harshly. "How many bottles of vodka did you get for the dresser my mother gave us? How many for the chairs, the carpets, the cooker, and all the rest? How many, Paul?"

Silence. Then the phone crashed in her ear.

Kate's hand shook as she replaced the phone and sank into a chair. The vision of Paul sitting there on the floor remained with her. Unless… She caught her breath. What if he wasn't at home? What if he was closer? At the end of the street in the kiosk there. No, she'd have recognized the metallic sounds at the beginning of the call. But he could be anywhere.

Kate let her breath out slowly as anger supplanted fear. Why did she let Paul do this to her? Why should she be afraid of him? She could take care of herself. In fact, she was probably physically stronger than he was in his present condition. And yet, she couldn't shake the feeling that something was about to happen. She had to know. She picked up the phone again and dialled.

"Rick? Sorry to trouble you, but you told me to ring if... No, no, it's just that I've had a phone call from Paul, and I wondered... You are? Outside the house? Oh, bless you, Rick. I know I told you there was no need, but I had a feeling you might be there. Is he still inside? You're quite sure? No, really, I'm fine. Honestly."

She put the phone down and let out a long breath. Rick was coming over, and she felt better knowing he would soon be there. She'd been so surprised the other night when he'd phoned to warn her that Paul might be on his way there. She'd been even more surprised when, ten minutes later, he'd been there himself to make sure that she was all right. Talked one of the night shift into driving him over, he said, after admitting, somewhat shamefacedly, that he'd been trailing Paul, but lost him. Later, much later, he'd called a taxi to take him back to where he'd left his car.

Until that night, she'd had no idea that he'd been watching out for her. She'd told him there was no need, but she knew he'd been sitting out there in his car night after night, watching the house, and she'd felt safer because of it. Rick was a nice lad. Well, hardly a lad. He was younger than she was—but only by two or three years.

Kate pushed herself out of the chair and went into the kitchen to put the kettle on.

PAUL MARSHALL SAT on the floor, knees drawn up, fists clenched, head resting on his knees. She'd been in the house! She knew! But when? How would she know when...?

Of course! It must have been when they'd taken him down to Charter Lane. She'd been there when they'd brought him in, and she'd gone straight back to the house. To get her clothes, most likely.

Marshall scrambled to his feet and flew up the stairs. Flung open the wardrobe, checked the drawers. Her clothes were still there. He stood there, frowning, pulled out a dress, crumpled it and held it to his face. A faint perfume still lingered. He breathed in deeply, then gripped the dress with both hands and tore it apart. Kept on tearing, and when that lay on the floor in shreds, he stripped the wardrobe bare, pulled underclothes from the drawers, and tried to shred those too.

Nylon. Stretched, refused to tear. In frustration he gathered everything up and took the bundle downstairs and out into the back garden. Black as pitch out there. High walls on either side. No one to see what he was doing. Ran back into the kitchen for matches; switched on the back-door light.

They wouldn't catch. The clothes refused to burn; smouldered and then went out. Furious at being thwarted, he ran to the shed, grabbed a spade and tried to dig. The ground was wet, heavy clay choked with weeds. In a blind rage he flung the spade into the night, then fell, exhausted, to his knees and wept.

SEVENTEEN

"I MUST SAY you're looking better than I expected, considering what you've been through," Bob McKenzie observed as he faced Paget across the table. He was a big man, ruddy-faced and heavyset, with tangled eyebrows and a thick mane of grey hair. "All that country air must agree with you. How do you like it down there in the back of beyond?"

"Best move I could have made," Paget told him, "and I have you to thank for it. And speaking of moves, congratulations, *Chief* Superintendent. When did this happen?"

"Three months ago, and thank you. Davenport retired—he's been ill for a long time—and I'd been acting for best part of a year. So when he went, they decided it was easier to leave me there than go through another shuffle."

"I'll bet Eve's pleased."

"She is. And she'd like to see you while you're here."

"We'll have to see," Paget hedged. "I'm not sure how long I'll be here."

McKenzie nodded and let it go. He sat back and looked around. "I haven't been in here for at least a year," he said, "but nothing seems to have changed. Doctor's got me on a diet—high cholesterol, touch of blood pressure. Nothing serious."

"You should have told me on the phone. We could have gone somewhere else."

"And miss an opportunity to dig into a decent meal for a change? Not on your life. This is something of an occasion, and I intend to enjoy it."

The waiter appeared and they ordered wine. "Do you still do the fettucini with the veal and the blue cheese sauce?" asked McKenzie.

"Ah, yes, sir." The waiter pointed to one of the items on the menu. "But it is *very* rich, sir," he warned.

McKenzie rubbed his hands. "Good! I'll have that," he said as he snapped the menu shut. "And don't you dare tell Eve," he warned Paget.

Paget smiled. "I'll have the chicken tetrazzini," he told the hovering waiter, more to be rid of him than because he was interested in eating.

The chief superintendent waited until the waiter was out of earshot, then leaned forward across the table. "Now then, Neil," he said, "tell me what this is all about? You weren't exactly forthcoming on the phone last night."

McKenzie listened attentively as Paget told him of the attack that had been made on him outside the police station in Broadminster, but he looked mystified when Paget told him what had been said.

"It was *your* fault Jill died?" he echoed. "Where did they get that idea? It was an accident, pure and simple. You weren't even in London at the time. And I don't understand the bit about you and all the others. What others? And who's behind all this? Even if someone has got it into his head that you were somehow responsible, why wait till now to try to kill you? As I recall, Jill didn't have any relatives, so who…?"

Paget shook his head in weary resignation. "Believe me, Bob, those same questions have been plaguing me for days."

The two men sat back as the waiter appeared with their orders. McKenzie tucked in with evident relish, but Paget merely picked at his food.

"So tell me why you're here, Neil. What is it you hope to find?"

"A connection, I suppose, between what's been happening

to me in Broadminster and the events surrounding Jill's death.''

''Tell me again exactly what you heard—or you believe you heard.''

''*Believe* I heard?''

McKenzie nodded. ''Bear with me for a minute. As you said yourself, the words don't make any sense. There *is* no connection between the two events, so let's suppose, just for a moment, that you've got it wrong, and those words are coming from your subconscious rather than from the person who tried to kill you. What does your doctor say?''

''I haven't told him. I felt this was something I had to pursue on my own.''

McKenzie set his knife and fork down, and shook his head. ''Don't you think you're being a bit foolish, Neil?'' he said carefully. ''Perhaps even paranoid? I know how you felt about Jill. God knows, we all felt her loss and feel it still, but you've allowed this guilt about not being there the day she died to take over your life, and now you've got it mixed up with what happened during the attack. Yet you're too damned stubborn to ask for help. It's not a sign of weakness to ask for help, you know.''

The chief superintendent picked up his knife and wagged it at Paget. ''Not only did you have a concussion, but from what you've told me, you damned near bled to death. Between the two, it's no wonder you are hearing and seeing things. For that matter, you shouldn't have driven all this way today—we've got enough mayhem on the roads as it is without you fainting or falling asleep at the wheel. And now you tell me you haven't even mentioned any of this to your doctor. What about Alcott? What does he have to say about all this?''

''Nothing, because I haven't told him,'' Paget said somewhat sheepishly. He felt like a schoolboy shifting from foot to foot before the headmaster.

''Because you were afraid you might wind up in a psycho ward as you did when Jill died,'' said McKenzie with uncanny accuracy. He shook his head dismissively. "But that was different, as well you know. You came away with a clean bill of health. You'd have never got the transfer to Broadminster if you hadn't.

"However," McKenzie continued, "having said that, I still think you need professional help, and for starters, I think you had better talk to this doctor of yours. I'm sure he's run into this sort of thing before, and he'll probably put you onto someone who can help you."

"A psychiatrist?"

"That's right, a psychiatrist," said McKenzie firmly. "I'm sure you were grateful for the professional help you received when they stitched up your throat and pumped blood into you, and patched up your head, so where's the difference when it comes to matters of the mind?"

"It's just—oh, I don't know. I suppose you're right, but I'm still left with the problem of who wants me dead so badly that hitting me over the head with a piece of pipe wasn't enough—they had to slash my throat with a razor as well."

"A razor?" McKenzie grimaced. "You didn't mention that before. I assumed it was a knife. That's a bit unusual out your way, isn't it? Even here in London, we rarely see razors used these days. Too awkward. It's all knives nowadays." He indicated the flesh-coloured dressing on Paget's neck. "Still painful, is it? I see you're pretty careful about the way you turn your head."

"It pulls," Paget admitted, "but it's getting better. I was fortunate, though; I'm told that the collar of my mac was cut completely through, so the razor didn't slice quite as deeply as it might have done."

McKenzie sat back, frowning. "Funny," he said ruminatively, "but that's the second time in the last couple of weeks I've heard of a razor being used—except in this case, the victim died. I was talking to one of our AMIP superintendents—chap by the name of Bellamy; I don't think you'd know him; he's relatively new to the Area Major Investigation

Pool—and he was telling me about a case he has in Richmond. Two women living together. One of them is a psychologist, the other was her stay-at-home partner. Apparently everything was normal when the doctor went off to work that morning, but when she returned that night, she found her friend dead, sitting in a pool of blood in the middle of the living room. Her throat had been slashed twice. No sign of a struggle. The prime suspect is the doctor, but so far they've been unable to find a motive, and there were no physical clues. Bellamy is convinced that the doctor did it, but there is no way he can prove it.''

''I presume, then, that the doctor has an alibi for the time of death?''

McKenzie pursed his lips. ''Bellamy says the timing is tight, but he still believes she could have done it, although everyone from her receptionist to her patients insists she acted normally throughout the day. No witnesses have come forward, no one saw anything, and despite exhaustive enquiries among the neighbours, they've come up with nothing.''

''What time of day was she killed?''

''Sometime between nine and ten in the morning. Bellamy said the doctor claims her partner was alive and well when she left the house at nine-fifteen. It would have been fully daylight.''

''And no one saw anything? When was this?''

''Late October.''

''*Yours and all the others,*'' said Paget thoughtfully. He spoke so softly he might have been talking to himself. ''*Now it's your turn, Chief Inspector.*'' His eyes narrowed as he looked at McKenzie. ''You know,'' he said earnestly, ''I've been concentrating so hard on what he said about Jill that I'd almost forgotten what else was said. What he said was, 'It's your fault Jill died the way she did—yours and all the others. Now it's your turn, Chief Inspector.' Doesn't that suggest that others have been killed, or are about to be killed?''

McKenzie shot Paget a quizzical glance. "Are you sure you aren't clutching at straws?" he asked quietly.

"When all you have are straws, what do you have to lose?" said Paget. "Do you mind if I come back to the office with you after lunch? It's probably a waste of time, but I'd like a word with this Superintendent Bellamy."

EIGHTEEN

"JACK REESE." The inspector shook hands with Paget and invited him to sit down. Reese was tall and thin, and round-shouldered from spending too many hours hunched over a desk. His dark features were sharp and well defined, suggesting a Middle Eastern background, but his speech was that of a true Londoner. "Superintendent Bellamy told me to expect you," he said when they both were seated, "but he was a bit vague about what it is you're looking for. Something to do with an attack on you in Shropshire having a connection with our Tessa Knowles case?"

Paget smiled. "I'm afraid he thinks I'm some sort of crack-pot, and perhaps he's right. But when I heard that the weapon used in your case was a razor, I felt it wouldn't hurt to find out if there was anything else about the case that might have a bearing on mine. Still, you can judge for yourself," he concluded, and spent the next few minutes sketching in the details of the attack in Broadminster.

Reese shook his head emphatically. "If you'll permit me to be blunt, Chief Inspector, I don't think you have a hope in hell of connecting the two cases," he said. "You said yourself that the only thing they have in common is the type of weapon, and even though we don't see many razor attacks, they are used from time to time. Besides, you said the person who attacked you said it was because you were to blame for the death of your wife, so how do you connect that to the Knowles murder? How did your wife die?''

"It was an accident. She was killed in an explosion in Crighton Street. A gas leak in one of the shops. She went in to rescue someone, and—''

"Off-duty policewoman?'' Reese put in sharply. "She was a DS at Bethnal Green. I remember that because I was at Stoke Newington at the time, and I attended the funeral. Full honours. Just about everyone in the Met who could go was there, weren't they? It was a good turnout. So, she was your wife? You must have been proud.''

Proud? The word struck him as incongruous, but Reese had meant it as a compliment. He nodded mutely.

"So, what's the connection?'' Reese asked again. "I don't understand.''

"I'm beginning to think that either it's a red herring, or that what I believe I heard was wrong,'' said Paget. "But I *am* sure he spoke of others being responsible in some way, and he spoke of it being 'my turn,' and one way of interpreting that is that there were others who had either been killed or would be killed. I know it sounds weak—it *is* weak—but I have nothing else to go on. So I'm asking you to indulge me and let me see the file on the Knowles murder. I know it's a long shot, but I might see something that means nothing to you, but might mean something to me.''

Reese was sceptical. If one of his own men had come to him with such a half-baked idea, he would have told him to get his head examined and stop wasting his time. On the other hand, what harm would it do to let Paget see the file? If the DCI wanted to waste his time trying to tie the killing of Tessa Knowles in Richmond to the attack on himself in the depths of Shropshire, good luck to him.

PAGET KNOCKED LIGHTLY on Reese's open door. "Got a minute, Inspector?'' he asked.

Reese lifted his head from a report he was studying and

motioned for Paget to come in. "Any luck?" he asked perfunctorily.

"Nothing yet, but perhaps you can help me with this." Paget laid the open file on Reese's desk. "It's down there at the bottom of the statement Dr. Braun made the day following her partner's death." He pointed the passage out to Reese. ' It's where she volunteers the information that she received a phone call early the next morning following the murder. She claims the caller said, 'Now you know what it feels like to lose someone you love.' Do you know if that was ever followed up? I can't find any further reference to it."

Reese didn't look at the page. Instead, he closed the file. "It was followed up," he said coldly, "but we could find no evidence of Braun ever receiving such a call."

Paget frowned. "She was at home, was she, when she claims to have received the call?"

Reese shook his head impatiently. "We were treating the entire house and garden as a crime scene, so she spent the night of the murder in a hotel. That was where she claimed to have received the call. Naturally, we followed it up, but we found no evidence that the call had ever been made, and quite frankly, we didn't expect to. Make no mistake about it, Chief Inspector, it was Braun who killed her lover, and she knows we know it. She made up that call to divert suspicion, but no one believed her for a minute."

"Still, the wording is unusual."

"The woman's a psychologist," Reese reminded him. "She wouldn't be satisfied with just any old message; she had to give it that extra bit of a twist. Take my word for it, she made that story up."

Paget gave a non-committal shrug, and rose to his feet. "Thanks for your help, Inspector," he said. "I'll be leaving in the morning, but just in case something does come up that you think might be of interest to me, I'll leave you my card. And if there is ever anything I can do for you, please don't hesitate to give me a call."

Reese gave a wry smile as he half rose from his chair. "Not much chance of that, is there, sir? Not with you being in a place like Broadminster."

KRISTA BRAUN slipped off her reading glasses, slumped back in her chair, and rubbed her eyes. She was having trouble staying awake; understandable, of course, considering she had hardly slept at all these past weeks—six weeks to the day, she reminded herself. She'd done everything she could to keep her mind occupied; she'd taken on new clients, worked right through the weekends, and gone to bed exhausted, only to lie there staring into the darkness as the memories flooded in. As always, her eyes were drawn to the spot where Tessa had died. She'd had the carpet taken out and another one put in, but she couldn't erase the image of the fragile body surrounded by a dark and ugly stain.

She tasted salt, and realized she was crying.

The doorbell rang. Krista Braun wiped the tears from her face and looked at the time. Eight o'clock. She wasn't expecting anyone. Unless…? Surely not the police again. But who else could it be? She pushed herself out of the chair and made her way to the front door, switched on the outside light, and pressed her face to the peephole in the door.

She'd not seen this one before, but there was no doubt in her mind that the man who stood there was a policeman. Still, it didn't hurt to be cautious, not after what had happened to Tessa. Braun pressed the button on the newly installed intercom. "Who are you, and what do you want?" she demanded.

She saw him turn to the unit on the wall beside the door, then push the Press to Talk button.

"My name is Paget," he told her. "Detective Chief Inspector Paget from Broadminster in Shropshire." He held up the now familiar warrant card. "I am not associated with the local investigation into the death of Miss Knowles, but I would like to talk to you about the telephone call you received at the hotel the night following her death. May I come in?"

The telephone call! He'd said "the call *you received*," not "the call you *allegedly* received," the way Superintendent Bellamy and Inspector Reese referred to it—if they referred to it at all. On the other hand, it could be just another ploy. Broadminster? Shropshire? But if it was a ploy, it was certainly a very different approach, and she didn't think the locals had that much imagination.

She pressed the button again. "You sound more like a Londoner to me," she said.

"I am," he replied, "or was before transferring to Broadminster a few years ago."

He could be lying, but what would be the point? "I'm going to open the door on the chain," she said. "Hand me your ID when I do. I can't see it well enough out there." She undid the bolts, top and bottom, slipped the chain on, and opened the door.

Paget passed the card through. A moment later the chain was removed, and the door opened.

"Thank you, Doctor," he said as he stepped inside and closed the door behind him. "I can't say I blame you for taking precautions after what happened here. The intercom is a good idea."

Braun eyed him neutrally. "Broadminster?" she said with a rising inflection. "What possible connection does it have to the telephone call I received that morning, Chief Inspector?" She glanced once more at the warrant card before handing it back.

There had been several photographs of the doctor in the file he had studied so assiduously that afternoon, but none of them did the woman justice. *Striking* and *handsome* were words that came to mind, yet neither quite described the woman whose dark eyes appraised him now. Eyes still moist from crying, if he was not mistaken.

"To be honest, Doctor, I don't know," he told her frankly. "Which is why I'm hoping you can help me. Do you mind if we go inside?"

The doctor led the way into the large front room overlooking the street. It was a pleasant room, comfortably untidy, but welcoming. "Please, sit down," she said, indicating a well-worn armchair beside the hearth. She sat down facing him, crossed her legs, placed her elbows on the arms of the chair, and laced her fingers beneath her chin. A natural yet professional pose.

By rights, he thought, he shouldn't be there at all. Not only was the doctor a suspect in a murder investigation, she was the *prime* suspect, and he could be severely reprimanded for unwarranted interference in the case. At the very least, he should have told Reese what he had in mind, but he'd known the inspector would have balked at the idea, based as it was on such flimsy evidence. For that matter, it wasn't even evidence; it was little more than a gut feeling that there might—just *might*—be a connection between the murder of Tessa Knowles and the attack on him.

He said, "I've read the police reports and your statement about what happened here, Doctor, but I'd like to concentrate on the telephone call you received the morning after Miss Knowles died, and the wording of the call itself, as near as you can remember."

"Why this sudden interest in that call?" she asked. "No one seemed interested when I first told them about it. In fact, they as good as told me I was lying."

"Believe me, Doctor, there is a reason," he assured her, "but I'd rather not tell you what it is until I've heard what you have to say. My reason for being here has nothing to do with the local investigation, and the reason I'm holding back is because I don't want to influence what you might tell me. So I would appreciate it very much if you'd bear with me for the moment."

Krista Braun had spent much of her life judging whether people were telling the truth or not, and she felt that this man was being straightforward. On the other hand, he was a policeman, and it was her belief that they would go to any lengths to build a case against her. Still, she didn't see how the truth could harm her, so why not tell him what had happened?

The house, she told him, had been cordoned off by the police, and she was told she must find other accommodation until they had concluded their investigation. "Not that I could have stayed here that night after what had happened," she explained, "but, since I had nowhere else to go on such short notice, I took a room at a small hotel not far from there."

"Littlewhite's."

"That's right. As you might imagine, I slept badly, but I was asleep when the phone rang just after six in the morning. It took me a few seconds to remember where I was, and I was still half asleep when I picked up the phone. Even so, I remember thinking that the only people who knew I was there were the police, and they might have some news for me. But when I answered there was silence for a moment, then someone said, 'Dr. Braun?' I said, 'Yes,' and as soon as I said that, they said, 'Now *you* know what it feels like to…'" The doctor's voice grew husky, and she took a deep breath before she was able to continue. "'…to lose someone you love.' Before I could reply or even get my breath, I heard a click and the caller had gone."

"Man or woman?" Paget asked.

Krista Braun shook her head. "I've puzzled over that for weeks," she said, "and I still don't know. It was an odd voice; harsh, hollow-sounding, rasping. It's very hard to describe."

It *had* to be the same person! Different words but essentially the same message, and Braun's description of the voice was uncannily like the one he'd heard himself. But he needed more.

"What about the caller's accent?" he asked, recalling how she had picked up on his own.

"Definitely a local," she said promptly.

"A Londoner like myself?"

"Not quite as well educated, I shouldn't think, but yes, a Londoner."

Paget let out a long breath. "That's what it sounded like to me," he said, and went on to tell her about the attack on himself, and the telephone call he'd received. "Which, when I put it together with what you've told me, suggests either a highly unlikely coincidence, or a connection between the two cases. Assuming for the moment it's the latter—and I realize that is a very big assumption—what is the link between us? In my line of work, threats are not uncommon, but what about you? Have you ever been threatened by anyone? Perhaps by one of your patients?"

"Clients," Dr. Braun corrected automatically, then shook her head. "No, not by a client," she said, "at least, not by any I have now, but there was a time when I would get the odd threat." She shrugged. "But then it was all part of the job, as it was in your own case."

"Which job was that?"

"I used to prepare psychological assessments of suspects, sometimes for the prosecution, sometimes for the defence, but that was years ago. Other than that, I don't see a connection."

For the next half-hour, Paget and Krista explored other possibilities. They compared where they had lived in London, where they had worked, organizations to which they had belonged, but there was nothing to show where their paths might have crossed. "Except in court," Paget concluded. "That seems to be the most likely place. I wonder...?" He broke off and stared into space for several seconds. "Do you know if anyone was ever convicted on your testimony alone?"

Krista Braun smiled. "I think you know better than that, Chief Inspector," she chided. "Psychological profiles are treated with deep suspicion in a courtroom, so at best—or worst—my testimony might help tip the scales in the minds of some jurors or judges, but I think it's fair to say that no one has ever been convicted or let go on my testimony alone."

Paget nodded. He knew all too well how such reports were treated in the courtroom. "Do you still have records of those assessments you presented in court?"

"Even if I do, the contents of those files would still be confidential."

"I'm not so much interested in what's *in* the files as I am in the *names* of the people you assessed, and when you gave that assessment in court. That information will be in the public record, but sifting through thousands of cases to find the ones at which you testified would be a monumental task. It would save so much time if you could compile a list of those people, and the dates they appeared in court."

"Assuming I have such records, how do you intend to use the information?"

"Compare it with records of my own appearances in court," Paget told her. "All I would need from you are names and dates."

Dr. Braun nodded slowly. "I'll have to think about the names," she said, "but if I give you dates, and locations of the courts, that should give you what you want. I do have records, so I will see what I can do. Are you staying here in Richmond?"

"No. I think it might be best if I return to Broadminster as soon as possible and begin a computer search from there. I have the feeling that I might run into trouble if I asked the local people here to do it. I don't think they would approve of my visit here tonight. I'll leave my card."

"A computer search? For what exactly, Chief Inspector?"

"For cases similar to yours and mine," he said. "Because if our two cases are linked, as I now think is possible, there may have been others who have been killed. Not only that, but there may be others yet to come."

NINETEEN

BEFORE LEAVING Richmond the following morning, Paget paid a visit to Littlewhite's Hotel, where he spoke to the manager about incoming telephone calls. Yes, the manager assured him, all incoming calls came to the desk first, and were forwarded to the individual rooms from there. The local police, he said, had questioned Miss Harding—the person on duty that morning—and were satisfied that no such call had been received.

"What about room-to-room calls?" Paget asked.

Ah, yes, well, they didn't have to go through the desk, but Littlewhite's was a small hotel, and the police had checked on everyone there that night, apparently without result. Paget thanked the manager, and made as if to leave the hotel. Instead, he stepped into the small lounge off the reception area, and found what he was looking for. He picked up a house phone and dialled a number at random.

"'Allo?"

"Is this room fifteen?"

"Yes, but noboby 'ere. All gone. Still cleaning room. Not ready yet."

Paget replaced the house phone and left the hotel. No one paid the slightest attention to his departure.

After leaving Dr. Braun the night before, he had called Tregalles at home to pass on what he had learned. "So, what I want you to do first thing tomorrow," he concluded, "is—"

"What the hell are you doing in London?" Tregalles broke in, adding a belated, "If you'll pardon my French, sir. You're supposed to be resting at home for the next few weeks, not getting involved in the case. Jesus Murphy, if I'd gone into someone else's manor like that you'd have had my balls. The super's going to go spare when he finds out.''

''I became involved the moment someone tried to kill me,'' said Paget testily, ''and I am well aware of my position with regard to the Richmond case, thank you, Tregalles.'' He was annoyed that the man he thought of as his sergeant should presume to question him in such a manner—until he realized that perhaps Tregalles was really concerned about his well-being, to say nothing of his future as a DCI.

''Sorry,'' he said roughly. ''I didn't mean to jump down your throat, Tregalles, but this is important, and the sooner we get started, the better. You may find something on HOLMES 2, or you may not, so I want you to send out a blanket RFI on any attacks where a razor was the weapon used, and someone close to the victim received a telephone call from the killer or killers shortly afterward. Those two elements are important: the razor and the telephone call.''

HOLMES 2—the Home Office Large Major Enquiry System—was a useful tool in collating evidence on major crimes, but not every crime was recorded, especially if the police were convinced they knew the identity of the killer.

''Ask them to go back six months. We can go back further later on, if necessary, but let's try that time frame for a start. You can disregard any slashing to disfigure, or where money was demanded, just concentrate on those where the victim died or almost died.''

There was a lengthy pause before Tregalles said, ''It's not much to go on, is it, sir? I mean, perhaps it would be best if you came in and talked it over with the super before we put this on the network.''

''And you know what he will say, don't you, Tregalles? That's why I want you to do it now. Damn it, man, I know it's not much to go on, but it's better than anything you've got so far!'' Paget regretted the words as soon as they were

out of his mouth. Tregalles had worked hard; it wasn't his
fault that there were no leads left to follow.

"Look," he went on in a conciliatory tone, "I didn't mean
that to sound the way it did. It's just that I believe it's possible
that we have a serial killer on our hands. I know the case is
weak; I know I may be wrong, but I can't afford to ignore
the possibility that I'm right. Now, will you help me?"

"I suppose, if you put it that way," Tregalles said grudgingly. "But what am I supposed to tell the super? I mean, I'll
need his authorization to start pulling that sort of information
in from all over the country. As you say, some of it may be
on HOLMES 2, but if it's not, and I send out a request for
information, that means everyone will have to check their local records."

"Which is why they have computers in the first place,"
Paget told him brusquely. "Look," he said, softening his
tone, "there's no need to tell Alcott anything. Just get that
request out as soon as possible, and I'll square it with him
when I get back."

Which was all well and good, Tregalles thought as he hung
up, but if Paget didn't sort it out, or if he was wrong, the DCI
wouldn't be the only one for the high jump; he would be right
up there beside him.

BEFORE LEAVING LONDON, Paget visited the cemetery on the
hill where Jill was buried. The grass between the rows of
gravestones was long and beaten down with all the rain, but
apart from that the hillside cemetery was well maintained. But
there were no trees. Pity about that, he thought. Jill would
have liked trees.

The headstone, small, unobtrusive, tasteful, was made of
polished granite, a gift from Bob McKenzie and his wife. Bob
had arranged everything while Paget was in hospital, and he'd
had pictures taken of the funeral, the honour guard, the uniformed pall-bearers, the church, the grave site—pictures Paget
could never bring himself to face before. But he'd brought

them with him, and now, after placing flowers on the grave, he took them from their envelope and looked at them, tears pouring down his cheeks as he said his last goodbye.

TRAVELLING UP the M40 was something of an ordeal. Traffic was heavy, and Paget could feel the tension building. A dull ache at the base of his skull became more pronounced; his vision blurred and his hands began to shake. He looked for a convenient lay-by, but as people were so fond of saying of policemen, they were never there when you needed them.

So it was with a sense of relief that he turned off the motorway east of Oxford in order to skirt the city on a quieter B road, but even then, he had to continue on for several miles before he was able to pull off into the car park of a roadside pub. He glanced at the time: half an hour to go before opening time, and there was no one about. He switched off the engine and lay back in his seat. It was as if every bit of energy had suddenly drained away. Bob McKenzie had been right—he shouldn't be driving, at least not long distances. Andrea had warned him it would take a long time to regain his strength, as had DeWitt, but he'd ignored their warnings.

The pale December sun cast shadows on the windscreen, and he could feel its warmth inside the car. He closed his eyes....

THUNDER. He could hear it rumbling, faint at first, then louder, until it seemed as if it was directly overhead. He opened his eyes; the noise stopped. Strange faces peered at him anxiously through the windows.

"You all right, mate?" one of them called.

Paget struggled to sit upright, blinking against the light; fumbled with the door handle and found it locked. He must have done that automatically before he'd dropped off to sleep. The men stood back as he opened the door, eyeing him curiously. There were four of them.

"Thanks for waking me," he said groggily. "Stopped early for lunch. Must have dropped off."

"You quite sure you're all right?" one of the men asked. Big man, red-faced, wheezing around his cigarette as he spoke. "Thought you was dead, you looked so pale."

Paget mustered a smile. "No, just a bit tired from driving, that's all," he assured the man. "Are they open yet?"

"Been open more than an hour. Saw you when we came in, but thought you was having a bit of a nap, so we left you alone. But when we came out and you were still there, well… You *sure* you're all right? You don't look too good to me. You been ill?"

"A bit overtired, that's all," Paget assured the man as he got out of the car and locked it. "Thanks for waking me. I could have missed my lunch, but for you."

"Looks like you could do with a bit more than lunch," one of the others observed.

"Can I buy you all a drink?"

The men looked at one another, then at the red-faced man. "Thanks," he said with some reluctance, "but we've got to get on. Got a job on up the road, and if this lot has any more to drink, they'll be sloping off by the middle of the afternoon. Some other time, mate, eh?"

"Some other time," Paget agreed. "And thanks again." He watched them climb into a rusted white van, then entered the pub and scanned the chalked menu at the end of the bar. Most of the items had been crossed off, but there remained a choice of an egg salad sandwich or roast beef. He ordered the beef, together with half a pint of Guinness. Red meat was supposed to help raise his red blood cell count. As for the Guinness, he didn't know if it contained iron or not, but reasoned it would probably do him more good than coffee, tea, or beer.

Before leaving the pub, Paget telephoned DeWitt's office to say he'd been detained and wouldn't be able to keep his afternoon appointment, and with that out of the way, he continued his journey at a more leisurely pace. He'd intended to go on to Broadminster to try to—as he'd told Tregalles—''square things with Alcott,'' but by the time he reached the turn-off to Ashton Prior, the light was fading, and it had begun to rain. Still somewhat shaken by his earlier experience, he decided he'd pushed his luck far enough for one day, and turned the car toward home.

There was a note taped to the front door. It was from Mrs. Baker, the woman who had filled in for Mrs. Wentworth once before while she was away. The note said that she had tried to ring him several times, and asked him to ring her as soon as possible, as she needed to know if he would be requiring her *professional services* next week. The wording brought a smile to his lips, and he wondered who else might have read the note, and what interpretation they would put on professional services. At least it would give the postman something to ponder while he did his rounds.

He glanced at the clock as he entered the house. Ten past four. Still time to call Alcott. He'd make a cup of tea, then ring him.

He set his small suitcase down and went through the house, flipping light switches on as he went. It was good to be home again, but he knew if he sat down and allowed himself to relax, he'd probably fall asleep. He wandered into the kitchen with some vague thought about making a meal, not because he was hungry, but because Andrea had impressed upon him the importance of eating not only wisely, but well. ''You must in order to get your strength back,'' she'd said.

He shivered. The kitchen was ice cold, and the back door was open.

''TREGALLES? Just what the devil is going on down there? I've just had a call from a Superintendent Bellamy of the London Met. He wants to know if there is a connection between the RFI originating in this office, and DCI Paget's interest in a case in Richmond, and I can tell you, he was not a happy man. He was even more unhappy when I had to put him off by telling him I was awaiting Paget's latest report, and I would have to call him back."

There was a pause, and Tregalles was sure he could hear the superintendent sucking deeply on his cigarette as he prepared to deliver another verbal blast. "I can explain—" he began, but Alcott cut him off.

"My office," he snapped. "Now! And you can explain to me why I should be the last to know that Paget is in London meddling in someone else's case." Alcott's phone crashed in the sergeant's ear.

Tregalles put the phone down and grimaced at Ormside. "I just hope to hell that nothing's happened to Paget," he said worriedly. "He assured me he would be in to talk to Alcott as soon as he got back, and it's not like him to be late. Try ringing his house again, will you, Len? And if he doesn't answer, maybe you should check to see if there've been any road accidents. He should never have been driving that distance in the first place, not in his condition."

Ten minutes later, having listened to the sergeant's halting explanation, Alcott sat back in his chair, fingers drumming on the desk. There was no question that Paget had overstepped the mark by going off to London without telling him, to say nothing of sticking his nose into someone else's case. On the other hand, the investigation had all but ground to a halt, and almost anything that might breathe life into it would be more than welcome. As for the sergeant's willingness to go along with Paget...

He scowled as a knock on the door interrupted his thoughts, and Fiona, his secretary, poked her head inside. "I know you said you didn't want to be disturbed," she said quickly before he had a chance to speak, "but Sergeant Ormside's on the phone. He says to tell you that Mr. Paget came home to find that someone had broken into the house while he was away."

"THEY CAME IN through the back door," Paget explained when Tregalles arrived. "Pried the door open, broke the lock and the jamb. Must have made a hell of a racket doing it, so they must have known I was away. Been through the whole house, poking through drawers, cupboards, desk, but they don't seem to have taken anything. It's certainly not a professional job.''

"Kids, maybe?''

Paget shook his head. "They would have either stripped the place or trashed it. No, I doubt if it was kids. I suspect it's the same people who attacked me.''

"But why? What's the point?''

"To remind me that they're out there, waiting to have another go at me, perhaps. I don't know any more than you do, Tregalles, but I can't think of any other explanation. Have there been any other reports of break-ins around here?''

"Not that I know of.''

"I thought not.''

The two men went through the house together, but they both agreed there was little to be gained by calling Charlie's people out before the following morning, and even then Paget doubted they would find anything of value. Besides, all he wanted to do was sleep. He had secured the back door with six long screws before Tregalles arrived, and as he'd told the sergeant, he doubted if the intruders would be back now that they'd made their point.

"Maybe not, but it's pretty isolated out here,'' Tregalles observed as he opened the front door and looked out into the night. There wasn't a light to be seen in the immediate vicinity, and the village, half hidden in the valley, was almost a mile away. "They were probably watching the house, and saw you leave. The thing that puzzles me, though, is why they haven't had another go at you. I mean, you're out here on your own, and assuming you're right and it was them who broke in—whoever *they* are—what's holding them back? Sorry to put it that way, sir, but I'm wondering what they're waiting for.''

Paget massaged the back of his neck. "So am I," he said wearily. "Believe me, Tregalles, so am I."

TREGALLES HAD GONE, and Paget went round the house turning out the lights. The trip to London had taken more out of him than he'd imagined possible, and he was halfway up the stairs to bed when the telephone rang. He trudged back down again and answered it.

"Neil?" It was Andrea. "You sound half asleep. Are you all right? I didn't wake you, did I?"

"No, of course not," he said, pleased to hear her voice. "I'm fine."

"Are you sure? I was worried about you when I heard you'd cancelled your appointment with DeWitt this afternoon. I was going to ring you then, but his nurse said you had called from somewhere out in the country, and she understood you to say that you wouldn't be able to drive back in time for your appointment. I felt sure she'd got it wrong, so I rang the house, but there was no reply. Unfortunately, I had to work late this evening, so I've only just got round to ringing you again."

"No, she didn't get it wrong. I phoned from a pub near Chipping Norton."

"You *drove* there?" Her tone was sharp.

"Yes, but—"

"By yourself? Oh, Neil, you know you shouldn't be driving yet. Are you still having headaches?"

"Not enough to worry about, no."

"But you are still having them." Andrea's sigh of exasperation could be heard clearly over the phone. "Look, Neil, I know you hate being cooped up, but please be careful. The effects of that blow on the head are far from over, and with your low red blood cell count causing fatigue, that's a bad combination."

"I know," he said contritely, "and I will take care, but there was something I had to do. So, since I have to come in

Monday morning to see DeWitt, why don't we have lunch afterward, and I can tell you all about it?''

"Monday? Let's see. I have a session with Mr. Stone first thing, and then there's morning rounds, but yes, I think I can manage that. What time?''

"I should be through by twelve, twelve-thirty at the latest. I'll come to your office as soon as I'm finished.''

"Right, I'll see you then. And for heaven's sake go to bed. You sound very tired. Good night, Neil.''

"Good night, Andrea.''

He was still thinking about their conversation as he settled down in bed. Andrea had sounded quite concerned about him, and that was a good sign. It seemed like ages since he'd had a chance to sit down with her and really talk. Perhaps on Monday...

Which was as far as he got before falling asleep.

KATE REGAN STIRRED uneasily in her sleep, turned over and buried her face in the pillow. She was running—from what she did not know, but she knew she had to get away. Fog, thick black fog engulfed her, blinding, choking her as she ran. She gasped for breath, wheezing, coughing, coughed herself awake. And yet the dream continued. Tears streamed down her face as she struggled to sit up. She sucked in air.

Smoke! The room was full of smoke!

"Linda?'' she screamed as she scrambled from her bed. Drew in her breath to cry out again and began to cough once more. Her eyes were burning as she found the door and pulled it open to a thunderous roar as flames leapt up the stairs. The floor was hot beneath her feet as she crossed the tiny landing to Linda's door and flung it open. She fumbled for the light switch, found it, lost it, snapped it on. Nothing!

Kate's shadow danced across the wall as flames shot up the stairs behind her. Linda Bryce lay sprawled across the bed, still fully clothed, except for shoes, head back, mouth wide open, dead to the world.

And dead drunk, if Kate knew anything.

"Linda!" she gasped, and slapped her face, but Linda merely grunted and tried to pull away.

Get down near the floor, that's where the coolest air is; that's what she'd been taught. Kate dropped to her knees, tried to breathe, and almost tore her throat apart with coughing. Great theory. Not worth a shit in this situation. She pulled Linda off the bed, hoisted her bodily across her shoulders, and tried to rise. She staggered beneath her friend's dead weight. Her bare legs were burning, and she half expected the floor to burst into flames beneath her.

She lurched across the room and through the door. The flames licked at the banisters halfway up the stairs. No way down. Holding her breath as best she could, she carried Linda into her own room and slammed the door behind her. Stumbled over her own shoes, and went sprawling across the floor with Linda's weight on top of her.

"Wake up, you useless bitch!" she screamed as she pulled herself up and staggered to the window.

It wouldn't move. She pushed, she cursed, she wept as she struggled to open it, but still it failed to yield. Her feet felt as if they were on fire. Trainers. Where were they? She had to get something on her feet. Under the bed. She shoved Linda's body aside and felt beneath the bed. One. Thank God. And there was the other one. She tried to pull them on while kneeling, but the floor was too hot and she had to sit on the bed. Got up, tripped on the laces, lost precious time stopping to tie them.

Linda moaned. Kate dragged her onto the bed, then grabbed a blanket, wound it round her arm, and smashed it against the window.

Glass shattered. Cold air! Lifesaving air, but she didn't have time to do more than gulp a few quick breaths before returning to her task. Broke more glass. Raised her foot and kicked cross-pieces into the night.

The fire behind her was thundering at the door. The whole

room was ready to explode in flames. Kate dragged Linda to the window, pushed her through, saw blood streak down her arm, cut by the jagged glass.

A four-foot drop to the sloping roof below? Or was it six? Too late now to think about it; there was no other way. Kate gritted her teeth and let Linda go. Reaching back to the chair beside the bed, she found her dressing gown. No time to put it on. She scrambled onto the sill, crouched in the frame, sent up a silent prayer, and jumped.

TWENTY

VOICES. THE SOFT ringing of a bell somewhere. Kate opened her eyes and tried to focus. Lights on the ceiling, a corridor. Hospital, she knew the smell. People moving past, talking low. She tried to turn her head, but her neck was stiff.

"Kate? Kate?"

Oh, God! She must still be dreaming. The fire… She hoped it was a dream.

"Kate? It's all right, my love. You're going to be all right. I've come to take you home."

She could smell him. Stale, rancid, just like the house. She forced her head around, tried to snatch her hand away, but he held on tightly. "Don't," he said. "Your arm is broken. And you've torn the ligaments in your right ankle. See?" His knuckles rapped the cast.

"Go away!" she hissed. "Leave me alone! I'm not going anywhere with you."

He patted her hand. "You're upset," he said soothingly. "It's all arranged. They say you can be released in a few hours, and we'll go back home together. Just like it used to be."

"For God's sake, Paul, get it through your head. It's over, and that is not my home."

He smiled. "But you don't have anywhere else to go, do you? Not since Linda's house burned down. You have to come home with me."

"No!" Kate raised her head. "Nurse! Nurse!" she called, and began to cough. Her throat was raw. "Nurse!"

"Ssshhh! They're very busy, Kate. Just lie back. You'll hurt yourself."

She struggled harder, almost sat up. Saw someone in a white coat. "Doctor!" she screamed.

"Shut up, for Christ's sake!" Paul leaned over her, pushed her down on the bed, clamped a hand over her mouth. She bit his hand.

"Bitch!" He raised his hand to strike.

"What's going on here?" a voice demanded. "What are you doing, sir? Please move away from the patient."

"She's hysterical. I was just trying to calm her. It's the anaesthetic. She's not out of it yet."

"Who are you, sir?"

"I'm her husband. I was just…"

"Get him out of here," Kate panted. "Please. I've left him and he's been stalking me ever since. For God's sake get him out of here. He's the one who set the house on fire."

Paul lunged at the doctor, who went sprawling across the bed. Kate screamed as he landed on her leg. People were running. Paul was shouting.

The doctor pushed himself off the bed, reached for his pocket phone. "Security to Casualty. Security to Casualty. Now!"

"BUT HOW DID he know I was here?"

They had whisked Kate out of the corridor and placed her bed in an alcove behind the Casualty desk. No ward beds available. Not enough nurses even if there had been a bed. A security man paced the floor nearby. Rick Proudfoot stood beside her. She'd asked them to call him.

"Apparently Linda gave them his number when they asked about your next of kin, and they called him."

Kate groaned and closed her eyes. Trust Linda to do the wrong thing. "She is all right, isn't she, Rick? They said she was, but…"

"She's fine. You know Linda. When I spoke to her there

were two blokes fighting over which one she was going to stay with until she gets things sorted. She'll be along to see you as soon as they've finished with her, but she looks all right. No bones broken; just cuts and bruises, and a hell of a hangover. They tell me you got her out. She doesn't remember a thing about it.''

"I'm not surprised. She was unconscious the whole time. I found her lying on her bed, fully dressed. I remember screaming at her, but she never did wake up."

Rick said, "When I showed the doctor my ID, he told me you said it was Paul who set the fire. Is that true?"

Kate shivered. "I don't know. He could have. I just wanted them to get him away from me. He kept going on and on about taking me home. I suppose the house has gone?"

"Linda's house? I spoke to one of the uniforms who attended the scene. He said it didn't look too bad from the front, but the back is completely gutted, top and bottom."

"Do they know where it started?"

"They'll need more time to determine that, but it looks as if it started in the room directly below your bedroom. Could have been someone left the fire on, or..."

"We don't use that room. At least, not usually. And the fire's never on in there."

"Linda smokes. And she was drunk."

"Not in there. You know as well as I do, Rick, we use the kitchen and the front room. Linda's still got some of her stuff in boxes in the back room. She calls it the junk room."

Rick Proudfoot stood looking down at her. "If only you hadn't persuaded me to stop watching Paul, this might not have happened," he said quietly. "You could have been killed, Kate, and so could Linda." He drew in a deep breath. "Anyway, someone from our lot as well as the fire investigator will be talking to you about it. And Paul."

"I can't tell them much. I was asleep when it started. Woke up smelling smoke, and the fire was already partway up the stairs by then." She sagged against the pillows. "Everything

I own, apart from the car, was in that room," she said huskily. "What am I going to do, Rick? My mother lives in Oxford. I suppose I shall have to go there and stay with her until I can get everything sorted out. Would you ring her for me? Tell her I'm all right, but ask her if I can stay with her at least until I'm a bit more mobile. I should be able to manage crutches. I can't drive with these on"—she indicated the casts—"so she would have to come and pick me up."

"I can call her," he agreed, "but there's no need for her to come and get you. I have the weekend off. I can drive you down there—that is, if you still wish to go. But they'll want to talk to you here, and I can help sort things out for you. If you don't mind roughing it a bit, you can stay at my place. It doesn't look much—it's over a shop that sells second-hand clothing—but it's clean, it's close in, just off the market square, and best of all, it's cheap. The shop is run by two old dears, one of whom is my landlady. No strings, I promise. There's a sofa that's quite comfortable. I'll sleep on it and you can have the bed. I'll get you a cell phone, and anyone who needs to can contact you on that without knowing where you are. And I suggest you tell no one, and I really mean *no one!*—at least until we have Marshall behind bars."

Kate shivered. She found it hard to believe that Paul would go to such lengths, and yet, when she thought about his behaviour here in the hospital, what else could she think? "It's very good of you, Rick," she said hesitantly, "but..."

"But nothing," he said firmly. "Now, what about clothes? Did you get out with anything at all?"

"A dressing gown, that's all. Other than that... Oh God, Rick, what am I going to do? I didn't even have time to save my handbag. My money, ID, driving licence, credit cards, all gone."

"Look, Kate, don't worry about it. One thing at a time. They can't sling you out of here without any clothes, so why don't I get Mrs. McKinnon—my landlady—down here to take a look at you and get some idea of size and what you'll need, then we'll nip out and get you enough clothes to be going on with. And I don't mean from the second-hand shop. OK?"

Kate reached for his hand. "Thank you, Rick," she said simply. "I don't know what I would have done without you, but are you really sure? I mean, look at me. I'm barely mobile."

"I am looking," he said quietly, "and I'm very sure." He wanted to take her in his arms, but now was not the time. Instead, he said, "Besides, I don't see that you have much choice. There's bound to be an investigation, and they'll want you here, not in Oxford. Not only that, but it will make things simpler when you apply for your new driving licence and the rest."

She was tired. Too tired to argue. She just wanted to close her eyes and go to sleep—and wake up to find that this had been nothing more than a very nasty dream.

"ARSON. THAT'S WHAT this is, mate," the fireman pronounced. He and a uniformed constable stood side by side surveying the still-smouldering house. "No doubt about it in my mind. It'll have to be confirmed, of course, but you can smell the petrol. I'd say someone smashed the window, poured petrol inside, then tossed something like burning rags in after it. Chances are you'll find the petrol tin not far from here. Amateurish job, but those women were lucky to get out of there alive. Good job the neighbour saw it and turned in the alarm before it spread."

PAUL MARSHALL WAS watching television when they arrived. He denied having anything to do with the fire; denied that he'd been out during the night, and said the first he'd heard about the fire and his wife's narrow escape was when someone phoned him from the hospital.

As for causing a disturbance at the hospital, the doctor had misunderstood. Of course they weren't fighting. Ridiculous idea. Kate was his wife; why should they be fighting? He'd found her unattended in the corridor, thrashing around as she came out from under the anaesthetic, and there was no one there to help her. He'd simply tried to prevent her from hurting herself.

Why had he run?

"I was scared," he confessed. "Kate was screaming, the doctor seemed to think that I was trying to harm my wife, and he was calling for security. So I left. I didn't *run*. I just walked away quickly because I didn't want to upset Kate any more than she was. Anyway, there should have been someone there to take care of her."

"And you know nothing about the fire?"

"Absolutely not!"

They searched him; they searched his clothes; they searched the house; they searched the garden and found a sodden mass of clothing slashed to ribbons and partly burned. "Like burning things, do you, sir?"

"The wife's clothes. I told her to come and get them but she said she didn't want them, so I burned them, all right?"

They searched the garage, but couldn't find so much as a whiff of petrol.

"Why would there be?" he asked. "Kate took the car when she left months ago. Why would I need petrol?"

They took him in for further questioning, and held him overnight. He was questioned again the next morning, but his story remained the same. His picture was taken to every garage and filling station to see if anyone recognized him as someone who had bought petrol recently. But by two o'clock on Sunday afternoon, the best that they could do was charge him with causing a disturbance before they let him go.

CHARLIE, ACCOMPANIED BY two of his people, arrived on Paget's doorstep just after eight on Saturday morning. Paget had thought Grace Lovett might be there, until he remembered she'd said something about going to see her parents in Sheffield this weekend.

They checked the approach to the back door and examined the door itself, checked every room and dusted virtually every surface in the house for prints; and after they had gone, Paget was left with the job of cleaning up. He was partway through the task when he remembered Mrs. Baker's note.

He rang her, and began by thanking her for offering to fill in for Mrs. Wentworth while she was away, but went on to explain there had been a break-in.

"They made a mess of the place," he told her. "Probably kids, but you never know, so I'd rather you not be here alone until we know more. I'm sure it won't take long. I'll let you know as soon as I feel it's safe for you to come."

"But you'll be there, won't you, Mr. Paget? I mean, I wouldn't be alone in the house, not with you there, would I?"

"I have to be away quite a bit of the time," he hedged.

"But you're ill, and Mrs. Wentworth told me…"

"Ah, yes. That's right, Mrs. Baker, but we didn't know about the therapy then, did we? Takes quite a bit of time."

"Oh, I see. Yes, well I'm obliged to you for letting me know, but I was rather looking forward to it, what with work being so hard to come by these days."

"I'll let you know as soon as I think it's safe for you to come," he assured her, "but as I say, I wouldn't want you to be at risk should the same people return. No telling what they might do."

"Well, no, there is that, isn't there? But you will be sure to ring, then?"

"As soon as possible," he assured her.

By four o'clock, the headache had returned, and the now familiar lassitude descended on him. He couldn't stop yawning, then realized that he'd eaten almost nothing since breakfast, and forgotten to take the tablets he'd been given on leaving hospital. So much for his promise to Andrea.

As usual, when it came to the matter of the preparation of a nutritious meal versus convenience, it was no contest, and four rashers of bacon and two fried eggs later—plus a couple of slices of toast, marmalade, and a mug of tea—he felt much better. The dietitian wouldn't approve, he thought, but then, she wasn't there, was she?

PAGET LEFT THE HOUSE early Monday morning and drove into town. His appointment with DeWitt wasn't until eleven, but he wanted to talk to Alcott first. He'd spoken to him on the phone shortly after reporting the break-in on Friday, but the superintendent had not been in a receptive mood. In fact, his response to Paget's theory that they could be dealing with a serial killer had been, to say the least, somewhat cool.

To his surprise, Grace had rung on Sunday night, saying that she had just returned from Sheffield, and she was anxious to know how he was and how things had gone in London. She had tried to persuade him not to go, at least until he was stronger, and when he'd mentioned going by car, she'd all but called him an idiot. She had been right, of course, as had Bob McKenzie, but if he hadn't gone, he would never have met Krista Braun.

He hadn't intended to bore Grace with the details, but she was insistent, and he found himself recounting everything that had happened. Or almost everything. There was no way he was going to tell her that he'd felt so shaky driving back that he'd had to pull off the road.

"Was this old boss of yours able to add anything to what you already knew about your wife's death?" asked Grace.

"Not really, but after talking it through with him, I must admit I feel much better. Not about Jill's death, nothing will change that, but he did make me see that there was nothing I or anyone else could have done to prevent it. As for the connection between what happened here and what happened in Richmond—assuming there is a connection—I'm beginning to believe that the motive behind these attacks is to inflict as much pain and suffering as possible. I think the real target in Richmond was Dr. Braun, and the killing of Tessa Knowles in the home they shared was staged to cause Braun the greatest pain, and to make it appear as if she had killed her partner. In my own case, I think the person who attacked me knew about Jill and the way she died, and he wanted to twist the knife, so to speak, even as he was trying to kill me.''

"That," said Grace huskily, "is a terrifying thought, and I don't think you should stay out there, Neil, especially after the break-in while you were away."

"How did you know about that?" he demanded sharply. He hadn't mentioned it.

"I called Charlie to let him know that I was back in case we had a call-out overnight," she explained. "He told me. You weren't going to tell me, were you, Neil?"

"Nothing much to tell," he said lightly.

"Neil Paget, you are the most exasperating man! Staying out there by yourself is just asking for trouble. It's only by the grace of God that you're alive now. What if you'd been there when they broke in? At least move into town until this is over."

"I don't think they would have tried it if I'd been here," he said. "I think the purpose of the break-in was to rattle me, and I don't intend to let them do that."

"God! But you're stubborn!" The frustration in Grace's voice was palpable. "No matter what I say, you're not going to change your mind, are you? If this was happening to anyone else, you would tell them exactly the same as I'm telling you, wouldn't you? So why is it that when it comes to yourself, you can be so utterly…'' Grace bit the words off before she said something she'd regret.

"Stupid?" he supplied.

"Pig-headed was the word I had in mind."

He tried to reason with her, but Grace cut him off. "You've made up your mind, so there's not much point in talking about it, is there?" she said sharply. "If you're not going to listen to reason, I'm not going to waste any more breath trying to make you. So I'll say good night before this discussion gets out of hand, and one of us says something we might regret. Good night, Neil.''

She hung up before he could reply.

Thinking about it now, he wished he'd called her back. But what could he have said?

TWENTY-ONE

SUPERINTENDENT ALCOTT looked up from the report he was reading to see Paget standing in the open doorway. "Come in," he said tersely. "I'll be with you in a minute." He didn't offer the DCI a seat as he returned to his reading, but Paget sat down anyway.

Alcott sat back in his chair and tossed the report aside. He crushed a cigarette that had been smouldering in the ashtray, and lit another. "I don't know how you do it," he said at last, shaking his head, "but if you had come through that door ten minutes ago..." He broke off, at a loss for words. He picked up the report again and tossed it across the desk.

"Read it," he said. "It just came in from Thames Valley, and if I didn't know better, I'd say that you and Tregalles had made the whole thing up between you."

Paget scanned the page. Olive Driscoll, a seventy-eight-year-old widow, had been found dead in the house in which she lived with her son, Lionel Driscoll, QC. Her throat had been cut, and Lionel Driscoll was the prime suspect, although he had never been charged. Driscoll admitted being in the house shortly before the estimated time of the murder, but claimed that when he left to go up to London for the day, his mother was preparing to go out to 'do the daily shopping. No one else had been seen entering or leaving the house that morning. In one of his statements to the police, Driscoll claimed he had received a telephone call on the night of his mother's death, quoting the caller as saying something like:

"It's your fault she's dead. Now you know what it's like to lose someone you love."

A neighbour and friend of the victim was quoted as saying that Olive Driscoll had been devoted to her son, as he was to his mother. In fact, she had described Lionel, now in his middle fifties, as something of a mummy's boy.

Despite that statement, Lionel Driscoll was still considered to be the prime suspect, but the report ended by saying that DI Radcliffe of the Thames Valley Police Authority, Reading Division, would like to be kept informed of any further developments.

"So I was right," said Paget, trying not to sound too self-congratulatory as he handed the report back to Alcott. "This is exactly what I was hoping for. And the sooner this is followed up, the better, because God knows how many more may be on the list. Someone has to go down to Reading, and since I know something of the background—"

But Alcott cut him off. "And since you are on sick leave, Chief Inspector," he said heavily, "it won't be you—that is, if anyone goes at all. I can't afford to have people running all over the country on the basis of a single report that may or may not have anything to do with the case in hand."

"But it fits," Paget protested. "The same MO, the same sort of phone call after the killing. Anyway, I'm seeing the doctor later this morning, and there's a good chance he'll clear me to come back to work. I could be on my way by this afternoon."

"Judging by your appearance, I doubt that," Alcott told him bluntly. "You look as if you haven't slept for a week, and the last thing we need is you collapsing on the job, or worse still, running head-on into someone on the road, so forget it." He drew in a long breath and let it out again, and his tone was less belligerent when he continued.

"Look, I know you want to get back into the game, but damn it, man, your injuries were serious; you should be at home, resting, not chasing all over the country. Until you're cleared by your doctor, stay out of it. *If,* and I repeat, *if* we receive more reports of a similar nature, and your doctor clears you for work, I'll consider bringing you back." His voice hardened. "But make no mistake about it, I'm putting you on notice—you and Tregalles. Sick or not, I'm warning you: if you come by any information concerning this case, I want to be the first to know, not the last. And anything involving other Regional Forces, requests, discussions, visits, whatever, are to be authorized by me, personally. Understood?"

Paget stood up. "Understood, sir," he said. "But I would like to say that Tregalles can hardly be blamed for something I told him to do."

But Alcott dismissed that with an angry gesture. "You may have put him up to it," he growled, "but he's been around long enough to know the rules. He knew you had no authority over him while you were on sick leave. He should have come to me for clearance."

"Which you would have denied," said Paget grimly, "and we wouldn't have that report from Thames Valley on Olive Driscoll."

Alcott's voice was dangerously low when he replied. "That will be all, Chief Inspector," he said. "Don't let me keep you; I wouldn't want you to be late for your appointment with your doctor. But when you've finished there, I suggest you go home and get some sleep. You're supposed to be convalescing, and you look like hell!"

KATE WAS DISCHARGED from hospital Monday morning, and Rick took time off work to take her to his flat and get her settled in. "I have to go back in to work at lunchtime," he told her, "but you'll be safe here. I put two bolts on the door yesterday, and I want you to use them when I leave. Now, are you sure you can handle the crutches with your arm in a sling like that?"

"It's awkward," she admitted, "but I can manage." Kate

smiled as she looked around the tiny flat. "It's not as if I have far to go, is it?" she quipped. "So I'll be all right. And thanks, Rick. You've no idea how grateful I am."

He waited outside the door until he heard the bolts shoot into place before making his way downstairs. But he didn't go straight back to work as he'd led Kate to believe; instead, he drove across town to the house in Bridgewater Road.

"SUPERINTENDENT ALCOTT tells me I look like hell," said Paget as he and Andrea sat down at their table in the Selkirk Inn. He'd chosen the place because it was close to the hospital, yet quiet and secluded, and the tables were spaced well apart. Ideal for quiet conversation. "Do I really look as bad as all that?"

Andrea eyed him critically, but avoided a direct answer. "What did DeWitt say?"

"Not much. You know what he's like. He sort of rambles on to himself rather than the patient. But he seems to be satisfied that I'm making progress."

Andrea slowly shook her head. "That's not the impression I had when I spoke to him after he'd seen you this morning," she said. "He felt you were not getting enough rest, and he also felt that you weren't as forthcoming as you might be."

"About what, for example?"

"That's the trouble, he didn't know. He just felt that you were holding back. I gather you didn't tell him about your trip to Chipping Norton?"

He forced a smile. "Do we have to talk about me?" he asked lightly.

"You didn't tell him, did you?"

"No," he said, and wondered what Andrea would say if he told her he'd driven to London and back. "He didn't ask, and I didn't volunteer the information. Besides, I don't see that it's done any harm. I feel fine." He tried to lighten his voice. "So, shall we order and talk about something more pleasant than my problems?"

Later, as he was driving home, he replayed their lunchtime conversation in his mind. Once he had managed to get Andrea off the subject of his health and state of mind, they had chatted amiably enough throughout the meal, but Paget had the feeling that they were circling each other like a couple of sparring partners, each wary of the other.

When the coffee arrived, he decided he could wait no longer. "I've missed you, Andrea," he said quietly. "What with work and everything, it seems we hardly ever get together. Which is why I asked you to lunch. So we could talk about us for a change."

Andrea seemed to hesitate for a second, then smiled brightly as she picked up her cup. "It has been pleasant, hasn't it, Neil," she said. "And it has been a long time. But you mustn't blame yourself. It's my fault too. We do work terrible hours, and just lately it seems I never have a minute, what with helping Sten get settled in his place, and having Heather over. She and Sarah get along so well together, and she's no trouble."

She set the cup aside without drinking. "And Sten…" Andrea smiled ruefully and shook her head. "I don't know how he's managed to look after himself since his divorce. I made photocopies of about fifty recipes and took them over to his flat the other night and spent most of the evening going over them with him. And we spent hours the other day looking at wallpaper for his place. It really needs brightening up. In fact, I told him I'd come over and help him put it up this weekend, because the sooner it's on, the better. And you should see the kitchen! Cramped doesn't begin to describe it."

And that, thought Paget as he pulled up in front of his garage, had been the way the conversation had gone until it was time for Andrea to go back to work. It was Sten Wallen this, and Heather that, on and on and on. Had she told him that she and Sten had gone out together during that first year in university? No? Well, they had, and he was still the same. Big, bluff, and easy-going. Nothing ruffled Sten. He should never have married Shirley Clapton; everyone knew what she was like. Except Sten, apparently, Andrea had said. "I knew when they got engaged that it would end in disaster. Shirley just could not settle for one man. Fortunately, Heather takes after Sten. She's such a gentle child."

Paget switched the engine off and listened to it die. Somehow that seemed appropriate, because he had seen something in Andrea's eyes when she spoke of Sten Wallen that had not been there when she looked at him. Sten Wallen was probably a nice enough guy, but by the time they left the Selkirk Inn, Paget was wishing he'd never heard of him or his gentle daughter who got on so well with Sarah.

THE CHILDREN HAD LEFT the table, and they were enjoying their second cup of tea. "That was a grand dinner, love," Tregalles told Audrey as he settled back in his chair. "Nice bit of pork, that. Not a bit dry like that last one, and that stuffing and apple sauce…" He sighed contentedly.

"Yes, well, I thought I'd try that new butcher's in Crossley Street for a change. It's a bit more expensive than the supermarket, but I think it's worth it."

"Certainly was tonight," Tregalles agreed as he sipped his tea. "And there's a good bit left for tomorrow. Might even get a sandwich or two out of it."

Audrey stood up and began to clear the table. "No, sit still," she told him as he, too, began to gather plates together, "and tell me about your day."

"There's not all that much happening at the moment," he said. "Paget was in to see Alcott, and I gather they had a few words, but at least the super seems a bit more willing to follow up on a lead we got from Reading. In fact, I think there's a chance that he'll send me down there sometime this week. Fiona said she thought she heard Paget say he might be back to work soon, but I don't think he's ready for it yet. He still looks rough."

"Reading?" Audrey grimaced. "Will you be gone long, do you think?"

"Shouldn't think so. Maybe stop overnight, but that's about all."

"Overnight!" Audrey seized on the word. "That reminds me—I almost forgot." She pulled a folded paper from the pocket of her apron. "We had an email from Philip this morning. About Christmas."

They're not coming for Christmas! was the first thought that flashed through his head, but it died stillborn. He should have guessed something was afoot. It was unusual to have a pork roast on a Monday, and Audrey had seemed preoccupied during dinner.

"So, what did Philip have to say? Nothing wrong, is there?"

"Oh, no. It's just that—well, they're still coming, of course…"

Of course!

"…but Philip says he has an assignment in Shrewsbury with the Radio Shropshire people early in the New Year, so, since he'll be here over Christmas, he thought he might as well see to it while he's here. Ordinarily they wouldn't work over the holidays, but there's some sort of push on due to Radio Shropshire going digital—whatever that means. Anyway, you can read it for yourself. Philip explains it all in the email."

Audrey handed the sheet of paper to her husband, but Tregalles ignored it for the moment. There had to be more. "So what does that mean?" he asked cautiously.

"Oh, well, it doesn't really change anything, at least, not about Christmas. They'll still be here Christmas Eve as planned, but he'll be going back and forth to Shrewsbury each day, beginning the day after Boxing Day. He reckons it will take about a week, and he wanted to make sure it would be all right if they stayed on."

"They? You mean Lilian will be staying on here"—his voice rose—"for a week?"

Audrey sighed. "I know," she said, mistaking the reason for his concern, "it won't be much fun for her, will it, love? Not after London. Which was why I thought it would be a good time to take some of that leave they owe you, so we could take her round a bit. You know, Ironbridge, and maybe the Royal Worcester factory. A day out here and there."

"Won't be much open Christmas week," Tregalles said. It was an automatic response. He was still trying to digest the news that Lilian would be in the house for a week or more. The thought sent shivers down his spine, and the last thing he wanted was to be on leave while she was there. "Besides, the way things are at work, I don't thinks there's a snowball's chance of getting time off."

"But you could at least *try*. I mean, it will be something different for the kids as well over the holidays. For me as well. Lilian likes to look round the shops, and it will be nice to have someone like her to go round with." Audrey stacked the last of the dishes and carried them out to the kitchen.

Tregalles unfolded the paper and pretended to read. He could see it all now. The kids had been to Ironbridge more times than he cared to remember, so they would be bored stiff for a start, and he couldn't see it as a great attraction for Lilian. Olivia had been round the factory at Worcester twice already, and Brian wouldn't be interested. Five of them in the car, and Audrey was bound to insist on sitting in the back and giving Lilian the front seat. And with her roving hands and the kids' sharp eyes… He shuddered. It didn't bear thinking about.

"We'll give it some thought," he called after her. "When does Philip need to know?"

Audrey came to the door. "Oh, that's all settled," she told him. "I knew you wouldn't mind them staying over, so I've already sent a reply telling him it's all right."

TWENTY-TWO

PAGET WAITED impatiently until the middle of the afternoon before phoning Len Ormside to ask if he'd heard from Tregalles. If the sergeant had left for Reading first thing this morning, he should have reported in by now. But Ormside seemed surprised by the question. "Heard from him?" he said. "Well, yes, in a manner of speaking, but he's in with the super at the moment. Would you like me to have him ring you when he comes out, sir?"

"You mean he hasn't gone to Reading?"

"Been here all day, sir," Ormside told him.

"Then who has gone to see this man Driscoll?"

"No one, sir. Superintendent Alcott said he wanted to wait until we have more information."

"More information or more killings?" Paget demanded.

"I wouldn't know about that, sir," said Ormside neutrally, "but more information has come in today, so I should think someone will be following that up tomorrow. Tregalles is upstairs briefing the super now."

"Exactly what sort of information… ?" Paget began, but stopped himself. There was nothing to be gained by involving Ormside, and possibly getting him into trouble. "Never mind, Len," he said. "I'll have a word with Mr. Alcott myself— but I won't be mentioning this conversation."

"Thank you, sir." The sergeant was clearly relieved. Not that he could see any harm in what he'd told Paget, but you were never quite sure where you stood with Alcott, so the less said, the better.

Paget hung up the phone and looked at the time. Alcott rarely left the building before six, and it would only take twenty minutes or so to drive into Broadminster. He hesitated, held out his hands and looked at them. They seemed steady enough.

Half an hour later Alcott looked up to see Paget standing in the open doorway once again. He sat back in his chair, shaking his head as he regarded the DCI. "I'd hate to be your doctor," he said wearily. "What is it now? Been talking to Tregalles, have you?"

Paget looked surprised. "No. Isn't he in Reading?" he asked innocently. "But speaking of my doctor, I just wanted to let you know that he's cleared me for light duties, and I was wondering if—"

"Light duties?" Alcott eyed Paget suspiciously. "Which means what, exactly?"

"Just that. Can't do anything too strenuous yet, but he told me I can do most normal things." In fact, what DeWitt had said, at Paget's prompting, was, "I don't see any harm in your doing light duties *around the house*. It will be up to you to listen to what your body is telling you, and make sure you don't overdo it. It's important that you eat properly, continue with your iron supplement, and get plenty of rest. Your blood count is still low, and it will take time to build it back up again." And it had been at that point that Paget had changed the subject by asking an unrelated question.

"I'm glad to hear it," Alcott said cautiously. "But that doesn't mean you can come back to work. God knows I could use you, but I don't want you back until you are completely fit. All right?"

Paget nodded. "But while I'm here," he said, "I would like to know if we've received any other replies to our RFI, and what, if anything, you've heard from Reading."

Alcott grimaced and lit a cigarette. "It's beginning to look as if you might be right," he said. "Mind you, there's no proof of any connection yet, but there does seem to be a pattern. A razor was the weapon used in several killings in the past six months. What appears to be lacking is a clear motive. There are suspects, but no one has been charged in any of the cases we've heard of so far.''

"Well, at least we've made a start with Reading," said Paget. "Has Tregalles had a chance to talk to this man Driscoll yet?"

Alcott eyed him suspiciously. "We don't have anyone in Reading," he said, "but then, I suspect you know that. Tregalles wanted to go down this morning, but I told him to hold off until we had more information. He'll be going down first thing tomorrow."

"Tomorrow." Paget looked thoughtful. "It might be useful to have someone go with him," he said. "Mind if I go along, sir? As an observer, so to speak," he added hastily. "Since I did spend some time with Dr. Braun in Richmond, I would be in a better position to spot similarities or differences between her story and Driscoll's. Tregalles could take care of the driving, so I wouldn't be doing anything more than I would if I were at home."

Abruptly, the superintendent swung his chair around to face the window. It was pitch-black outside, so the only thing he could see was the mirror reflection of the office. But it was here that Alcott retreated when he needed time to think, and Paget was wise enough in the superintendent's ways not to speak.

"Tell me," Alcott said after a lengthy silence, "what would you do if I ordered you to go home and stay there?"

"If you *ordered* me to do that, I would be facing a very difficult choice, sir," said Paget quietly, "but I'm hoping I won't have to do that. I was very nearly killed by these people, and if there is a link between me and victims in other parts of the country, I have a better chance of spotting it than anyone else. As I see it, sir, you can't afford to keep me out of it, not when there is the possibility of others being killed."

Alcott swung round to face Paget. "I hope to God you

know what you're doing," he growled, "but it seems I don't have much choice in the matter. Go down and see Tregalles. He'll brief you on what we have, and you can accompany him tomorrow. But"—Alcott raised a warning hand as Paget was about to speak—"you go as a passenger. Nothing wrong with giving Tregalles the benefit of your experience, but let him do the donkey work. And I want your word that you'll pack it in at the first sign of fatigue. Understood?"

"Understood, sir. And thank you."

"Just one thing more before you go. I had our doctor speak to your doctor yesterday afternoon, and we have a full report on your condition. So if you like your job, and you want to remain involved in this case, don't try to con me again. Is *that* clear?"

"Very clear," said Paget meekly as he closed the door behind him.

EARLY THE FOLLOWING morning, Tregalles made a detour through Ashton Prior on his way to Reading. He had briefed Paget the night before, and their visit to interview Lionel Driscoll had been cleared with the Thames Valley Police, and Driscoll had been notified. "By the book," Alcott had stressed, and Tregalles had no intention of incurring the superintendent's displeasure again.

They chatted in a desultory fashion for a while, but it soon became apparent that something was bothering Tregalles. A frown creased the sergeant's brow, and he seemed more and more preoccupied as time went on.

"Are you going to tell me what's bothering you, Tregalles," Paget finally prompted, "or are we going to continue the journey in silence?"

Tregalles let out a long breath. "It's just that… Well, this isn't going to work, is it, sir?" Instinctively, Paget felt he knew what the sergeant was about to say, but he waited for Tregalles to spell it out. "I mean this business of me doing the leading when we get down to Reading. I know what Mr.

Alcott said, but when a DCI and a sergeant walk in together, nobody's going to look to the sergeant, are they? It's only natural that they'll look to you, and that's how it should be. Then everybody knows where they stand, including me."

The same thought had been in the back of Paget's mind, but he hadn't wanted to bring it up himself. "What do you suggest?"

"I think we should go back to the way we've always worked. It's not that I'm trying to shirk my responsibility, it's just that it makes more sense. What do you say, sir?"

"If you're sure that's the way you want it, I have no objection."

Tregalles glanced across at Paget. "Like I said, sir, it's not that I want to shirk my responsibilities; I could have done it if I were on my own, but with you here… Well, it changes things, doesn't it? See what I mean?"

Paget smiled. "No need to worry on that score," he said. "I have to admit, I've been wondering how well it would work ever since Alcott agreed to my coming down with you."

"But you didn't say anything."

"Because I didn't want you to think I was trying to take over. It's your case; it had to be your decision."

"What if I hadn't brought it up?"

"But you did, didn't you?"

Tregalles grinned. "In that case, welcome back, sir. And thanks."

"Thank you, Sergeant. Glad to be back. Now, wipe that silly grin off your face and pay attention to your driving."

Twenty minutes later, Paget was asleep. Best thing for him, Tregalles thought, and fell to thinking about the information they had received in the past couple of days.

Responses had been varied to the initial RFI, but by the end of the day on Tuesday, several disturbingly similar killings had been reported, including one that had taken place in Hertfordshire eleven days after the attack on Paget. A young man by the name of Gerald White had been attacked and killed for no apparent reason as he was walking home late one evening. It was believed at least two people were involved in the attack, because his body had been carried or dragged some distance from where he was killed, and deposited inside the gate in front of his mother's house. He had suffered an injury to his head, and his throat had been cut with a razor.

Until receiving the enquiry from Broadminster, nothing had been known of a telephone call to White's mother, but when questioned again, she said yes, there had been such a call, but she'd been so distraught at the time that she had put it out of her mind. She couldn't remember the exact words, only that the person had taunted her about the loss of her son.

From Bournemouth came the information that a nineteen-year-old girl by the name of Penelope Crofton had died in a similar manner in September, killed in her flat where she lived alone. Her body was discovered by her grandfather, a retired judge by the name of Harmer, who suffered a stroke shortly after talking to the police, and had since died without regaining consciousness. Once again, the weapon was believed to be a razor. The grandfather told the police he'd received a frantic telephone call from his granddaughter, pleading for him to help her, but she was cut off before he could reply, and was dead by the time he arrived.

Harmer told the police that within minutes of his finding his granddaughter, the telephone in her flat rang and kept on ringing. When he answered it, he said, someone had mocked him, saying it was his fault his granddaughter was dead. He hadn't been able to recall the exact words, but he did remember the caller asking him how he felt about losing someone he loved.

Despite an intensive investigation into the girl's background, no motive could be found, and no arrest had been made. But as far as Tregalles was concerned, a pattern was emerging. It now appeared that Penelope Crofton, Tessa Knowles, Olive Driscoll, and Gerald White had all been killed for the same reason: to cause pain and suffering to those closest to them. And in each case, those left behind appeared to be associated in some way with the courts. Harmer was a former judge; Driscoll was a QC; Braun was a psychologist who had worked on suspects' profiles; Gerald White's mother worked for the Prison Service; and then there was Paget himself.

Except in Paget's case, the killer had been unable to find a victim whose death would cause him the same level of pain and suffering that had been inflicted on the others, so Paget himself had become the target.

There had been other reports, but they hadn't quite matched the profile. From Southampton—no distance at all from Bournemouth—came the report of the death of a twenty-three-year-old prostitute by the name of Shirley Lampson. She had been killed in the back seat of a stolen car after being sexually assaulted in a place called Netley Marsh. Her throat had been cut with a thin-bladed weapon, although not, in the opinion of the pathologist, a razor. Lampson was known to the police, and known to have associated with a rough crowd, but no clear suspect had emerged thus far.

A twenty-one-year-old student by the name of Marjorie Williams, attending York University, had been attacked and slashed across the face as she was walking home one night late in September. However, it appeared that disfigurement rather than murder was the objective, and an ex-boyfriend was still being sought in connection with the attack.

And in Rotherham, Derbyshire, a twenty-eight-year-old woman by the name of Lydia Dalmer had been killed ten days ago. She'd been stabbed several times, and her head had been all but severed by a thin-bladed weapon, possibly a razor, although this was by no means certain. Dalmer's ex-husband was being sought in connection with the murder, and an early arrest was expected. Tragic as it was, until more information became available, this case, too, would be excluded.

TWENTY-THREE

FOLLOWING DIRECTIONS given them by the local police, Paget and Tregalles found the house without difficulty. It was on a tree-lined street on the outskirts of the town: large, three storeys, set on a slight rise well back from the road.

Lionel Driscoll was a short, plump, grey-haired man with small but sharp, intelligent eyes, and heavy jowls that wobbled when he talked. Paget had hoped he would recognize the man as someone he'd seen in court, but the face was unfamiliar. Neither did Driscoll give any indication that he recognized the chief inspector.

The two men followed Driscoll into a large, high-ceilinged room lined with paintings and crammed with heavy, Spanish-style furniture, dark and old. The padded seats of the chairs, once rich in texture, were so worn and faded that it was hard to tell their original colour, while the chairs themselves, straight-backed and solid, looked extremely uncomfortable.

They were.

Driscoll sat down facing the two detectives, and set a tape recorder on the low table separating them. "You'll forgive me for being cautious," he said as he flipped the switch to On, "but when Inspector Radcliffe told me you wished to talk to me because you believed there might be a connection between my mother's death and an attempted murder in Broadminster, I didn't know what to make of it. I know she's convinced that I killed my mother, so I suspected her motives, but finally decided I had nothing to lose by hearing you out, so here we are.''

Paget nodded. ''Fair enough,'' he said. ''And to make sure there is no misunderstanding, I have agreed to share anything we might learn here today with Inspector Radcliffe. So if you don't mind, sir, we will record this conversation as well.'' He nodded to Tregalles, who took a tape recorder from the small case he was carrying and set it on the table.

Driscoll smiled. ''Touché,'' he said. ''So, now that's out of the way, shall we get on? What is it you wish to know?''

''I've seen the file on the investigation,'' Paget told him, ''but I'd like to hear an account of what happened in your own words.''

Driscoll's account was straightforward and succinct, and as far as Paget could tell, deviated not a whit from the statement the man had given to the local police. On a Tuesday early in October, Driscoll had left the house a few minutes before nine to drive up to London. His mother was preparing to go out to do some shopping, something she did regularly two or three times a week.

''She always walked, rain or shine,'' Driscoll explained. ''She could have taken her car, but she liked to walk. It's half a mile to the shops, and sometimes she would meet a friend and they would stop and have a coffee together.''

But that day, Olive Driscoll had never left the house.

Driscoll went on to say he'd returned home just after six to find his mother lying in a pool of blood on the kitchen floor. His eyes filled with tears as he described the scene.

''According to police records, you didn't ring them until six-forty-four,'' said Paget. ''Why was that, sir?''

Driscoll grimaced and shook his head. ''Inspector Radcliffe keeps coming back to that,'' he said disdainfully, ''and I'll ask you the same question I asked her: What would you do if you came home to find your mother dead, her throat cut, and lying in a pool of her own blood? Well, I'll tell you what

I did during that time: I sat on the floor beside her and held her hand and cried!''

He wiped his eyes and put away his handkerchief. ''Now, can we get to the point, Chief Inspector? What is the connection between my mother's death and an attempt on someone's life in Broadminster?''

''Believe me, I'm coming to that, but first, let me ask if you recognize me as someone you've met or seen before—perhaps in court?''

Driscoll eyed Paget carefully, then shook his head. ''I have the feeling I *may* have seen you before,'' he said carefully, ''but it's no more than an impression. Sorry.''

''Does the name Braun mean anything to you, sir? Dr. Krista Braun? She's a psychologist. You may have called upon her for a professional opinion on the state of mind of one of your clients.'' He took a folded paper from his pocket and opened it. ''I had Dr. Braun fax me this picture last night. It's not the best, but she is quite recognizable.''

Driscoll studied the picture, then shook his head. ''Sorry,'' he said again. ''I don't remember her, but that's not to say she hasn't had dealings with the firm. She may have given a written assessment of a client without my actually seeing her. I'm going up to London tomorrow, so if I could have a copy of that photograph, I could show it to some of my old colleagues and the staff. They might remember her. Was she killed also?''

''No, but someone very close to her was,'' said Paget, handing him the picture. ''You can have this; we have more.''

Driscoll folded the picture and tucked it away in his pocket.

''In your statement to the local police, you mentioned receiving a telephone call shortly after your mother's death. Can you tell me about that?''

Driscoll eyed Paget suspiciously. ''Why do you want to know about that?'' he demanded. ''Radcliffe thinks I made it up.''

"I'd prefer to make up my own mind about it after I hear what you have to say."

"Very well then." Driscoll lowered his head and stared at the floor. "Whether anyone believes it or not, there most certainly was a phone call, and I shall never forget those words, or the voice. He said, 'You didn't defend your mother very well, either, did you, Mr. Driscoll? Now *you* know what it's like to lose someone you love.'"

Tregalles, who had remained silent until now, spoke up. "You said 'he,' sir. Are you quite sure it was a man speaking?"

"I think it was, but I'm sure he tried to disguise his voice."

"Could you describe it? Was there anything distinctive about it? Anything at all?"

Driscoll took his time thinking about that. "It was an odd-sounding voice, harsh, but the words were clear enough. I thought at first he had a cold, but it was coarser than that; unpleasant, grating. I don't know how else to describe it."

Tregalles cast an enquiring look at Paget, who nodded. Driscoll might well be describing the voice he'd heard himself.

"What about the words themselves?" Tregalles continued. "What did they suggest to you?"

Driscoll shrugged wearily. "I don't think there can be much doubt about their meaning. And the thought that something I did in the past may have caused my mother to be killed in such a brutal fashion has haunted me ever since. I've gone over everything in my mind a hundred times, but the truth is that clients who are found guilty invariably blame it on a poor defence. I've received my fair share of threats, as have most of my colleagues at one time or another, but I've never known of anyone who carried out those threats."

"You're retired now, are you, sir?" asked Paget.

"No, but I spend much less time in London these days. Most of my work is done from home now, but I still have ties to the old firm."

"Do you still have access to your old chambers' records?"

"To a limited degree, yes, I suppose I do. Why? What did you have in mind?"

"The records are computerized, are they?"

Driscoll gave a wry smile. "If you're talking about the past four or five years, the answer is yes, but before that…" He shrugged. "In my profession, change has always been viewed with deep suspicion, and approached with extreme caution, so we were slow to accept anything as radical as computerized records. We played around with the idea for years, but we didn't really get into it until shortly before I came down here. What is it you would like me to look for, exactly?"

"Any reference to Dr. Braun, and the case or cases for which she was retained. I have asked Dr. Braun to do the same."

Driscoll sat forward on his chair, shoulders hunched, his eyes fixed on Paget. "It was you, wasn't it?" he said softly. "You're the one who was attacked in Broadminster. That's why you asked me if I had seen you before. That's why you believe me about the phone call. You heard the voice; you know I'm telling the truth." His voice rose. "You must have *seen* him!"

"For the moment, let's just say there are similarities," Paget cautioned. "There is no *direct* evidence as yet to connect the incidents. As for seeing the person who attacked me, it was dark and it was raining. I was hit on the head from behind and blinded by a bright light." He touched the covering on his neck self-consciously. "Fortunately, the person who attacked me was scared off before he could finish the job, or I wouldn't be here now, asking questions."

"But you heard his voice," Driscoll insisted.

"Yes, but as I'm sure you understand, sir, that is not worth much in a court of law." He smiled thinly. "A good brief would tear it to ribbons."

"What about this Dr. Braun—did she receive a similar call?"

"All I can say at the moment is that there appears to be sufficient circumstantial evidence to warrant further enquiries."

Driscoll grunted. "Spoken like a true policeman," he said, "but at least you seem to have more of an open mind than Inspector Radcliffe."

Paget took out a card and handed it to Driscoll. "If you do find a reference in your files to Dr. Braun—or to me, for that matter—please contact me or Sergeant Tregalles immediately. We can both be reached twenty-four hours a day on one or the other of those numbers. Oh, yes, and I'd like a photograph of you. Preferably one taken a few years ago. In fact two photographs, if possible: one in your court robes, and one in ordinary clothes."

Driscoll left the room, returning a few minutes later with two pictures. One had been taken in brilliant sunshine against a background of what looked like orange trees. Beside him was a white-haired woman. She was smiling, and there was no mistaking the family resemblance.

"Your mother?" Paget asked.

Driscoll nodded. "Taken in Spain four years ago." His eyes were moist as he thrust the second picture into Paget's hands. It was a group picture taken, Paget supposed, outside one of the Inns of Court. "It's the only one I have of me in robes," Driscoll explained. "I was a bit thinner then. I'm in the second row, third from the right."

Paget looked at both pictures closely, but if he had ever encountered Driscoll before, he had no memory of the occasion.

IT WAS FOUR O'CLOCK and already dark when they left the house to make their way back to the centre of town. It had begun to snow, and large wet flakes spattered the windscreen. "I think we'd better split up tomorrow," Paget suggested. "I'll see if I can wangle a car from the locals here, but if not I'll hire one. First thing tomorrow morning, I want you to go down to Bournemouth to find out what you can about the death of that young woman, Penny Crofton. Meanwhile, I'll go across to Potter's End and talk to Gerald White's mother. We can meet back here tomorrow night to compare notes."

"You shouldn't be driving," Tregalles told him. "There's no reason why I can't do both."

"Except it will take an extra day, and we can't afford to waste any more time."

"Still, traffic could be heavy, and you're not exactly fit, are you, sir?"

"I made it to London and back without incident last week."

Tregalles shook his head stubbornly. "You know what Mr. Alcott said," he reminded Paget. "You were to come strictly as an observer. He made that very clear to both of us."

"In that case, when you report to him this evening, you can tell him that I shall stay behind and rest while you go down to Bournemouth tomorrow."

"Rest?"

"Rest. I'm on sick leave, remember?"

"You won't get much rest if you plan on driving to Potter's End."

"As far as you are concerned, Tregalles, I shall be resting tomorrow, and that is all you need tell Alcott. So let's just leave it at that, shall we?"

There was no point in arguing with the man. Paget would do what he wanted anyway, and the less Tregalles knew about it the better.

TWENTY-FOUR

BROADMINSTER

RICK PROUDFOOT CAME out of a deep sleep to the sound and smell of frying bacon. He struggled upright and groaned aloud. The sofa wasn't bad, but it was narrow and didn't do a lot for the back. He squinted in the direction of the cooker, where Kate stood propped between a single crutch on one side, and the counter on the other.

"Kate! You shouldn't be doing that," he protested as he slid off the sofa. "Here, let me do it before you have an accident."

"I'm doing all right," Kate assured him. "My arm may be broken, but I can still use my hand. Besides, I want to do it. I need the practice. I can't sit around doing nothing all day."

"There's television," he offered, and was met with a withering look.

"Have you watched daytime television lately?" she asked. "If those programmes are any indication of the level of intelligence in this country, then God help us, Rick."

"All right, all right," he said soothingly. "It was only a suggestion. Anyway, if you're sure you can manage, I'll have a quick wash and get some clothes on. Are you sure you don't want me to…"

"Just go, and be quick about it or your breakfast will be cold."

Ten minutes later as they sat facing each other across a small table, he said, "Remind me I still have to shave before

I go to work. I didn't want to hold up breakfast. It's good, Kate. Thanks.''

"It's the least I can do," she told him. "I know I'm being a nuisance, so I want to…''

"Kate. Please get it through your head you are not a nuisance. Believe me, this flat has never been as welcoming as it has since you've been here. I feel as if I have a reason for coming home now, whereas before…'' He ended with a shrug. "Anyway, as I said last night, I've arranged to have a couple of hours off this afternoon, so we can get you sorted out at the bank, and see about your driving licence. I'll work through till two, then come and pick you up.''

Kate reached across the table and gripped Rick's hand. "I really don't know what I would have done without you," she said softly. She began to take her hand away, but Rick held it for a moment longer.

"Kate…'' he began earnestly, then stopped, afraid he would be making a fool of himself if he continued. He let go of her hand and looked away.

"What is it, Rick? You look so serious.''

"Sorry, Kate. I'm afraid my mind was wandering again. I'm convinced the fire was set by Marshall, but where did he get the petrol from? The man has no transportation, and it's not as if he could lug the stuff around on a bus, is it? We've drawn a blank as far as garages and filling stations are concerned, but I suppose there is always the possibility that he stole it from somewhere close at hand; siphoned it out of someone's tank, for example.''

Kate folded her hands. She was sure that was not what Rick had been about to say. She wished… What did she wish? For Rick to speak the words she believed were in his heart? And what about her own heart? Could she trust the feelings stirring there? Could she ever trust any man again after what she'd been through?

"I still can't believe he would do such a thing," she told him. "He used to be such a…'' She stopped and spread her hands in a helpless gesture. "But then, he's not what he used to be, is he? He needs help, Rick. I wish there was something I could do. I wish…" Whatever it was Kate wished, it ended in a sigh of resignation, but she sounded most unhappy.

She's still in love with him! he thought. She must be. Why else would she talk and look like that?

Abruptly, Rick pushed his plate away and rose from the table. "I'd better have that shave," he said gruffly, "but leave the washing-up; I'll do it when I get home."

Kate opened her mouth to speak, then closed it as Rick left the room. She sat there frowning. What had she said to upset him? Why the sudden change? She struggled to her feet, found her crutches, and began to clear the table.

"Men!" she muttered fiercely as she hobbled to the sink.

RICK GOT INTO his car and sat there, fingers drumming on the steering wheel. Was is possible that Kate could still be in love with Marshall after all he'd done? It defied all logic if she was, and yet there had been that faraway look in her eyes when she spoke of him at breakfast.

He slammed the wheel hard with the heel of his hand. What was it going to take to convince her, for God's sake? He looked at his watch. There was time, he decided; time to make a detour on his way to work.

A HAND DESCENDED hard on DC Jimmy Fletcher's shoulder. "Things a bit slack, are they, Fletcher?" Ormside enquired. "Got nothing better to do than read the paper?"

"Just glancing at the headlines, Sarge. Was there something…?"

"I've had no progress report from you on this woman who visited DCI Paget's housekeeper—the one who claimed she was doing a survey."

"Ah!" Fletcher folded the paper and pushed it aside. "To be honest, Sarge, I haven't had much luck with that. I've phoned everyone I could think of, but like I said, no luck."

"Let's see the list, then?"

"The list?"

"The list of people you've phoned."

The colour rose in Fletcher's face. "I didn't…"

"…make a list," Ormside finished for him. "In fact, I wouldn't be at all surprised to find you've done bugger all about it since Molly gave the job to you. Right?"

Fletcher took one look at Ormside's face and decided against another lie. "Right, Sarge," he said, and waited for the blast.

"Then I suggest you get off your backside and get out to Ashton Prior and start canvassing DCI Paget's neighbours. Find out if they were visited by this woman." He looked out of the window; it was pouring rain. "Better take your wellies with you," he advised. "Most of his neighbours live on farms."

BOURNEMOUTH

"TENTH OF SEPTEMBER, it was, when Penny died," said Harriet Crofton. "Just turned nineteen, she had, with her whole life in front of her. She and her granddad used to…"

Her voice broke and she looked away. She was a plain woman, yet gentle-featured, and Tregalles could see a likeness around the eyes and mouth as he looked at the picture in his hands. Penny Crofton, bright-eyed and smiling. She made him think of his own daughter, Olivia. He couldn't begin to imagine what it would be like to lose her in such a brutal fashion.

He waited, hard-pressed to keep his own emotions under control as he continued to stare at the picture.

"I'm sorry," the woman said as she turned back to face him. "I'll be all right now. What was it you wanted to know?"

Tregalles set the picture aside. "I've read the reports, which tell me the facts of the case, but I'd like you to tell me a little bit more about Penny and her grandfather. Mr. Justice Harmer was your father, was he?''

''That's right. Came to live with us when my mother died just before he retired about four years ago. Penny was fifteen, and they took to each other straight away. You see, my husband died when she was three, so she'd never really had a father. She and Dad just clicked. He was always fond of her, but it wasn't until he retired that they saw much of each other, because he was always so busy and lived in London. Penny needed a father, and Dad needed someone to take Mum's place.''

''The local police say Penny called your father on the phone, and he rushed over there. You weren't here at the time, I take it?''

Harriet's eyes misted once again. ''If only I had been,'' she whispered. ''I don't know if it would have made a difference, but it might. I might have rung the police while he went over there. They might have got there in time to save her. But I wasn't here, was I? I was at the church, and when I got home the first thing I saw was the phone hanging there and the newspaper on the floor by Dad's chair. I knew something was wrong. I knew it, but it wasn't until later that I...''

The woman's eyes were brimming with tears. ''I might have saved her if I'd been here,'' she burst out, ''but I wasn't, and now she's dead.'' Tears spilled down her face. ''Oh God! I haven't cried like this since Penny died,'' she wailed. ''I'm sorry. I'm sorry.''

Tregalles rose from his chair and stood beside the woman. He put his hand on her shoulder. ''You've nothing to be sorry for,'' he told her gently. ''You couldn't have known. It's not your fault that Penny died, so please don't blame yourself. But we have to find whoever did this before he has a chance to kill again, which is why I need your help.''

Harriet dabbed at her eyes and nose as she rose unsteadily to her feet. ''What must you think of me?'' she said, annoyed with herself for breaking down in front of this policeman.

She'd always been the strong one in the family, but it was as if a dam had broken, and there'd been no holding back.

Tregalles said, "I think what you need is a good strong cup of tea, and I wouldn't mind a cup myself. Would you like me to pop the kettle on?"

Harriet smiled weakly through her tears. "You're very kind," she said, "but I think I can manage that." She started toward the door, then paused. "If you'd like to come through, we could talk while I make the tea."

Tregalles followed her into the kitchen. "Do you have children?" she asked as she filled the kettle.

"Two," he told her. "Olivia and Brian."

"How old are they?"

"Olivia's nine, going on ten, and Brian's seven."

Harriet ran the water until it was hot, then filled the teapot to warm it while she waited for the kettle to boil. "I used to think I'd like a large family," she said, "but when Penny came along she seemed to fill our whole lives. Then, like I said, her dad died, so now"—she drew in a deep breath and let it out again—"I have no one except my sister, and I don't see much of her these days, now that Dad's gone."

The kettle boiled and Harriet made the tea. She set cups out on the kitchen table, then looked at Tregalles. "Do you mind?" she asked. "I never thought. I'm so used to having my tea in here."

"That's where we always have it at home," Tregalles assured her.

"Good. Care for a biscuit?" Harriet pulled the lid off a tin. "They're bought ones, I'm afraid. I don't do much baking anymore."

"Garden Creams. Yes please."

Harriet found a couple of small plates and set them beside their cups of tea, and Tregalles helped himself from the tin.

"So, your father and your daughter were very close, were they?" Tregalles prompted.

Harriet Crofton's eyes took on a faraway look. "She was

everything to him," she said softly. "I know I shouldn't, but I used to envy him. You see, I've always had to work, so there were many times when I couldn't be here for Penny when she came in from school and things like that. But he was always here, and they got along together so well despite the difference in their ages. And yet he never spoiled her— well, perhaps he did a bit—but he never tried to come between Penny and me. He taught her a lot. He loved her very much, and she loved him. And when she died…well, I sometimes think that it was just as well that he had that stroke when he did. He wouldn't have been able to live with himself, having seen the way she died."

He would have felt the pain; he would have been made to suffer, had he lived, thought Tregalles. Paget was right. To the killer, Penny's death was incidental. Her grandfather had been the intended victim in this case.

BACK ONCE MORE in Reading, the two detectives compared notes. "So," said Paget, "we have Dr. Braun, who has testified in court on behalf of both the prosecution and defence; Driscoll is a QC; Harmer was a judge; and Theresa White, the mother of the young lad who was killed in Potter's End, is a psychologist who has worked in various prisons."

"And then there's you," Tregalles put in.

"That's right. So, assuming we were all involved in the same case, all we have to do now is find out which case that was."

Easier said than done, Tregalles thought. There was no easy way of collating information of that sort. According to Harriet Crofton, her father had served on the bench for nine years before retiring four years ago, so what they were looking for could have happened anywhere from four to thirteen years ago. And the further back they had to go, the less chance there was that the records would be in a database. Paper, microfiche perhaps, but it would be a daunting task. On the other hand, at least it was a place to start.

BROADMINSTER

PAUL MARSHALL slouched in his chair in front of the television set, nursing a half-empty bottle of vodka. He stared blankly at the images on the screen, but what he was seeing on his inner eye was a heavyset young man who had roused him from his bed this morning by pounding on the front door. Marshall shivered as he remembered stumbling down the stairs, still half asleep, trying to get to the door to stop the man from breaking it down. The chain was on, but the moment he'd opened the door a crack, the man had put his shoulder to it and the chain had snapped.

"Sorry about that," the man said as he pushed his way inside. "Must have stumbled on the mat. I should get a better chain if I were you. These cheap ones are a waste of money."

Marshall backed away, hands outstretched before him as the man advanced. "You can't come in here like this," he stammered. "This is my house. I'll call the—"

"Police?" the man suggested. "I *am* the police, Mr. Marshall." He'd shoved his warrant card under Marshall's nose. "Why don't you ring Charter Lane. I have a lot of mates down there who'd love to come round and have a chat with you. Go on, ring them now."

A tremor ran through Marshall's body as he relived the scene. His hands were clammy; he lifted the bottle to his lips and drank deeply. What he *should* have done was stand up to the man, he thought resentfully. What he *should* have said was... But then, he'd not had the chance, had he?

It might not have been quite so bad if he hadn't tripped over his own feet and fallen. He drew in his breath as he remembered the man standing over him, smiling. He'd pulled up his knees and covered his face, waiting for the blow.

But the blow never came. Instead, the man had spoken quietly, and the words had been running like an endless tape through Marshall's head all day.

"We all know you set that fire, my friend, and one way or

another I am going to prove it. Until then, I'm warning you: if you ever come near Kate again, I will personally break every bone in your miserable body.''

Marshall tipped the bottle up and drank deeply, then drank again until it was empty. He hugged the bottle to him as he would a child, and began to rock gently back and forth. Fear receded, replaced by bravado, for the man had made one very big mistake. Marshall knew his name. He'd seen it when the man had thrust the warrant card in front of his face. Proudfoot. Shouldn't be hard to find. There couldn't be that many Proudfoots in Broadminster.

TWENTY-FIVE

IT WAS BEGINNING to make sense at last, thought Paget as they drove back from Reading. The killings were connected, the motive most likely stemming from a court decision in the past, a decision in which he, Braun, Driscoll, and Harmer had been involved, although Theresa White must have come into the picture later. Where their paths had crossed was still unknown, but at least now he felt there was a sense of direction—something that had been missing in this investigation far too long.

Before leaving Reading, the two men had used the police facilities to make a copy of the taped conversation with Lionel Driscoll for Detective Inspector Radcliffe. She had listened to it, then sat back and continued to listen as Paget explained his theory.

"If we assume that Harmer was the presiding judge," he concluded, "what we have to do now is search for cases where Driscoll was defending, and then see if we can match any of those to Dr. Braun's records and my own appearance in court. And once we have that, no doubt we will find a connection to Theresa White. But we must move quickly, because the thing that troubles me is this: how many others are on this killer's list? Who was prosecuting? Who were the witnesses?"

Radcliffe nodded slowly. She'd found it hard to let go of the idea that it was Lionel Driscoll who had killed his mother, but the evidence Paget had presented appeared to make sense. "So, what is it you want from me?" she asked cautiously.

"I'm not sure there is a great deal you can do from here," Paget told her, "but I would like to get these pictures of James Harmer and Lionel Driscoll faxed to Dr. Braun. If she recognizes either one of them, it could save us a lot of time. The last thing I want to hear is that there has been another razor killing, so we need to get things moving. If I can use one of your phones, I'd like to talk to Dr. Braun, let Inspector Reese in Richmond know what we're doing, and call my own superintendent."

Thinking back to his conversation with Alcott, Paget couldn't help smiling to himself. The superintendent hadn't known whether to sound pleased that progress was being made at last, or annoyed that Paget had managed to slip back into the system through the back door.

"You're still on sick leave," Alcott reminded him, "and I don't want to see you back here until you have a clean bill of health. I know you have a personal stake in all this, but we are quite capable of following up on the information that you and Tregalles have given us. Now, let me speak to him."

"He says I'm to drop you off at your house on the way in," the sergeant said as he hung up. "And I'm not to let you talk me into doing anything else."

BROADMINSTER

PAGET ROSE EARLY Sunday morning to catch up on the washing and ironing. He'd slept late on Saturday, drained of energy after the long drive home on Friday. They'd encountered everything from rain to sleet to snow and icy roads. But that wasn't the only reason for his lassitude. He'd paid almost no attention to his diet for the past three days, and neither had he been drinking anywhere near the amount of liquids recommended by his doctor.

Fortunately, Tregalles had reminded him to pick up a few things on the way home on Friday. It was just as well he had, because there were no fresh vegetables in the house, no bread, and the milk in the fridge was definitely off.

On Saturday afternoon, he'd made himself an omelette consisting of eggs, cheese, and tofu for protein, together with tomatoes, onions, spinach, and grated carrots, which took care of the vegetables; and several slices of toast and a very large pot of tea. That took care of the carbohydrates, and he'd read somewhere that tea was supposed to help ward off cancer. Not quite, perhaps, what the dietitian had had in mind when she'd given him the food guide, but it seemed to do the trick. At least he felt better, and after a hearty breakfast of sausage and eggs on Sunday morning, he felt fit for work again.

But by noon he could feel his newfound energy slipping away, and he stopped to make himself a cheese sandwich and a pot of tea. As he sat there sipping tea, his thoughts turned to Andrea, and he wondered if she had finally got this Sten whatsisname settled into his new place. Funny how she'd managed to find the time to do that, yet he and Andrea had always found it difficult to get together because of the unsociable hours they were forced to work. An unworthy thought, he told himself. It was only natural that she should do everything she could to help the man she'd known since childhood, especially when he was trying to make a new life for himself and young daughter.

Paget poured himself another cup of tea, picked up the phone, and punched in Andrea's number.

"Yes? Who is it?"

"Ah! Mrs. Ansell. Neil Paget here. Is Andrea there, please?"

"No, I'm afraid she's not, Mr. Paget. She's out. There's just me and the two girls here. Can I take a message? She'll be back about four. She's helping Mr. Wallen redecorate his flat. They were at it all day yesterday, but they reckon they should be done by four today, so they're coming back here for dinner. There's a joint roasting in the oven, and I'm keeping an eye on that as well as looking after the girls. Not that they take much looking after. They play ever so well together. I love watching them. Just like sisters, they are, and young Heather was ever so thrilled when her dad told her she could sleep here for a night or two until the smell of the new paint is gone in her bedroom.''

Mrs. Ansell paused briefly for breath. ''Was there a message for the doctor, Mr. Paget?''

''No, thank you, Mrs. Ansell. I'll probably talk to her later in the week.''

''I'll tell her you called, then,'' the woman said, ''but it was nothing special. Goodbye, Mr. Paget.''

Paget put the phone down and picked up his tea. Mrs. Ansell was right, he thought wryly. It *was* nothing special. Nothing special at all.

THE GRANDFATHER CLOCK in the hall had just finished striking the half-hour when he heard a car pull up outside. Two-thirty. The sky had cleared, but dusk and lowering clouds were nudging daylight from the stage.

He opened the door. ''Grace, this is a pleasant surprise,'' he greeted her as she ran lightly up the steps.

''Can't stop long,'' she said as he closed the door. She stripped off her gloves and rubbed her hands. ''Heater in the car is on the blink,'' she explained, ''and it's very cold out there.''

''Got time for a cup of tea?'' he asked. ''The fire's on in the living room. Why don't you go in and get warm while I put the kettle on.''

She glanced at her watch. ''That sounds lovely,'' she said, but instead of going into the living room, she followed him into the kitchen and undid her sheepskin-lined coat. The high collar and her golden hair framed her face; her cheeks were pink with cold, and her eyes…

Paget caught his breath. It was as if her presence there had brought new light and life into the house. He stood there, eyes fixed on her face, the kettle in his hand forgotten.

Grace eyed him suspiciously. "What?" she asked, touching her hair self-consciously. "I know my hair's a mess. I must look as if I've been dragged through a hedge backward, but it's been one of those days."

"No, no, really," he assured her hurriedly. "You look absolutely marvellous." He felt his face grow warm, and turned away so she would not see the rush of colour. "What brings you out this way?" he asked to cover his confusion.

"I came to see a neighbour of yours about the New Year's Day walk. Jack Collins. He's our chief marshal. Perhaps you know him. He and his wife, Mary, plan most of the walks for the Border Patrol—that's what we call ourselves since most of our walks criss-cross the Welsh border—and I sometimes give them a hand. We're starting and finishing at the old Claybury Station. It's not a long walk, seven or eight miles, something like that, but for those who feel it's a bit too much"—she grinned—"like convalescing DCIs, there are a couple of optional shortcuts that bring it down to five or three."

Grace settled into a chair. "So, since you've broken in your boots again, and rediscovered the joys of tramping in the hills, I thought I'd pop in and ask if you'd care to join us."

"That was thoughtful of you, Grace. Ummm…" He could barely remember the question. "Can I let you know later?"

A shadow crossed her face. "What is it, Neil?" Her voice was filled with concern. "You sound… I don't know…different. You've been overdoing it again, haven't you? Charlie said you'd been running around the country with Tregalles, and I did wonder." She shook her head in mild exasperation. "Honestly, Neil, you need a minder. You are supposed to be resting. Why don't you relax and let Tregalles and Alcott and the others do their job? They do know what they're doing. I know you hate to be on the sidelines, but there's no telling what damage you might do to yourself if you keep this up."

"It's not that," he said distantly. "It's… Well, perhaps I did overdo it a bit." The words came from some preprogrammed part of the brain that had nothing to do with what he was feeling—an emotion so powerful, so completely unexpected, that he was sure it would betray him if he dared to show his face. He concentrated on the task of warming the teapot, while trying desperately to make sense of what had happened in that moment when he'd looked at Grace just now. It had, quite literally, taken his breath away.

He opened a cupboard and took a deep breath to steady his voice. "Like a biscuit with your tea?" he asked. "Or some of Mrs. Wentworth's shortbread? She made such a lot before she left. I sent some home with Tregalles, but I still have far more than I can eat—or should. It's very good." He arranged an assortment on a plate and set it on the table. "Tea will be ready in a minute."

"There's something wrong, isn't there, Neil? This isn't like you."

He sank into a chair and forced himself to face her across the table. "I'm just tired, that's all," he said. "Sorry I'm such poor company."

"You know," said Grace, "for a man with a reputation for being brilliant, you can be awfully dense when it comes to your own well-being." She smiled when she said it, but concern showed in her eyes. "Please, Neil, let the case alone and let the others do their job. Just concentrate on getting better."

Later, as he saw her to the door, Grace turned to him. "Promise me that you'll get some rest," she said, pulling on her gloves.

"I will," he assured her. "And you take care yourself. How are the roads?"

"A bit icy in spots, but not bad. See you, Neil."

As the car disappeared from sight, Paget was about to close the door when something caught his eye. A flash of light from partway up the hillside on the opposite side of the road. It was gone in a second, but he was sure he hadn't imagined it.

He closed the door and went in search of his binoculars, then moved to the front window and stood behind the curtain.

Adjusting the range, he scanned the hillside. Nothing moved. He'd seen sheep there earlier in the day, but now there wasn't the slightest sign of life. He focused on the spot from which he thought he'd seen the flash of light, slowly working his way up the hill.

There! Tucked almost out of sight was some sort of covering, canvas by the look of it, probably army surplus, and in the dark opening, Paget could see what looked like a man's head. Someone was watching the house.

He set the binoculars aside and picked up the phone.

THE LIGHT HAD GONE, and so had the watcher on the hill. "Lost the trail on the other side of the hill," the dog handler explained. "Must have packed up before we got there and had a car waiting on the track that leads down the back of the hill to the village. We could try asking if anyone down there noticed a strange car coming off the track."

"And tomorrow he'll have another car," Paget snapped angrily, while silently berating himself for not following his instincts and going after the man himself. But it would have taken him at least half an hour to circle round behind the watcher's hide if he were to avoid being seen, so he had done it by the book. He'd called for assistance, explaining what he needed. But it was Sunday, and more than an hour later by the time two constables and a tracker dog arrived in a police car you could spot for miles.

No wonder they'd lost the watcher. He'd even had time to roll up his pup tent or whatever it was and take it with him. All the searchers found was a flat patch in the grass. No cigarette butts, no matches, no empty pop cans or sandwich wrappers. Nothing!

So much for doing it by the book!

TWENTY-SIX

THERE OUGHT TO BE *something* we can do from here," Alcott complained. "This whole thing is taking far too long. The morning briefing was over, and now Alcott, Tregalles, and Ormside stood before the whiteboards containing the information gathered over the weekend.

"I'm afraid it's pretty much out of our hands," Ormside told him. "But we are getting good cooperation from the Met. Since Mr. Paget spoke to him last Friday, Chief Superintendent McKenzie has assigned someone to assist Driscoll with his search of chamber records, while someone else is searching court records for Mr. Justice Harmer's cases. I spoke to DI Reese in Richmond, this morning, and he tells me Dr. Braun spent the weekend working on her records, and she hopes to have a complete list ready for him later in the day. He's going to fax a copy to us, as well as to Mr. McKenzie, who is coordinating things up in London."

"Is he, now?" Alcott muttered as he butted a cigarette. "I suppose Paget arranged that as well, did he?"

"Doesn't hurt to have a friend in high places, though, does it, sir?" Tregalles observed. "Cuts through a lot of unnecessary red tape. As a matter of fact, I was talking to Mr. Paget a few minutes ago, and he said he'd be in later on today—just to see how things were going, like," he added hastily as he saw the look on Alcott's face.

"Then you'd better ring him back," the superintendent told him, "because, despite what he may think, he is not running this show. DCI Paget is on sick leave, and you can tell him from me that if I see him in here today or any other day until he's been given a clean bill of health by his doctor, he'll no longer be on sick leave, he'll be suspended until further notice.''

Tregalles winced. ''Bit drastic, isn't it, sir? I mean, you can hardly blame him; he does have a personal interest in all this.''

But Alcott was adamant. ''I am well aware of that,'' he told Tregalles, ''but I am also aware that DCI Paget has been told over and over again that he could do himself real harm if he persists in disregarding orders. I had a call from his doctor on Friday, asking if I knew where Paget was. He'd been trying to contact him at home, but of course he was with you on your way back from Reading. I didn't tell his doctor that, but, as he pointed out quite forcefully, that's the second time in two weeks that Paget has missed his appointment, and he regarded that as nothing short of irresponsible.''

The superintendent lit another cigarette and drew deeply on it. ''If I'd known he had another appointment, I would never have agreed to his accompanying you to Reading. Now half the people involved in this case think they should be reporting back to him rather than to us. So get on that phone, Tregalles, and make that clear to him. I meant what I said. If he shows his nose in here, he'll be suspended!''

THEY HAD FINISHED morning rounds, and Andrea had been about to escape to the safety of her office when Ivan Stone, her boss and mentor, caught her roughly by the arm and spun her round to face him.

''Just where in God's name were you this morning, Doctor?'' he demanded angrily. ''Because you certainly weren't with me or your patients. You weren't even listening half the time.'' His voice softened slightly. ''That's not like you, Andrea. Are you in some kind of trouble?''

''I'm sorry…'' she began, but he brushed her words aside before she could continue.

"I don't want 'sorry,' I want an explanation," he said brusquely. "And I want to know why you didn't tell me before we started rounds?"

Andrea took in a deep breath and let it out slowly. She found it hard to stand her ground against this man, especially when he was right. She should have begged off this morning. Instead, she'd said nothing, but she'd been unable to hide the turmoil in her mind.

"It...it's personal," she hedged.

"Not when it affects the way you do your job," he snapped. He looked at her for a long moment, his eyes like jet beneath the shaggy brows. "All right," he said at last. "I can't force you to tell me what's troubling you, but I am disappointed that you don't feel that you can trust me. Damn it, woman, if you have a problem at least tell me so that I know what to do. Frankly, this morning's performance was embarrassing for all of us, and if I'd known ahead of time I'd have had you stay behind. So, whatever it is, get it sorted out, because you're no good to me in your present state of mind."

With that, he'd turned and walked away.

His words had stung, and she felt she'd let him down. Stone was a hard man to work for, a demanding man, but she'd learned a lot from him. She'd worked hard to earn his respect, and she believed she had. But she had come very close to losing it this morning—if it wasn't lost already.

Now, in the safety of her office, she sat with her eyes closed, trying to sort out her emotions. Somewhere in the last twenty-four hours, her planned and ordered world had come tumbling down around her.

When had it started? Last night? A week ago? Or was it twenty years ago? And did it really matter? What mattered was that she and Sten had spent the night together, and for the first time in many years she'd felt alive. She hadn't wanted to leave this morning, hadn't wanted him to go; but with the girls stirring in the next room, they'd had no choice.

All she could think of this morning was Sten. It was no

wonder Ivan Stone had been so upset. She'd been on cloud nine—or ten or twenty or nine hundred and ninety-nine! she thought wildly, and stifled the urge to giggle. The moment passed. Stone had every right to be annoyed. Her mind had not been on her job this morning, and she would have to apologize for her behaviour.

Her thoughts returned to Sten. She'd been pleased to see him again after all those years, but she'd never thought of him in, well…that way. He was just a friend, a friend she had known for a long time. They'd had much in common in their earlier years, but both had gone their separate ways. Yet, now that she thought about it, it was as if they had never been apart. Somehow those intervening years didn't matter. She felt comfortable with him.

Last night…Andrea sighed as she thought about last night. She hadn't meant it to happen. *(Hadn't she?)* Sten had stayed on after the girls had gone to bed to make sure that Heather wouldn't have second thoughts about remaining there overnight. The girls had settled down and finally gone to sleep. She and Sten had talked and had another glass of wine, and then Sten got up to leave. She saw him to the door *(had she really wanted him to leave?)* and he'd said good night. She'd pecked him on the cheek…and suddenly she was in his arms and she never wanted him to stop.

Dear Sten. Dear, wonderful Sten. She could hardly wait for the day to end. He'd said he would be waiting.

She opened her eyes and sighed again. She really must apologize to Stone.

KATE REGAN eased herself into a chair and poured herself a cup of tea. She had spent the last hour cleaning and vacuuming, and she was exhausted. Trying to hobble about on crutches when you could only put pressure on one hand was, to say the least, difficult, and vacuuming was an exercise in contortionism, if there was such a word—and if there wasn't, there should be, she thought. Trying to push the beast around while balancing on one foot and propping herself up with one crutch had resulted in some creative postures, but she had managed it. Rick would tell her she shouldn't have done it, but she had to do *something* to pass the time, and it made her feel less of a burden.

She set her cup down. Her arm had started to itch again, and it was driving her mad. She thumped her cast several times with her other hand, flexed her fingers, rolled the cast against the table, but nothing worked. She really must remember to ask Rick to get her a long knitting needle. She had searched the flat for something thin and pliable she could slide down inside the cast, but there was nothing long enough to reach the spot.

Sammy—short for Samantha—Rick's ginger cat, poked her head round the door leading to the bedroom to which she had fled the moment Kate had switching on the Hoover. She looked at the silent machine, then looked at Kate.

"It's all right, Sammy, it's safe to come in, now. I've finished for the day."

Sammy uncoiled her tail and raised it as she padded into the room, then jumped up on the sofa, turned round three times, then settled down and closed her eyes.

The phone rang. Sammy didn't so much as stir. Kate waited. If it was Rick, he would hang up after two rings, then call again in thirty seconds. But the ringing didn't stop. It kept on and on and on as it had twice before that morning. It seemed silly to just sit there and not pick it up, but Rick had been deadly serious when he had told her not to.

"It's for your own good, Kate," he said. "No one knows you're here, so there's no chance of Marshall finding out where you are. As far as those at work are concerned, you're staying with friends, and anyone wishing to contact you can do so by leaving a message with your mother, and she'll pass it on to you."

It had made sense at the time, and she'd agreed to the arrangement after talking to her mother, but now it all seemed

so melodramatic. Even after all the trouble she'd had with
Paul, it was hard to believe that it was he who had set the
fire. After all, there was no actual *proof* that Paul had set it.
Even Rick admitted that he could find no evidence against
Paul. But he'd summed it up succinctly when he said, "Who
else do you know who wants you either back home or dead?"
and to that she'd had no answer.

The phone stopped ringing. She just wished the itching
would stop as well.

Paul Marshall stepped out of the call box at the end of the
street. Still no answer, and he'd seen no movement at the window of the flat, but he felt sure she was there. Even if she
wasn't, he was sure that Proudfoot would know where she
was. There had been something very personal about the way
he had spoken of Kate when he'd barged into the house the
other morning, and sooner or later the man would lead him
to her.

THE BREAK CAME that afternoon, when the contact man in the
Met phoned to say a fax was coming through. "I think this
is what you're looking for," he told Tregalles. "A woman by
the name of Mary Carr was convicted of killing her husband
ten years ago. She was released last April. Driscoll was coun-
sel for the defence, Harmer was the judge, Dr. Braun was the
consultant hired by Driscoll's firm, and Paget was the officer
in charge of the investigation. And since this appears to be
tied in with the killing of Tessa Knowles in Richmond, I've
been instructed to turn everything we have over to AMIP's
Superintendent Bellamy. Any further enquiries should be directed to his office. You'll find his contact number in the
fax."

Tregalles scanned the information as it came through, then
went up the stairs two at a time to Alcott's office. "Looks
like this is it, sir," he said as he laid the message on the desk
in front of the superintendent. Alcott picked it up, read it, then

tossed it on the desk. He lit a cigarette, then sat back in his chair and regarded Tregalles with brooding eyes.

"Go on, say it," he grated harshly.

Tregalles drew a deep breath and plunged straight in. "In that case, the way I see it, sir, is it's all very well for London to say they're heading up the investigation, but everything points to the killer being here, and the sooner we know who we're dealing with, the better."

"Go on."

"Well, sir, there's only one person who can tell us that, isn't there? I'd like to ask DCI Paget to come in as soon as possible."

Alcott drew deeply on his cigarette. God knows he'd tried to keep Paget out of it for the sake of his health, but the man was like a bloody eel and always seemed to find a way to slip back in. But in this case, Tregalles was right. Not only did they need the information, but it was Paget's life that was at risk.

"Very well," he said brusquely. "Let's get him down here." He glanced at the clock. "And tell him not to hang about. We don't want to be here all night."

MARY CARR! Paget remembered the name with something akin to sadness. Good-looking woman; late thirties, dark hair, dark eyes, volatile and high-strung. A successful business-woman and owner of something like half a dozen hairdressing salons, as she liked to call them. Killed her husband of only a few months, stabbed him when she found out he was having an affair with a former secretary. Paget hadn't thought about the woman in years, but he remembered her vividly now as he drove through the narrow lanes late in the afternoon. Daylight was almost gone; broken clouds moved swiftly across the darkening sky, and there were snowflakes in the air.

A far cry from the muggy night in July some ten years ago when he'd been called out late in the evening to a house in

Grenville Crescent, a quiet backwater on the edge of Hampstead. He'd been a DI, then, working out of Rosslyn Hill.

It was a three-storey house, extensively remodelled, with a glassed-in sun room and extended patio at the back, beyond which was a lawn and garden completely enclosed by high, vine-covered walls of stone. The sun room itself was full to overflowing with white rattan furniture, plump, colourful cushions, and semi-tropical plants in large earthenware pots.

The victim was Donald Carr, Mary's second husband. He lay on his side, knees drawn up, hands clasped to his belly as if trying to stem the flow of blood that stained the surface of the parquet floor. He was a small man, slim, sinewy arms and legs, sandy-haired, fortyish. Gold-rimmed glasses lay bent and twisted beneath his head, and there was a cut below his right eye. He wore baggy shorts, cinched in tightly at the waist, a pale blue short-sleeved shirt, and sandals. Cushions from a lounge and one of the chairs were on the floor beside the body.

There was no sign of a weapon.

When the doctor arrived, Paget remained with him only long enough to establish the location and nature of the wounds—three distinct punctures made by a broad-bladed knife just below the ribs—before making his way to the living room to talk to the wife of the victim.

A policewoman met him as he entered the room. "This is Mrs. Carr," she told him, "and her daughter"—What *was* the girl's name? Janet? Jeanette? No, but it was something like that—"and this is her brother, Michael."

Mary Carr was seated on a cushioned high-backed sofa, one arm around the shoulders of her daughter, whom Paget judged to be twelve or thirteen years old. The woman's eyes were red from crying, mascara streaked her cheeks, and her dark hair looked as if she had been running her fingers through it over and over again. She wore a flowered summer dress, sleeveless and very short, revealing shapely legs, and her high-heeled shoes lay on the floor beside her feet.

The girl, in sharp contrast to her mother, was slight, fair-skinned, and blonde. She, too, had been crying, and strands of her long hair were stuck to the side of her face. She wore a rumpled T-shirt, jeans, and trainers, and she pressed closer to her mother as he approached, as if she feared he was about to pull them apart. The boy was fast asleep in a deep armchair. A sturdy lad, dark-haired, and older than his sister by about a year.

In answer to his questions, Mary Carr told him she had been out all evening with a friend, returning shortly after ten o'clock to find her husband lying dead on the floor of the sun room. She said she couldn't believe it at first, but once it did sink in that Carr was dead, her first thoughts had been for the children. She said she'd taken the stairs two at a time, frantically screaming their names—and then there they were at the top of the stairs. Paget remembered her words: "Gillanne was looking at me as if I'd gone mad, then Michael came up behind her, and I just collapsed in a heap on the steps, crying and laughing. I was so thankful to see them alive."

Gillanne…

Paget caught his breath. It was winter; it was snowing; his eyes were on the road, and yet what he was seeing was from another time, another place.

"Oh my God!" he breathed softly. *"Gill-aaanne,"* the name drawn out as if they were two separate names. Said quickly in guttural tones as a razor slashed toward his throat, they had sounded like… *Jill and*…

He spoke the words aloud. *"Jill and… It's your fault Jill and…died the way she did. It's your fault Gill-anne died the way she did. Now it's your turn, Chief Inspector!"*

He didn't know whether to feel relieved or angry. Gillanne! Until tonight he had forgotten the girl's name completely. Almost forgotten Mary. And, assuming it was she who had attacked him, she hadn't been talking about Jill at all. She'd been talking about her daughter, Gillanne. *He* was the one who had misinterpreted the words. He and his paranoia, his guilt complex, or whatever it was that refused to let him see beyond the death of his wife.

It was cold in the car, but he found himself sweating. If it was Mary Carr behind that light, what had she meant when she'd said, "It's your fault she died the way she did"? Gillanne hadn't died—at least, not as far as he knew.

TWENTY-SEVEN

BY THE TIME he reached the junction with the main road, it had begun to snow in earnest. It was the end of a working day, and a steady stream of traffic flowed toward him, headlights flared against the falling snow. His eyes were fixed intently on the road, but he was seeing images from the past.

Gillanne Carr was a child in transition. Thirteen years old, a beautiful child on the verge of becoming a beautiful young woman. She was very tense, but slowly, carefully, Paget had coaxed information from the girl while her brother slept. When Paget asked why he was sleeping, Gillanne said he'd taken an antihistamine tablet earlier in the evening, and it always made him sleepy. "Allergies," she explained. "They're always bad for Michael in the spring and summer."

She went on to tell him that she and her brother had been upstairs all evening, building a model destroyer. She said Michael loved to build models, but sometimes he had trouble with the instructions, so she would help him. There was something about the way she glanced at her mother when she told him this that made Paget curious, but Mary Carr anticipated the question, and spoke first.

"It takes Michael a bit longer than others to learn things," she said in a tone of voice that closed the subject.

But Gillanne wasn't content to leave it there. "He is all right," she assured Paget earnestly. "I mean he's not retarded or anything like that. It does take him a bit longer to pick things up, but once he's got them, he does as well as anyone else, doesn't he, Mum?"

Her mother had given her a brief hug. "The inspector's waiting," she said. "Just tell him what you told me."

There had been little enough to tell. Working in Michael's room, Gillanne said, she'd heard the doorbell ring, then heard her stepfather talking to someone as he let them in. No, she hadn't seen who it was—she hadn't left Michael's room all evening—but she was quite sure it was a man's voice she'd heard. No, she hadn't heard him leave.

When asked if she could tell him what time it was when the visitor arrived, Gillanne said she thought it would be about nine o'clock. She hadn't looked at the time, but thought it would be about an hour before her mother had come home.

Asked about possible enemies or if Carr had been threatened, Mary brushed such thoughts aside completely. "He was a very kind and gentle man," she said. "Everybody liked him. He was my first husband's partner in the firm for twelve years, so I think I'd have known if he had any enemies."

"Which firm is that?"

"Lawrence and Carr, Printers and Stationers, in the High Street, not far from where you work, Inspector. Not the sort of business where you make enemies, is it?" A fleeting smile. "That is unless you're late with someone's wedding invitations."

He had let Michael sleep, then spoken to him the following morning, but the boy proved to be even less helpful than his sister. He said he didn't remember hearing anyone downstairs. Too busy working on his model.

The post-mortem established that Donald Carr had died of a single stab wound penetrating the heart. The other two wounds had done a fair amount of damage, but would not have been fatal by themselves. The weapon was a thin, broad-bladed knife, such as an ordinary kitchen or carving knife, and several bruises on Carr's neck, arms, and shoulders suggested that there could have been a struggle. But most disappointing, as far as Paget was concerned, was the lack of certainty about the time of death.

It had been a hot and humid night, and Carr's body had been found in the sun room. By no means an insurmountable problem as far as establishing the approximate time of death, but the police surgeon, who had first examined the body, made an error in recording the body temperature. To compound the problem, Carr was a vegetarian, and he tended to eat sparingly, paying little attention to what others considered normal mealtimes. While Mary and the children all agreed that Carr had not eaten dinner with them, they had no idea what or when he had eaten. The pathologist, therefore, allowed for a wide margin of error and placed time of death between eight-thirty and eleven.

The police canvassed the neighbours, but no one had noticed anyone entering or leaving the Carrs' house after Mary left. Her next-door neighbour said she had spoken to Mary when she left the house around seven o'clock, and she had seen Mary's car in the driveway later on. "But I've no idea what time it was," she confessed. "Mary comes and goes at all hours."

On the assumption that the killer had taken the knife with him, and would want to dispose of it as quickly as possible, Paget had had the gardens searched on both sides of the street, and when that proved fruitless, he had turned his attention to the victim. Mary described Donald Carr in glowing terms. Not only had he been her first husband's partner, she told him, but he'd been a friend of the family for years, and when Trevor Lawrence suffered a stroke and died at the age of thirty-nine, Carr had helped her through a difficult time. They had become close friends, and were married a year later.

"I shall always miss Trevor," she'd said somewhat defensively, "but it wasn't as if I hadn't known Donald for a long time."

Tracy Morgenson—the friend with whom Mary Carr said she'd spent the evening—was a woman of about thirty-five, small, brisk and forthright, yet she had seemed strangely uneasy when answering Paget's questions; so uneasy, in fact, that he'd had her come to the station for further questioning. Once there, and realizing that everything she said was being recorded, she'd changed her story.

She told Paget she had worked as a secretary for the two partners for several years before leaving to get married. But prior to working as a secretary for Lawrence and Carr, she had been trained as a hairdresser, and later, when she was looking for a part-time job, Mary had asked her to work for her. Three years later, when Mary opened another salon, she had asked Tracy to run it.

"Mary was devastated when Trevor died," she told him, "and Don did a lot to help her through it, but I was really surprised when she told me she and Don were to be married."

"Why was that?"

Tracy looked uncomfortable. "Look, Mary is my friend, and I don't want to talk behind her back, but…" She'd looked at the tape, then back again at Paget. "You see, Mary looks strong and self-sufficient, but she's the sort who needs a man; she needs to be told that someone loves her, and to be honest, I wasn't sure that Don was the right man for her. But what could I say? I mean, they got on well together, and the marriage seemed to be working out all right at first."

"But something changed?"

Tracy nodded. "I didn't know anything was wrong until a couple of weeks ago, when Mary came round to see me. She was upset. Said she didn't think Don loved her anymore, and wanted to know if I thought there was something wrong with her. See, Mary…well, she enjoys the sex, and from what I gathered Don was keeping her very happy, both before and after they were married. But she said he'd gone off her these last few months. Kept making excuses not to have sex, and she was worried.

"I knew then that Don hadn't changed since I worked there. He always had some woman on a string; sometimes more than one at the same time, and believe me, I know, because I used to take some of their phone calls. It might have been all right while he was single, but not once he'd married Mary, and I told her so. Big mistake. Mary certainly didn't thank me for it, I can tell you. Went off in a high old dudgeon, but I think deep down she knew I was right.''

''This was a couple of weeks ago, you said?''

''That's right.''

''So what about the night Donald Carr was killed?''

''Mary rang me about one o'clock in the morning to tell me what had happened. It was after the police had gone. She was in a blind panic, and wanted me to swear that she had been with me all evening until ten. She swore to me that she'd had nothing to do with Don's death, but said she couldn't tell the police where she'd been; said she would explain everything later, and she did when I spoke to her the next day.

''She told me I'd been wrong about Don. She said she'd spent the last few nights sitting in her car in the car park of the supermarket at the end of their road, watching the house, but Don had never left it. She said if I considered myself her friend, the least I could do now was back her story up and say she was with me that night.''

''And you agreed.''

Tracy shrugged. ''I didn't see any harm in it at the time. I mean, I've known Mary a long time, and I like her, but... Well, now I don't know what to think.''

There were five people on staff at Lawrence and Carr, Printers and Stationers. Four of them had expressed shock and sorrow and shaken their heads when asked if Carr had any enemies, but the fifth one, a short, stout, grey-haired man by the name of Lou Hines, painted a very different picture.

''Not *enemies* as such,'' he said thoughtfully, ''but if you'd told me it was Mary who killed him, I wouldn't have been surprised, 'specially if she'd found out about his bit on the side. Mary's not the sort to put up with that.''

''Are you saying that Donald Carr was having an affair?'' Paget asked him. ''Do you have any proof?''

Lou took out a battered tin of tobacco and papers, and

began to roll a cigarette. "If it's proof you want, you won't have to look very far. It's young Robyn. Used to work here in the office until Mary persuaded Don to get rid of her. Liked to think she was posh because she spelt Robyn with a *y*. Proper little cock teaser, she was. Just a bit of a thing, but really built, if you know what I mean. Skirts up to her bum, blouse open down to her belly button, or close to it. Talk about fallout when she bent over; I mean, she was a safety hazard around here every time she opened the filing cabinet."

"Where is she now?"

Lou stuck the cigarette in his mouth and lit it. Paget watched with fascination as the paper flared and burnt halfway down the cigarette.

"Got a flat over on Norfolk Street." He jerked a thumb over his right shoulder. "Don set her up there. Goes over there most afternoons—or he did. She can't be more than half his age. Wonder he didn't die of exhaustion, what with keeping her happy and Mary as well. And she must have cost him a packet. I reckon that's why he married Mary. Her business makes more money than ours; has done for years. He married Mary, but Robyn was pulling his chain."

"Do you know if Mrs. Carr had any idea about what was going on?"

Lou took the limp cigarette from his mouth and eyed it critically. "Dunno." He shrugged. "Somebody could've told her, I suppose."

"How do you know about this set-up with Robyn…what's her last name?"

"Summers. Robyn Summers. And it's not just me; everybody in the shop knows. Just ask 'em. You could hear him on the phone to her all the time."

By the time Paget left the print shop, Mary Carr's description of a warm and caring husband had taken on a completely different meaning, and if Tracy Morgenson and Lou Hines were right, it could be argued that Mary could have killed her husband in a jealous rage.

The scene faded from his mind as the lights of Broadminster appeared over the lip of the hill and he began the long descent into the valley. He geared down, slowed to a crawl, then stopped behind a line of cars. Flashing lights ahead marked the scene of an accident. Uniformed police were milling about in the road, and an ambulance, lights flashing, was grinding its way up the hill, forcing cars to the side as it tried to get to the scene.

He settled down to wait, his thoughts drifting back in time.

He had spoken to Robyn Summers. She was all Lou had said she was as far as looks and figure went, but her main concern had been for her own future: things such as who was going to pay the rent, and what was going to happen to her now that Carr was gone.

"Mind you, I'm sorry he's dead," she said perfunctorily, "but I knew something was up. I mean, he used to come round three times a week regular as clockwork, even after he married that cow, Mary, but I haven't seen much of him lately. Kept saying he had a lot of work on, but I didn't believe him. To tell you the truth, I began to think he actually preferred her to me—I know it's hard to believe, but she isn't all that bad looking, considering her age, and even Don said she wasn't bad in bed. But when she came round here last week and accused me of taking him away from her, I didn't know what to think. She was in a right old mood, I can tell you. Started screaming at me the minute I opened the door. You wouldn't believe the things she called me!"

"Mary Carr came round here? She knew about you and her husband?"

Robyn Summers lit a cigarette and blew a stream of smoke toward the ceiling. "Somebody told her. I reckon it was Lou down at the shop."

"Why do you think it was him?"

She shrugged. "Getting his own back. He used to try to grope me when I worked there, so I slapped his face in front of everybody. He didn't like that, but he deserved it. Randy old sod. Mind you, I wasn't going to let Mary have it all her own way, not after what she called me. I gave her something to think about, believe me.'' Robyn Summers grinned maliciously. "I told her Don said he always thought of me when he was humping her, because that was the only way he could manage it.'' She chuckled. ''That stopped her, I can tell you. If you think she was mad before, you should have seen her then. I thought she was going to explode. She went red in the face and just stood there shaking. To tell you the truth, she scared me. I thought she was going to fly at me, so I slammed the door on her and locked it.''

Mary Carr's version of her encounter with Robyn Summers was somewhat different. She said that Donald Carr had told her of what he'd called a brief affair with Summers, but had assured her it had ended long before he married Mary, and she believed him. But Summers couldn't accept the fact that Donald was finished with her, and had tried to stir up trouble between them, so Mary had gone round to warn her off.

"You say you trusted your husband, and yet you have admitted spying on him by watching the house. That doesn't sound like trust to me,'' Paget told her.

"I wasn't *spying*. I did trust Donald. I knew he loved me, and he'd finished with her, but I just had to be *sure*, that's all. And I am sure. He never did leave the house while I was out.''

"Did you kill your husband?''

"No! Donald was dead when I got back. It was a man. Gillanne told you she heard him downstairs with Donald long before I got home.''

"But you were watching the house from the end of the road. You would have seen someone going up to the house.''

"Well, I didn't.''

"Neither entering nor leaving the house? Strange. Was that because there was no man? Was your daughter lying when she said she heard a man enter the house?''

"No! Why should Gillanne lie?''

"I should have thought that was obvious—to protect her mother, of course."

Even now, so many years later, Paget remembered the stubborn set of Mary's jaw as she said, "I know you won't believe me, but the truth is I fell asleep. You know what it's like when you are concentrating hard on something. I'd hardly taken my eyes off the house all evening, and suddenly I came awake, and I had no idea how long I'd been asleep, but it was going on ten o'clock."

"I do find that hard to believe, Mrs. Carr. Very hard indeed. Why didn't you tell us this in the beginning?"

"Because I knew you wouldn't believe me, but it's the truth."

They searched the house and garden, and found a knife buried in a flower bed at the edge of the patio. It had been wiped clean, but Forensic found enough traces of blood between the blade and handle to identify it as matching that of Donald Carr. Although not part of a set, the knife did match others in the kitchen drawers, but more damning was the fact that the blade matched exactly the wounds in Donald Carr's body.

Paget remembered as if it were yesterday going to the house two days later, accompanied by a WPC and a social worker, and Mary Carr's reaction. She'd seemed almost resigned to the idea of being taken into custody, but when she realized the children were to be taken into care, she'd gone berserk and attacked the policewoman who had tried to calm her down.

It had been bedlam; mother screaming, daughter crying, the boy, clutching his sister's arm, bewildered by what was happening. Mary Carr was still screaming as she was half carried, half dragged to the car, calling her daughter's name.

Paget squeezed his eyes shut and opened them again. His head was beginning to throb, and the lights surrounding the accident ahead seemed to dance before his eyes. He leaned back against the headrest and closed them, and saw the distorted face of Mary Carr as she screamed her daughter's name, *Gill-aaanne… Gill-aaanne!*

He heard engines starting up, and opened his eyes. The cars were moving. The ambulance had gone, and a yellow-jacketed policeman was calling him on. The images of the past dissolved as he started his engine and slipped it into gear.

TWENTY-EIGHT

THEY WERE GATHERED in Alcott's office, Paget, Tregalles, and the superintendent himself. It was ten past six; the snow was beginning to thicken on the ledge outside the window, but no one had given a thought to going home, listening in silence as Paget recounted what he remembered of the case.

"I find it hard to believe that Mary Carr is behind these killings," he concluded. "Certainly the voice I heard bore no resemblance to that of the woman I remember. When was she released?"

"Last April," Tregalles told him. "Apparently she could have been paroled after eight years, but the board asked for a psychiatric evaluation, and she was held back for another couple of years."

"Which means we probably have a nutcase on our hands," Alcott observed grimly.

"Even so, she has to have a motive that makes sense to her if not to anyone else, and if something did happen to her daughter while Mary was in prison, she may have transferred the blame to those who put her there."

"Was there ever any doubt about her guilt?" asked Alcott.

Paget blew out his cheeks and shrugged. "Everything we had *pointed* to Mary as the one who killed her husband, but the evidence was all circumstantial, and I can't say I'm ever very happy about presenting a case based on that alone. But you know how it works: we gather the evidence and present it to the CPS, and they put it under their legal microscopes and decide whether or not to proceed. In this case, they felt the case was strong enough to go ahead.''

Alcott eyed him narrowly. ''Tell me this,'' he said. ''If you'd been on the jury, would you have voted to convict on the evidence?''

''I don't know. As I say, everything pointed to her guilt, but there was always a bit of a question mark in my mind about what did happen there that night. The one thing that did bother me was how Mary could have killed Carr, then left the house again while the children were still upstairs.''

''Perhaps they knew. Perhaps she coached them—or at least the daughter—to say she'd heard a man in the house.''

''Perhaps,'' said Paget neutrally as he turned to Tregalles. ''Do we have anything on the children?'' he asked. ''Anything on where they are now or what happened to them? The one thing I do remember about Mary Carr is that she seemed to be far more concerned about their fate—especially that of Gillanne—than she was about herself. She wanted them to go to their grandmother, but there was some reason why that couldn't be done; the grandmother was ill or something, so they were sent to a foster home. I don't remember the details, but I do remember Mary was most upset when she found out what had happened to them.''

''I don't have anything,'' Tregalles said, ''but I can check to see if the Met has anything on them.''

Paget nodded. ''Especially Michael. If we are dealing with Mary Carr, she had an accomplice, and that could be Michael. But no matter who it is, the sooner we find Mary, the better, and one of the first things we must do is contact Dr. Braun and Lionel Driscoll and ask them to dig up everything they have on the case. Also, Theresa White may be able to help us, because one of the things she mentioned when I spoke to her was that she had worked in Holloway for several years, which may prove to be the connection there. So tomorrow, we should—''

But Alcott cut him off with an impatient wave of the hand.

"We will take care of it tomorrow," he said firmly. "*You* are still on sick leave, and you wouldn't be here now if it weren't for the fact that we needed your input. For which," he continued as Paget started to protest, "we are very grateful. But this is not your case, so the sooner you go back home and get some proper rest, the sooner you'll be back to work. In the meantime, we—"

The phone rang. He glanced at the time and scowled as he scooped it up. "Alcott," he said tersely. He listened for a couple of moments, then said, "He's here now, as it happens, but he is still on sick leave, so… Yes, I do understand, but it's not…"

Alcott looked grim as he placed the palm of his hand over the transmitter.

"It's Superintendent Bellamy," he told Paget. "Since you were directly involved in the Mary Carr case, he wants you to come to London to assist with the investigation. Personally, I don't think you should go. You've been pushing yourself too hard already, and your doctor—"

"My doctor told me I could do whatever I felt comfortable doing," Paget interjected, "and I think you will agree I've managed to cope so far. I'll admit I'm not completely up to par, but if it will help in any way, I'm quite prepared to go."

Alcott eyed him for a long moment, then sighed resignedly. Even as he had warned Paget to stay home and rest, he'd known very well that the DCI would not be content to stay there. So why not give in gracefully, give the man his blessing and be done with it? Besides, it wouldn't hurt to have someone in the Met indebted to him, someone with a bit of pull like Bellamy. You never knew when you might want a favour in return.

He put the telephone to his ear. "He'll be there," he told the superintendent. "I'll put him on, and you can tell him where and when."

SOMEONE HAD tipped off the press, and despite the cautious wording of the official press release the following morning, the headlines came out screaming: SLASHER TERRORIZES COUNTRY, WOMEN STALKED BY SERIAL KILLER, RAZOR RAMPAGE, and more.

Superintendent Bellamy went on national television at noon to assure everyone that the police had matters well in hand, that there was no danger to the general public, and he was confident that an early arrest would be made. He answered questions in measured tones, and made sure the cameras did not see his fingers crossed beneath the table.

ALTHOUGH HE'D ALLOWED himself ample time, it was midafternoon by the time Paget arrived in London. He had turned south at Burford after hearing reports of mile-long tailbacks on the M40 due to fog, but between patches of wet snow and ice-slick hills around Wantage, he'd made no better time. And when at last he managed to make his way over to the M4, the traffic was so heavy he began to wonder if the entire population of the West Country had decided to migrate to London.

He reported to Superintendent Bellamy at his office in Scotland Yard, where the superintendent greeted him by looking at his watch and saying, "You cut it a bit fine, I must say, Paget. The others are already here, so the sooner we get on with it, the better."

"The others?" Paget queried.

"Dr. Braun, Driscoll, and Dr. White. They're waiting for us in the conference room. I have the court records of the trial of Mary Carr, but not her prison records or progress reports. They should be here later on today. Between us, I'm hoping we can work up some sort of profile that will help us find her. Do you have any ideas?"

"Just one thing. Do you have anything on the whereabouts of the children? Michael would be about twenty-four or -five by now, and Gillanne would be a year younger."

"No. Anything else before we go in?"

"Just that I think we should warn anyone else who might have been involved in Mary Carr's conviction. Driscoll was leading the defence, but what about her solicitor, and whoever it was that led the prosecution?"

"Gordon Billingsley was her solicitor. He'd done quite a bit of work for the printing firm over the years, and was a good friend of her first husband, Trevor Lawrence. He still works out of the same office in Finchley Road. He's been contacted, but says he hasn't heard from Mrs. Carr, and isn't particularly worried. He says he always got on well with her, and can't believe that she's behind the killings."

Paget grimaced. "I'd have been inclined to say the same thing about her until recently," he said.

"Brendan Carrington, QC, led the prosecution," Bellamy continued. "Died three years ago. I don't see any danger there, but the family has been warned just in case."

"What about Mary's relatives?" asked Paget. "We might get a lead through them. I believe her mother lives somewhere in North London, at least she did then, and there may be others."

"Golders Green," Bellamy confirmed. "A Mrs. Edith Chambers. DI Wallace is out there now. Perhaps he'll get lucky and find Mary Carr out there, but I'm not counting on it."

EDITH CHAMBERS LOOKED older than her seventy-five years. Her hair was white and her face deeply lined, and her skin was dry and yellowed like the colour of ancient parchment. She looked and sounded frail, but DI Wallace detected a stubborn streak beneath the surface. While others searched the small house for anything that might lead them to her daughter, Mrs. Chambers sat quietly beside the electric fire, seemingly detached from the activity around her.

Wallace leaned forward in his chair. "Look, Mrs. Chambers," he said earnestly, "we know that Mary spent several days here with you when she came out. We also know that you withdrew six thousand pounds from your account three days after Mary's release. Did you give that money to Mary?''

"So what if I did?" the woman said defiantly. "It was my money; I can do what I like with it. After all she's been through, she needed it to get a fresh start."

"And what sort of start would that be, Mrs. Chambers?"

The woman sighed heavily. "Not that it's any of your business, but an old friend of hers offered her a job when she came out. She's got a little shop up north somewhere. Sheffield or Leeds, I don't remember exactly, and she told Mary that if she could bring a bit of money into the business, she'd expand the shop and Mary could come to work as a partner."

"What's the name of this friend?"

"I don't know," the woman said irritably. "She did tell me, but my memory's that poor since my husband died and I've been living on my own. I can't remember things like I used to."

"What kind of shop?"

"Hairdressing salon. One of them unisex places. Not that she should have to start all over again at her age, but she had to sell her shops to pay the lawyers. She still had her share of the print shop, but it went bankrupt six years ago, and she was left with nothing."

"When did you last hear from her?"

"She's been very busy, I expect," the woman hedged. "I mean, it stands to reason. There'll be work to do on the shop, and she'll need time to get her hand in again. She'll ring when she's ready."

"Are you telling me she hasn't contacted you since last April? Not even a letter or phone call?"

Edith Chambers lifted her chin. "Like I said, she'll ring when she's ready."

Wallace shook his head. "Frankly, Mrs. Chambers, I have trouble believing that. You say you loaned her a substantial sum of money to help her get started again, and yet she's never so much as spoken to you since then? Nobody is *that* busy. Now tell me, where is Mary, really? We have to talk to her.''

"So's you can put her back inside? That's all you want, isn't it? Don't you think you've done enough? She's done her time, and paid dearly for something she didn't do, so leave the girl alone.''

A constable entered the room. "Excuse me, sir," he said, "but I think you might like to see this." He held up a clear plastic bag with what looked like letters inside.

"No! No! You've no right! They're mine!" Mrs. Chambers protested as she pushed herself out of her chair and started forward. But Wallace was there before her.

"Where did you find these?" he asked.

"Hidden beneath some underwear at the bottom of a drawer in the bedroom. They appear to be letters from Mrs. Carr to her mother. There are seven of them, and one of them was posted in Poole, September eighth. Right next door, you might say, to Bournemouth, where Penny Crofton was killed September tenth.''

"You leave them be. They're mine!" the woman cried again as she tried to snatch the letters, but Wallace easily fended her off. "Leeds, eh?" he said. "Or maybe Sheffield? I think you'd better get your coat, Mrs. Chambers. My super's going to want to have a chat with you.''

SUPERINTENDENT BELLAMY sat at the head of a long rectangular table. He was fiftyish, narrow-faced and lean; his deep-set eyes reminded Paget of a watchful bird as he looked at each of them in turn.

Seated on the superintendent's left was Dr. Braun, crisp and businesslike in tweeds, plain white blouse, dark stockings, and sensible shoes. A slim leather pouch lay on the table in front of her. Next to her was Lionel Driscoll in his dark blue business suit, still looking slightly red in the face after lugging a heavy briefcase up the stairs—his one and only concession of the day to his doctor's advice to get more exercise.

Paget sat on Bellamy's right, and next to him was Theresa White. Short and heavyset, she wore an oatmeal-coloured pullover, dark brown corduroy trousers, and thick-soled boots.

She spoke now with bitterness. "The woman should never have been let out onto the streets," she said flatly. "I found Mary Carr to be one of the most recalcitrant people I've ever had to deal with. Stubborn, sullen, hard to handle. She showed no remorse for what she'd done, and flatly refused to accept responsibility for her crime. Right to the very last she maintained that someone else had killed her husband, and she'd been imprisoned falsely. And that was what I told the parole board on both occasions when her application came up. I told them I believed she was mentally unstable, and couldn't be trusted. I managed to persuade them to have her sent for psychiatric assessment the first time round, but not the second. Mary could be very cunning, and she managed to fool them all the second time, and what with a favourable psychiatrist's report, and playing on the sympathies of some of the bleeding hearts on the board with that voice of hers, she persuaded them to let her go, and it was my Gerald who paid the price."

"That voice of hers?" said Paget sharply. "What do you mean by that, exactly, Doctor? I don't recall your mentioning that when we spoke a few days ago."

"I had no reason to, did I, Chief Inspector? We didn't know at that time that it was Mary behind these killings, did we? You asked me about a telephone call, and I told you it was a man's voice. Mary wouldn't have dared ring me herself, I would have recognized her voice immediately."

It was true. When Paget had asked her about the phone call, she had told him she had been extremely distraught at the time, and all she could tell him was that she believed it was a man who called. She had become quite emotional while telling him, and he had not pursued it further.

"How would you describe Mary's voice?"

"Hoarse and rasping like that of a heavy smoker," she told him. "Most unpleasant."

"She certainly didn't sound like that when I knew her," he said. "What happened, Doctor?"

"It's in her record," she said impatiently. "I should have thought you'd have those details at your fingertips, Chief Inspector."

"If you mean her prison records," Bellamy broke in, "we don't have those yet, so please tell us what you know."

"Oh, very well," the doctor said, and sighed resignedly. "It happened when she tried to hang herself after her daughter committed suicide. I wasn't there then, of course, but I've read my predecessor's notes. Personally, knowing Mary, I doubt if she really meant to kill herself at all. I think it was just another pathetic attempt to gain sympathy. Pity she didn't complete the job, if you ask me. At least my son would be alive."

One corner of Theresa White's mouth lifted upward in a twisted smile. "Broke her larynx doing it, though, and she never could talk properly again."

Paget was staring in stunned amazement at this bitter woman. A dozen questions crowded into his mind, but all he could say was, "Gillanne committed suicide? When was this, Doctor?"

"About six weeks after her mother was sent down. But you must have known. You were the arresting officer. I don't see how it could have escaped your attention."

Paget cast his mind back, conscious of everyone's eyes upon him as they waited for an explanation. Six weeks after... Suddenly it was clear why he had never known of Gillanne's suicide.

He turned to Bellamy. "That was the time of the IRA bombing in the West End," he said. "If you recall, every available officer was brought in to aid in the search. I was one of them, and I had nothing to do with the case from that point on. My assignment went on for weeks, twelve to sixteen hours a day, and when it was over, I was transferred to Brompton to fill a vacancy there."

Superintendent Bellamy turned to Krista Braun. "What was your assessment of Mrs. Carr at the time of her trial, Doctor?"

The doctor put on her reading glasses and picked up a single sheet of paper. "I must admit I don't remember the woman well at all," she said, "but I was reminded of two things when I was going through my notes: first, she steadfastly maintained that she was innocent of any crime, and second, she was more worried about what was going to happen to her children, especially her daughter, than she was about her own fate. I had three sessions with her in all, but by the time we started the third session, she had become so despondent and unresponsive that it was hard to get a straight answer from her. In fact, at one point she accused me of being part of a conspiracy to 'fit her up' for the murder of her husband, as she put it, and told me to go to hell. I recommended a psychiatric evaluation at that time, but it was never acted upon to the best of my knowledge."

Krista Braun took off her glasses and set the paper on the table. "I would have liked to spend more time with her, but there were other pressures, and it wasn't possible, I'm afraid."

"Thank you, Doctor." Bellamy turned to Driscoll, who was nodding. "What can you tell us about Mary Carr, Mr. Driscoll?"

The man smiled grimly as he pulled a file from his briefcase and opened it. "Interesting," he observed, glancing at Braun, "because Mary Carr said much the same thing to me. She accused me of being on the side of the police, but when I asked her if she wanted someone else to defend her, she said there wasn't any point, since we were all against her. And I can confirm what Dr. Braun said about the children. I don't know how many times we would be in the middle of a discussion when she would suddenly break off and say, 'Gillanne. Where is she? I want to see Gillanne. We're a family; we should be together.'"

"She didn't mention Michael?" Paget asked.

"She did, but it was always my impression that it was her daughter she was most concerned about."

He set the file aside and looked around the table. "I had several sessions with the girl before the trial, because I wanted to be certain in my own mind that her testimony would stand up to cross-examination. She was just a little slip of a thing, but fiercely protective of her mother, and I had a hard time convincing her that all we wanted from her was the simple truth and nothing more. Which was, of course, that she had heard a man enter the house that night."

Driscoll said, "She did well at first, but when Carrington challenged her on what she claimed to have heard, she began to embellish the story, and it became clear to everyone that the girl would say anything if she thought it might save her mother. I knew then that we'd lost the case, and I think she realized that as well."

It's your fault Gillanne is dead! Yours and all the others.

Paget shivered. It was as if an icy finger had touched his spine. There could be little doubt now that it had been Mary Carr who had tried to kill him, blaming him and the others for her daughter's death.

"You must have known of Gillanne's suicide," he said to Driscoll.

"Oh, yes. The girl left a note saying that she had told the truth at the trial; that there was a man in the house, and her mother was innocent. I launched an appeal based on it, but the appeal was denied, I'm afraid."

"On what grounds?"

"The court was sympathetic, but said the girl's statement was disjointed and rambling, and simply restated what she had said at the trial, and that testimony had been discredited."

"Tell me, sir, how did Gillanne die?"

A shadow darkened Driscoll's face. "She returned to her mother's house and slashed her wrists. She wasn't found for several days."

"I DON'T KNOW WHERE Mary is, and even if I did, I wouldn't tell you," Edith Chambers said defiantly. "Not after what you did to her."

"We have to find her," Bellamy insisted. "You can see for yourself what she did to Chief Inspector Paget, and there have been others—one a very young woman just starting out in life. She didn't deserve to die simply because her grandfather was the judge at Mary's trial."

Edith Chambers flicked a glance at the raw scar on Paget's throat, now exposed for all to see. It had been Bellamy's idea to leave the covering off. Her eyes slid away, but her mouth remained set in a stubborn line.

Paget said, "I didn't understand what your daughter was saying at the time, Mrs. Chambers, but I realize now that she was telling me it was my fault that Gillanne died. Tell me about Gillanne and her brother. What happened to them after Mary went to prison? There was some reason why they couldn't stay with you, wasn't there?"

Edith Chambers looked down at her hands. She remained silent for a long time, then slowly lifted her eyes to meet Paget's own. Her thin lips quivered, and a tear rolled down her cheek.

"I *wanted* to have them," she said, "but they wouldn't let me. I tried; I really did try. I pleaded with them, but they wouldn't listen. Took both kids away, they did. Then Dad got worse, and I had to look after him; there was no one else, no one to help. Later, Gilly ran away from the home and came round to help. She loved her gramps, and she wanted to stay, but they came and took her back again, and it didn't matter what I said or anyone else said, they knew best."

She took a proffered tissue from Bellamy and wiped her eyes.

More to clarify the record than because there was any doubt in his mind, Bellamy asked, "Who knew best, Mrs. Chambers?"

"The social people." She sat forward in her chair. "See,

Dad had lung cancer, and it was only a matter of time before he died. He didn't want to be stuck in hospital when his time came, so I was looking after him at home. It was a full-time job, I can tell you, 'specially near the end, but I didn't mind. Neither did the kids. Gilly and Michael would have been glad to help, but the Social Services wouldn't have it. They said I was supposed to be looking after the kids, not the other way round, so they were fostered out. Gilly ran away twice and came to me, but they took her back and put her somewhere else so's I wouldn't know where she was. They even told me I could be arrested if I didn't report her if she came again.''

Edith Chambers shook her head sadly. "Poor child. She was at her wits' end. Her mother was in jail, and there was talk of moving Michael to another home. I've never seen a child as upset as she was. She kept saying, 'I've got to do something, Gran, but I don't know what to do.' She and her mother were very close, 'specially after Trevor died. Then, of course, Donald came along and things were a bit different then.''

"How do you mean?"

"Well, they just are, aren't they? Not that it made any real difference. Donald was a lovely man. Oh, I know what they said about him and that tart in court, but she was just out for what she could get. Splashed all over the papers; made a bit of money out of it, and then she was off after someone else, I shouldn't wonder. Thought the world of the children, Donald did.''

"What did they think of him?" Paget asked. "Coming in to take their father's place.''

Mrs. Chambers made a face. "Gilly wasn't all that keen at first, of course. She'd had her mum all to herself for a good while, but she soon got over it. She was a sensible girl." Her eyes misted over as she looked from Paget to Bellamy and back again, and when she spoke again, her voice was pitched so low they had to strain to hear. "I still wake up in the night and hear her screaming as they dragged her away that first time. Screaming for me to do something. Anything. But what *could* I do? I was exhausted, what with looking after Dad and everything.''

She fell silent. The tape whispered on, and when she spoke again, her voice was flat and toneless. ''The last time I saw her, alive, was the day of Dad's funeral. Somehow or other the kids knew, and they both turned up at the house. But the police came round looking for them. Gillanne managed to get away, but they took Michael. Accused me of hiding Gillanne, but I hadn't.

''Took 'em three days to find her. Back at the house where she grew up. It had been locked up after the police were finished with it, and Mary's solicitor had the key. But Gilly knew where the spare was, and she went in the back door and locked it behind her. She went upstairs and took out the box of things that belonged to her dad—her real dad, Trevor— things Mary had saved. She found his razor. She must have known it was there.''

Edith Chambers raised her eyes to look beyond the room to a distant time, a distant place. ''He always used a straight razor, Trevor did. Real ivory handle, carved with his initials on it. They said Gilly went upstairs to the bathroom, got undressed, laid her clothes all neat and tidy in a pile, then tried to cut her throat. They said there were marks where she'd tried, but when that didn't work, she ran the bath, then got in and cut both her wrists. First I knew of it was when the police came round and said they wanted me to identify the body. Nice as pie, they were then, of course.'' Her eyes hardened. ''Bastards!''

TWENTY-NINE

HAD MARY CARR been innocent? Had Gillanne been telling the truth? Or had she lied to save her mother? Had Mary coached her daughter? Was that why Mary had held Gillanne so close while she was being questioned? Alternatively, had Gillanne killed her stepfather, then made up the story about a man being in the house? But if that was true, why hadn't she said so in the note she left behind? These and other questions crowded into Paget's mind, but the biggest question of all was: What had driven the girl to take her own life? She'd said in her note that it was because no one believed she was telling the truth, but there had to be more to it than that.

Michael had to be considered as well, although there was nothing to suggest that he had been involved; in fact, he had seemed almost oblivious of what was going on around him.

Paget rubbed his face with his hands. He was going round in circles. What mattered now was finding Mary Carr.

Using the resources of the Met, he had checked the date of Gillanne's death, and found that he was right. The girl had killed herself the day after the West End bombing in which seventeen people were killed and dozens injured. Consequently, the death of a single child hadn't received much attention from the media or the police.

Together, Paget and DI Wallace had gone over the letters Mary had sent to her mother, but they were of little value. All but one—the one postmarked Poole—had been posted from various places in the Midlands, with no return address. She might as well have used postcards for all the information they contained. They all said roughly the same thing: It's me again, Mum. How are you? I'm fine. Keeping busy. Not much to tell at the moment, but I'll write more later. Love, Mary. No mention of where she was, what she was doing, or whether Michael was with her. It was as if Mary knew, or at least suspected, that the police might one day be reading them.

She had never written much more than that, but Bellamy had obtained an order to intercept mail addressed to Edith Chambers, and a warrant had been obtained to monitor her phone calls, and round-the-clock surveillance was set up on the house.

As for Michael Carr, a computer search turned up the information that he was known to the police in Lambeth. According to their records, Michael had first come to their attention when he was fifteen. He had run away from a foster home and joined a local band of tearaways. He was regarded by the police as non-violent but easily led, more of a hanger-on than a true member. He'd been involved in petty crimes, shoplifting, joyriding, theft from cars, and things of that nature, but nothing major as far as was known.

As to his present whereabouts, they had no idea. There had been nothing on his record for the past nine months, which was unusual, they said, because Michael was not the brightest star in the heavens, and was easily caught.

The last nine months. His mother had been released from prison in April. A check with the prison authorities showed that Michael had visited his mother in prison on a number of occasions, the last being a week before her release, which strengthened Paget's belief that the two of them could be working together.

Edith Chambers had been a regular visitor. Twice a month, year in, year out. She denied knowing anything about Michael, where he was or what he was doing, and insisted that she had not seen him since he'd been taken away by Social Services.

Paget didn't believe her, and neither did Bellamy.

BROADMINSTER

LEN ORMSIDE SHUFFLED through the pictures of Mary Carr
that Paget had sent through on the fax machine. Three of them
were prison pictures: full front face, left and right profiles.
The rest had been modified and enhanced by computer. Subtle
changes had been made. In some pictures she had short hair,
in others long, each done in several different styles, and the
harsh shadows had been softened. It might not have been
Mary Carr who had called on Paget's housekeeper, but the
age and description she had given Molly Forsythe were close
enough to make it worth checking.

Ormside faxed the photographs to Bristol, asking them to
have Mrs. Wentworth see if she recognized the woman who
had called on her, purporting to be doing a survey. The pictures were all numbered, and, assuming it was Mary Carr who
had come to the house, he asked Bristol to have Mrs. Wentworth choose the photograph that most closely resembled her
appearance now.

HE COULD TELL by the way Audrey was stacking the plates
for washing up that she was annoyed. Audrey wasn't given
to moods, but she certainly hadn't been pleased when he told
her his application for extra leave at Christmas had been
turned down.

"It's just that with this woman on the loose, it's all hands
on deck, Christmas or not," he explained. "I mean I did ask,
but we're short-handed, and…"

"Seems to me that's always the excuse," Audrey muttered
as she turned on the water. "And I don't see why young Ron
King from down the road can get time off at Christmas, and
you can't. I met his mother in Sainsbury's the other day, and
she was telling me that Ron and that new wife of his are off
to Spain for a week at Christmas. Casa something-or-other.
Supposed to be the best there is, according to her. He doesn't

seem to have any trouble getting time off, and he's only been there three years, if that.''

"Ron King? Spain? On his pay? Never! Not unless he's got some fiddle going on the side."

Audrey clucked her tongue impatiently. "His mother's paying for it," she told him. "Why do you think she went out of her way to tell me? It isn't as if we know them very well, is it? She just wanted to make a point. Anyway, all I'm saying is, he got time off, but you with all your seniority can't get time off, and I don't understand why. God knows you've got enough time owing."

"Well, yes, but that's different, isn't it? I mean, he's uniforms. There's more of them to go round. Besides, I'll be having the four days off."

"But you'll be going back on the Wednesday, just when we could have all gone round together."

"Well, it's only Lilian who'll be here, isn't it? Philip will be in Shrewsbury all day doing whatever it is he does for the BBC, so you can take Lilian round. Be nice for you and the kids. Be better, really. The two of you can have a good natter."

Audrey scowled as she pulled on rubber gloves and plunged her hands into the hot water. "I really think you could have tried a bit harder to get leave," she grumbled. "I mean, I know you're not all that keen on Philip, but he'll be off in Shrewsbury most of the time, and it's not as if you and Lilian don't get on, is it? When I spoke to her on the phone the other night, she said she was looking forward to seeing you again. She'll be ever so disappointed."

"As will I, love," Tregalles said earnestly, "but you know how it is when duty calls. I mean, how do you think I'd feel if this madwoman had another go at Paget while I was off on holiday? No, sorry, love, but it wouldn't be right, would it?''

"Well, put that way, I suppose you're right," Audrey conceded grudgingly, "but they'd better not do this to you again, or I'll be having a word with Mr. Alcott myself."

THIRTY

"I CAN'T SEE ANY point in keeping you here," Bellamy told Paget. "I appreciate your coming up to London, and thank you for your help, but as your Superintendent Alcott keeps reminding me, you are supposed to be on sick leave. We have things well in hand. Mary Carr's picture has been circulated, and it's only a matter of time before someone spots her. So you might as well go home, get some rest, and enjoy your Christmas there."

The trouble was, he thought as he drove out of London on Thursday morning, there was nothing for him to go home to. No doubt Andrea would be spending Christmas with her friend, Sten, and his wonderful daughter who got on so well with Sarah, so any thoughts along those lines were out. Even Mrs. Wentworth's cheery face would be absent this year, so it looked as if he would be spending Christmas...

Good God! Mrs. Wentworth! He'd forgotten her completely. Here it was the twenty-first already, and he hadn't even sent a card, let alone a gift.

He groaned aloud. What to send her? He'd never been any good at this. It had been different when Jill was alive. She always seemed to know exactly what to get for everyone, and he'd been quite happy to leave it all to her. But he would like to get Mrs. Wentworth something other than a box of chocolates this year, something a bit special. Perhaps Grace...?

The thought cheered him. Grace would know. He hadn't thought about it before, but Grace was a lot like Jill in many ways.

He could phone her from the car, but it might be better if he could talk to her face-to-face before asking her advice about choosing a gift for someone she'd never met. He should invite her out to dinner. He owed her that much after all the things she'd done for him, and he did enjoy her company. He looked at the time. He'd be home by three; he'd phone her then.

A FEEBLE SUN slid behind the western hills, and darkness began its swift descent upon the fields as he crested the last rise before the run down to his house. He pulled up to the garage door, switched off the engine, then sat there for a moment, looking, listening, before getting out to circle the house. Nothing seemed amiss. No windows broken, the doors locked as he had left them; no footprints that he could see in the fading light.

A swift inspection of the inside of the house satisfied him that nothing had been disturbed while he was away, and he began to relax, happy to be home again. He'd only been in London a short time, but it was enough to convince him that he much preferred the country now. But he did miss Mrs. Wentworth. Not so much her actual presence, because even when she was there, they seldom saw each other; it was simply knowing that she'd been in the house while he was away.

He made a mental note to phone her Christmas Eve.

In the meantime... He picked up the phone and punched in Grace's number at work.

She wasn't there. Left yesterday for Sheffield, he was told. Be back on Wednesday after Christmas. Paget set the phone down and stood there looking at it for a long moment. Grace hadn't mentioned going home again—but then, why should she? There was nothing to keep her here, and it was only natural for her to want to be with her family at Christmas.

So why did he feel so put out? It wasn't just the fact that Grace hadn't been there to help him decide on a present for Mrs. Wentworth; it was more than that. He'd been looking forward to talking to her, hearing her voice again, and it had never crossed his mind that she might not be there.

His footsteps sounded hollow on the wooden floor as he made his way to the kitchen and stood there in the doorway. He thought of Grace as she had looked last summer when, after driving up from Worcester in the worst thunderstorm of the year, they had stumbled into the house, soaking wet and exhausted. In his mind's eye, he saw her standing in the middle of the kitchen, posing for his inspection. She'd been wearing one of his shirts tucked into a large bath towel wrapped around her waist. A second towel had been twisted into a turban, revealing her long, slender neck normally masked by shoulder-length hair. And on her feet, she'd worn Paget's hiking socks.

"You look stunning," he remembered telling her, and he had meant it.

The vision faded, but there was turmoil in his mind. Had he had an inkling then? he wondered. Had he pushed the idea aside because he was still clinging to the hope that he and Andrea might one day find some common ground? He and Andrea had been good friends once. Perhaps that was the trouble; perhaps he should have been content to leave it at that.

But Grace... He groaned aloud. He'd been such a fool! A blind fool! Memories. He had wrapped himself in memories of Jill and the time they'd had together until that was all that he could see. Comforting as they might be, they had chained him to the past.

He slumped into a chair and steepled his fingers beneath his chin. Perhaps he'd needed time, even this recent brush with death, to clear his mind. His lips twisted into a wry smile. And now that it was clear, it seemed ironic that, at the very moment it had finally penetrated his thick skull that he was in love with Grace, she wasn't there.

PAGET ARRIVED in the office early the following morning in order to sit in on the briefing conducted by Tregalles. The sergeant began by taping three pictures on a whiteboard. Front, left, and right side face, each labelled with the number 6.

"We have confirmation from Mr. Paget's housekeeper that this is what our killer looks like," he said. "This is the same woman who came to Mr. Paget's house early in November, pretending to be doing a survey, but in reality she was pumping Mrs. Wentworth for information. Copies of these pictures will be in the hands of every copper in the country by the end of the day; they'll be on TV, and in most newspapers by tomorrow morning, so with any luck at all we should start hearing from the public very soon."

Tregalles continued with an overview of the investigation to date, but since control of what had become a nationwide hunt for a serial killer had shifted to London, he asked Paget to bring them up to date on what had happened there.

Paget did so, concluding with, "The problem is, there may be others on her list, minor players who were involved in putting her away, people who, in her mind at least, were directly or indirectly responsible for the suicide of her daughter. But what we *do* know is that she wasn't satisfied with what she did to me, otherwise why take the trouble to phone me to say she hadn't finished with me yet, and break into my house while I was away? As I see it, the whole point is to make everyone suffer in the same way she suffered when Gillanne took her own life, but in my case, since she couldn't find anyone close enough to me to do that, I believe she won't be satisfied until I'm dead."

There was silence in the room for a long moment until someone said, "This Michael Carr, sir. You say he's a loony as well?"

"Mentally challenged, Bert," someone else put in. "Can't say loony these days."

"That is *not* what I said," Paget told the man. "Michael Carr was, and may still be, perfectly normal in most respects.

My recollection of him is that of a nice kid who simply had more trouble than most in grasping a concept or course of action. But once he'd got it, he could apply it as well as anyone else. One thing I do remember about him is that he was always looking to his mother for approval, and he was very attached to his sister, and she to him. It's my belief that he would have been just as devastated by her death as Mary was, so he might be just as keen to avenge her.''

"So what do we do now, sir?''

"First, familiarize yourselves with these pictures. Study the features carefully, because once these pictures are out, Mary Carr will probably try to change her appearance. Different clothes, make-up, change of hairstyle, colour, a wig, whatever, so concentrate on the features she can't change, such as the eyes and shape of the nose, but especially her voice. We know she can't change that. As for Michael, the only picture we have of him was taken several years ago, but I doubt if he'll have changed that much. In any case, if we find Mary, I think we'll find him with her. Local teams will be covering the areas from which Mary sent letters to her mother; copies of these pictures will be taken round to all the hotels, motels, B and Bs, estate and letting agents, and so on, as you will be doing here. Other than that, there isn't much else we can do but wait and hope for a break. But make no mistake about it, Mary Carr is extremely dangerous, and she has nothing to lose by killing again.''

"What about you, sir?'' asked Molly Forsythe. "What precautions are you taking? You're pretty isolated out there in Ashton Prior. Shouldn't you have someone out there with you to, well, watch your back, so to speak?''

"You applying for the job, Molly?'' someone called.

"Better brush up on your judo,'' someone else suggested.

"Bedside manner, more like.''

"You can watch my back, Molly.''

Paget ignored the banter. "I'll be watching my back,'' he assured her, "but if I can persuade Superintendent Alcott to let me return to work, I shan't be spending much time out there on my own. Meanwhile, I will take every precaution." He smiled. "In fact, I've taken one already. You may have noticed I'm wearing much higher collars these days."

Chuckles around the room as Paget turned the floor back to Tregalles, but Molly wasn't smiling. She didn't think it was funny at all.

"ABSOLUTELY NOT!" Alcott leaned back in his chair and shook his head. "It's just not on," he added firmly. "We all appreciate everything you've done—that goes without saying; but you've been pushing yourself to the limit as it is, and I'll admit that I am partly to blame for allowing you to do so. But things are under control now, so go home, put your feet up, and stay there, at least until after the New Year. Tregalles has done a credible job in your absence, and is quite capable of handling things here; in fact, he's volunteered to come in each day over the holidays to monitor progress and give Ormside a break."

Paget raised an eyebrow in mild surprise. This wasn't like Tregalles. In previous years, he'd fought hard to make sure he spent Christmas with his wife and children. Unless, of course, having been given the extra responsibility by Alcott, he'd decided it was time to look toward promotion. If so, good luck to him.

Alcott was speaking again. "One other thing before you go. Tregalles tells me the point was raised this morning about your safety over the holidays. It's a valid point, but there is no one I can assign to you. However, I spoke to Mr. Brock, and he's agreed—reluctantly, I'll admit, but nevertheless agreed—to pay your expenses if you will move into a hotel in town, at least for the next few days. After that, we may be in a better position to assign someone to…"

But Paget was shaking his head. "Thank you very much, sir," he said. "I appreciate the thought, but I'd much prefer to be on my home ground. I don't intend to take chances, but

I hardly think Mary Carr will try to tackle me in the house. Besides, she will have enough to worry about when her picture appears in all the newspapers tomorrow morning. Thanks, but no thanks.''

Alcott wasn't surprised by Paget's reaction. He would probably have said the same under similar circumstances, but at least he'd tried, and Brock would be delighted that he wouldn't have to spend the money. ''In that case,'' he said, ''go home and get some rest. And try to enjoy your Christmas.''

Paget rose and made for the door. ''And a Merry Christmas to you and the family, sir.''

Alcott grunted. ''Not much chance of that,'' he growled. ''We're spending Christmas with Marion's parents in the Rhondda Valley. Poky little cottage miles from anywhere, damp, no central heating, and you have to go outside if you want to smoke. Oh, yes, and they always have a goose, and I can't stand the bloody bird!''

Paget grimaced. ''Not a pleasant thought, sir,'' he agreed solemnly. ''No way out of it, I suppose?''

''Not a hope. Been putting it off three years in a row, so we'll have to go.''

''In that case, good luck to you, sir.''

Alcott grunted. ''Just one more thing. I had a call from Mr. DeWitt this morning. Wanted me to remind you that you have a two o'clock appointment with him this afternoon. Apparently he doesn't trust your memory.''

THE BELL ABOVE the door jangled as he entered the shop. Shop—it was more like a miniwarehouse with its racks of clothing and narrow aisles. It smelled of disinfectant, slightly musty, slightly damp. He closed the door behind him and the bell jangled again.

A grey-haired lady with too much rouge on her wrinkled face popped her head above a rack of clothing and said, ''Good morning, sir. What can we do for you today?'' She ran an expert eye over the man: decent enough anorak, but ill used; trousers, what she could see of them, had seen better days, as had the man himself. She couldn't see much of his face beneath the hood, but what she could see made her wonder if he was ill. She hoped he didn't have anything catching.

"Something warm, perhaps?" she ventured. "We have several nice cardigans and pullovers, and very reasonably priced. And boots," she added, looking at his shoes.

Marshall shook his head as he looked around. It had not taken him long to find the addresses of the four people named Proudfoot in Broadminster, but he'd thought there must have been some mistake when he'd first checked this one. Number 12 Church Lane was a shop that sold second-hand clothing, and that couldn't be right. It was only when he'd come back a second time that he'd noticed the narrow passageway between the shop and its next-door neighbour. Further investigation revealed a faded number 12A on a recessed door halfway down, a door that must lead to stairs and living quarters above the shop.

"It's about the rooms to let," he said hesitantly, then pointed upward. "Upstairs."

The elderly lady looked puzzled as she came out from behind the rack. "Rooms to let?" she repeated. "I'm sure there must be some mistake."

"It was in the paper. I believe the name was Proudfoot or something like that."

"Oh, no, dear, I think someone must have got it wrong. Besides, it isn't Mr. Proudfoot's to let. It's Mrs. McKinnon's. She owns this shop and the flat upstairs, but she's not here at the moment."

"Perhaps I should have a word with Mr. Proudfoot." He turned as if to go.

The woman sighed and fluttered her hands. "I'm sorry, my dear, but he's gone as well. Left early this morning, and he'll be gone all day. But I'm glad you reminded me. He came in just as we were closing last night to ask if I'd see to Sammy—that's his cat—while he's away.''

Marshall, who had been around the back to make sure Proudfoot's car had gone before he'd ventured in, pretended to look perplexed. ''You say he'll be gone all day?''

''That's right, my dear. He's taken that poor young woman who was injured in the fire the other week to see her mother. You probably read about her in the paper—the young policewoman, I mean, not her mother. She's staying there for Christmas, but he'll be back tonight. Not that I think it will do you any good to come round then, because as I said, it's not his flat to let, and if he'd said anything about moving to Mrs. McKinnon, I'm sure she would have told me.''

Marshall shrugged resignedly. ''Ah, well, as you say, someone must have made a mistake. I suppose I shall have to keep on looking. Sorry to have taken up your time.'' He turned to go, then paused to ask, ''Would you mind very much if I had a look round while I'm here?''

''Not at all, my dear. You just have a good look round while I pop out the back. It's been a bit slack this morning, and I'd just put the kettle on when you came in.'' She hesitated. Now that she'd had time to size him up, she decided he looked more undernourished than sick, and he was quite nicely spoken. ''Would you like a cup of tea?'' she ventured. ''It's not very nice out there, and to tell the truth, I wouldn't mind a bit of company. I'm afraid it's going to be one of those slow days; what with everybody dashing about doing their last-minute Christmas shopping, there won't be many come in here.''

''That is very kind of you,'' said Marshall. He'd found out much of what he'd wanted to know, but it would be even better if he could see what was in the back of the shop as well. Much better.

RICK PROUDFOOT PARKED the car behind the shop and made sure the doors were locked. A fitful wind stirred litter in the narrow passage between the two buildings as he made his way to the side-door entrance to his flat. The passageway was a natural funnel, and leaves and litter had a habit of collecting there.

He closed the door behind him and leaned his back against it, thankful to be home. He was cold and tired; persistent rain and sleet had dogged him all the way from Oxford; a three-car pile-up on the other side of Evesham had held him up for the best part of an hour; and the heater in his car was acting up again.

He crossed the tiled floor to a second door that opened directly onto stairs. It was a strange little hallway, four feet wide and no more than six feet in length. It was as if the architect had tried to make what was essentially a back door into a miniature front entrance hall. The tiles were chessboard black and white, and slippery when wet, as they were now. He must get a proper mat, he thought for perhaps the hundredth time as he plodded up the stairs.

He reached the landing at the top and let himself into the flat. It seemed strange, now that there was no one there to greet him. He'd become used to Kate being there, and the flat seemed empty without her. Still, he consoled himself, he'd done the right thing by taking her to her mother's for Christmas. He would be working through the holidays, and it wouldn't have been much fun for Kate to be cooped up here all by herself. She'd had enough of that already, and it would do her good to get out.

Today had been his day off, so he had driven her to Oxford, where she could relax and spend Christmas with her mother. It had been his idea that she should spend the holidays there, and he had phoned Kate's mother without telling Kate until everything was settled.

"But you'll be here all on your own over Christmas," Kate had protested. "It doesn't seem fair for me to go off and leave you. After all you've done for me, the very least I can do is be here to see that you have a proper Christmas dinner when you get home." She smiled wryly to take the sting out of her next words. "I mean, you're not exactly the world's greatest cook, now are you? What will it be? Frosted chicken or some such thing? I'll talk to Mother; I'm sure she'll understand."

"Don't you want to spend Christmas with your mother?"

"Of course I do, but..."

"Then it's settled," he'd told her firmly. "She's dying to see you, and you can't disappoint her now. As for me, I'll be all right. I spent last Christmas with Gerry Findlay and his wife and kids. After all, I am their sort-of uncle, and Gerry's invited me there again after I've finished work. Told me to bring a girlfriend if I like."

Alarmed, Kate said, "Oh, Rick, you didn't tell him I'm here, did you?"

"No one knows you're here," he assured her. He grinned. "I'll have to dig into my little black book and see who's available."

Kate reached out and took Rick's head between her hands and pecked him on the cheek. "Thank you, Rick. You've been so good to me. I don't know what I'm going to do without you when I have to leave."

"Then why leave?" he'd said softly—too softly, perhaps, because she had turned away without responding. Perhaps she hadn't heard, but if that was the case, why had she tried to hide the colour rising in her face?

As Rick removed his coat, Sammy jumped off the bed and came to meet him, rubbing against his legs as he bent to scratch behind her ears. He sighed. At least the cat was there to greet him, but it wasn't quite the same.

"No offence, Sammy," he told the cat as he picked her up, "but it's not the same at all."

THIRTY-ONE

SUNDAY, AND A SMALL band of children, using everything from strips of cardboard wrapped in bin bags to sheets of tin and plywood as makeshift toboggans, swooshed and tumbled down the hill above the village of Ashton Prior. They'd been at it all afternoon, each run a little shorter than the last as the patch of snow receded beneath a watery sun and the pounding of many feet. Now the light was fading, and the children began to drift away, stopping now and then to scoop up snow and try to ram it down someone else's neck. They'd be soaking wet and half frozen by the time they got home, but Paget doubted if that would bother them for very long. All they would remember was that they'd had fun on Christmas Eve.

Which was more than he was having, he thought glumly as he set the binoculars aside. There had been no sign of the watcher since the police had searched the hillside, and no wonder, the way they'd arrived on the scene. Even so, he had to assume that he was being watched at least some of the time, so he couldn't afford to let down his guard.

He slumped into a chair and put his head back. The dull ache at the base of his skull continued to throb, low, insistent, reminding him of DeWitt's words on Friday.

"It's your own fault," he'd said bluntly. "If you'd rested as I told you, chances are that pressure would be gone and you'd have been ready to go back to work by now. But no, you had to do it your way, and you're paying for it now. I know you've been telling me everything is all right, but I don't believe you. Whatever else you may be, Mr. Paget, you are not a convincing liar. And I suspect your eyes have been giving you trouble as well, haven't they?''

He hadn't waited for an answer. He didn't need to, for Paget felt rather like a schoolboy under the gimlet eye of a stern headmaster, and his face betrayed it.

''Go home and rest, and I mean complete rest this time!'' had been DeWitt's parting shot. ''Stop whatever you're doing at the least sign of fatigue, and lie down.''

Yesterday hadn't been too bad. He'd paced himself with household chores. He'd walked down to the village to shop for fresh food—walking was all right, but nothing strenuous, DeWitt had advised—and to arrange for a large bouquet of flowers to be sent to Mrs. Wentworth. He'd stopped for a ploughman's lunch at the White Hart on his way back, and spent much of the afternoon preparing dinner. It had passed the time, but by the end of the day, with no one to talk to, nothing on the radio or TV but bad news interspersed with endless carols, he'd gone to bed early and settled down to read *Sarum,* the book Grace had brought him in hospital.

Twenty past three: that was what the clock had said when he awoke this morning, cold and stiff, still propped up in bed, the book lying on the floor, and the light still on. He'd snuggled down in bed and tried to go back to sleep, but kept thinking of Mary Carr's daughter, Gillanne, and the tragic way she'd died.

He got up at five and, for the lack of something better to do, loaded the washing machine with every scrap of clothing, sheets, and towels that he could find. By eight o'clock the clothes had gone through the dryer, and he'd had his breakfast, done the washing up, and set out to do the ironing. It had taken him twice as long as it would have taken Mrs. Wentworth, but at least it passed the time.

Mindful of the possibility that Mary Carr might not have finished with him yet, he had gone to the windows several times throughout the afternoon to keep a watchful eye on the road and surrounding hills. He noted cars and vans and trucks—even bicycles and the occasional walker—moving up and down the hill outside the house, but it seemed a bit silly after a while. The threat on the phone had been real enough, but that was probably all it was, a threat, just another way of putting him on edge, or in Mary's words, to make him suffer.

He was dozing when the phone rang. The sound startled him, and he was only half awake when he picked up the phone and said, "Hello?"

"Neil?"

"Grace?"

"Yes. Are you all right? You sound… Did I wake you?"

Paget shook his head to clear it, wondering why Grace was phoning from Sheffield. "No, no…well, yes, you did, actually. Nodded off in the chair. It's been a grey day. How are things in Sheffield?"

"Fine, except I'm not in Sheffield. I'm calling from home."

"But I thought… Someone said you'd gone home for Christmas."

"I did, but we celebrated Christmas a few days early. Mum and Dad are spending Christmas with my grandparents, who retired to the south of France a couple of years ago, so the plan was to have our usual family Christmas in Sheffield on Thursday. Unfortunately, my younger brother, Alex—you know, the one I told you about, the one who loves golf?— had an opportunity to go to Florida to play in a tournament there, and my other brother, Bob, went down with the flu on Tuesday, so it was a bit of a flop. Anyway, I'm back home again, and I have all this food I brought back with me, and I was wondering if you'd like to join me for Christmas dinner tomorrow?"

THE TEMPERATURE had plummeted overnight, and a fresh layer of snow blanketed the ground. A rising sun outlined the leafless trees in gold, and their shadows lay like lace upon the pristine whiteness. Everything was still. The air was crisp and clean, and Paget filled his lungs as he stepped outside and locked the door behind him. He stood there for a moment drinking in the beauty of the countryside, and listening to the muted sound of squabbling rooks across the valley.

He paused only long enough to brush the snow off the steps before getting the car out and making sure the garage door was securely locked. Tyres crunched as he backed into the road and set off down the hill, touching the brakes lightly to test the icy surface of the road. The village was deserted; not a soul to be seen this Christmas morning. He turned on the radio. More carols. "The Little Drummer Boy"—again. After listening to that particular carol for what must have been the tenth time yesterday, he could have cheerfully beaten the kid and his infernal drum into the ground with his own drumsticks, but today the words took on new meaning, and he found himself humming along with the choir.

It wasn't only the lifting of the grey skies that made him feel better, although the sight of the sun was a welcome change; it was the thought of seeing Grace again. Yesterday, the prospect of spending yet another Christmas alone had been a gloomy one; in fact, the sooner it was over, the better, as far as he was concerned. But Grace's unexpected invitation had changed all that.

She'd phoned again first thing this morning. "Come as soon as you're ready," she told him, "and bring your boots if you think you're up to a bit of a walk before dinner. It's such a beautiful day. The mist is on the river and all the trees are covered in frost, so I thought it might be nice to go through the park and take the path along the bank. You can tell me all about your trip to London, and this woman, Mary Carr."

He stood there for a long moment after he put the phone down. Was he doing the right thing? he wondered. Grace's reference to Mary Carr had reminded him that he could be putting her at risk if they were seen together. On the other hand, with her picture in every newspaper and on every television screen, chances were that Mary Carr had gone to ground until the heat died down. She'd hardly be out walking the river path on Christmas Day.

"So stop being so bloody paranoid and go out and enjoy yourself," he told himself, and went to find his boots.

THEY WALKED THROUGH the park behind the hospital and along the river-bank as far as the bridge. The path ran high above the river, and Grace tucked her hand under Paget's arm as they negotiated the icy patches close to the edge. He was reminded of the night Kate Regan had done the same as they walked around the building to their cars. He had tried to call her when he heard that she'd been injured, but no one seemed to know exactly where she was. Wherever she was, he hoped she was enjoying Christmas Day as much as he was. She certainly deserved a break.

They didn't talk much; there was no need. The mist had lifted by the time they came in sight of the King George Street bridge, but the frosted fairyland remained, and sunlight glinted on the sparkling waters far below. They turned as one, and walked back to a wooden bench that overlooked the river, and while Paget brushed off the snow, Grace took sandwiches and a flask of coffee from a shoulder bag.

"This wouldn't be Christmas dinner, by any chance?" he asked as she handed him a sandwich.

"You mean you expected more?" she laughed. "Sorry, but I could never quite get the hang of cooking. Far too complicated for me. Disappointed?"

He pulled a face as he poked at the empty bag. "What, no Christmas pud? Good Lord, woman, you can't have Christmas without the pudding. You could at least have picked one up at Marks and Sparks."

"There's no pleasing some people," she sighed as she poured the coffee. "Think yourself lucky I brought this along, but I was afraid that, in your delicate state of health, you might be too weak to make it back without some sort of sustenance.'' The smile faded from Grace's face. "But seriously, how are you feeling, Neil?''

"Never felt better,'' he assured her, and meant it. If the day had ended here, he couldn't have been more content.

"I'm glad.'' Grace handed him a mug. They sat side by side on the narrow bench, shoulders touching companionably, munching sandwiches, drinking coffee, and savouring the warmth of the winter sun. Grace closed her eyes and raised her face to the sun. "You haven't said a word about the case or what happened in London,'' she said quietly.

"To be honest, I'd just as soon forget it on such a lovely day,'' he told her, "but there is one thing you should know. I think the chances of my being watched are virtually nil at the moment, but if I'm wrong, just being seen with me could expose you to danger. And the more I think about it, the more I think I had no right to do this to you, Grace.''

She opened her eyes and turned to look at him. "Don't you think I knew that before I asked you to come today? I've been speaking to Charlie since I came back from Sheffield, and he's been keeping on top of things, so I'm think I'm pretty well up to date.''

"And still you asked me?''

Grace smiled. "As you said, chances are that Mary Carr is a good long way from here by now, so why not? Let's forget about her and enjoy the day.''

They remained there for a long time, reluctant to move or break the spell until the cold began to chill their bones. They rose to leave, and in what was almost an unconscious gesture, Paget took Grace's hand and tucked it under his arm as they started back. She wriggled her arm as if she found it uncomfortable, and he thought she was trying to pull away, but instead she linked her fingers with his own, and he felt a thrill of pleasure.

As they left the river path and came out on Edge Hill Road, Grace cupped her free hand around her eyes to shield them from the sun. A man in a dark blue anorak had left the path ahead of them and was scrambling up the bank to take a shortcut to the road above. He had his back to her, and she wouldn't have noticed him at all if it hadn't been for his abrupt departure from the path, when another ten yards would have brought him to the road.

Must be late for something, she decided as he jumped into a car. She heard the engine start, the grate of gears, and watched as the car shot round the corner into Barnfield Road and disappeared.

"What is it, Grace?" Paget followed her gaze across the road. There was nothing there of interest that he could see.

"Oh. Sorry." She took his arm again. "Just wondering what that man was late for, that's all."

"What man?" Apart from the odd glance round to make sure they weren't being followed, he'd hardly taken his eyes off Grace throughout the morning.

"The one who got into that car and took off in such a hurry," she explained. "I'm afraid I'm always doing that— watching people and wondering why they do the things they do. It was probably the clock."

"The clock?"

"The church clock just struck the hour a couple of minutes ago. He probably heard it and realized he was going to be late for dinner—or whatever."

"Speaking of which, shouldn't we be going?"

Grace shook her head despairingly. "You sound just like my brother Alex. He has an appetite like a horse. How he stays as trim as he does, I don't know. Me, I have to work at it all the time."

"Believe me, it works," Paget said with such sincerity that she squeezed his arm and said, "You'll do anything to get a Christmas dinner, won't you, Chief Inspector?"

"I will indeed," he said as they set off once more.

They continued the walk in silence, breathing in the fresh, clean air and listening to the squeak of snow beneath their boots. Paget was almost afraid to speak for fear it would break the spell, while Grace was trying to catch a fleeting memory as faint as a wisp of smoke before it disappeared. There had been something familiar about the man in the dark blue anorak, but for the life of her she couldn't think what it was.

TREGALLES COULDN'T understand it. Philip and Lilian had arrived on Sunday, loaded down with presents for the kids as usual, and Lilian had been on her best behaviour. She had greeted him with a chaste kiss on the cheek, and had been the model of decorum ever since. But she could still put away the wine, and he could see that even with the two extra bottles Audrey had prodded him into buying, Lilian would be into the *vin ordinaire* by the middle of the week.

She'd sat next to him at dinner, pulled crackers with him, and worn a paper hat, but not once had she made so much as a gesture that might be construed as an advance.

But then, he told himself, a year had passed; perhaps Lilian's flirtatious phase was over and he could relax. In fact, he was rather enjoying her company this time. She was still a little overweight, but it looked good on her. Good figure, trim legs—and she had a wicked sense of humour.

She was good with the children, too. She and Philip had no children of their own, but she joined right in the children's games. As Brian said later on his way to bed, "Auntie Lil's a super sport. Wish she lived here all the time."

Good for Brian, Tregalles thought when Audrey told him, but perhaps it was just as well Lilian was only staying the week. But even that prospect seemed less threatening now. Perhaps he should have taken a few days off after all.

Philip hadn't changed. Talked as if he were lecturing a class; explained every boring detail of his *very* important work with the BBC, and how much poor old Radio Shropshire was relying on him to guide them through this difficult transition to digital, a term he never did get around to explaining fully— and Tregalles was careful not to ask.

He also informed them that he'd developed a back problem,

and found it difficult to sleep in anything but a soft bed. Excruciating pain. Pinched nerve, his specialist had said, and not a hope in hell of having anything done about it under the NHS for at least a year. But he refused to go private as a matter of principle.

"To say nothing of parting with his money," Lilian had added quietly.

But Audrey's sympathy had been aroused. "Then you must have our bed," she said firmly, ignoring the startled look on her husband's face. "We'll be very comfortable on the pull-out bed down here, won't we, love?"

It wasn't so much a question as a command. The look she gave him dared him to say anything but yes.

"Oh, yes, very comfortable," he agreed, giving up all hope that three nights on the pull-out bed might have been enough to make Philip change his mind about staying on.

FRIARS WALK WAS one of the oldest and narrowest streets in Broadminster. The original Tudor houses at the top end of the street looked much as they had when they were first built. In fact, they were now merely shells, their facades fronting for boutiques, gift shops, a tea house, and a thriving sausage and pie shop, all of which attracted tourists. Those at the lower end of the street were much newer, having been rebuilt after a fire destroyed seven houses and the Odd Fellows hall on the corner in 1926. While similar in style and pleasing to the eye, they, too, were not what they seemed. They had started life as houses, but had evolved over the years into flats: two small rooms and a kitchen downstairs, and one bedroom and bath upstairs.

Grace lived in number 11, back to back with the houses facing the market square, "With a view of the minster ruins if you stand on tiptoe in the bedroom," she told Paget as she led the way inside. There was a Christmas tree in the corner, holly on the mantel, decorations strung across the living room, and the warm, delicious smell of a turkey roasting in the oven to greet them as they entered. "That doesn't smell like left-overs to me," he observed as he removed his hiking boots and replaced them with shoes. "Is there anything I can do to help?"

"I'm counting on it," Grace told him. "Come on through to the kitchen. You can test the turkey while I see to the vegetables."

Working so closely together in the confines of the tiny kitchen, Paget found it hard to concentrate on what he was supposed to be doing. He couldn't take his eyes off Grace; the way she moved, the curve of her neck, the softness of her cheek, the glint of light upon her hair...

"What?" Belatedly, he realized that Grace had been talking to him.

"I said the turkey needs one last basting before you take it out of the oven." She turned to face him. "You are all right, aren't you, Neil?"

"I'm fine," he assured her. "Never better. Honestly. Sorry, Grace, but I was miles away."

She eyed him suspiciously, then nodded. "In that case, I'd better baste the turkey while you open the wine. Freshen up our taste buds before we sit down to dinner."

Paget had brought the wine, but felt embarrassed for not having a gift for Grace. In fact, he had agonized over that very question more than a week ago, but talked himself out of it on the grounds that she might think it presumptuous of him, and be embarrassed for not having a gift for him.

So much for reason, he thought ruefully as he opened the wine.

GRACE SAT ON the floor, her long legs tucked under her, back against his chair as they listened to some of her favourite tapes from the seventies and eighties. The only light in the room came from the tree, soft, multicoloured rays that seemed to make her blonde hair flow like liquid gold around her shoulders.

He sighed softly. Grace looked up, a question in her eyes.

"That was a sigh of perfect contentment," he told her. "I don't know when I've felt so utterly relaxed and happy."

"I'm glad," she said as she rose to her feet and held out her hand. "Care to dance?"

"Dance?"

"Yes. It's a thing you do to music with your feet. I'm sure you must have heard of it. It's been going on for aeons."

"I haven't danced in years," he confessed. "I was never very good at it, and I suspect I've forgotten altogether by now."

"It's like riding a bike," she told him. "You never forget."

"Everyone always says that when they're trying to get you to make a fool of yourself," he grumbled as he got to his feet and set his glass aside. "It's a very small dance floor."

"It's big enough." Grace held out her arms.

"You're not wearing shoes," he objected.

"I like to dance without shoes. Any other excuses?"

"You'll regret this," he warned as he drew her into his arms.

"It's a waltz," Grace told him.

"I know it's a waltz. It's just that my feet haven't caught up yet."

He was rusty, but as their bodies melded together, he found himself responding to the music, and they moved as one. With the gentlest of pressures, Grace guided him around the small room, nudging chairs out of the way as they went. He could smell the fragrance of her hair, feel the warmth of her skin beneath his fingers.

They danced through three more numbers before the tape came to an end. It switched itself off, but they remained standing there in the middle of the room, bodies swaying as if to their own silent rhythm. Grace looked up at him; he drew her closer, kissed her gently.

Her arms tightened around his neck as she responded, and suddenly there was no time, no space, no dimension to a universe that was theirs, and theirs alone.

THIRTY-TWO

IT WAS RAINING again, but nothing could dampen Paget's spirits this morning. He had set the alarm for six-thirty, but he was in no hurry to get up. Lying there, listening to the rain, he was tempted to pinch himself to make sure he hadn't dreamt the last two days. Grace would be getting ready for work now. Should he phone her for no other reason than to wish her good morning? Better not; she wouldn't want to be held up. On the other hand...

He rolled over and picked up the phone.

"GOOD CHRISTMAS, then, was it?" asked Len Ormside, looking pointedly at the clock. "Audrey's brother and his wife get here all right?" Ormside had heard all about Philip.

"It was all right." Tregalles poured himself a mug of coffee from the pot Ormside kept beside his desk, then wandered over to survey the boards.

Sleeping on the pull-out bed for one night was tolerable, two nights were bearable, but last night neither he nor Audrey had had much sleep, and he wasn't looking forward to spending the rest of the week on it. And Audrey's reminders that she had been telling him for the past couple of years they needed a new pull-out bed hadn't done much to improve his temper.

But what had really annoyed him this morning was trying to get into the bathroom. Philip had taken it over early, saying he hoped no one minded, but he wanted to get off to Shrewsbury as soon as possible because he'd arranged to be at what he'd called a working breakfast meeting with the executive at eight-thirty. Even that wouldn't have been so bad if Lilian hadn't slipped in after him and stayed there for forty minutes. By the time he got in there, he was already late for work.

"And how was your Christmas, Len?" asked Ormside of himself as he came to stand beside Tregalles. "Very nice, thank you," he continued. "So kind of you to ask." He took a sip of coffee. "Get out of the wrong side of the bed this morning did we, Tregalles?"

"As a matter of fact, yes," Tregalles growled, "except it wasn't our bed, it was the bloody pull-out downstairs."

Dangerous ground, Ormside decided, and waited to see if Tregalles was going to elaborate—which he did at considerable length. "So, when do they go back?" Ormside asked.

"Sunday," Tregalles told him glumly.

Ormside switched to safer ground. "You might be interested to know that London had recorded one hundred and eighty-two sightings of Mary Carr as of eight o'clock this morning," he said, "and they're still coming in. We've had four from around here so far, but only one of them looks promising. A Mrs. Boxmore runs a B and B in Parkside. She says a woman answering Mary Carr's description, and a younger man purporting to be her son, stayed there for four nights. Came in on the Wednesday, November first, and left the following Sunday. She reckons the man would be in his mid-twenties, and they gave the name of Carleton. Maureen and Mark Carleton. Same initials."

"A couple of weeks before Paget was attacked."

"That's right, but we know that Mary Carr was at Paget's house talking to Mrs. Wentworth on the Friday of that week."

"Does this Mrs. Boxmore know where they were going when they left?"

"No. But they had their own car. A grey Renault. She couldn't tell us anything more than that, but her young son— he's eleven—says it was a Clio Oasis, L reg."

Tregalles grunted. "Which only leaves a few thousand to check," he said uncharitably. "Anything else?"

"I'm running a check on the chance that it was stolen," Ormside told him. "According to his record, Michael Carr used to nick cars when he was a kid in Lambeth, and with him and his mother moving about all over the country, I reckon they might be changing cars from time to time."

"It's possible, I suppose," Tregalles agreed grudgingly, "but without a number it won't be easy."

"Oh, I don't know," Ormside demurred. "Of all the cars in the world to choose from, how often have you heard of anyone pinching a Clio Oasis?"

"THIS IS THE LARGEST bag we carry, sir," said the man at the counter in the medical supplies shop. "It's for use at night; just put it on the floor beside the bed. It's very strong and quite leakproof, and as you can see, the tube that fits onto the catheter is extra long, allowing the wearer to move about in bed without worrying about disconnecting it. The handles make it easy to carry, and all you have to do to empty it is turn this spigot, and this short length of tubing allows you to direct the flow." He demonstrated. "We sell a lot of these," he continued, "but we do have the strap-on leg-bags as well. There's the regular size, and what we call—" He stopped himself in time. He had been going to say "the piddling size," an inside joke appreciated by some, but this one didn't look as if he'd smiled in years. "The small size. It's long and narrow; fits on the inside of the leg, and no one would ever know it's there."

Marshall picked up the larger bag. Very sturdy, very pliable. Rolled up it would fit into one of the large pockets of his anorak. To be used at night, the man had said. He snickered to himself. How very appropriate. He nodded. "That's the one I want," he said.

"Very well, sir. The tubing is non-latex, of course. No risk of an allergic reaction there. So many people have that problem these days. Just the one, was it, sir?"

"Just the one." He didn't care what the tubing was made of; it would be coming off as soon as he got home in any case, and he'd use the heavy-duty tubing he'd bought from the DIY Wine and Beer Shop earlier in the day.

"Anything else for you today, sir?"

"No, thank you." Marshall paid for the purchase and left the shop. Clever of him to think of this. He'd felt the plastic pouch, soft and pliable, yet strong. Much better than the bin bags he'd used before. Even using two of them together for added strength, he'd found them barely strong enough, as well as very awkward to handle. This would be much better for what he had in mind.

Later, as he rode home on the bus, he kept touching the package in his lap and smiling to himself. He'd soon have Kate home again. Once she realized she had no one else to turn to, and nowhere else to go, she'd come home. Proudfoot had made a bad mistake when he'd pushed his way into the house and threatened him.

Marshall snickered. Big man, throwing his weight around. Well, he hadn't been so clever, had he? Flashing his card like that. Because now he knew where Proudfoot lived. Not that he'd be living there much longer, he told himself, and laughed out loud. He patted the bag. Come to that, Proudfoot wouldn't be living anywhere much longer.

The woman next to him shifted in her seat and put both arms around her shopping bag as if she feared he might take it from her. That was the trouble with buses. You never knew who might be sitting next to you these days. If he'd any manners he'd stand up and let that old dear standing next to him sit down, but men didn't do that these days, did they? And he had a funny smell about him. Drink, most likely. In the old days she could have called the conductor and had him thrown off, but not today. Oh, no, not today.

The woman wrinkled her nose and sniffed her disapproval. She rubbed the misted window with her hand. Four more stops to go. She hoped that he would get off first.

THIRTY-THREE

MICHAEL CARR PEERED worriedly at himself in the mirror. He found it hard to get used to his new image. His thick dark hair had been cropped to within half an inch of his skull and, together with his eyebrows, bleached almost white. But was it enough to avoid recognition? It was all very well for his mother to keep telling him no one would recognize him, but he didn't have her confidence. He just wished she'd been able to change his appearance as much as she'd changed her own. From the dowdy, care-worn, grey-haired woman who had first gone to Paget's house, she'd become a handsome black-haired businesswoman, smartly dressed and looking ten years younger.

"Are you *sure* they won't recognize me, Mum?" he asked for perhaps the tenth time in the past few days. "I mean, my face is still the same."

Mary Carr bit back a sharp reply. "But it's not, Michael," she assured him soothingly. "You don't look a bit like the picture in the paper. You've changed a lot since that picture was taken, and they'll be looking for someone with dark red curly hair, not a blond with a close crop."

"But the eyebrows—they look...well, they don't look real."

"I could hardly leave them dark, now could I, Michael? Besides, no one pays any attention to things like that these days."

"But I still don't think—"

His mother came to the end of her patience. "For God's

sake, Michael, will you stop going on and on about it? That's all you've done since this began. You were keen enough at the start. Anyone would think you didn't care about what happened to your sister.''

''I do, Mum, honestly I do, but I didn't expect it to be like this. So much killing, and now we're in the papers and on telly and everybody's looking for us.''

''No they are not! How many times do I have to tell you, Michael? They are looking for those two people in the photographs, and we don't look a bit like them. They are looking for a mother and son travelling together, not for two single people living in different motels. And they have no idea what car to look for now.''

God! he could be thick at times.

Michael shrugged sheepishly. ''It's just that I don't want to go to prison like you did, Mum,'' he muttered. ''That place gave me the creeps when I used to come to see you.''

What the hell do you think it did for me, Michael? You'd be even more worried if I told you I don't give a shit what happens to either of us as long as we finish what we set out to do. I'm finished anyway, and you never did have a future.

Mary Carr put her hands on her son's shoulders and turned him to face her. ''It will be over soon,'' she said soothingly. ''There's just one more thing to do, and then it's finished. Do I really have to remind you that I spent ten long years in that prison for something I didn't do? Donald was such a gentle man. Even if what they said about him at the trial was true— which it wasn't—I could never have hurt him, let alone kill him. He loved me, Michael, I know he did, and I loved him. But Gillanne was my life, Michael—as well as you, of course—and they tore us apart.'' Her voice hardened. ''They destroyed our lives, Michael; they destroyed Gillanne, and I promised myself that they would pay for that, and keep on paying for the rest of their miserable lives.''

Mary's eyes bored into those of her son, and her fingers dug into his arms. ''They killed her, Michael. Always remember that. And I hold every single one of them responsible for her death. It's your *duty* to help me do what must be done. Do you understand, Michael?'' He winced as her fingers dug in deeper.

He nodded wordlessly and turned away, afraid that if he faced her a moment longer he might blurt out the truth. *Don't ever tell her, Michael. Promise me you'll never tell. Cross your heart and promise!*

He'd crossed his heart and promised. Gillanne always knew what was best, and he'd kept his word. He just wished... He pushed the thought away. What was the point of wishing for something that could never be? Gillanne had always been his mother's favourite, but it had never occurred to him to resent it. He'd adored his sister. Even though she was younger by more than a year, she'd always been there for him; always taken care of him, helped and defended him when others became impatient with him for being slow or making a mistake. He'd loved his sister, and cried for days when she died.

He just wished his mother would look at him the way she'd always looked at Gilly.

He'd thought things would be different when his mother asked him to help make those responsible for Gillanne's death pay for what they'd done. He'd felt such a glow of pride. This was his chance to earn her respect, and get back at those who had driven his sister to her death. Perhaps, then, his mother would look at him the way she'd looked at his sister all those years ago.

But it hadn't happened, and it was his own fault, because no matter how hard he tried, he could never seem to get it right. The trouble was, he couldn't stand the sight of blood, and his mother had had to do the girl in Bournemouth, and the two women in Reading and Richmond on her own, with him standing by with the car. But she'd insisted that he help her with Paget.

She'd been really pissed off about Paget. ''The man has no wife, no parents, no girlfriend,'' she'd said disgustedly, ''so

I'll just have to cut the bastard's throat and watch him die. But I'll need you to take him from behind, so don't let me down, Michael. Make sure you get it right this time. And for Christ's sake, don't be sick!''

It had been cold in that workers' hut, and they'd had to wait so long that he'd wanted to give up. But not his mother. She'd made him wait it out. But his fingers were so numb with cold by the time Paget arrived that he'd had trouble gripping the short length of pipe.

He'd got it almost right. He'd come up behind the man and hit him exactly as his mother had told him—except he didn't have quite the right grip on the weapon, and the man had moved his head as he was about to strike. Still, he had gone down.

But then they'd had to run when the police car came round the corner. His mother had raged for days when she learned that Paget had survived, and she blamed him for the failure, saying he hadn't held the man still while she slashed his throat.

They'd driven south that same night, and he'd thought that now, at least, they would have to lie low for a while, because the police would be out in force trying to track them down. But he was wrong—as usual, he thought bitterly.

His mother had planned to do Gerald White during the Christmas holidays. ''Give his mother a nice Christmas present,'' she'd said. ''All nice and neat on her doorstep. See how she likes *that* when she wakes up in the morning.'' But, still fuming over the bungled job on Paget, she'd decided she couldn't wait for Christmas. ''We'll have to let things cool down a bit before we go back and finish Paget,'' she told Michael, ''but we might as well be doing something useful while we're waiting. We'll do White now.''

Michael's stomach churned as he relived the awful scene. He'd vomited all over the road, and his legs had turned to water when his mother had ordered him to help carry the boy to the house. They'd ended up dragging him most of the way, and Michael felt his face grow hot with shame for being so weak and useless and letting his mother down.

Since then, he'd done everything she'd told him to do; watched the house, reported to her everyone who called there; followed the woman who had driven Paget home from the hospital, then followed her again after she'd stopped to ask if he needed help. He'd been scared when she spoke to him. He thought she was going to ask why he had been following her, but instead she'd asked if she could help him. She was nice, but when he told his mother that, she'd smiled for the first time in days.

"We'll keep an eye on her," she'd said. "Perhaps the good Lord is interested in justice after all, and we'll have another chance. If this woman means anything to Paget at all…" She left the rest unsaid, but her eyes glittered, and Michael wished he'd never told her.

G. Lovett was her name. It hadn't been hard to find out once he'd tracked her to where she lived in Friars Walk. She was beautiful, and he couldn't help thinking that Gillanne would have looked very much like her, had she lived. He didn't know the woman's first name, but it was curious that she should have the same initial as Gillanne. Not very likely her name would be the same, though; he'd never heard of anyone else called Gillanne.

They'd followed her out to Paget's house a couple of times, but it wasn't until Christmas Day that they had seen the two of them walking arm in arm.

"Beautiful," his mother had crooned softly when she returned to the car. She laughed, her voice grating even more than usual. "They make a lovely couple, Michael. I think the Lord's been kind to us."

She'd followed them as far as the bridge, walked past them as they sat on the wooden seat, before returning to the car. "I don't *think* he would recognize me now, not after all these years," she'd said, "but there's no point in taking chances, is there? So go down the path and keep an eye on them. But be careful, Michael. As soon as they show signs of coming back up to the road, get back here quickly and we'll follow them."

It wasn't as if he hadn't tried to do what she asked, but the river valley was such a breathtaking sight that he'd become engrossed in the frosty scene. Almost too late, he'd looked up to see Paget and the woman coming toward him. They couldn't have been more than fifty feet away, and he'd panicked. He didn't think they'd seen him—too absorbed in each other to notice—but he couldn't be sure. So he'd scrambled up the bank to get off the path, but when he'd looked back he thought he saw the woman watching him. He'd broken into a run crossing the road to where his mother waited in the car.

Michael cringed inwardly as he recalled the way she'd looked at him as he scrambled into the car and started the engine. She hadn't said a word, but she didn't need to; he knew what she was thinking. He'd failed her once again.

THIRTY-FOUR

MARSHALL HAD BEEN ready to leave at midnight, but he'd forced himself to wait until two o'clock before slipping out of the house. The bag and tubing were tucked away inside his heavy winter parka, while a tightly rolled newspaper was jammed into one of the pockets. He'd hadn't thought of using paper until earlier that day—which meant he'd had to go down to the news agent's to buy the thickest one they had. He touched it now as he left the house, and smiled.

He'd thought of everything.

Except for the occasional passing car, the streets were empty, but Marshall kept to the lanes and back streets as he made his way into the older part of town and the alley behind the shop in Church Street.

Proudfoot's car was in its usual place behind the shop. Marshall crouched down beside it and pulled off his gloves. His fingers were cold, but he didn't mind that; they'd be warm soon enough. He chuckled at the thought.

He pried the cover off the petrol tank and unscrewed the cap, then pushed one end of the plastic tubing into the tank. He sucked on the other end of the tube to start the liquid flowing, then stuffed it into the bag. The taste of raw petrol in his mouth was foul, but it was a small price to pay for what he was about to do. And the idea that Proudfoot was supplying the petrol from his own car was one that appealed to him.

When the bag was full, he clipped the end of the tube, removed it from the bag, and left it hanging out of the tank to be used again. He closed the bag and carried it down the narrow passageway to the doorway leading to the stairs of Proudfoot's flat, and set it down carefully. Working swiftly in the dim light filtering into the passage from Church Street, he pulled pages from the newspaper and stuffed them into the crack between the door and sill until he was satisfied that nothing could escape. Then he picked up the bag, pushed the short length of tubing through the letterbox, and opened the spigot.

The bag took only moments to empty. Marshall closed the spigot and withdrew the tube. Let Proudfoot try coming down the stairs with that lot alight, he thought grimly. Of course, he could always jump from the window, but it was a fifteen-foot drop onto concrete, so good luck to him. Perhaps that would teach the bastard to leave other people's wives alone.

But he wasn't finished yet. If Kate thought she was coming back here to live, she had another think coming. With this place gone, she would *have* to come back to him.

Unless she decided to stay on in Oxford.

The thought gave him pause, and then he shrugged. He would find a way to get to Oxford and burn her out of there as well.

Whistling tunelessly beneath his breath, he returned to the car and began to fill the bag again.

RICK KEPT THINKING about Kate. He was back in his own bed again, but he'd been tossing and turning for what seemed like hours. Sammy, who normally slept on the foot of the bed, finally stalked off to curl up in a chair.

He couldn't get Kate out of his mind. He'd had girlfriends before, a couple of whom had shared his flat for a while, but it had been like playing house—pleasant, even fun for a while, but never anything more than a game.

But Kate was different. He couldn't say why; she just was, and he missed her.

THERE WERE NO bolts on the back door. Marshall had taken special note of that when he'd followed the woman into the kitchen at the back of the shop after she'd offered him a cup of tea. It was a sturdy door, heavy, solid, and the old-fashioned lock looked formidable. But the top half of the door was a multipaned window, and a sharp jab with his elbow was all it took to break one of the panes. It made surprisingly little noise, but Marshall paused for a moment, listening for any signs of movement from above the shop before reaching inside and turning the key.

Using a small torch to guide him, he moved swiftly through the kitchen into the shop itself. Clothing, racks of it. Couldn't be better, he thought as he opened the spigot and began sloshing petrol around. Dresses, they'd catch quickly, so would the blouses. Trousers, jackets... He laid a trail to the door between the shop and the kitchen, lit a match, and tossed it and the bag inside before closing the door. Within seconds he was across the kitchen and out of the door.

He dashed down the passageway to the side door to finish the job, panting hard. The adrenaline was pumping. God! he was clever. He wished he could stay to admire the results of his handiwork, but he'd have to get back to the house before the police decided to pay him another visit. Oh, they'd be there all right, same as last time, but they wouldn't be able to prove anything, and without proof, they couldn't touch him.

He lit a match, cupped it in his hands, then dropped it through the letterbox.

"WHAT THE HELL...?" Rick Proudfoot came out of a deep sleep to find the ginger cat pawing at his arms. "Sammy! For God's sake, what's the matter with you? What do you think you're doing?" He tried to push the cat away, but Sammy ducked aside and clawed his wrist.

Angrily, Rick shoved the cat off the bed and sat up, vaguely aware that something was wrong. Then he heard it, a dull, roaring sound that seemed to be coming from below.

Fire! He slid off the bed, picked up the cat, and was half-way across the room when he felt the tremor beneath his feet—and a split second later, heard the explosion.

A SLAP ON the backside from Audrey brought Tregalles awake. "Come on, love, time to get up," she told him. "I let you sleep as long as possible, but Philip has already gone and I think Lilian has just finished her shower. I want this bed put up before she comes down."

Tregalles groaned. What was today, anyway? Thursday? Three more nights of this before he and Audrey could go back to their own bed again. At least three more nights, because Philip had said something last night about staying on a couple of extra days to tie up a few loose ends in Shrewsbury. And all Audrey had said was, "Oh, that *will* be nice, Philip."

He struggled to his feet, wincing as he straightened out the kinks in his back. He could hear Audrey in the kitchen, humming away to herself as she went about preparing breakfast, and he wondered how she could be so bloody cheerful after a night on the damnable pull-out bed. He pulled on his dressing gown and plodded up the stairs.

Three years ago, they'd had an extension put on the bathroom, taken out the tub, installed a bigger water heater, enlarged the airing cupboard, and put in a full-sized shower. It had been expensive, but it was a luxury they both enjoyed, and as Tregalles climbed the stairs, he looked forward to the relief hot water would bring to his aching shoulders.

Still only half awake, he went into the bathroom, turned to shut the door, and was confronted by a grinning Lilian in a filmy nightgown.

"Jesus Murphy, Lil!" he began, eyes suddenly open wide, but Lilian's hand shot out to cover his mouth. "Shut up, you fool. She'll hear you," she whispered fiercely, and began to push him into the bathroom. Tregalles took a step backward, then stopped himself and began to push back.

"For God's sake, Lil, what do you think you're playing

at?'' he whispered hoarsely. "Look, this isn't funny. Philip—"

"Philip has gone to work," she interrupted, pushing back, "and Audrey will think you're in the shower by yourself. Come on, Johnny. Be a sport. It'll be fun."

"For God's sake, Lil!" he said, now deadly serious. "This may be a game to you, but this is one game I'm not playing."

Lilian stared at him for a long moment, brows drawn together and a hurt look in her eyes. "You've always played the game before," she pouted, "and I know you like me, so I thought that we could…"

"*Like* you, yes, Lil. I really do like you, but not…"

"Enough to screw me," she finished for him. "And I really thought…" She jumped as Audrey's voice came up the stairs.

"John? You there, John? It's getting late and I haven't heard any water running yet. You all right?"

Lilian turned quickly to seek refuge in the bedroom, but she stumbled and went sprawling across the landing. She screamed, and Audrey came charging up the stairs. "Oh my God, Lil, what have you done?" she panted as she reached the top.

"It's my wrist," Lilian said through gritted teeth. "I think the sodding thing is broken."

Audrey looked up at Tregalles, who stood frozen in the doorway. "Well, don't just stand there, John," she snapped. "Come and help me get Lilian up."

Between them, they got Lilian on her feet. "It is swollen," Audrey agreed, "but are you sure it's broken, Lil?"

"Of course I'm bloody sure!" Lilian grated. "Do you think it normally looks like this?" She shot an angry glance at Tregalles over Audrey's shoulder. "And if it wouldn't be putting you out *too* much, Johnny, perhaps you could spare the time to drive me to the hospital. Or will that make you late for work?"

"Of course he'll take you, won't you, John?" said Audrey soothingly. "But we'd better get some clothes on you before you go. You can hardly leave the house in your nightgown, can you, love?'' She frowned. ''But how did you come to be out here dressed like… Well, in your nightgown, in the first place?''

Tregalles held his breath.

Lilian looked at him for a long moment before she said, ''I thought I'd left something in the bathroom, and I was going to slip in and get it before Johnny came up. I didn't know he was there already.''

''But what made you fall?'' Audrey persisted.

By now the pain was making Lilian lose patience. ''It was your shouting up the stairs at Johnny,'' she said baldly. ''It startled me and I fell.''

''Oh! Oh, dear, I am sorry, love. I didn't mean to… Well, like I say, I'm ever so sorry, Lil, but let's get you into the bedroom and get some clothes on you. And you'd better get dressed as well, John. There's no time for a shower now.''

''That's right, Johnny,'' Lilian said in a little-girl voice as she moved away. ''No time for a shower now, is there?''

''I'll get my clothes,'' Tregalles said, and scuttled down the stairs.

DETOUR SIGNS had been set up at both ends of Church Street because the section in front of the second-hand shop was blocked by a fire engine and police cars.

Rick Proudfoot, still holding Sammy, stood at the Church Street entrance to the passageway, talking to a fireman named Tate. They fell silent as two men carrying a stretcher containing a PVC body bag edged by them.

''Crazy bastard!'' observed Tate, shaking his head. ''Built himself a bomb, then stood in the way of it when it blew.''

Rick said, ''I still don't understand exactly what happened.''

Tate shrugged. ''We won't know till they've done the investigation, but one thing's for sure. He was standing in front of that door when it blew, and it flung him across the passage and smashed him against the wall. Must have died instantly.''

"But why didn't the stairs catch fire?''

''That inside door at the bottom of the stairs is what saved you,'' Tate told him. ''That stopped most of the blast from hitting the stairs and forced it outward; the walls are plaster, so they didn't catch, and whatever flammable material was left—petrol I suspect, from the smell of it—was blown outside along with the door. But I can tell you this, mate: you were bloody lucky; it's a damned good thing the shop had sprinklers in, or we could have lost half the street.''

''Thanks to your boss or whoever does fire inspections,'' Rick told him. ''It was only after he threatened to close the shop last year that Mrs. McKinnon had them put in. I remember her going on and on about the expense at the time, but I'll bet she's thankful now. I know I am. Even then, I might not have been so lucky if it hadn't been for Sammy. She woke me up.'' He held up his wrist for Tate to see the scratches.

Sammy raised her head at the mention of her name, then snuggled into Rick's shoulder once again and closed her eyes.

THIRTY-FIVE

IT WAS AFTER SIX on Friday night by the time Grace was able to get away. The office had closed at three-thirty, and she'd been about to leave when Charlie told her he'd accepted an invitation on behalf of his staff to join the New Year's Eve party put on by the insurance agency office staff on the floor directly below them. Grace would have preferred to go home—there were things she wanted to do—but felt she could hardly refuse.

To be fair, it had been a very pleasant way to end the old year—the old year as far as the office was concerned, anyway. There were drinks, but bearing in mind that the police would be out, no one had gone overboard, and there was more than enough to eat. At least now she wouldn't have to spend time preparing a meal when she got home, she thought as she left the building.

The streets were all but deserted. The shops were shut, office workers had gone home early, and there was hardly any traffic. Head down against a bitterly cold wind funnelling through the narrow streets, Grace was glad to reach the comparative shelter of Friars Walk and the recessed entrance to her flat. Mounting the worn steps, she threw back the hood of her parka and stood there for a moment to catch her breath before delving into her handbag for her keys. She began to slide the key into the lock, but met no resistance as the door swung open.

They came at her from behind, propelling her through the open door. She fell forward into the tiny hall, banged against the umbrella stand as she went down, flung out an arm to save herself as the floor came up to meet her. Hit her face on something hard. Heard someone in the distance say, "Shut the door!" Heard it slam, then...nothing.

PAGET HAD CLEARED AWAY the remnants of the evening meal, and was about to start the washing-up, when the phone rang.

Grace? He hoped so, although she had said she wanted this evening to herself. "The house hasn't been cleaned properly since before Christmas," she told him, "and I have ironing that's been staring me in the face for the best part of a week. If we are going out on Saturday *and* Sunday, I don't want to come back to a dirty house and a basketful of ironing. I want to go into the New Year with a clean house and clear conscience."

"I'll come in and help you," he'd offered, but she'd smiled and shaken her head. "I'm sure you mean well, Neil, but let's face it: if the past few days are anything to go by, we wouldn't get much work done, would we?"

"True, but it would be a hell of a lot more enjoyable."

Or it could be the office, he thought as he picked up the phone and said, "Paget."

"Chief Inspector Paget?" A man's voice, hesitant, unsure.

"Yes."

"Ah, good. My name is Nelson. I live in the flat next door to Miss Lovett. She asked me to ring you. I'm afraid she's had a bit of an accident, and—"

A chill ran through him. "What happened?" he demanded before the man could finish. "Is she badly hurt?"

"Oh, no, sir, it's not as bad as all that, it's..." The man paused, and Paget thought he could hear someone speaking in the background. "It's just that she's taken a bit of a tumble on the stairs. I heard her call out, so I went in. She's lying down. I wanted to ring for the ambulance, but she said I was to ring you instead. Can you come?"

"I'm on my way," Paget replied. "Please stay with her

until I get there. Is there someone else there with you? I can hear someone in the background.''

''It's—it's another neighbour. You see—''

But Paget interrupted him again. ''I'll be there in twenty minutes,'' he told him, ''and if there is any change for the worse before I get there, call an ambulance, and never mind what Miss Lovett says.''

''Right, sir.'' The man sounded relieved.

Traffic was light, but there was ice on the road, and after almost sliding into the ditch on a curve, he was forced to slow down. But his imagination refused to slow down. The stairs in Grace's flat were steep and narrow, and if she'd fallen from the top… He shuddered at the thought. At least she must be conscious if she'd asked Nelson to ring him.

He should have asked to speak to Grace. She had a cordless phone.

He picked up his own phone and punched the numbers in with his thumb.

Engaged! Was Nelson phoning for the ambulance? If he was, that meant Grace had taken a turn for the worse. He pressed redial and heard the engaged signal again. He waited a couple of minutes, then tried again.

Still engaged! What the hell were they doing? It shouldn't take that long to have an ambulance dispatched.

He set the phone aside as he started down the long hill leading into the town. He needed steady hands on the wheel to negotiate the treacherous curves.

Friars Walk appeared to be deserted as Paget pulled up outside number 11 and parked on a double yellow line. The temperature had dropped rapidly with the setting of the sun, turning the slush of the afternoon into jagged chunks of ice, and he almost fell in his haste to get out of the car. No ambulance outside, and nothing to indicate one had been there, but whether that was a good sign or not, he didn't know. The curtains were drawn, but a chink of light suggested that someone was still inside the flat.

He hurried up the worn steps, pausing only for a second to peer at the name above the bell-push beside the door of number 10. Nelson. Right.

He was about to ring the bell beside Grace's door, then tried the handle. The door opened to his touch and he stepped over the sill. The short hall was in darkness, but a wedge of light spilled from the partly open door leading to the living room. "Grace?" he called as he pushed the door open. "It's Neil. Are you...?"

Someone shoved him violently to one side as he entered the room, and the door slammed behind him. He stumbled to his knees, started to get up, and was knocked down again with a vicious kick to the side. He hit his head against the wall; his vision blurred.

"Stay where you are! Don't try to get up!"

It wasn't so much the words that held him there, but the voice. He recognized it immediately as the one he'd heard as a razor slashed at his throat—hoarse and rasping like that of a heavy smoker, Dr. White had described it—and the sound of it chilled his blood.

"Stand away from him, Michael," the voice commanded. "And watch him."

"Mary Carr!" he breathed as he raised his head.

Grace sat facing him on one of the dining-room chairs. Her arms were drawn behind her, tied or taped, no doubt, and a wide strip of tape covered her mouth. Her face was pale, one cheek was bruised, and the eye was partly closed.

Behind her stood Mary Carr. Smartly dressed, well groomed—a far cry from the woman in the pictures that were circulating throughout the country. Older, certainly, and her face was more heavily lined, but there was no mistaking the grim set of her mouth, or the hard look in her eyes.

But Paget's eyes were drawn to her hands. Strong, capable hands, the left firmly entwined in Grace's hair, while the right held an open razor. He watched in horror as she drew the gleaming blade lightly across Grace's throat, and a trickle of blood ran dark against the pale skin.

"Just so there is no misunderstanding, Chief Inspector," the woman said, eyes fixed on Paget, "you know what this blade can do, so please don't try anything foolish. She'd be dead long before you or anyone else could do anything about it. You do understand, don't you?"

He nodded slowly.

"Good," the grating voice continued. "Now, take off your coat, lie face down on the floor, and put your hands behind you. Don't try anything with Michael while he is taping your hands, because I shall take that as a signal to cut deeper into this lovely throat."

Paget tried to hold his wrists apart as much as possible, but Michael pulled them tight, and wrapped the tape several times before tearing it from the roll.

"Step away, Michael, and let the Chief Inspector stand up."

The young man moved back against the door while Paget rose awkwardly to his feet. "Your quarrel is with me," he said. "I think you know that Miss Lovett has nothing to do with this, so I'm asking you to let her go."

Mary Carr smiled. "And I think *you* know very well that Miss Lovett has everything to do with this," she told him. "So we might as well begin." Her hand tightened on Grace's hair. "On your feet, lady," she ordered, "and don't try anything stupid or I *will* cut your throat. And if you think I won't, just ask your man there. He'll tell you. Understand?"

Grace nodded, insofar as she was able, but it was enough for Mary Carr.

"Good. In that case, here is what we're going to do. Paget, I want you to move over to the far wall opposite the door. Michael, you stay close to him but watch his feet. I don't think he's fool enough to try anything, but watch him anyway. Miss Lovett and I are going upstairs, and I want you to follow and do exactly as I say."

Paget took up his position opposite the door while Mary guided Grace through the doorway into the hall and to the bottom of the stairs. "All right, Michael," she called. "Have him come out in front of you."

"Do as she says…" Michael began, but Paget had moved so swiftly across the room and into the hall that Michael had almost to run to catch up with him.

Mary stood with her back to the bottom of the stairs. "Now," she rasped, "Miss Lovett and I are going up these stairs backward, so I will be watching you all the time. I'll go first, one step at a time, and Miss Lovett will follow when I tell her. This razor will be at her throat all the time, and I'll use it if I have to. You, Paget, will face me and follow five steps behind, and Michael will follow you. Is that clear?"

Paget couldn't take his eyes off the razor at Grace's throat. Through some sort of telepathic empathy, he could feel the touch of steel against his own throat, and he had to stop himself from flinching. He looked into Grace's eyes, and tried to send a silent message of encouragement with his own.

"I *said,* is that clear?" Mary's voice rose; her hand trembled as her eyes bored into his own, and for one sickening moment, he thought she was going to use the razor.

"Yes! Yes, it's clear!"

"That's better."

Grace felt the prick of the blade as Mary took one step backward. Oh, God! Don't let her slip or fall backward, she thought frantically as she put one foot back and felt for the step. She found it and moved up.

"Very good, my dear," said Mary. "Just keep that up and you'll be all right."

For how long? And why are we going upstairs?

Grace's mind was working furiously, trying to work out why Mary wanted them upstairs. She was all too familiar with what the woman had done with the rest of her victims, so unless she could think of something…

"Aahhgg!"

The strangled sound was muffled by the tape. She'd almost lost her balance as she'd felt for the next step, and the blade had nicked her throat.

Mary was pulling hard on her hair. "Pay attention!" she grated. "One more move like that and your precious Paget will find your head in his hands."

As the pair moved up the stairs, Paget followed as instructed, with Michael close behind, too close. Even with his hands bound behind him, Paget was sure he could take him down. But a move like that would only infuriate Mary, and she wouldn't hesitate to slit Grace's throat.

But there *had* to be a way.

"It's over, Mary," he told her quietly. "You and Michael can't possibly get away, so why make matters worse. You need help…"

"Shut up!" The razor pressed closer to Grace's throat. A silent but effective warning. He saw Grace's eyes close, thought she was going to faint; but she opened them again as Mary pulled her up one more step.

Paget mounted the next step, careful to keep his distance, eyes on Mary as he did so. But why, he kept asking himself, was she so intent on going upstairs at all? As far as he knew, all of her other victims had died where she'd found them.

Mary reached the top. She pulled Grace up after her, then walked her backward to the bathroom door. At first he thought she'd made a mistake, but it soon became clear she knew exactly where she was going, and Paget had a sudden premonition.

The thought chilled him to the bone, and he prayed that he was wrong.

With hardly a glance behind her, Mary kicked the door open and, still walking backward, pulled Grace through. "All right, Michael, bring him in," she ordered, "but make sure he keeps his distance."

Paget paused in the doorway. Considering the age of the house, the bathroom was surprisingly spacious. Immediately in front of him stood a pedestal washbasin, with a towel rack beside it. Above the towel rack was a small frosted window, and to the left of that was a large, old-fashioned bathtub, supported by cast-iron feet in the shape of lion's paws. Behind the door was the lavatory, an airing cupboard, and a hot-water tank.

Mary stopped with her back against the airing cupboard. "Close the door and lock it, then come over here," she told her son. "You, Paget, back up and stand with your back against the door, and don't move. Not one inch! Understand?"

"I understand," he told her, and moved back against the door.

"Fill the bath, Michael."

"But, Mum, you said you weren't going to—" he began, but his mother cut him off.

"Be quiet, Michael, and fill the bath."

With an unhappy glance at his mother, Michael Carr turned on the taps.

"Hot water, Michael."

This was the first real opportunity Paget had had to study Michael. The quiet lad with the dark red hair that he remembered looked much different now. He wasn't as tall as Paget, but he was heavier, and his hair had been cut to within an inch of his scalp, and bleached. But there was something servile about him, and although he must be twenty-four or -five, Paget couldn't help thinking of him as a boy—but this boy, it seemed, would do almost anything to please his mother. If he could find a way to drive a wedge between the two...

It was a slim chance, but even a slim chance was better than no chance at all.

The bath was filling slowly. Steam swirled above the water, and Michael stood beside it, staring into it.

"Don't just stand there, Michael," said Mary sharply. "You know what you have to do next."

Alarm flared in Michael's eyes. "Oh, no, Mum. No. You promised me you wouldn't—"

But Mary cut him off. "I know what I said, Michael." She spoke with the exaggerated patience of a mother to a five-year-old. "But I've changed my mind. I want Chief Inspector Paget to see exactly how your sister died. Now, get her clothes off, and be quick about it!"

"No… Mum, no! You promised me you'd…" He was close to tears.

"Would you rather I cut her throat now, Michael? Would you like that?"

"No! Please, Mum…"

"Then get on with it. We haven't got all…" Mary's voice dropped ominously as Paget started forward. "Don't even think about it unless you want her dead this instant," she warned. "Get back against the door."

Paget could see the pain in Grace's eyes as he held them with his own. But how could he relay encouragement and hope when they both knew there was no hope?

Michael was fumbling with Grace's skirt, eyes averted, afraid to look at her as he pulled it down. "Step out of it carefully," his mother told Grace—her hand tightened on Grace's hair—"and I shouldn't try it if I were you," she warned ominously.

It's as if this woman can read my mind! thought Grace despairingly. She'd tensed, bent her legs, ready to shove Mary backward as hard as she could against the cupboard, then try to duck out from under the razor. She would probably be cut, but if Neil could get a couple of good kicks in… It might not succeed, but anything was better than letting this woman send her to her death without a fight. But Mary had sensed the move and was ready for it.

"Now the tights, Michael. And the shoes."

He shook his head; his cheeks were wet with tears, but he did as he was told.

"You'll have to cut the blouse off. And her bra. Use your

knife, but carefully. I want her clothes folded just as your sister folded hers. And for Christ's sake, hurry up!''

If Michael would just block his mother's view, even for an instant, there might be a chance, thought Paget. He could charge them both, knock Mary back against the cupboard—too bad she wasn't standing in front of the bath.

The thought died. It would take at least a second to cross the floor—more than enough time for this determined woman to use the razor on Grace's throat. And even if he did succeed in knocking Mary over, what then? Would Michael stand by and do nothing? Would Grace be bleeding to death while he stood there and watched helplessly? Given time, he might—just might—get his hands free, though even that was doubtful. Already his wrists were raw from trying, but the tape hadn't budged an inch.

"Why are you doing this?" he asked Mary.

Her eyes narrowed. "Oh, I think you know why," she said softly. "You were there the day they took my Gillanne away from me. You stood by and let them take her. You testified against me in court; you sent me down for something I didn't do. You killed my daughter, and now you're going to pay."

Her voice dropped as she jerked Grace's head back. "But then, she doesn't know, does she? So I'll make it very clear."

Her eyes remained on Paget's face, but her words were for Grace. "Someone—I still don't know who—came into the house while I was out, and killed my husband, Donald. I loved that man and he loved me. I wouldn't have harmed him for the world, but this man said I did it. He's the one who arrested me and stood by while they dragged my children off."

Paget shook his head. "You say you loved him, but if that's true, why were you out there night after night, watching to see if he was sneaking off to meet his lover?"

"But he wasn't, was he?" she flung back at him. "He'd finished with her. He never left the house, and I should never have listened to my so-called friends who said he was still seeing her. Donald was a good man."

Mary let out a long, shuddering sigh. "Do you know what it's like inside?" she asked, but it was clear she didn't expect an answer. "Do you know what it's like to be shut away for something you haven't done, knowing it will be eight or ten or twelve years before you can be with your child again? Do you have any idea what it's like to be told, quite callously, that your only daughter committed suicide because no one would believe her?" Her voice rose. "Have you any idea at all what's it's like not to be allowed to die when you have no reason to live?"

Her eyes glittered. "But then I found a reason, didn't I, *Chief Inspector?* And I vowed that you and all the others would suffer as I have suffered all these years."

"Did you hear that, Michael?" asked Paget sharply. Michael was trying to fold Grace's clothes, but he had to keep stopping to brush tears away from his eyes. "Did you hear what your mother said? She wasn't worried about you, was she, Michael? Just Gillanne. She's never cared about you, has she? She doesn't care about you now. She's using you, and when she's finished here, she won't care whether you live or die. It was always Gillanne, wasn't it, Michael? Never you. It was—"

"Shut it, or I'll kill her now!" Mary screeched the words, and Michael flinched. "Don't listen to him, Michael. He'll say anything to try to save his precious girlfriend." She drew a deep breath and made an effort to control her voice. "And for God's sake stop fiddling with those clothes, and turn water off."

Head down, Michael left the clothes and turned off the taps.

Mary Carr wrenched hard on Grace's hair, forcing her to arch her back as she was manoeuvred into position beside the high curved end of the tub. "Now then, my dear," she said, "Michael is going to cut the tape on your wrists, so stand perfectly still, and don't move your arms until I tell you." Her voice rose sharply. "Well, Michael? What are you waiting for? You heard me. Get on with it. Cut the tape."

"You won't *really* do it, will you, Mum?" he said in such a quiet voice that only Grace could hear. "You did promise."

For a brief, hopeful moment, her spirits rose. Was it possible that this was simply some sort of ghastly charade? A demonstration of how Gillanne had died? But no sooner had the thought entered her head than she remembered what had happened to the other victims, and whatever hope she might have had vanished with Mary Carr's next words.

"Cut the tape, Michael, and stop asking foolish questions."

Grace felt the cold hard steel of the knife against her wrists; felt the trembling hands that held it as the boy sawed carefully at the tape.

He was trying not to hurt her! If only there were some way she could get him on her side. But how could she when she couldn't speak? But the biggest question of all was, why were they cutting her hands free now?

The tape parted, and the boy began to pull it carefully from her wrists, but his mother stopped him with a sharp, "That's enough, Michael. Now, step away and keep your eyes on Paget."

Grace's head was pulled back, and she felt the edge of the razor on her throat. "Now, then, lady, I want you to raise your hands above your head and step into the bath, left leg first, then the right, and sit down carefully. If I even think you are going to lower your hands, this blade will take your head off. I'm sure you get the picture."

Grace felt the sting of tears behind her eyes, and used every ounce of willpower she had to hold them back. She'd be damned if she would give this woman the satisfaction of seeing how scared she was. Even so, she flinched as her foot entered the water, and she pulled it back again.

"A bit too hot, is it?" Mary asked solicitously. "Never mind, my dear; you'll be glad of the warmth later on, so get on with it. Sit down carefully, and keep your hands up where I can see them. Not too far down, now," she warned as Grace's body slid beneath the water. "Bend your knees, and keep your feet away from the other end of the tub. If you were thinking of using them to push back suddenly and try to grab my arm, forget it!''

Mary Carr had sunk to her knees at the head of the bathtub as Grace lowered herself into the water, her hand still firmly entwined in Grace's hair. Now she looked at Paget, and her voice turned almost soft.

''This is how my daughter died,'' she said, ''and this is how your lady's going to die.'' Her right hand shot out, the razor flashed, and Michael screamed as blood spurted from both of Grace's wrists. She snatched them away, but it was too late. ''Stop or you'll have her head!'' Mary rasped as Paget started forward. The razor was back again at Grace's throat, and one look into Mary's eyes told him she meant exactly what she said.

He pulled up short. ''For the love of God, Mary, she's done you no harm. Finish the job you did on me, but let her go. There's still time.''

She knew what he meant, but she merely smiled and shook her head. Slashed wrists leak blood more slowly than do carotid arteries, but the water was swiftly turning red as Grace tried desperately to press her wrists against her body to stop the flow.

''And for God's sake, stop blubbering!'' Mary snapped at Michael. ''You're no damned good to me in that state. You wanted this as much as I did, so take a good, hard look, Michael. This is how your sister died. This man, Paget, killed her—or might just as well have done—and he is going to remember this moment for the rest of his life!''

''While you spend the rest of your life behind bars, Michael,'' Paget put in swiftly. He eased forward. The bath was red with blood, and it seemed as if Grace was finding it harder to keep her head from falling forward. He tried to tell himself that she couldn't have lost all that much blood in such a short time, but... *Half a step more.* If he could get in one hard kick to Mary's head, he'd take his chances with Michael. Grace would probably be cut, but she couldn't last much longer as it was. He raised his voice. "She doesn't care what happens to you, Michael." *Weight on the other foot.* "There's no escape, Michael. There's no—"

"Stop right there, Paget, or she's gone this instant."

The razor pressed hard against Grace's throat. Even the slightest movement sideways would cut very deep. "Back against the door. You know I'll do it. I've got nothing to lose."

"But Michael has, and he doesn't want to see an innocent person die."

"Gillanne was his sister! He wants what I want."

"Stop it! Stop it! For Christ's sake stop!" Michael screamed. Tears were streaming down his face. He seemed to be fighting for breath. "It wasn't his fault or any of the others," he panted. "It was yours! You were the one who married him. You were the one who said everything would be all right. Gilly tried to tell you, but you wouldn't listen, would you? She killed herself because she didn't want to hurt you or me, and she didn't know what else to do."

Mary stared at her son, colour rising in her face. "Don't you *dare* take that tone with me," she grated. "You don't know what you're talking about."

But Michael was shaking his head. "You thought you were so bloody clever, didn't you? Sitting out there in the car every night, watching to see if your precious Donald was sneaking out of the house while you were gone."

"He *didn't* come out! He loved me. He would never…"

"He didn't *have* to go out!" shouted Michael. He dashed a hand across his face to wipe away the tears. "He didn't have to, Mum, because every time you left the house he was screwing Gilly!"

Mary's face was livid as she lunged toward her son. Paget seized his chance, but in trying to avoid his mother, Michael got in his way. Paget kneed him in the back. The boy went down, but Mary was almost on her son when Paget kicked as he'd never kicked before. His foot caught Mary on the elbow. The razor clattered to the floor, and Mary fell back screaming.

"Grace!" She was sliding down; her head was nodding and she seemed barely conscious. "Grace!" he screamed again, and saw her try to lift her head.

But Mary was reaching for the razor. Her right arm was shattered at the elbow, but her left hand was only inches away from the gleaming weapon. Paget moved to intercept her, but Michael got there first. She had the razor in her grasp when he brought his foot down on her wrist. Hard! Bone snapped beneath his heel.

His mother screamed, tried to rise, then fell back. Michael knelt beside her, picked up the razor, and grasped his mother's hair.

"Michael, no!" Paget's throat had suddenly gone dry, and he had trouble getting out the words. "Don't make it worse. She can't harm anybody now, but Grace will die if we don't get her out and stop the bleeding. You don't want her to die, do you, Michael? Cut me free and help me get her out."

Grace's eyes were closed and her head was sinking lower on her chest. Paget screamed her name. Her eyes fluttered, and she tried to lift her head, but the effort was too much, and it fell back again. Her mouth was underwater. Only the tape was saving her, but another inch lower and she would drown in her own blood.

"Go on, then, do it!" Mary panted. The words rattled in her damaged throat, and her lips curled in contempt. "But you haven't got the guts, have you, Michael? Never had and never will."

"Don't do it, Michael. Cut the tape," Paget pleaded. "You can't get her out alone."

The boy looked up at him through his tears. "She never loved me," he sobbed. "She loved Gilly, but she never loved me. Gilly was the only one who loved me."

"Gilly wouldn't want you to let Grace die, would she, Michael?'' said Paget desperately. "She'd want you to save her. Cut the tape on my hands and let me help you."

Michael stared at him for a long moment, then, slowly—so slowly that Paget wanted to scream at him—he released his hold on Mary's hair, and stood up. "Turn round," he said, and moments later Paget's hands were free.

"Pull the plug, then help me get her out," he told Michael as he tried to get a grip under Grace's arms. The boy did as he was told, but lifting her out of the tub was an almost impossible task. Her blood-soaked skin might as well have been smothered in grease, and she kept slipping from their grasp. Slowly, painfully slowly, they managed to pull her over the lip of the tub, and from there onto the floor.

"Give me the roll of tape," said Paget as he pulled yards of toilet paper from the roll and began to bind Grace's wrists, "then toss me those bath towels and sheets from the airing cupboard. We've got to keep her warm." He peeled away the strip of tape from Grace's mouth, then, with Michael's help, rolled her into the towels and sheets.

"We need an ambulance," said Paget, still on his knees. "Will you go down and ring them for me, Michael? Tell them that it's urgent." He would rather have gone himself, but he wasn't sure enough of Michael to leave him alone with Grace and his mother.

Michael nodded slowly, then took the folded razor from his pocket and handed it to Paget. "You'd better have this," he said, and left the room.

Paget raised Grace up and held her in his arms. He wiped her face and kissed her brow. Tears welled in his eyes. "Don't die on me now," he whispered softly. "Please, God, don't let her die."

THIRTY-SIX

TREGALLES FOUND PAGET in the Casualty waiting room, hunched forward, head bowed, hands together beneath his chin. If he hadn't known the man better, he might have thought the DCI was praying.

Paget had phoned him from the car as he followed the ambulance to the hospital, and told Tregalles to meet him there. "Mary Carr's been injured, and I have her son, Michael, with me. Better let Alcott know as well."

"Bloody hell!" Tregalles breathed as he saw the state of Paget's clothes. "What happened? Are you all right, sir?"

Paget raised his head. His face was grey and drawn. "It's a long story," he said softly, "but in a nutshell, Mary Carr came close to killing Grace tonight, and now they're both in there. He nodded in the direction of Casualty. Mary will recover, but Grace… I just don't know."

"Grace? She tried to kill Grace Lovett? Why? What…?"

But Paget was shaking his head. "Not now, Tregalles," he said wearily. "I'll fill you in later, but in the meantime, you'd better have someone come and take Michael in." Paget indicated the young man sitting a couple of seats away. "This is Michael Carr," he explained. "He's agreed to turn himself in, but I suggest you delay specific charges until I've given you my statement."

"But he *was* working with her, wasn't he? His mother, I mean."

"As I said, it's a long story."

"Mr. Paget?" A nurse appeared beside him. "The doctor would like a word."

"How is Miss Lovett? Is she going to be all right?"

"No doubt the doctor will be able to answer that better than—" the nurse began, but Paget's hand shot out and grabbed her arm.

"I want to know if she's still alive!" he said roughly. "Surely to God you can tell me that!"

A protest rose to the woman's lips, but when she saw the look in Paget's eyes, she nodded quickly. "But she's lost a great deal of blood," she said. As if he didn't know. "Are you a relative?"

"No, but I'm the closest thing she's got to one right now. If she needs blood, I'm quite prepared…."

"You *will* have to ask the doctor about that," she said firmly.

"Don't go away, Tregalles," Paget called as he followed the nurse. "And you'd better see about placing Mary Carr under arrest as well, before she walks out of here."

BY THE TIME Paget returned to the waiting room, Michael Carr was being led away by two uniformed constables, and Molly Forsythe had arrived. She would stay close to Mary Carr until the woman could be taken into custody and charged. Alcott, it turned out, was in Birmingham, and wouldn't be back until sometime on Saturday, but Tregalles had issued instructions to track the superintendent down and inform him of the apprehension of Mary Carr and Michael.

"What about Chief Superintendent Brock?" Paget had asked. "Does he know yet?"

"I was hoping to contact the super in Birmingham before talking to Mr. Brock," Tregalles told him. "I thought it would be best if he were the one to tell Mr. Brock, rather than the other way round. What do you think, sir?"

"I think you're learning," said Paget, "but don't leave it too long, or you'll have Brock on your back. Better Alcott than Brock."

PAGET REMAINED at Grace's bedside throughout the night. The nurses recognized him from his own stay in hospital the month before, and brought him cups of tea to help him stay awake. The doctor had advised him to go home and get some rest, but he had stubbornly refused.

They had given Grace a transfusion, but she still looked deathly pale, and the bruise on her cheek looked almost black against the pallor of her flesh. The cuts to her throat looked worse than they really were, and the doctor assured him there would be no lasting scars. Unfortunately, the same could not be said of her wrists. The cuts, he said, were deep, but even they would fade…eventually.

But what of the scars within? The trauma of the mind? How long would it be before the horror of what she'd been through faded from her memory? Grace was strong, but even so…

He'd stroked her hair and taken her hand and held it to his lips as he offered up a silent prayer.

WHILE GRACE WAS receiving a blood transfusion the night before, Paget had prevailed upon the casualty officer to let him have a shower and lend him a hospital housecoat until he could get hold of clean clothes of his own. He had given his key to Tregalles and asked him to have someone go out to the house and bring him a complete set of clothing, because, as he told the sergeant, "I'm not leaving this hospital until I know that Grace will be all right, and I don't want to go round wearing this thing any longer than I have to."

Tregalles, accompanied by Charlie Dobbs, returned to the hospital just after eight o'clock on Saturday morning. They both looked shaken, but their first questions were about Grace.

"They're being pretty cautious, but they seem to think that, barring complications, she'll be all right—at least physically, but after what she went through last night, I just don't know what that will do to her mental state.''

"We stopped in at her flat on the way here,'' Tregalles said in hushed tones. "Charlie's people are there now collecting evidence.'' He grimaced. "The bathroom looks like an abattoir.''

"What I don't understand is why she attacked Grace,'' said Charlie. "Why would Mary Carr go after her?''

"It was my fault.'' Paget's eyes were bleak as he shook his head in self-recrimination. "Mary Carr chose Grace as a way of getting at me. We—we've been seeing each other recently, and Mary and her son must have been stalking us. I should have realized I was putting her in danger when I saw someone watching the house last week, but I chose to ignore it for my own selfish reasons.'' He took a deep breath before continuing. "Mary Carr intended to kill her while forcing me to watch.''

"Bloody hell!'' Tregalles breathed.

A grim smile touched Paget's lips. "It's an apt description,'' he said tonelessly. "Did you get anything from Michael?''

"We have his statement, yes.''

"And...?''

"He pretty much confirms what you told me last night, but we're going to need a statement from you as well.''

"You'll get it,'' Paget assured him, "but unless you want to take it here, it will have to wait until I know for sure that Grace is out of danger. And I'll want to talk to Michael about the night his stepfather was killed. He said something last night that made me curious. What about Mary? How is she?''

"In custody and spitting mad. Swears she's going to kill Michael if she can get her hands on him. She has a full-length cast on her right arm, and a smaller cast on her left wrist— which she tried to use on Molly as a club. Caught her a nasty clip on the shoulder. But Molly soon sorted her out. The woman's as mad as a bloody hatter, of course.''

But Paget demurred. "I'm not so sure she is," he said, "at least not legally; but she is dangerous, and I wouldn't let her get too close to Michael or she will try to carry out her threat."

HE WAS DOZING in the chair when he felt someone give his hand a shake. He opened his eyes, and blinked against the light.

"Can I have my hand back?" someone said.

He raised his head. "Grace! You're awake," he said. "Thank God!"

He took her hand between his own. "How do you feel?"

"Hungry," she said with a tired smile, "which is why I need my hand back."

"But how do you *really* feel?" he asked anxiously. "Oh God, Grace, I'm so sorry for what happened. I don't know how…"

Grace slipped her hand free and pressed her fingers against his lips. "It's not your fault," she said softly, "so for heaven's sake don't try to take the blame upon yourself. I'm fine. I am a little shaky, and it will take time for me to get my strength back, but apart from that…" She shivered and her eyes grew dark. "But I don't think I shall ever take a bath again."

"Oh, Grace. I was so afraid…" The words died in his throat.

She took his hand again and drew him close to her. "I love you, Neil Paget," she whispered, "and if you can negotiate your way through these tubes and needles, I'd like you to hold me."

"I thought you said you were hungry?"

"Oh God, you really are hopeless," she told him as she drew him down to her.

Andrea McMillan, who had been about to enter the room, turned back and walked off down the corridor. Later. She would look in later on the patient, but right now it seemed best to leave Grace Lovett and Neil alone. She was very fond of Neil, but not in love with him. Grace, on the other hand, was in love with him. Andrea had known that from the very first time she'd met Grace, but what she hadn't known was if Neil was in love with Grace. She sighed contentedly. From what she'd just witnessed, there didn't seem to be much doubt.

Neither was there any doubt about her feelings for Sten. After years of trying to distance herself from the past, the past had caught up with her in the form of Sten Wallen. Although it was he who had found her, she felt as if she'd come home at last.

PAGET WENT DIRECTLY from the hospital to Charter Lane, where Alcott and Tregalles both sat in while his statement was being recorded.

The superintendent sat back and sucked deeply on his cigarette as Tregalles turned the tape recorder off. "I think both you and Miss Lovett had better spend some time with our trauma counsellor," he said. "I know, I know," he interrupted as Paget started to protest, "no one likes to think he or she might need help when it comes to the mind, but better to make sure at the beginning rather than have nightmares about it later. I should think you've had enough of those already."

"True," said Paget absently. He hadn't thought about it until Alcott mentioned it, but he hadn't experienced any of the dreaded flashbacks since before Christmas. Perhaps it was the realization that Mary Carr had been talking about her daughter rather than Jill that had banished them. On the other hand, perhaps it had something to do with Grace.

"You'll do it, then?" Alcott sounded surprised.

Paget nodded. "I can't speak for Grace, of course, but if you think it might help, I'll give it a try."

"Good." Alcott rose to leave, but Paget stopped him. "I'd like to talk to Michael Carr about the death of his sister," he said. "Something he mentioned last night about why she killed herself. I think he knows more about what happened the night his stepfather was killed than he told us at the time."

"His mother was convicted of the crime."

"And has consistently denied that she was guilty."

"Are you saying you believe her now?"

"I don't know, but I would like to know the truth."

"I see." Alcott drummed nicotine-stained fingers on the table. "Very well," he said. "Let's have him in, Tregalles."

Michael Carr looked apprehensive as he was brought into the room to face the three men. Alcott dealt with the preliminaries, then turned the interview over to Paget.

"Last night you told your mother that Donald Carr didn't have to go out the night he was killed, because he was sexually assaulting your sister. Is that true, Michael?"

Michael Carr swallowed hard. He'd expected to be questioned about his role in the recent murders, not about this. "I…" His mouth was dry. A sheen of sweat appeared on his brow, and he looked as if he might cry.

"Is that true, Michael?"

He managed to nod.

"With her consent?"

"Jesus, no!"

"You mean he was raping her?"

"Yes… No…" The boy gulped air. "I don't know," he said miserably. "I suppose he was. He threatened her with a knife. The one you found in the garden."

"Was that the first time he'd done that? The night he died, I mean?"

"No." Michael's voice was husky as he tried to explain. "He'd been doing it for a long time. It started not long after he came to live with us. Even before that, Gilly tried to tell Mum she didn't like him, but Mum wouldn't hear a word against him. He kept touching Gilly, stroking her hair and telling her how beautiful she was. Gilly didn't like it. She told Mum it made her feel funny, but like I said, Mum wouldn't listen. She told Gilly it was just his way of showing affection.''

"Where was your mother while this was going on?"

"Out. She'd go out most nights to visit her shops, talk to the managers and check the day's takings."

"But you knew?"

"Not at first. I knew something was wrong, but I didn't realize... I mean, I was a kid; I was fourteen, and Gilly was thirteen. I—I didn't know that grown-ups did that sort of thing. I knew he kept going to her room and she would be crying afterward, but it had been going on for a while before she told me."

"And you said nothing? Told no one?"

"How could I? Gilly said he'd told her he'd kill all of us if it ever got out, and she made me promise never to tell."

"But there must have been times when Carr was out of the house and you or your sister could have told your mother."

"Gilly was afraid. She said Mum might think that what was happening was her fault, and she wouldn't love her anymore. See, Mum was really gone on Don. He could tell her anything and she'd have believed him. Besides, Gilly was afraid of what he'd do if she said anything."

"An impossible situation for two children," Paget said, and Michael nodded mutely. "So one night, when it became too much to bear, Gillanne managed to get hold of the knife, and she killed him. Isn't that right, Michael?"

"No!" The boy stared at him in horror. "No!" he tried to say again, but the word stuck in his throat.

"Which is why she killed herself," Paget went on. "She couldn't live with what she'd done. She..."

He stopped. Michael's head was shaking so hard that his whole upper body was twisting as if in torment. "It wasn't Gilly," he gasped. "It was me! She was screaming. He was hurting her, and I couldn't stand it any longer." Michael brushed the tears from his face with the back of his hands. "I'd always tried to pretend it wasn't happening. I didn't want it to be true. I used to go to my room and put a pillow over my head, but this time…'' Michael lifted his head and met Paget's gaze head on. ''But this time it was different. I went downstairs. He was on top of her. The knife was on the floor beside him. I tried to pull him off, but he knocked me down. I grabbed the knife, and when he started to get up I stabbed him. But he didn't stop. I was scared shitless, so I kept stabbing until he fell over. It wasn't Gilly. It was me.''

THEY STOOD AROUND the car, Tregalles, Audrey, and the children, as Philip put the last suitcase in the car. He wasn't in the best of moods; he had wanted to stay on to finish what he'd started with Radio Shropshire, but Lilian had been adamant; she insisted on going home, and that was that.

''But it's New Year's Eve!'' he'd objected.

''So it's New Year's Eve. It's not as if we'll be going dancing, is it? Not with this cast on.''

''You could,'' Philip said unwisely. ''I mean, it's not as if it's a very big…''

He never did finish the sentence. The look he received stopped him dead in his tracks, and he began to pack.

''Well, must be off,'' he told his sister, glancing at his watch. ''It will be getting dark by the time we get home.''

''So glad you could come,'' said Audrey, ''but I am sorry about your wrist, Lilian. I do hope it will be better soon.''

''So do I,'' Tregalles told her, giving her a hug. Lilian put her arm around his neck, and in doing so managed to drag the rough cast across his ear.

''Oh, I am sorry, Johnny,'' she said contritely as tears welled in his eyes. ''I hope I didn't hurt you.''

''It's nothing,'' he said huskily. ''Take care, now.''

''Oh, I will,'' she assured him. ''I never make the same mistake twice.''

THIRTY-SEVEN

WHEN PAGET RETURNED to the hospital late Saturday afternoon, the doctor was at Grace's bedside. "If all goes well overnight, I don't see why you can't go home tomorrow," he told her. "How are you feeling now?"

"Fine, apart from feeling weak."

"You lost a lot of blood," he said, "but you're responding well. Is there someone at home who can keep an eye on you for the next few days?"

"I..."

"Yes, there is," said Paget firmly.

"Good. In that case, Miss Lovett, I'll look in on you first thing tomorrow morning."

Now, as Paget drove into town to take Grace home, he thought about what Michael Carr had told them.

They had all been wrong, tragically wrong, and Mary Carr had spent ten years of her life in prison, convicted of a crime she didn't commit. Enough in itself to send anyone round the bend, but to have her daughter commit suicide on top of that had been more than she could bear.

There was no way anyone could condone what she'd done since her release, but he was acutely aware that he, along with everyone connected with the case, must bear some of the blame for what had happened.

Gillanne was only thirteen at the time, but it had been she, Michael said, who had recovered first and told him what they had to do. "Gilly was always a lot cleverer than me," he said wistfully. It was Gillanne who told him to wipe the knife clean and bury it in the garden. It was also Gillanne who made up the story about hearing someone come to the house that evening, and having an argument with Donald Carr, and it was she who had insisted he take two of his antihistamine tablets so that he wouldn't be questioned by the police when they arrived. "She was afraid I might get it wrong, you see," he explained.

But when the police turned their attention to her mother as the prime suspect, Gillanne hadn't known what to do. If she remained silent, her mother could go to jail, but if she spoke out now about what Carr had been doing to her, and the police thought that her mother had found out about it, the case against her would be even stronger. If she told the truth, Gillanne was afraid her mother would hate her, and her brother would go to jail.

On the day of their grandfather's funeral, Michael said Gillanne had made him promise once again to keep silent about what had really happened, because she knew what she had to do to get her mother off. "I didn't understand what she meant at the time," he said, "but she told me she'd read somewhere that if a person said something when they knew they were going to die, everyone had to believe it."

"A dying declaration," Alcott said softly.

"When the police came to get us," Michael continued, "Gilly gave me a big hug and said I mustn't worry, because everything was going to be all right, then ran out the back. That was the last time I saw her. I didn't even know she was dead till about a month later. They moved me to another foster home and no one told me, so I never even got to go to her funeral."

The girl had sacrificed herself to save both her mother and her brother, and it had all been for nothing. She had done what she'd thought best—with disastrous results.

Paget parked the car and sat there for a moment before

getting out. There would be an enquiry, of course, and he, like everyone else, would be called upon to defend his actions. He was on record as having voiced concerns about the evidence at the time, but that was of little consolation now. Nor did the fact that he had been deliberately misled by the children bring any comfort.

Not only had Mary Carr and her family suffered because of a gross miscarriage of justice, but many innocent people had died as a result, and he must share the blame. If he had done a more thorough job; if he'd spent more time with the children...

He got out of the car. No matter what the outcome, he would always know that he had failed. He could dwell on it, take on the guilt, allow it to overshadow every decision he would make from this point on, but that would change nothing that had happened in the past. He, and the others, had done their jobs to the best of their abilities, but they were human, and humans make mistakes. He would always feel the guilt, but dwelling on it would accomplish nothing. Better to learn from it, and let it serve as a reminder of what could happen if he failed to do a better job.

It would not be easy to put all this behind him. Every time he looked in a mirror, every time he looked into Grace's eyes, he would remember. But when all was said and done, he had a job to do, and there was nothing to be gained by dwelling on the past. He'd been down that road before.

"I WASN'T SURE what clothes to bring, so I brought as much as I could carry for you to choose," he told Grace. "I'll wait in the corridor while you get dressed. Do you need a nurse to help you?"

Grace shook her head, but he saw her hand was shaking as she pulled back the bedclothes and swung her legs over the side. "I think you do," he said. "I'll ask someone to help you."

"No. No, Neil, it's not that. I know it's silly, but the thought of going back into the flat, especially the bathroom, sends shivers up my spine."

"You're not going back to the flat," he said as he took her by the hand. "For a start, the place is a hell of a mess, and some of your people are still working there, so, if you've no objection, you're coming home with me. I'm still on sick leave, remember, and my doctor thinks I've been overdoing it a bit, so we can recuperate together."

Grace let out a sigh of relief. "I'd like that," she said simply. She slid off the bed, and would have fallen if he hadn't been there to catch her. She stood there blinking and shaking her head while he held her. "This is ridiculous," she said, annoyed at her own weakness. "It's not as if I've been ill."

"You have to learn not to move too fast while your blood levels are so low," he warned. "Now, why don't you sit in this chair while I try to find a nurse to help you dress?"

But Grace held on to him. "They're awfully busy, Neil," she whispered. "It seems a shame to trouble them. If you'd like to draw the curtain, I can manage—with a little help from you."

RICK PROUDFOOT and Kate Regan turned away from the open grave. Kate, still on crutches, picked her way carefully down the slope to where Marshall's old boss, Frank Talbot, waited by Rick's car.

He extended his hand. "I try to remember Paul the way he was when he was on the road," he told her. "I hope you can do the same."

Kate gripped his hand. Her eyes were moist as she looked back toward the grave. "The Paul we knew died long ago," she said. "I don't know the man we buried here today."

Talbot nodded and turned away.

"Do you need a lift?" Rick called after him, but Talbot

shook his head. ''It's not far and I like to walk,'' he said, and plodded on. A breeze stirred in the leafless trees, and it looked as if it might snow again.

Kate took one last look around, then took Rick's arm. ''It's over,'' she said softly. ''It's time to go. Please take me home.''

BETTY WEBB

DESERT WIVES

Arizona private investigator
Lena Jones is hired by a frantic
mother desperate to rescue her
thirteen-year-old daughter from a
polygamist sect. But when the
compound's sixty-eight-year-old
leader is found murdered, Lena's
client is charged with his murder.

To find the real killer, Lena goes
undercover and infiltrates the dark
reality of Purity—where misogynistic
men and frightened women share a
deadly code of silence.

**"...this book could do
for polygamy what
Uncle Tom's Cabin
did for slavery."**
—*Publishers Weekly*

*Available July 2004
at your favorite retail outlet.*

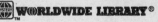

katie's gold

Tom Mitcheltree

When his office and apartment are ransacked and he's blindsided by an unknown assailant, Paul Fischer realizes that the saga of legendary pioneer Katie Baker is far from over! Returning to Oregon's Rogue River Valley to reopen a case he thought long closed, Paul must outsmart a brilliant and dangerous enemy long enough to find out what Katie Baker was so desperate to hide...and why.

*"Interesting characters, solid storytelling....
works well as a stand-alone."*
—Kirkus Reviews

Available July 2004 at your favorite retail outlet.

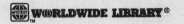

WORLDWIDE LIBRARY®

WTM498